DARKEST KISS

A COMPLETE VAMPIRE ROMANCE COLLECTION

MILA YOUNG

FOREWORD

I grew up watching vampire movies. Every single one I found, then I moved onto books. These tempting creatures of the night have been my weakness for so long. And it was only a matter of time that I'd finally write my own series.

What makes this series special, is that I wrote it with my husband :)

Our plan is to make this a LONG series and I can't wait for you to meet these four bigger than life characters, a new world crawling with dangerous monsters, and an enemies to lovers tale.

If you love action packed stories with strong, sassy heroines and dominant males, you've found your next addiction.

CONTENTS

MOON KISSED

BLOOD KISSED

CHOSEN VAMPIRE SLAYER

A vampire. A fallen angel. A demon. Me.

I'm supposed to slay the monsters, not jump into bed with them. But that's exactly what happens when my work as a private investigator forces me to collaborate with three of the sexiest most deadly fiends I've ever set eyes on. And they do things to my body I've never felt before, but can I trust them with my life?

...Or my heart?

Darkest Kiss is a three-book series full of kick-ass heroines with sass to match, scorching hot monsters who take what they want, and is perfect for devourers of enemies to lovers books. Expect steam, action, and a supernatural world filled with vampires, demons, shifters, angels... and unhinged alphas who will do anything to protect their woman. Lovers of Anita Blake and True Blood, this is your next addiction.

Darkest Kiss is the complete collection of the Chosen Vampire Slayer books.

NIGHT KISSED

CHOSEN VAMPIRE SLAYER

Seth had started to walk away in the direction of the house. Veronica watched him leave, and a hot spike of jealousy rammed into my chest. I grasped her chin and turned her face back to me. "Don't look at the jester in the presence of his king," I advised her curtly.

Heedless of my words, she said, "Who is that?" Her eyes flicked in Logan's general direction. "And that?"

"If you're a good girl, you might find out."

BOOK ONE

To say I'm killing it at my job is an understatement… Literally.

Monsters. I hunt them. I kill them.

And I enjoy it, ridding the world of the vicious supernatural killers who stalk innocents and destroy lives.

Like mine. Like my family's.

That was years ago. But I'm strong now. I'm not the victim anymore. I've fought hard to become the thing they should fear—a vampire slayer. When I'm called in to investigate a chain of suspicious deaths across Alaska, I meet three of the hottest, and most dangerous, monsters I've ever seen.

Just one problem.

They're the things that go bump in the night—a vampire, a fallen angel, and a demon. Enemies I must trust with my life if I'm to solve the dark trail of mysteries before more lives are lost.

But just as hard as solving the murders is denying my attraction to them all. And as things heat up in more ways than one, I know I'll never be the same again…

That is, if I survive the evil I'm sworn to kill… and the ones I've let into my heart.

Night Kissed is the first book in the Chosen Vampire Slayer series.

This is your kind of book if you love kick-ass heroines with sass to match, scorching hot monsters who take what they want, and is perfect for devourers of enemies to lovers books. Expect steam, action, and a supernatural world filled with vampires, demons, shifters, angels... and unhinged alphas who will do anything to protect their woman. Lovers of Anita Blake and True Blood, this is your next addiction.

PROLOGUE

VERONICA

I realized he was staring at me. The boy with turquoise eyes, who sat two seats from me in our seventh-grade math class, who never noticed me. Why would James pay attention to a nobody in a school with two girls in beauty pageants?

But when I glanced across the snowy street in the middle of Anchorage while shopping with my parents of all people, I met his gaze. I wanted to die of humiliation that he saw me with my parents, and I quickly looked down at the old, fraying brown coat I wore.

I took in as much air as possible into my lungs, then I held it for a few seconds to slow down my racing pulse. Maybe he hadn't seen me.

I glanced up as I tripped over my own feet. Lurching forward, I felt like the biggest idiot in the world, and my cheeks flushed brutally.

"Veronica, watch where you're going," Mom reprimanded me, her voice sharp.

My father didn't say a word, but I felt his heavy stare on my back.

I flung my gaze back across the street to him. The most beautiful boy I'd ever laid eyes on was walking away, head low, no longer seeing me. My stomach knotted.

"Did you hear your mother?" Dad asked.

I nodded, but struggled to concentrate on what he said next when I kept thinking about James and if he saw me or just stared right through me.

Our car lay another few blocks away and we'd long ago left the crowds behind, when a chill swept around me. The main parking area at the shops was still closed after a man had been found butchered there over the weekend. And being close to Christmas, everyone was out shopping. Which was why we parked a million miles away. The murder got me thinking about the sheer number of killed people in our town, more than the police could explain. For the past few years, Alaska had become the state with the highest murder rate per capita as a result.

I tugged down my hat over my ears, and we moved with haste as I scanned the sidewalk behind us in case anyone followed. Mom placed her arm around me, and we hurried past closed office buildings in this area. The hairs on the back of my neck raised.

A shiver ran down my spine. It was freezing.

Finally, spotting our sedan a block away parked on the curb, we rushed forward. I wanted to get out of here and just hide in my room.

Movement from an alley we passed caught my attention.

A blur that came so suddenly, so unexpected out of the darkness that I flinched around, startled.

Three deathly pale men charged out of the alley and snatched us right off the sidewalk.

Fear iced my veins and I swallowed the terror like barbed wire.

Mom screamed; Dad twisted to punch the man. I thrashed wildly, fingers digging into another's face, crying out, "Get off me!"

A hand slapped over my mouth, shutting me up. His strength was unimaginable, the touch cold as marble.

In a blink, we were deep in the alley where the inky darkness concealed us from anyone passing along the sidewalk.

My gaze swung left and right to see where my parents were, my body shaking under the arm of my attacker. Suddenly, the man squeezed me against him, his face inches from my neck. My feet tangled, and I lost my balance as I drove my fists into his chest.

I couldn't breathe or think straight. We were trapped, stolen, and all I could remember were the news reports about the dead man in the parking area. His throat ripped out. I shook frantically, fighting the monster who watched me like a predator did prey. Dark eyes with bushy eyebrows, pale skin, a short flat nose.

An ear-piercing shriek sliced through the darkness, and I knew it was my mom. A terrifying coldness wrapped around me, numbness crawling through my limbs. I twisted my head to find her slumped on the ground, a man's mouth attached to her neck. Father lay near her, another monster on his neck, slurping, drinking his blood. Tears blurred my eyes.

Mom's eyes, wide and glassy stared at me, and tears spilled down my cheeks, knowing her life had slipped away.

I screamed against the hand on my mouth. Rage and heartache twisted around me, shredding me to pieces.

I loathed these monsters… loathed this town… loathed myself that I couldn't save my parents.

The bastard yanked my head aside. I shoved my hands at his face, and fought with everything I had, kicking and punching, going ballistic.

The fiend grunted like an animal as he gripped one of my arms and twisted it behind my back.

Adrenaline pushed and pushed me. I felt nothing but the desperation to escape, to help my parents. My body shuddered.

With my scream, the monster bit into my neck. Sharp fangs dug into my neck, teeth sinking into me.

It hurt so badly, I cried, pummeling my fists against him, but he was a mountain. Breathing grew harder, but I still never stopped fighting.

A strange lethargy flared over me, flooding me with an unbearable exhaustion. My knees buckled out from under me instantly, but the monster held me pressed against him, slurping and licking my blood. He drew me deeper into the dark mass feathering the edges of my vision.

Crackling electricity flared down my arms, a snap of power I didn't understand. It came faster and hard, the hairs on my nape standing upright.

The vampire shoved me away so violently, I flew backward and slammed into a trash can. I collapsed on the ground, struggling to move from exhaustion.

The fiend's mouth gaped open, blood dripping out as he unleashed a horrendous screech of what sounded like pain.

I trembled, my vision fading faster and faster. The alleyway tilted around me and suddenly, my world blackened.

1

VERONICA

8 Years Later

*H*ow many forensic science students could say they went to class *and* hunted vampires on the side? It wasn't really kosher to brag about that sort of thing, and yet I did take pride in it. Even if I was the only person who knew.

After a long day at college, I stood in front of the bathroom mirror and stared at the face of a girl who'd foolishly structured her schedule into dense, impenetrable walls of learning and was now paying the price. At the beginning of the semester, it had seemed like the best idea not to tempt myself with breaks between classes. Ten weeks later, it felt like walking over and over into a wall of sharp bricks.

I sighed deeply, trying to ignore the darkening circles under my eyes. After a shower, I retrieved my bag and chugged down a third of my undiluted coffee as soon as I sat in the chair at the desk. The bitterness forced some life back into my sleepy brain.

"Okay." I sucked in a deep breath. "I can totally do this."

First, I reached over to the corner of the desk and switched on my trusty police scanner. It was an older model, like a fax machine with an antenna, and it crackled as I fiddled with the dials to get a signal. It was old but affordable and that helped as money wasn't exactly streaming in when I lived off the small inheritance from my parents. But I made do with everything I had, and even worked at a local café over the Christmas season for extra money.

It only took about half a minute to pick up on a reliable signal. I'd gotten pretty good about finding the right channels. Satisfied, I turned the TV on too, just to cover my bases. The local news was in the midst of a story about the rash of graffiti "decorating" the downtown cityscape as of late.

"The police have said they can't rule out occult activity as of this report," the reporter said. She had a look of professional concern pasted onto her face.

"Well, they'd be half right," I answered.

No breaking news flashed across the television, no intrusions of sudden, horrific, and puzzling violence.

The next thing I heard was a very loud, angry buzz. I managed to trace it back down to my ringing cell phone.

I picked it up quickly, without checking the caller ID. Every fiber in my body was prepared to turn down an invitation to a night out, no matter how hard my friends ragged on me. A dozen excuses ran through my mind as I thumbed the answer button. *I'm sick. I'm studying. I accidentally microwaved a spoon and the whole thing blew up.*

"Hello?"

"Veronica? Hi, it's me."

I paused. The voice on the other end of the line was not one I would have expected to hear at this hour. Not least because she and I were currently separated by about two thousand miles. And at least one time zone.

"Uh, hey." I leaned back in the chair and ran my fingers through the tangled nest of my hair. "What's up, Lian? Is everything okay?"

"Sorry for calling so late." Lian stifled a yawn. "We've had a really busy day, but I didn't think this could wait until morning." She paused. "Wait, let me back up and explain."

"I'd appreciate it." Despite the remnants of sleep still fogging up my brain, I was suddenly determined to stay awake. Under normal circumstances, Lian Zhao was much too polite to call anyone after midnight, including me. Even though she'd been my closest friend for the last decade of our lives. I knew something serious was up.

"Okay, listen." She paused to take a sip of something. I could see her as clearly in my mind's eye as if we were sitting across from each other: cross-legged on her bed or sofa, the phone tucked neatly between her shoulder and her ear. She was almost certainly keeping her hands busy somehow; she had to whenever she talked for longer than two minutes.

"I'm listening," I said.

"I think there's a new tribe in town." Lian had never been one to mince her words. It was one of the characteristics I loved most about her.

Now I sat up a little straighter. "What do you mean by 'tribe'?"

"Well...all right, so they've been here a while. They're bears, V. Bear shifters."

"Oh, shit." I stared absently at the channel numbers on the scanner. "How'd you find that out?"

She took a moment to reply. "Because they work for my parents. A lot of them, anyway. Let's just say I happened to witness an event one night and have kept it a secret until now."

"You saw one of them change." I chewed on my lip.

"I saw one of them change," she confirmed. "Totally didn't mean to; kind of wish I hadn't, to be honest with you. Those guys are incredibly hairy."

I chuckled. "Did he see you too?"

"Mm-mm. I don't think so." Again, she hesitated. "God, I hope not. That'd be embarrassing at best."

"I don't see the problem, then," I admitted. "Unless you just wanted to burden me with your awful confession so I'd also be haunted by the mental image of a man who looks like he's been glued to a carpet."

"No!" But I heard her grinning in spite of herself. "Shut up for a second. Look, they're working on a lot of our boats, and my dad says they really know how to haul ass. He likes them, apparently. I think they've worked out some sort of bargain."

"Uh huh. So, he knows what they are?"

"If he doesn't know directly, I think he's got to suspect they're weird in some way. All they do is hang around the boats, get smashed at the bars, and sleep. They could be cult members. But he just cares about the work ethic. You know him."

I did. Mr. Zhao was a man whose love for efficiency bordered on the fanatical. He wasn't so strict about the rules themselves, as long as things got done correctly. The fact that he wasn't bothered by a horde of extremely productive bear shifters did not surprise me at all.

"Right…" She was warming up to the point. I felt it approaching.

"The problem is, they're not very popular with anyone else. Especially not the vamp clan." Lian sighed. "There's been a huge uptick in violent crime recently. That's what I'm worried about."

I tensed. "Do you think your parents are in danger?" The notion made my blood run cold. The Zhaos were like my second family. Before losing my parents, I spent nearly every weekend at her place. We were inseparable. I couldn't live with the idea that vamps might be out to hurt them. "Are *you* in danger?"

"The shifters are super territorial and aggressive. Since their arrival, a couple of girls were found assaulted and dead locally too," Lian replied. "Then there are the vamps in the same area pissed at the bears' presence. I don't know." She shifted position, her voice waxing and waning as she moved. "It seems like they *hate* each other. Like, a lot. And right now, the vampires are winning." In the background, a keyboard clicked away. "Two bear shifter bodies have been found so far. The first one was like, last month, but the last one was two days ago."

"You can tell they're shifters?"

"Yeah. I've seen enough to recognize them by now. They're pretty obvious around the docks and in town. Not as good at blending in as the vamps tend to be." Lian let out her breath. "I'm worried, V. About a lot of things, but especially about what will happen if things keep escalating. I remember what you've told me about everything happening in Seattle, and I always thought Anchorage would be safe from that."

"I'm sorry." It was the only thing I could think to say in the moment. "What can I do to help? Name it." If she had asked me to reposition the sun, I would've died trying. That was how much this family meant to me.

"It's a lot to ask." Lian sounded sheepish. "And I'm kind of ashamed for even bringing it up, but…you're the best slayer I know."

"The only slayer you know," I corrected, smiling.

"That's not the point, smartass," she shot back. "We're like, leagues out of your jurisdiction, but I wanted to see if you could maybe come up north for a while and try to sort this out. Someone has to nip this in the bud before it spins out of control, and if anyone's going to, it'll probably be you."

I was already typing Anchorage, Alaska into the GPS on my phone.

It was not a good time to take a trip, academically speaking, but I couldn't have cared less at the moment. For once in our lives, Lian needed me instead of the other way around. I was determined to be there and find out what was going on.

"This thing says it will take me forty-two hours to drive." Two days in the car wouldn't be much of a party, but again, those details were inconsequential. "Do we have that much time?"

"I mean, I hope so, but that's a hell of a drive. Let me send you a plane ticket instead."

"Come on, I can't ask you to do that," I protested.

"Oh, whatever. Mom and Dad are rich, and I'm the one asking the enormous favor of you. How soon can you leave?"

Fifteen minutes of grudging travel arrangements later, a one-way ticket to Anchorage showed up in my email inbox. A small buzz of mixed emotions surged through me to be going back to where I grew up, where I'd get to see my best friend again. I had gone back a few times since moving to Seattle after the vampire attack, and each time, my stomach churned with nerves and excitement.

I had fifteen hours to get my shit together before takeoff. That meant packing—and figuring out what to do about school while I was gone.

"Thank you, V. I appreciate this so much."

"Don't even worry about it, seriously. But I've gotta go if I'm going to make this work. We'll talk when I get to Alaska."

"Sounds good. I'm excited to see you!"

The feeling was mutual. I could count on one hand the number of times I had actually gotten to spend time with Lian since I'd moved back to Seattle with my grandma after my parents were killed and I miraculously survived the vampire attack. Before that, Lian and I were together all the time.

I pulled my laptop over and opened up the email client, copied all my professors onto a blank message. The words flowed from my fingers as automatically as if I had planned them out for days.

"Dear Professors. I regret to inform you that I need to take an immediate leave from all classes, due to an unforeseen personal emergency..."

Outside the bedroom window, the smallest sliver of moon continued its slow sail across the darkened sky. In a matter of hours, I'd be on the train to SeaTac Airport, headed into the unknown without so much as a backward glance.

A flare of unease spiked through me... Anchorage brought back many memories that for so long I tried to push to the back of my mind. But I couldn't let that stop me from helping Lian.

2

———

SETH

*P*arked on a stool at the Rabbit's Foot bar, on the south side of Anchorage, I could see the blurry shapes of wet snowflakes hitting the window. I scowled. If there was one thing to complain about on the mortal plane of existence, the lousy weather occupied a place high up on my list.

But I had been promised rich rewards dependent on my ability to follow through on this mission, and I was never one to miss collecting on a debt once it was owed.

Nor did I turn down a chance to shed blood. The very thought made the edges of my mouth pull into half a smile.

The thing was, Orion, the local vampire clanmaster of Anchorage had found himself in trouble recently. The territory he'd been ruling over for decades was under threat by the vampire master from Seattle who sent over a tribe of shifters and vamps to claim the place on his behalf.

So, Orion hired me and one other guy to be the muscle and help remind these intruders the area wasn't for the taking. A brutal, violent reminder that would terrify the asshole to stay back in Seattle where he belonged.

And tonight we were rolling out the beginning of our retribution with me kicking us off. I couldn't wait.

I was ready to do what was needed to get my reward; Orion

promised me my own realm in which to indulge without any rules hindering me, or others sticking their noses in my business. I had faced my fair share of shit down in the Underworld, fought to climb the hierarchy of legions, and it still got me betrayed by those closest to me. My gut churned at the thought of everything I lost...

Including her.

An ache sharpened in my chest.

Grinding my teeth, I shoved the memories aside, loathing how they made me feel sick to my stomach.

Fuck everything and everyone. After I finished the mission with Orion, I was on my own.

As I sat back on the stool and stretched my powerfully muscled arms and shoulders, stiff from hunching for the last few hours, I glanced around the room. My mark still sat stuffed into a booth in the far corner— I could only see the edge of the man's burly right shoulder, leading down into an arm like a tree trunk. No signs of movement, let alone an intent to depart.

I resented the jackass more with every passing minute for making me wait. More than anything I wanted to march over there and finish already, but that wasn't my plan. I sighed and kept waiting for him to leave.

Twin tendrils of smoke slipped from my nostrils into air already choked by cigarette fumes. The bar was proving to be the perfect cover, in a way. Dark, hazy, full of transients and weirdos. Nobody thought twice about some guy in a long coat blowing smoke at the corner of the bar.

The whiskey had almost disappeared by the time my mark finally struggled up out of his seat. The testimony of his partial silhouette proved truthful; he was a giant of a man. A bear, one might say. I tracked the man's lumbering movement toward the door leading out into the unpleasant Alaskan night. As soon as it began to swing open, I made my long-awaited move.

The glass clunked down onto the bar, cushioned by a bill. "Keep the change," I muttered to the barkeep.

My gaze cut through the miserable, snowy night to the shadow trudging away from the Rabbit Foot's dim circle of radiance.

The hulking shadow moved slowly, weighed down by the massive quantities of alcohol percolating through his system.

When I exhaled, jets of smoke poured from my nose and leaked from the corners of my mouth. I had been instructed not to throw my strength around if I could help it.

Too bad. Showing off was one of my favorite things to do. I was always performing, whether my audience was going to live through it or not.

The mammoth stranger staggered to a halt at the side of the road. I watched with a mix of amusement and disgust as the man bent forward, hands on his knees. He coughed and sputtered.

Pathetic.

I was standing within arm's reach by the time my quarry finally caught on to my presence.

"Who're you?" The words slurred from the depths of a silvered brown beard, aimed lazily over one burly shoulder. "And what the hell d'you want?"

My left hand emerged from my pocket to scratch the side of his jaw. Wreaths of steam had started to billow up from where the soles of my feet melted snow back into clear rivulets of water. I stared into the man's unfocused eyes and saw the fury smoldering there, but I'd still caught him off guard.

My right hand closed around the hilt of a long knife bearing a sharp, mean blade. If I struck true, it could puncture the heart of this giant and bring him down in seconds. On the other hand, if I was feeling exceptionally cruel…

Still sheathed inside the coat, the knife's hungry blade began to glow, first fire-orange, and then white-hot. As I drew it, the weapon lit me from beneath.

But the beast-man was undeterred. He faced me, rising to his full, impressive height. The cotton fibers of his shirt strained to contain masses of muscle beneath. "I said, what the hell do you want?" His gaze narrowed into dark slits, all traces of sickness chased away by the rush of adrenaline.

I raised the blade and its arc streaked through the night like a meteorite, drawing a trail of fire behind it. I saw a hand coming up to meet it, but his counter was far too slow.

I plunged the knife into his chest, the blade sinking into soft flesh.

Still, five huge claws raked into the flesh of my forearm, drawing a slow stream of black blood.

The stench of burning meat and hair lingered in the air, and I hissed at the second of sharpening ache before it started to heal.

The man, whose arm had morphed into a great, mauling paw from the elbow down, dropped his chin. He looked at the hilt sticking out from the left side of his chest, at the torn fabric and forest of coarse hair singeing and smoking in the heat. It was as if he didn't feel the pain at all, for a moment.

"Demon!" he snarled at me. He wasn't wrong there.

Then he let out a choking, garbled cry. It was hoarse, and it wouldn't carry far. I grinned and twisted the knife in the wound. I wrenched the knife deeper, my hand coming flush against the beast's hairy skin. I put my weight behind the blade and shoved.

The body was dead weight before it hit the ground. I glanced back at the bar, distant but not out of sight for any intruders, at the moment of impact. A tremor ran through the frozen ground. Then all was still. I glanced down at the lifeless, sprawling figure at my feet. A trickle of red ran from the parted lips into the silver-brown beard. The hand that had been a huge bear paw lay open in the snow, returned in death to its human form. Two dark eyes stared upward, glassy, unseeing.

In the end, the beast-man hadn't stood a chance. *Like always.*

I tightened my grip on the knife hilt. It was buried so deeply that for a moment, I thought it might not emerge. But then my grasp tore it free, cutting a wide swath across the upper torso.

My job was complete, and a sense of satisfaction flooded me. The vampire, Orion, who sent me on the kill reiterated that this dead bear shifter was part of the tribe trying to claim his Anchorage territory, plus had slaughtered two humans since arriving in town. More reason for him to be wiped from existence.

Five minutes later, I had slipped into the trees along the roadside, out of view of any unlucky bastard who might happen to pass by. For the moment, the kill lay shrouded in relative darkness, but the Rabbit's Foot wasn't far away. It would only be a matter of hours, if that, before the scene was discovered.

That was the vampire's intention all along. *Kill him near the bar,* he'd ordered me. *The other shifters and vamps in his tribe need to see the warning so they leave town.*

"It's done. Part one of your plan is complete," I murmured. I spoke aloud into the quiet darkness, knowing the others heard me. In answer, an impatient whisper returned on the breeze.

"What took you so long?"

I glowered at the trees around me. I recognized the vampire's maddening condescension at once. "Me? I'm not the one who picked the slowest target in this gods-forsaken city." My sudden burst of rage manifested in a quickly suppressed flash of fire. "You asked. I delivered. Come see the proof yourself."

"Fine. You're through for tonight. We'll take care of the rest."

I bristled but managed to swallow the brunt of my anger. "Don't wait up for me," I growled. The footsteps I left as I stalked off into the woods melted and ran across the crunching snow.

No reply came from the vampire. It was just as well. I had no further interest in whatever that freak had to say.

Logan

*M*oments ago, Seth had announced his triumph over the bear shifter, which meant I was up to implement part two of our sordid little act to get these assholes out of Archorage. Now I stood outside Golden Klondike club, at the edge of the spread of lights out front. A larger establishment that seemed to attract supernaturals for a drink.

A whisper touched my ears. "Where are you?" The voice was mildly impatient. It belonged to Orion, the local clanmaster who'd hired me.

"I'm coming in," I answered.

Orion never responded, but it didn't matter. I already knew our time had just become limited. He'd spent weeks planning out the impending confrontation; its effectiveness hinged on the element of surprise. We weren't there to engage in a spectacle. The example had already been made of their bear shifter friend—they simply did not know it yet.

Now, it was my turn.

I slipped through the main door. An acrid haze of smoke threatened to blur my vision, mingled with the thick scents of sweat and cloying perfume.

The front room was dark and looked small, despite its size. Its main source of light were the muted lamps illuminating a handful of barely-clad women on a raised stage in the center. They rotated to hypnotic beats before a throng of admirers. Money littered the floor at their feet. I looked away.

"Not your problem, Logan," I muttered. Indeed, *my* problem occupied the circular booth in the back corner, which was stuffed to overcapacity with the club's most raucous patrons. The glint of raised glasses frequently caught my eye as I made my way closer, accompanied by loud laughter. This was the group of shifters and vampires ordered here from the Seattle clanmaster to claim Anchorage from Orion. To lay his stake, not to mention the vamp seemed to have some personal vendetta against Orion. Regardless, I was about to instigate their removal.

I stepped up to the end of their table and gradually their mean dark eyes swept over to me, six or seven sets in all.

"Can we help you?" The one who spoke smiled thinly. The very tip of a hefty fang protruded from beneath the edge of his upper lip. His arms were covered in coarse hair; tufts of it poked out from the open collar of his work shirt. In the low light, he could easily have been mistaken for some kind of bestial mutant—which is exactly what he was.

"You're making too much noise," I said.

The daggers in their gazes would have been practically lethal, were they aimed at someone prone to fear. I just stared back and grinned.

"Who're you?" The same shifter asked this question as well. He fought to keep his smile, but it was quickly curling into more of a sneer. "I can't imagine you'd do something so damn dumb on purpose, boy. You don't want to start nothin' with us tonight, I promise."

I raised an eyebrow. "Does it look like I'm playing?" A mortal man would have struggled to hear me over the awful cacophony of the music. To him, I knew my words rang clear as a bell.

He scowled deeply. Dark furrows materialized in his forehead. One hand, the fingers like a vise of flesh and bone, clenched fiercely on the edge of the table. "That was my one attempt at bein' polite," he growled. "I ain't gonna make another."

The shifter's cheeks and neck flushed a deep, searing red. A feral wildness seeped into his expression, to the point where the human shape of his body felt like a deviation, a gross mismatching of forms. I smiled at the strangeness of it all.

"Something funny, wiseass?" One of the others leapt to his feet, knocking over a glass in the process. The flood of beer doused the tablecloth, dripping in amber rivulets onto the floor. Some of the group jumped back, shouting outrage over wasted drink. I resisted the urge to roll my eyes. These creatures were nothing more than instinct and raw emotion. Heads empty of everything other than hunger, thirst, and base brutality.

How pathetic. These enemies of Orion's were neither interesting nor entertaining.

"Answer me!" This one was younger than the others at the table, more rambunctious and lithe. Before I'd even had a chance to think of a reply, he shoved his way out of the booth, sending one of his companions sprawling.

A bark of warning went up from the kid's elders. "Control yourself, boy!"

But it was too late. Blinded by inebriated rage, the boy leapt toward me, reaching with balled fists toward the front of my shirt.

He never got a chance to finish his sentence. I stepped deftly back from the side of the table. The motion unbalanced his already unsteady feet, allowing me to turn his considerable momentum against him. In one swift shift of my arm and shoulder, I condemned him to fall on the floor. He stared up at me, stunned.

"Enough!" The oldest beast had risen to his feet. His fists slammed down onto the tabletop. Silverware jumped. Another cup tipped. The club's surrounding patrons had started to turn toward the commotion, curious and judgmental. Spittle flew from the corners of the elder's mouth. "I don't have to take this shit from you!" He pointed a finger at me. "And you can bet I'm never gonna forget that ugly mug."

"Yes, you will forget," I said. "By the time I'm done with you."

The shifter's massive, meaty face went purple with fury. Using both hands, he swept up the largest, heaviest glass he could reach and hurled it at me. I dodged and heard a shriek, followed by an explosive impact.

He let out a roaring battle cry, leaping with surprising agility over his group to get to me. I grabbed him first by his shirt, breathing in the potent stench of everything he'd drunk.

"I didn't come here to start a fight," I said. That was a lie. The fight was my sole objective. "But I can finish one."

He bared his teeth. "This is about to be the worst night of your life, boy." The others were pulling in on all sides, so tightly that I couldn't see the rest of the club anymore. I welcomed the fury, the readiness to finish them. I lifted my opponent off his feet and thew him back. He staggered backward into the laden table, dropping to one knee.

The rest of his party fell on me. Punches, bites, kicks. I took it all, and the pain came and went just as fast. But I launched at them, striking them, one after the other, my hits cracking into their faces and chests. It sent them flinging backward. It all blurred into one great heap of chaos, and as messy as it grew, I started to understand why Seth loved fighting so much. The adrenaline was addictive.

I grabbed a vamp by the throat and hurled him into a bear shifter, both of them thrown off their feet.

A fist came flying toward my face. I grabbed it midair and twisted the attached arm away. I threw a vicious knee to another attacker's groin. It all would have been so much easier if I was allowed to kill them.

But no. Except for Seth's mark, Orion typically liked to reserve lethality for himself. And he had made it extremely clear that the only choice we had was to follow his egotistical whims if we wanted to see our rewards.

"Gentlemen!" The word rang out across the room, reverberating almost like a musical note. It was too late to stop the right hook I had already aimed at a vampire's face, or else I would have. The crack of my knuckles against his jaw echoed in the abrupt lull that followed Orion's interjection. We all turned.

He stood amid the wreckage of the booth unruffled, looking as though he were floating above the torn vinyl and splintered glass in a long black coat. A fork stuck out of the seat at an angle; he pried it out and set it down. Then he looked at me. We nodded slightly at the same time. An implied passing of the baton.

Like Seth, I had done my part, messily or otherwise. Now Orion had control, just the way he wanted. I stepped back, smoothing the wrinkles out of the front of my shirt and running my fingers through my hair. No worse for the wear. All I'd lost was another night catering to Orion's whims.

In the end, a small price to pay for the spoils he had promised.

Back in heaven, I had everything. The perfect life. Friends. Future. Job. Except, I made a terrible mistake that cost me everything and got me thrown out. Each time I thought back, I kept thinking about falling literally out of the sky.

The ferocious wind tearing at my hair and wings.

My heart carved, and it took me too long to accept I'd become a fallen angel. That I was alone.

The only world I'd known had dissolved around me and my choices rapidly narrowed. I didn't have a clue how to even begin atoning for my past mistakes when I remained furious at how fast I was tossed aside.

So, I did the next best thing to survive...I had struck a deal with a vampire.

3

ORION

"Gentlemen." I repeated myself to make sure I had captured their attention. "Is this really necessary?" From the corner of my eye, I saw Logan do his usual disappearing act. Gone into the shadows, only to reappear at a moment's notice. Sometimes I envied him for being able to shift between the mortal realm and his.

The sharp heat of the raging inferno he had stoked was focused on me, and only me. A lesser being might have crumbled beneath the pressure, been reduced to a quivering pile of ash.

But I had been burned countless times before.

"You…" The alpha shifter glared at me through the swollen mask of bruises decorating one side of his face. Parts of his beard had been torn out, one patch clear down to the skin. There was blood in the hair; I could smell it. For all his reserve, Logan had done a decent job. "I ought to have known you were creeping around here somewhere. They told me you were a coward."

"Oh, did they?" I smiled, hiding the chill of rage that rocketed down my spine. "I'm afraid you've been misinformed."

"What the hell is going on here?" the head bouncer from the club bellowed. He was a mountain of a man who might have willingly wrestled a bear, shifter or otherwise. He grabbed two of the pack by their thickly muscled shoulders. "Actually, you know what? I don't give a rat's ass! You're out, all of you!"

It was at this point that Logan materialized again to help herd the unruly group out the front door, including their Alpha. The rest of the club patrons who hadn't already run out, stood their distance and watched us. I marched after them outside into the icy night.

I felt a little sorry for whoever ended up with the thankless task of cleaning up the mess at the club, but not sorry enough to regret a single moment. Collateral damage was a necessary, perhaps even an integral part of the way business was done in certain shadowy circles in Anchorage.

I would know. This place was my city. Mine, and no one else's. I had worked hard to keep it as mine for a long time. And I would do everything to keep it that way, and out of the hands of these intruders from Seattle.

"What kind of bullshit do you think you're pulling?" The alpha lumbered to his feet, drawing up to full height. He was taller by a significant margin, and clearly thought the difference signaled an advantage for him. He moved up into my space, deliberately casting the bulk of his shadow over the spot where I stood. "Anchorage is going to be under new management real soon. I'd pack my bags if I were you." By the time the last word left his lips, less than two feet separated us on the snowy asphalt.

"I'll paint the streets with grizzly blood before I let that happen." It took every ounce of willpower I had not to clench my fists until my knuckles hurt. "Don't ever forget who was here first."

The alpha shrugged. He grinned again. The patches of skin showing through on his chin and jaw had slowly begun to shrink as new hair grew over. His teeth lengthened. Massive, cruel claws sprouted from the tips of his fingers. The seams of his shirt swelled near to bursting.

"Someday soon," he snarled, "it'll be like you never existed." He dropped his jaw open wide and let out the beginning of a grizzly bear's primal roar. The back of his shirt ripped under the pressure of four hundred extra pounds of muscle.

"If that's a challenge, I accept." My whole body tensed in preparation for a wild fight. Behind the alpha bear, others had begun their transformations, though they were somewhat less intimidating. Shifting did nothing to counteract the effects of alcohol.

The alpha was on his hind legs, briefly silhouetted against the pale wash of moonlight spilling across the lot. One great paw arced downward toward me, claws poised to maul. I dashed in to meet him, but before I had the chance to connect, he faltered in his swing. A tortured gasp left his lungs, eyes widened, and he suddenly struggled for breath. A moment later, the shifter alpha crashed to the ground. His eyes bulged from their sockets. I watched the fur thin and gray, giving way once more to skin that now bore a sickly pallor.

"What are you doing to me?" he wheezed. The veins stood out on his neck and forehead.

At his back, his friends had scattered. There was only one figure standing behind him now. Logan's face betrayed as much as the calm surface of a lake when he withdrew his open palm from the alpha's back. Two black wings had sprouted from his shoulders, spread wide to help him channel the ethereal forces of life and death that he controlled. He'd driven his energy into the bear shifter, ripping his soul from this life and back again.

Logan's angel wings blocked out the moon, throwing us all into near pitch darkness.

I couldn't help but bristle. Hadn't he seen that I was ready to take the alpha on myself? His little show of appalling power felt like a deliberate slight, a way for him to show that no matter who was technically in charge, he had no real reason to fear me. His grin confirmed it, and my hands curled into balls.

He stepped back, melting away from my sight. My flash of anger passed as quickly as it had arrived. I knelt down to look the bear shifter in the eyes.

"Unless you want to endure that for the rest of your miserable life, I suggest you rethink who's doing the packing around here. Understand?" The hunting knife at my side sang a cold, one-note melody as I slid it from the sheath. The alpha tracked it with his unfocused gaze. "Or do you need more convincing?"

The tip of the blade found its way underneath his heavily bearded chin, slicing through the forest of silvered hair until its point found skin. The shifter's jaw clenched visibly. I prodded him, just a little. Enough to smell a fresh trickle of blood.

"You know," I said thoughtfully, "I'm sober as a mortal judge tonight. But I bet I could get a nice buzz off of you." It wasn't a joke. The pungent odor of beer lingered beneath metallic iron. I could almost taste it already.

"You're a bunch of sick freaks. All of you."

I chuckled. "Including the ones you work for."

The alpha grabbed the hilt of the knife and wrenched it away indelicately. He cut himself deeper in the process. A bright, jeweled stream of blood ran down the front of his throat, but he was undeterred. The scent of his alcohol tainted blood filled my nostrils, driving my own hunger, except I had control. My intentions had been to show those in charge back in Seattle that I wasn't taking their threat lightly and that meant leaving behind a scared tribe.

"Consider your point made," he growled. "And leave us the fuck alone."

"I'll consider my point made, and therefore expect never to see you again." I straightened up. "Or else I'm afraid things won't end so diplomatically next time."

He sneered but said nothing. His tribe had all but abandoned him for the shelter of the dark tree line at the edge of the lot. I stood my ground for as long as it took to see him shamble off into the night. Until I couldn't smell his thick, boozy blood any longer.

I did, however, smell something else. And then I heard it, the frantic sound of something running. It was too light to be a bear shifter. The lack of a beating pulse was what ultimately gave it away.

I kicked at the air, darting toward the intruder, and dragged him down to the wet earth, no more than a few feet from the end of the asphalt. Ten more yards and he might have made it to safety, but alas. I had overcome him.

"No!" He struggled feebly in my grasp. "Wait!"

"Why?" Adjusting my grip, I hauled him toward the edge of the woods. "You were there in the parking lot, weren't you? Listening to what was said?"

"Yes." He attempted to free his arm but succeeded even through dislocating his shoulder. "Ah, God!" His face scrunched up with agony.

"Then you should know I'm all out of mercy." The trees loomed before us, inescapable. He saw his fate written large upon their silent trunks. "Especially for a rat like you."

"They're coming for you," he said. "And you might think you're the big dog now, but you are nothing compared to the storm on the horizon. I guess you could call that a warning."

"Thank you," I said. "But there is no clemency for traitors."

I lashed forward, the blade in my hand biting across his chest. I made quick work of destroying his heart.

Twenty minutes later, Logan and I made our way down toward the inlet shore. I wiped the blood off my sleeve as we walked in silence.

I didn't recall everything from before I had been turned in to a vampire, but I'd grown up in a cold place with snow and storms. It was a hard life. And my father had once said, *it was better to stand and fight. By running, you'd only die tired.*

That was why I dug my heels in and had no intention of leaving my home. I'd experienced great loss, rebuilt, and lost even more. Including part of myself. That stopped now.

At the intersection in front of the Golden Klondike club, a body lay beneath the traffic light. A bear shifter. Ghastly pale, eyes wide and staring, thanks to Seth's handiwork. An example for the others to see, that they might know what retribution lay ahead. It was a warning they would never heed. I counted on their ignorance.

That was all part of the fun. My plan had been set in motion to eradicate these bastards from my territory.

4

VERONICA

*A*rriving at the Anchorage Grand Hotel less than twenty-four hours after Lian had called me in Seattle was a mildly surreal experience. The taxi dropped me off in front of a building whose sharp, modern angles stood in stark contrast to the rugged mountains in the background. If not for the fancy gold, '50s-era script adorning the front of its façade, I might have taken the place for a hospital or a school. Strange place, but I was too tired to complain.

The door to my room—number 502—opened to a surprisingly spacious suite of rooms. Lian had insisted upon these particular accommodations, and as soon as I saw the living room and kitchenette, I began to understand why. The drawers and cupboards had even been stocked with plates and flatware.

I called her five minutes after putting down my stuff. "Hey, it's me. Just wanted to let you know I made it."

"Great!" She laughed slightly. "You sound beat. How was the flight?"

I stifled a yawn, exhaustion raking through me. "It was fine. TSA only frisked me a little, which was nice of them."

She snorted. "It's got to be the hair. Unless you've dyed it since the last time I saw you. Again."

"Don't know what you're talking about." I ran my fingers through my hair as I talked. It had always been incredibly pale, even when I was a kid. The first time I colored it was to stop classmates from teasing me about my "grandma hair." My mom had made sure I stuck to normal colors then. Now, it was cotton-candy pink, and I kept it up because I liked it. "This is my natural color."

"Right." Lian chuckled. "Okay, go get some rest, V. We'll meet up tomorrow, but not too early. I promise."

My place in Seattle lay fifteen hundred miles south along the cold and rocky coast. Lying in Anchorage in the king-sized bed, it felt like I had stepped onto the set of a Twilight Zone episode—or maybe something just a little more sinister. The cold eye of the moon peered through a sliver in the heavy drapes. I was too tired to get up and pull them shut, but the feeling of being watched made me uneasy as I finally fell off to sleep.

Whatever was out there chased me through my dreams. A shadowy, relentless beast. Not far behind, and always gaining ground.

In the morning, I woke with my head full of fog, unable to recall anything from those dreams other than the barest feelings. My body felt like it had been filled with wet sand. By the time I was dressed and set my brush down, my phone was ringing.

"Morning," I answered without looking at the screen, secure in the knowledge that Lian was on the other end of the line.

"Hey babe. I've sent a car and there will be coffee waiting when you get here. Ten minutes. You good with that?"

"Yep, ready to go."

"See you soon!" The call ended before I could say anything else, and I launched into preparing my backpack now devoid of my schoolbooks. I threw my laptop, a fresh notebook, some pens... and for good measure, my camera and digital recorder.

Last but not least, I grabbed my keys from the corner of the desk beneath the window. The ring wasn't large, but it was weighted down significantly by one particular item: a slender, silver shape that looked for all the world like a penlight. And it was just that, as long as you only pressed the button nestled in the rounded end.

The keys went into my jacket pocket, and I thought about them the whole way down to the lobby. That secret knife brought memories flooding back into my mind. It looked like a timeless little trinket, the kind of thing sitting at the front counter of souvenir shops. But it was actually years old, a relic of my past.

Grandma gifted it to me shortly after vampires had killed my parents. She insisted I use it to protect myself. Shortly after the attack in the alleyway, I left Anchorage to live with her in Seattle.

My chest clenched at how much I missed my parents. They didn't turn into vampires but died from being completely drained, and by some miraculous fate, I survived. It shouldn't be possible and I still didn't understand why I didn't change into one of them, why the vampire freaked out after tasting my blood.

It took me years to come to terms with losing my parents, years to embrace the new ability I'd gained from the vampire attack… a strange power to sense death and the supernatural. I still didn't fully understand why I ended up with such power, but I used it to fight the bastards. Anything to get back at what they took from me.

The vehicle that eventually pulled up in front of the hotel was an Escalade, with its windows tinted so dark they had to be illegal. I got into the back seat anyway and watched the downtown city streets roll past in muted, subdued colors. Apart from confirming my identity, the driver said not a single word. I was grateful for that.

Pulling into the long, curving driveway felt a little bit like coming home. I passed him an extra tip as I hopped from the car. With a thanks, he pulled away less than ten seconds later. I made the journey up to the wraparound porch alone, my footsteps crunching in the loose gravel of their driveway. The house was huge and rounded at the front, and the shadow it cast bathed the grass in darkness. I vividly recalled Lian's father half kneeling as he replaced the front steps in years past. Before my parents passed, I had spent just as much time here as I did at home. And being here had my stomach turning with a strange feeling. Being in Anchorage brought back heartbreaking recollections about what I'd lost, yet it also held my fondest memories from before the attack. It was a strange thing to feel both anxious and excited about a place.

"V!" The door flung open before I got the chance to reach for the bell. Lian burst out in a flurry of energy and threw her arms around me. She wore black leggings, boots, and a white puffy sleeved shirt with gold buttons down the front that suited her so perfectly. "Oh my God, it's so good to see you!" She pulled back to look me in the eye. "I can't believe you're here again."

"Honestly, neither can I." I tried to keep my voice light, but we both heard a somber tinge. The second time she hugged me, Lian squeezed hard, and I hugged her back. There was something comforting and reassuring to visit her, and when we met up, I always wished I'd done it more often.

She pulled back and studied me, grinning. "Damn, how have you been, girl? And did you dye your hair brighter, as it's super pink and super amazing. Maybe I'll get these," she flicked her short hair, "colored. Been thinking of going green." She'd cut her dark hair into an adorable pixie hairstyle, and it suited her cute face. Lips pouty and cherry red, she smiled wildly at me.

"Do it." I laughed at how adorable she looked. "How's life with you, anyway?"

She shrugged. "Okay I suppose. Dad's been getting me into the business a lot more as he wants me to get more involved in the managing side of things."

"That's exciting."

"Yeah, I guess. Anyway, let's get inside before we freeze."

I glanced indoors through the front door. "Are your parents home?"

She shook her head. "They don't even know you're here yet. I wasn't sure if you'd want me to tell them right away." She grabbed me by the hand and pulled me into the front hall. "Come on in. The coffee's all ready." And as I followed my best friend through to the enormous kitchen with the granite countertops, the tension I'd been carrying began to melt away.

"Remember that night we tried to make popcorn and started a small fire on the stove," I mused.

Lian cut me a narrowing gaze. "Mom still reminds me of that. She didn't pay me pocket money for months."

"Which was why, I gave you half of mine." I wrapped an arm around her shoulders. "I missed you, babe."

She blew me a kiss. "I'm so excited you are back. We need to do one of our b-grade movie nights. No one will watch them with me." She pouted.

"You got yourself a deal. It's been a while since I've watched any movies. College assignments are whipping my ass."

I sat at the island, basking in the late morning sunlight pouring in from the picture windows with the idyllic view of their lawn.

She served us a cup of steaming coffee with cream, then joined me.

"You're doing incredible, babe. You'll soon be one of those forensic detectives like on CSI."

"Let's see if I can pass the exams first." I laughed as I unloaded the contents of my bag and sat with my pen poised above the paper. "Okay, let's get this out of the way, then we can sit and catch up properly. So, tell me about the murders."

She beamed, but then instantly put on a serious face. Her eyes grew deadly serious. "I've never seen anything like it, V. I swear on my life." She sighed, glancing out the window. "They're butchering each other." She pushed a newspaper, a few days old, across to me. It was open to a story about the rash of violent crimes plaguing the city. The center photo depicted the edge of a local road, dirty snow banked into drifts. Swaths of dark, bloody red cut across the surface. I stared at the unmistakable imprint of a body in the snowfall.

"This doesn't look like a vamp scene," was what I told her at first. For one principal reason. "They never leave that much blood behind."

"It doesn't look like a human scene either," Lian countered.

"I don't know…" Some of my forensics books would have disagreed. "Even good old mortal men can do some serious damage to each other."

But Lian would not be persuaded otherwise. "I think they must be beefing pretty hard," she said. "Otherwise, why kill like *that?* Doesn't it seem like someone's trying to send a message?"

I couldn't hide the skepticism in my voice or face. "I mean, I guess so." My gut told me her vamp assumption might not be completely correct. I knew that she was worried, and Lian was my best friend. "Listen, I can't promise I'll find anything out. But you need me, and I'll try to figure out what the hell is going on."

Instantly, she relaxed and smiled. "Oh, thank God. I thought you were going to bail on me for a second there." She took a sip of her coffee. "To be honest, I'm more worried about the business than anything. These are my dad's employees turning up dead. No one's going to want to work with a company where everyone's on a hit list."

The point was salient. Still didn't mean the vamps were the ones behind the carnage. Nonetheless, I had already made my commitment. "All right. If you've got any leads, I'd love to hear them. It'd help to hit the ground running." I couldn't imagine Mr. Zhao's fishing empire going belly up, but the rumor mill was a powerful force, even in the city. It wouldn't do to let shady gossip spread out of control.

"Not much," Lian admitted. "Only that someone moved into one of the big houses down along the inlet recently. It's been empty for months, but apparently there's been recent traffic. Neighbors have seen comings and goings at night."

It was only a blip on the radar, and an uncertain one at that. Still, it was the only crumb we had. "That's a start." I jotted down the address of the formerly empty house, as well as a few of the crime scene locations. "Anything else?"

Lian was quiet for a few minutes. "I really care for you, V," she said softly. "So much. And I missed the hell out of you. Please be careful out there. I want you safe so we can grow old and move to Florida together as we agreed."

I laughed lightly. "No promises," I teased.

My friend rolled her eyes, walked around the island's granite surface, and dragged me into a hug. Her breathing quickened as I knew she worried about those close to her a lot. "I'll keep my eyes peeled for more," she assured me. "Let me know if there's any other way I can help you. Money, food, whatever."

I pulled back. "Actually, you know what would be really helpful?" I grabbed my notepad and flipped it over to a clean page, then turned it toward her, offering the pen as well. "A map."

"You got it." She beamed a smile and studied the addresses she had just given me and then began to sketch.

Collecting my cup, I sipped my hot coffee as I watched her label landmarks and streets, an odd sense of foreboding crept up into my stomach. And no matter how hard I tried, I couldn't push it back down.

5

ORION

$\mathcal{I}$ had a love-hate relationship with the house on the inlet shore. It rose three stories and an attic above the beach, and if I looked out the bedroom window on the top floor, I could see the slate-gray tide glimmering under the moon. That was the nice part.

My problem lay in the company I had chosen. Once spacious, the place had become crowded with conflicting energies, always at a high simmer. Some days it seemed as though one of us might end up a cadaver on the nightly news. Were I a betting man, my money would have gone on the demon. Nonetheless, I held my tongue. They were necessities for the moment, inconvenient generals in a war against the fools intruding upon my stronghold.

Rageful vengeance was my constant companion. I was the one who held Anchorage in the palm of my hand, who watched this microcosm spin on its axis. No one else had the right.

And I'd prove it—in any way I needed to. Fire burned through my veins with the need to hold onto it and not be driven from my home. Plus, I detested the Seattle clanmaster. Our pasts had clashed before. He took from me someone dear long ago. For that, I would destroy everything and everyone connected to him. Then I was going for him.

My enemies were relentless and always growing in number. I'd fought to claim this land for myself long ago from another clanmaster, and there was no way I'd let another take it from me.

39

Hence the present predicament.

If I closed my eyes, I could feel the angel and the demon in their opposite corners of the house, one brooding and cold, the other blazing with restless fire. More than once, the thought had crossed my mind that Seth might present more of an immediate threat than anything else, with the way he flung his flames around and never shut up. On the worst nights I fantasized about destroying the whole damn house—with him inside. But he offered the strength I needed, and beneath all the raging flames, Seth dealt with his own dark history. I did my research on who I asked to join me on this mission. Seth wore his fury as armor, but I trusted him to follow through on the plan as he needed a new start. I'd been there and I understood the desperation, so even if I wanted to kill him most days, a part of me sympathized with him and wanted to aid him. Though, I'd never tell him that as he'd gloat and use it against me at every argument we had.

Suddenly there was a knocking on the door. Through the peephole, I saw a lean, whipcord-tough young man, nattily dressed in a dark suit. His comb had left tracks in his oiled hair.

We stared at each other for a moment or two after I opened the door. He was obviously waiting for me to speak first, but I had nothing to say. He reeked of the rain-soaked artificiality of Seattle, the pollution and greed of the city. I knew exactly where he had come from.

"Clanmaster Orion?" The young vampire used the correct form of address, but he barely inclined his head, and he never broke eye contact. Rarely had I seen such flagrant disrespect from one who was little more than a toady in my eyes. An errand boy sent to do his own master's bidding.

I smiled as disingenuously as possible. "To what do I owe the pleasure?" There was something about this boy that managed to grate on every nerve. Maybe it was the way he continued to stare me full in the face, his flat, pale eyes issuing the weakest form of challenge. It was maddening that he refused to look away, and even worse, that I knew he couldn't back up any threat.

"I've come to request a negotiation on behalf of Clanmaster Steele."

Just the sound of the name made my hackles want to rise. Steele was one of the master vampires from the Seattle area. I fought to keep the lengthening fangs inside my mouth. The bare desire to forgo the thin veneer of diplomacy and give in to instinct, which was to rip him limb from limb and throw the pieces into the ocean, burned white hot just below the surface. He could see it, just as I could see how he wasn't really there to negotiate. He was just there to humiliate me.

"I'll see what I can do." Brusquely, I stepped back to allow the boy to enter. He kept his shoes on. From the moment I let him across the threshold of that house, a small voice in the back of my head told me how things were going to end. But he didn't have to know how limited his time had just become.

Neither he nor I dared to sit in the parlor with the massive fireplace taking up the center of the room. The logs in it were cold at the moment. A shame, but I supposed I could use one to beat him to death in a pinch. His emotionless eyes flicked to the heavy iron poker set sitting at the side of the hearth. Our thoughts had drifted to the same cruel place. Maybe the kid knew his destiny after all.

"Clanmaster Steele wants to…acquire your territory." If there was one thing I had to admire about this whelp, albeit grudgingly, it was his unabashed directness. He was rude and lacked decorum, but at least he didn't waste too much of my time.

I laughed. "That's very funny. How does he think he's going to make that happen?"

The young man shifted his weight from foot to foot. He was bored, annoyed, impatient. An insult to my very presence. "He's open to an act of diplomacy, but he'll take it by force if he has to."

Again, I let a smirk curve my lip. "I hope for his sake that whatever force he plans to use packs a harder punch than you."

Steele's messenger scowled. I could practically see his temper rise like the mercury in a barometer. He clenched his jaw, and then he opened his mouth. "Listen, asshole. You think you're so high and mighty, running your little Podunk backwater cult? Yeah, right. I bet my boys and I could clean you out ourselves in one night." His fists clenched at his sides, white-knuckled and tense. All of his energy had been drawn in to focus on not taking a swing at me.

"You call this a worthless place, yet Steele sent you to negotiate its takeover. Interesting." I held my ground, cool and calm. The air crackled dangerously between us. But I knew better than to be the one igniting the powder keg. Not when my opponent was so green and easily manipulated.

"I told him it was a bad move," the messenger boy spat. His flat eyes had finally lit with a baleful gleam that revealed him to be on the very edge of sanity. "I said he would only be wasting his time." He shook his head, bewildered. "But the guy insisted."

"And you had no choice but to follow his every command, whipping boy." Frank amusement colored every word I spoke. The boy was so close to the edge, the glorious point of no return.

Then his nostrils flared, and he tipped himself over. "Shut the fuck up! I came here as a favor to Steele, not to be insulted by some two-bit miniboss!" Unable to contain his fury any longer, he let out a frustrated roar. "That's it! I can't take this bullshit anymore. I'll just bring him your head!"

He flew at me in a rabid frenzy, a hail of rapid-fire strikes. Not intimidated, I met him with equal force, and I rushed at him, both of us clashing. I shoved my hand at his throat, hurling him across the room. But the kid was fast, and reasonably strong, but his unbridled arrogance crippled his charge. I dodged his haphazard charge and buried my fist in the pit of his stomach, so hard that I swore I could nearly feel his spine. He buckled over, gasping.

"Let it be known that I'm a merciful creature," I told him quietly, my lips close to his ear. "This is your one chance to walk away."

Seconds passed. He stood precariously on the balls of his feet, his right shoulder hunched down. The effort to keep his balance made his whole wiry body tremble. I drove my knuckles harder into the scant flesh of his abdomen. He made a strangled groaning sound.

"Steele will waste your rotten blood!" was what he choked out in response.

"That's harsh." Now we could both see the end approaching, as fast and as hard as a speeding train. Opening the hand that had punched him, I shoved the kid back hard. He stumbled, arms pinwheeling for balance. Predictably, I saw him try to grab for the poker set. It was a pure defensive reaction.

It was also too late. In the next instant, I had caught him by the face, gripping his jaw in the vise of my thumb and fingers. The nails on that hand crept upward toward his temples as they lengthened into vicious talons. This time, I put the fangs on full display.

He couldn't talk, although he did try. His hands clawed uselessly at my arm, feet scrabbling against the smooth wooden floor. I glanced down at the scuff marks left by his heels and shook my head.

The voice that left me was not the one that mortals heard. I spoke to Steele's doomed henchman in my true voice, the one that belied the depths of my age. When it touched his ears, the young vamp squirmed in terror.

"You were never a negotiator, boy." I propped his chin up on the razor-sharp tip of a claw. "No. You were a sacrifice."

His terrified eyes widened. Then I was the one grabbing a poker out of the stand, gripping it firmly in my palm. Its blunted end plunged through his chest with little fanfare. The dull light drained from his eyes. His mouth went slack. No blood whatsoever dripped from the brand-new wound.

I dropped him where I stood. Out of view of the sun's descending eye, he sprawled limply over the floorboards. Nothing but a wretched shell now, a lifeless ghoul. If I had the option of waiting until morning, he would simply be incinerated into dust and blown away. But there was no doubt he'd be missed before long. After the first outsider vamp had turned up dead in the street, they'd be keeping a close eye on the rest.

Gazing down at the body, I had to admit I felt something like a stab of regret. Not because he was dead by my hand, but because I had just created more work for myself by killing him. I grimaced, bent down, seized him by the leg, and dragged him unceremoniously toward the cellar door.

Other than the thump of the corpse on the steps, the house was quiet. I could count on Seth to be gone more often than not, but I wondered if Logan was hidden in his roost, silent and listening. The thought was only disconcerting for a moment. What could he do? We were in league with each other, all three of us. Hell, I could force them to help me take the garbage out, so to speak.

And maybe I would, if for no other reason than to remind them who was in charge.

Minutes later, I locked first the cellar door, then the front door of the house behind me. I needed to gain the upper hand against those who would come searching for him in hours, if not sooner. I needed to track their movements. And there was one place I knew the rats from Seattle loved to congregate—among the bars downtown.

The trail led me toward the run-down, unimpressive façade of a place called Inlet Drive. Neon signs flickered in the two front panes of glass as I approached. I could hear the faint strains of music coming from inside.

Then there was movement in the narrow alley on the left. All my senses went on high alert. I listened for the sound of a heartbeat, a pulse, the smell of blood pumping just beneath human skin. As a figure emerged around the side of the building, heading for the entrance, I melted back into the darkness. But I could still see her with all the intensity of a beacon, especially the strange, silvery rose glow of her hair.

And for some reason, I couldn't tear my gaze away. There was something hypnotic about the way she moved, the way her body seemed to glow in the dim light, giving off its own power. I almost wanted to call out to her before she reached for the door handle and disappeared inside. The words rose dangerously close to the top of my throat, though I refused to release them.

It didn't matter. All of a sudden, the woman's face turned in my direction. Her eyes, pale and piercing, bored straight through the night into mine with uncanny precision, as if someone had whispered my exact position in her ear. Her outstretched hand dropped to her side, the door forgotten. She turned slowly.

Our eyes remained locked. A blazing heat tore through my body as I watched this woman advance on me. The shape of her silhouette awoke something feral that had lain dormant inside for decades. All I could think about was how much I wanted her, how determined I was to have her.

It seemed like she was about to make things easy.

6

VERONICA

No matter how many times it happened, there was always a rush, a surge of adrenaline that pushed through my veins the moment I laid eyes on a vampire. Maybe it was my inner ability at sensing death, or just the knowledge that those creeps never made anything easy. This one had tried to catch me unaware as he stared from the shadows. But I'd gotten pretty good at spotting their eyes, even from a distance.

Sometimes the vamps did their little disappearing act once they had been picked out. It was the world's most annoying party trick, the way they seemed to be able to melt back into the darkness. This time, I knew immediately that things would be different. He stood almost in the middle of the street with his shoulders back and his head held high, dressed in black pants, boots, and a long matching coat that did nothing to conceal the width of his shoulders and chest. As I approached, the air grew thick with silent tension.

The vampire did not back down. Actually, he seemed to rise up taller the closer I got, standing at six-foot-six at least. His burning, gold-ringed, silver eyes, never left my face, and I studied him, hating to admit that this blood-sucker was extremely easy on the eyes. That old saying, tall, dark and handsome was wasted on him. He was ridiculously gorgeous in a rugged, going to tear your heart out, kind of way. Well, of course, vampires were ruthless killers. Yet, he had me pause long enough to admire him, the way he stood proudly, which I rarely did. I could hear the blood pounding in my ears, which meant he heard it too. We stared at each other, both of us defiant, unwilling to give any ground.

"You're new here." He spoke softly, but the chill in his low, silky voice would've carried a hundred miles. "That's interesting."

"Or maybe you haven't been paying attention," I replied, never taking my eyes off him.

He glanced over my body, and I found myself fighting against the ripple of a freezing shiver. What was it about his expression that needled its way so effortlessly under my skin? He looked at me like I was trash in the gutter he might choose to pick through. Like I was already dead.

But then his lips curled over into a smile. Half amusement, half annoyance, and totally infuriating. The short laugh that followed only made things worse. "Not likely, little one. There are very few who know this city as well as I do. And I'm sure I haven't seen that face before."

I could say the same to you. The words came within a breath of jumping out of my mouth before common sense took over. No name surfaced in my mind, but whoever stood in front of me was no run-of-the-mill grunt.

"Well," I said out loud, "are you going to introduce yourself, or should we stand here and savor the awkwardness?" For good measure, I folded my arms and shifted my weight to my back foot. He didn't seem like the typical vampire, and seeing I just arrived town, I needed to quickly work out who was who in the hierarchy of vampires. "It's up to you. I can go either way."

Once again, he appraised me. I could see the gears turning in his head, underneath waves of thick hair so dark it blended into the night. "I wouldn't normally allow someone like you to speak to me with such disrespect." The icy edge underneath each word compelled me to believe him. "But I'll forgive your ignorance—this time." The smirk returned to his lips. "I am the clanmaster of the Alaskan territory. My name is Orion." He paused. "You would do well to remember it."

I resisted the urge to roll my eyes. Most of the vamps I had met could not have pulled off a line like that without looking like corny idiots. This guy, however... He could've made the phone book sound like a death threat. I had known him for all of two minutes, and it was already way too tempting to get drawn into the sheer power of his energy. A shiver zipped down my spine at how my body reacted to him because that distracted me from focusing on who stood before me.

"All right, fine, Orion." I refused to give him the satisfaction of admitting how recently I'd arrived. "Let me just start out by saying, if you want to run me out of your town, you're in for a hell of a fight. I don't do anything quietly."

The way his eyes roamed over me was both uncomfortable and mesmerizing. It was like he had the power to see directly through me, and for the first time in my career as a slayer, I wondered if I might be in over my head. Eight years ago, I'd gained a supernatural ability that gave me an advantage against these fiends, but there was also my heightened strength I never gave too much thought to. I always wondered if that came after the vampire attack as well. That terrifying day of the attack had left me changed forever. It made me something I didn't understand. Someone stronger, more agile, and coupled with the energy to trace down death, I was a force to be reckoned with. Sure, all the research in the world gave me no insight into what I'd become after the attack, but it didn't stop me from using what I'd gained.

Yet the vibes radiating from Orion seemed different and over-powering.

The thought only lingered for a second, but it was long enough to shake me. The stake at my belt that I carried everywhere weighed heavier as a reminder it was ready to be used.

Orion chuckled. "We'll see about that." When he moved, my whole body tensed automatically, a motion he seemed to appreciate. I was ready for him to come at me, to start a fight right there in the street. In Seattle, we would have been at each other's throats already. But he surprised me by stepping backward rather than forward. "Don't get too comfortable," he warned. "I'm watching you."

The tone of his voice made my spine tingle. I was so used to vamps being vile, repulsive creatures, and Orion still was, in a way. There was no mistaking the monster lurking just behind his smooth exterior. But he was also enticing, which was a thought I had never dared to think before. Disgusted with myself, I shoved it as far away as possible.

"Do whatever you want," I said coolly. "I'm not going anywhere."

He nodded. "I know."

Then he was gone, so suddenly it felt as though he could have been a mirage. I took a deep breath and let it out slowly. The drum of my heartbeat was just beginning to slow down, and my cheeks burned hot against the cold Alaska night.

"What the hell just happened?" I muttered, shaking my head. I'd meant to spend a while in the bar, but now I wanted to get out of there. The vampire's appearance had thrown my whole night out of whack, and I couldn't shake the feeling he was still close by. With the hairs on the back of my neck standing up, I turned around and retraced my steps back to the hotel.

"Back so soon?" The night clerk glanced up from her post behind the reception desk, first at me, and then out the window. "It gets pretty cold out there at night, even this late into the spring. You'll get used to it." She had seen me leave minutes earlier.

"Yeah." I smiled sheepishly. "Thought I was ready for a night on the town, but…I decided I'd rather stay in and watch a movie."

She laughed. "I won't tell anyone."

It didn't hit me until I stood in my room three minutes later with the remote control in my hand that this jackass who called himself Orion had managed to make me into a joke without even trying. Instantly, my feelings shifted from muddled confusion to anger and resentment, as if a fog had lifted from my brain. If there was ever a time I realized how much I still had to learn, it was right in that moment.

"Shit," I whispered. The reality of the situation was that he had chased me back into the corner without taking a single step forward. And he probably knew it, too. Sighing in frustration, I raked both hands through my hair, letting it fall angrily down my back.

It was safe to assume that Orion hadn't been kidding about watching me—if he really was the regional clanmaster, he'd have eyes in a lot of places. And that meant he could pop up wherever he wanted, unannounced. I was determined not to be caught off guard again.

Next time, I vowed, *he won't be so lucky.*

---

*L*ian and I had mapped out more scenes of as many murders as she had information on, and in the days following my first encounter with Orion, I hit the pavement hard.

Most of the sites we had pinpointed, especially the older warehouses and rundown houses, were long since cleaned up or degraded, but the air still hummed with the residual energy of violence. Sometimes it was difficult to find a quiet moment away from the eyes of the city to commune with the spot, but patience and perseverance proved to be my best friends. I spent the next few days walking around in phantom worlds of blood and death, terror lingering like a memory in the fresh mountain air.

The work was haunting and draining in equal measure, and it left me chased by nightmares filled with creatures whose faces I couldn't see. But despite my best efforts, the perpetrators' identities remained unknown to me for days. If I saw any of them, it was only as silhouettes, vanishing like smoke on the wind. The thing that stuck was the power of their energies. Like Orion's, but not quite the same. His was unlike anything I had seen or felt before.

It made me certain that something bad was going down in Anchorage.

On my way back to the hotel, a shadow caught my attention from between two homes. A small passage, flanked by tall wooden fences.

When a scream tore free that direction, I sprinted toward the sound without hesitation. Fingering the stake on my belt, I retrieved it, and followed the curve of the passage. A thin layer of snow crunched under my quick steps when I happened upon two vamps cornering a young boy who hugged his school bag, shaking. Terror flooded his huge eyes when he looked my way with a pleading expression of help.

"For hell's sake," I started, lifting my stake, twirling it in my hand. "You bloodsuckers are so predictable."

The darkhaired one swept his gaze up and down my body, his attention stopping on my stake, then threw his head back with laughter. "Come over here, and I'll show you what a real weapon looks like."

I rolled my eyes at his cliché line. The second vamp sneered in my direction, nostrils flaring.

Just then the young boy slipped free and darted out of their grasp.

The fiends twisted in his direction, but I called out, "I bet you two can't take me on."

Vampires had egos to match their bloodlust, and as predicted, they both turned in my direction, leaving the boy alone.

A deep guttural sound tore from one of their throats, and with the wind growing colder, I didn't have time to tap dance with these monsters. They came at me.

Inches from their grasp, I threw myself into a low forward roll right between them.

Throwing myself to my feet, I spun around and drove the stake right into one of the fiend's back, right over the heart. He arched, his knees already buckling as he gurgled his protests.

Except, the second bastard moved faster than I expected. He tackled me and threw us both to the wet, cold ground. Stars danced behind my eyes from the impact, and I struggled to suck in a breath with his weight pressed down on my chest, laying on top of me. We were face to face, and I gagged at his putrid breath.

I shuddered as I stared into his dark eyes where only my death waited.

"Get off me," I growled, bucking against him, shoving a fist into his chest. I quickly slid my other hand down my side and grabbed my switchblade on the ring from my pocket.

"You chased away my meal," he snarled.

While I clawed at his face. His hands snatched my wrist, distracted enough as I rapidly slashed my weapon at his head.

He turned his attention to the attack, reacting a split second too slow. My blade jammed right into his eye. He flinched backward and there was a scuffle as I shoved him off me and I rolled to my feet. My heart thundered in my chest because I didn't have much time. My attack was a distraction, nothing else.

I threw myself to the first culprit, scrambling to pull the stake from his back.

A shadow fell over me.

Frantically, my fingers snatched the weapon, my muscle tightening, heaving out the stake.

I whipped around in a sliver of a second, weapon raised and swinging around toward my attacker.

Silvery eyes shone.

Lips peeled over razor-sharp fangs, his snarl echoed through the night.

No hesitation.

I plunged the stake right into his chest as he rushed into me, throwing me off my feet once more.

My lungs emptied of air, and I gasped as the dead weight slumped over me, trapping me. He gurgled over me, blood dripping into my hair.

Seconds was it all it took for such a fatal blow to a vampire to render them useless.

"Fuck!" With all my strength, I drove my palms into his shoulders, rolling him off me.

He slumped onto his back like a sack.

Up on my feet, I dusted myself of snow and used it to clean the blood out of my hair.

I stared down at the two vampires. That was what I should have done earlier when I crossed paths with Orion, not drooled over him.

I sighed at myself as I collected my stake and took out my phone to call the cops. I would report bodies found in the alley so they were collected before anyone stumbled over them. Dead vampires once staked remain withered husks of themselves, fangs withering away and only their human body remained. Meaning discovering they were vampires was close to impossible. Sure, there would be inconsistencies in the results, but not many humans jumped to the conclusion of vamps in autopsies. So, I did my best to clean up after myself as much as possible at each fight.

I walked away, the cellphone pressed to my ear, and headed back on the street to continue my checks.

The moment I hung up from the police, my phone suddenly buzzed in my hand, and I checked to find it was Lian. She checked in with me every day, to ask about my progress and make sure I wasn't going totally insane. "How are you?" she asked, barely veiling the concern in her voice. "Find anything useful?"

Inevitably, I sighed and shook my head, even though she couldn't see me. "Not yet. All I know is, they're a different breed up here. There's got to be something in the water."

"It wasn't always like this." Lian said that a lot, and always with the same combination of morbid wonder and disbelief. "I mean it. It has gotten worse recently."

"Even more reason then, I should get back to work. Got a couple more places to visit." It wasn't a lie. She still understood my meaning perfectly.

"Right. Let me know if you need anything. I'll call if I don't hear from you."

"Thanks, Li. Love you."

"Love you too, girl. Be careful out there."

I slipped my phone into my pocket and thought about how badly I could use a long, hot shower, and a drink. For some reason, I hadn't expected my return to Anchorage to be so fraught with complicated emotions. I saw now how naïve I was being.

The last of the crime scenes I visited provided a welcome distraction. I had followed them in chronological order from least to most recent, which meant the intersection leading away from the Golden Klondike gentlemen's club practically reeked of vampire-scented brutality. A few cars cruised through as I walked along the tree line off the side of the road. As soon as I was within range, I closed my eyes and began the reconstruction.

When I opened them again, the images I saw gripped my heart in an iron fist. There was no blood to speak of, but the ghostly afterimage of the body splayed in the middle of the road was so grotesquely clear compared to most of the others. The head, twisted around on a clearly broken neck, stared blankly toward me. All of a sudden, the breath caught in my throat.

"A vampire?" That was new. The previous victims had mostly been bear shifters, just as Lian had said, but there was no mistaking the sickly pallor or the metallic irises of the corpse, clouded in death as they were. He looked a lot more like the vamps I was used to—that is to say, like he'd crawled out from under a rock.

And straight into the true embrace of death.

Another car zipped along the road, passing straight through my vision. I crouched down in the snow to get a better look across the pavement, waiting for a lull in traffic. Two more sets of headlights went by, and then the street fell dark and quiet. Now was my chance.

Springing up out of the crouch, I ran, leaping the snowbank. Exertion made the conjured images flicker, but I had long since learned how to hold my concentration on the move. The nearer I drew to the spot where the slain vamp lay, the more I could sense in the atmosphere, past energies swirling together to create an approximation of the night he died.

That was when I felt something new and all too recently familiar, the bold trace of an aura I had come across less than a week before.

Orion.

He was somewhere in the vicinity.

And another thing I recognized all mixed in, a whiff that gave me flashbacks to rain and gray skies and the clutter of a rushing cityscape pierced by the towering shape of the Space Needle.

The vamp on the ground at my feet was from Seattle. Like me, two thousand miles from home. And I was pretty sure I knew now who killed him. That piece of information shifted my focus entirely. I straightened up, lifting my head into the breeze. The remnants of the Alaskan clanmaster's energy glimmered on the breeze. Not enough time had passed to dull them beyond recognition.

I turned back toward the woods and began to follow Orion's trail.

7

LOGAN

A body in the cellar was something of an unwelcome surprise to both Seth and me. It had been hidden for a few days now, by the state of the corpse and the reek, once Seth had unwrapped it from the plastic casing Orion arranged. Unsurprisingly, it was another vampire, rendered ghastly pale by the uncompromising touch of Death,

Seth caught my eye as I glanced down from the top of the cellar door and motioned impatiently with one arm.

"Hey, get down here, angel-boy. We're on corpse-hauling duty tonight."

I stared at him, into fiery eyes brimming with destructive energy. He was smiling, but there was a thin mask of cruelty behind it. He was constantly on the edge of raging frenzy, waiting for any excuse to spill over. I wondered if he would come up and try to fight me.

"Where are we going?" I asked.

He shrugged, a brief, irritated jerking of the shoulders. "Orion doesn't tell me shit, the son of a bitch. He said something about throwing it into the river." The smile began to turn down into a scowl. "What are you waiting for? Get moving."

Despite knowing it would give the demon satisfaction he did not deserve, I complied. He and Orion were each too much of a hassle to deal with at their worst—the easiest thing was to keep quiet. I had nothing to prove on the surface—if a line was ever crossed, they'd find out quickly how I could hold my own.

We pulled the corpse up to ground level. Just as we dropped it on the floor, arms and legs akimbo, Orion stepped around the corner to join us.

Seth made a face. "I thought the dead ones turned to dust," he remarked.

Orion laughed mirthlessly. "In the sun, my friend, so long as the sun is the thing that does the killing. I'm afraid I've stolen the privilege for myself this time. This asshole tried to negotiate with me. Didn't turn out well for him."

Seth leaned down to lift his side of the improvised litter. "Let's get this over with. I'm already bored."

"Don't worry. When they finally realize what fate befell him, I'm certain we'll all be busy." Orion's eyes lit with a strange, almost maniacal flame every time he spoke of his rivals. I half believed he had killed this doomed creature on purpose, to goad his enemies out of dormancy. They had spent the past weeks dancing around idle, fruitless negotiations as more and more turned up mysteriously dead.

At last, it seemed that the time for halfhearted diplomacy had passed.

We walked in silent formation, the body balanced between us, through the densely forested wood between the house and the shore. The Alaskan wind blew coldly through my hair and ran its frosty fingers along my neck. To me, the sensation was a comfort, though I noticed Seth shake it away in an angry blast of steam. For once, however, he declined to speak.

We heard the river before we could see it, its voice muddied by the slough of ice rushing between its banks. The ice rumbled as it struggled for position on the ever-shifting surface.

"Here." Orion stopped. "Wait for a break in the ice."

"And what do we do if he doesn't go under?" Seth demanded. The question was on my mind as well, but I let him have the honor of asking. Judging by the way Orion's gaze narrowed slightly, it was a wise decision.

"He will." The phrase rang with finality—our leader had spoken. Seth grumbled something else under his breath. Orion turned his attention to me. "Close your eyes," he ordered. The strangeness of his command didn't strike me until I had already done as he asked. His voice, low and insidious, now sounded in the back of my mind. "Do you sense that?"

At first, no. But then I caught a foreign vibration, hiding beneath the clutter of everything else. The aura hummed in the background, quiet, unassuming. The only thing I knew initially was that it belonged to a living creature.

"Who is it?" Even as I asked it, I understood the question to be moot.

"You are about to find out." Orion steered me firmly in the direction from which the unidentified aura emanated. "Go and teach our little visitor some proper manners. And bring her back when you're finished."

I left the riverbank and headed once more into the trees. Whoever she was, she thought she was hidden. In the hush of a thickening night, I sensed her heartbeat—a little too quick. Maybe she was scared. And, well, maybe she wasn't wrong to be. As I moved among the dark trunks, she began to move in opposition. The prey could tell she had been rousted out.

This knowledge would not help her. I was nothing if not far too adept in the search for and subsequent extinguishing of life. But Orion had said to bring her back, hadn't he? That was something new and intriguing. Who was this individual, that I had not been granted the typical permission to kill on sight?

The game of cat-and-mouse went on between us for only a couple of minutes—as long as I allowed. She had nowhere to go but away from me, and I was the faster between us. Her pulse grew steadily louder in my ears, until I could nearly feel it with my own. Silent as a shadow, I rounded the trunk of the next tree…and heard a tiny gasp.

The human girl knelt on the frozen ground, staring up at me through huge, moonlike eyes. She had taken the chance to remain inconspicuous, efforts that struck me as pitiable more than anything. The dark hat over her head struggled to contain unnaturally bright waves of hair. I reached out to touch one of the escaping locks, momentarily transfixed. She made a valiant effort not to flinch.

In that moment, an impossible note of familiarity sounded within me, like the chime of a sacred bell. I looked down into her wide blue eyes and wondered if it was possible that we might have something, anything, in common.

"Who are you?" Her impressively calm inquiry shattered the spell.

"It doesn't matter." I grasped her by the arm, though not as firmly as

I had meant to. She was small beneath my hands, but sturdy too. A woman of tempered glass and secret steel. And unlike the bodies I had grown so accustomed to handling, she was warm.

In a heartbeat, her free arm lashed forward, and she drove the heel of her palm into my chest, catching me off guard, which surprised me. She wrenched her other arm from my grip, and stepped back. I already liked her. She didn't let anyone push her around.

"Why not?" The girl planted her feet as hard as she could into ground. I looked into her then, at the face of her soul, the relative newness of her life. So young and vital, and yet oddly wise. Was that why Orion wanted her? I doubted it. He had never struck me as a man appreciative of depth.

"Because." I spoke in measured tones. "Ask me again, and you'll be dead." Briefly, I regretted my coarse phrasing; that type of rhetoric was usually enough to induce panic in the hearts of mortals.

She narrowed her gaze at me, her pose ready to fight me. "Fine. What do you want, then? Why are you tracking me?" The considerable weight of either courage or stupidity filling her voice was enough to give me a moment of pause. I turned halfway to see her once more. She *was* a mortal, wasn't she? The echo of that one clear note haunted me. Maybe I was misjudging her. There was something odd about her I couldn't pinpoint.

She stared at me, a cold, defiant fire now burning in her eyes. "I'm not afraid of you. If you're not going to talk, then you can be on your way."

This was partially a lie. I could feel it coming off of her no matter how deeply she drew from her well of strength. There was nothing she could have done to mask it any further; fear was a vital instinct for any being with the inconvenient ability to die.

"Yes, you are." I leaned down. Her breath caught slightly in her throat, and she recoiled out of my reach. "Just as you should be."

She chuckled grimly. "I don't think so." The next thing I knew, she had kicked at my ribs, ripped her hat off, and thrown it in my face. The flash of black cloth was just disorienting enough to lose sight of her as she took off in the first direction she saw. I blinked and shook my head. She hadn't gotten far, what with her fragile human legs.

And now I was getting annoyed, fire igniting in my veins. As usual, the living were proving to be far more difficult than the dead. Not that it mattered, in the long run. I gave her a few seconds to believe her flight had a chance of success, and then I drew in a breath, pulling my power from the other side of the veil. The world washed white around us. I watched her slow to a halt mid-stride, her hair suspended in a glorious pink banner behind her.

My wings, no longer hidden in the liminal space between my domain and hers, weighed heavy on my back. Often, I wished they weren't necessary to use what cursed gifts I had been granted, but they were always mine to bear. They unfurled slowly as I approached her from behind. Up close, I could see her moving a fraction of an inch at a time. The sole of her right shoe descended gradually through still air. One wing formed a wall in front of the fleeing girl.

I exhaled.

She ran into a cloud of black feathers at full speed—the hollowness of my wing-bones did nothing to cushion the impact. I caught her as she reeled back, stunned.

Pivoting on the spot, she threw a fist at my shoulders and drove a knee into my gut, then shoved herself away, breaking free past my wings caging her.

She was good, but I was better.

Each wing folded against my body, and I ran after her this time, refusing to have Orion make comment regarding a human outsmarting me.

A small clearing ahead, and I spread my wings wide. They snapped outward, catching the wind and beat. My feet lifted off the ground. In seconds, I swooped right behind her and looped my arms under her armpits, hauling her into the air.

"Put me the hell down!" She writhed against me, but I held on tight, my wings beating, carrying us over the trees. Her fingers dug into hands, pulling at my hold as she thrust for freedom.

I admired how she didn't let fear paralyze her at a time when most humans would panic.

By the time the river was back in earshot, she was kicking and shouting to be put down. I fought the sudden, vicious impulse to crush her right there, to break her delicate neck in one effortless snap. As much as I would have enjoyed it, something about her made me want to study her further, to understand who she was.

Less than a hundred feet ahead, Orion stood on the side of the water, awaiting my return. I had no doubt that if I delivered him a dead girl, she wouldn't be the only one who ended up broken. I may have held death in my hands, but as it turned out, it was harder to deal with one who was already there.

To that end, the girl was still fighting as I set her down in front of the others. Seth had just finished sending the body off downstream, and as he moved back toward us, he caught sight of the captive girl for the first time. She stumbled out of my reach, her body poised to fight. Against anyone else, she might have stood a chance.

Orion smiled. There seemed to be a hint of genuine pleasure in his expression. "Hello again, little one," he said.

The girl whipped around at the sound of his voice. From that moment on, her giant eyes never looked at anyone else.

8

ORION

I liked the way she stared at me in that moment of true recognition, her upturned face illuminated by a fall of silver moonlight, her full lips, and cheeks rosy from the cold. Behind the mask of bravery in her blue eyes, there was a hint of fear, and also innocence. She stood about five-foot-eight, toned, and my gaze traced the curves of her full breasts. My presence had surprised her, truly. That palpable element of shock was what I enjoyed most—a way to let her know exactly where dominance lay.

"A strange place for a girl to be wandering at night in this city," I told her calmly. "Perhaps you're lost."

The vulnerable openness of her expression instantly closed up. She seemed to age a few years as her soft mouth tightened into a straight, emotionless line and her luminous eyes hardened into stones. "I'm exactly where I planned to be." Much like she had at our first meeting, she lifted her delicate chin.

What was this pretty creature hoping to prove by pretending not to be afraid? She was no match for even quiet, brooding Logan. Had I wanted to, I could have torn the thin white skin of her throat before she had the chance to say a single word. Didn't she know she was living purely on the strength of my mercy?

Her stubborn foolhardiness elicited a grudging but genuine admiration. Seldom did I get the chance to meet mortals whose hearts and

60

minds were able to withstand the knowledge of my nature. This human girl, on the contrary, had sought me out, followed me to my home. And now she was caught, and she still refused to back down.

"I suppose you expect me to spare you?" I spoke somewhat sternly, so that she wouldn't know I was in any way pleased to see her again.

"And I assume you'll have a price," she shot back. "How about you tell me what you three are doing out here?" Her wits were as sharp as her tongue, even under these trying circumstances. She brushed an unruly lock of wild hair from her eyes, which burned into me. Were I any weaker, that gaze might have turned my bones to ash.

"Well." I smirked. "It's very doubtful you'd have anything material that would interest me. But I think we could work something out. A payment plan, if you will." Stepping forward, I reached out to touch her face with the backs of my fingers, running my knuckles from cheekbone to jaw. She was a beautiful little thing.

A tiny shudder cracked her wall as she took a deep breath.

"I don't want to know," she said, eyeing the three of us, and the brave little thing never recoiled, "but I have a sickening feeling you're going to tell me anyway."

I laughed, unable to help it. She found a way to deepen my burgeoning fascination at every turn. Reckless, ignorant, self-endangering, and funny! How had it taken so long for this rare sort of woman to fall—almost literally—into my hands? She could not be permitted to stray too far from watchful eyes unless I wanted to risk losing her. But at the same time, I suspected she'd come back on her own even if I set her free.

After all, she had been unable to stay away once already.

The girl glanced to the side as I appraised her. When she had spoken, there were no fangs of any kind I could see, just the smooth, ineffectual even pearls of her teeth all humans carried. Yet the longer I stood so close to her, the greater I sensed something unusual, a characteristic I didn't recognize in her. Not to mention, no humans would stand before me without trembling with fear.

"Who are you, gorgeous?" For now, I kept my tone gentle and safe. Those great, jeweled eyes shifted back to mine. Her brows knit.

"Save the compliments, Romeo. My name is Veronica." She paused, holding my gaze. How fascinating seeing I haven't even tried to charm her yet. "By the way, I'm not giving you anything. Especially not what it looks like you're thinking. And you didn't answer my earlier question about what you're doing here." Veronica's whole body was tense with frigid anticipation. One hand had curled into a tight fist. On the surface, she might have seemed calm, but underneath was a cornered animal, ready to fight her way out, tooth and nail.

"We're out for a stroll." I grinned. Not discouraged, I slid my gaze over the side of her neck and over her throat. The blood pulsed through her carotid artery. I could hear it, smell it at being only a couple of feet apart. A shadow of the rich, metallic taste hovered on the surface of my tongue. My mouth began to water. But beneath that lay something new, something dangerous, something tempting. I narrowed my gaze on her. Veronica was so much more than a human. I didn't quite understand it, but a shadow lingered beneath the surface. Who exactly was she?

"Is there nothing I can do to change your mind to come home with me?"

"You have nothing I want." She held her chin high, her hands stiff by her side, and I didn't miss her gaze sweeping over the three of us constantly. She was watching our every move.

Her words had told me one thing very clearly, but the signals from her body, the heightened heartbeat, the faintest hint of red shaded her cheeks said something else entirely. "It would be a damn shame to waste a body with so much potential."

"I'm not here for your entertainment." Veronica's face reflected disgust and disdain at the same time her pulse sped up.

I knew that I had her in the palm of my hand, no matter how hard a fight she thought she was putting up. Not to mention that all together, we had her outnumbered and outclassed.

"Then what do you want? To spy on us?"

She gave no response, but the truth showed itself at the corner of her mouth, curling upward ever so slightly. The fire was back in her eyes as she stared daggers, first at me, Seth, then at Logan. Ever dispassionate, they gazed back at her.

"I could have you killed," I replied.

"For crossing paths with you out here?" She pursed her lips in a mocking expression looking like she might break out laughing.

"You *should* just do it." Seth spoke up at last, pushing his way into our sphere. He stood at my shoulder and glowered down at the captive. Smoke rose from his nostrils, wreathing around his face. "What a waste of time. Bring her home, or let's chuck her in there too." On the last word, he jerked his thumb over his shoulder toward the icy river thundering along at his back. I glanced at the surface of the water just in time to see the last of a pale, slightly mottled hand disappear below the current.

"Enough," I warned.

The demon grunted and fell silent, but I noticed that he, too, was transfixed by her sensuous beauty. His expression betrayed the naked lust I felt stirring within me. To see him want her so openly enraged me.

That was the moment I decided that I wanted to make her mine—in body and in spirit. Turning new vampires was a practice I had abandoned for decades, that I had, in fact, sworn never to repeat. Mistakes had been made in my careless youth, and they had cost me dearly. On the rare occasions I allowed my mind to venture back to those days, I remembered little more than brokenness and shadow, a constant crisis of faith.

One look at Veronica and those long-held convictions flew out the window. All I could think about was how she'd taste and the feeling of her death and rebirth in my arms. So many times it had been orgasmic in its own way. Pleasure mingling with pain. The thought of experiencing that moment with her filled me with a fiery passion I hadn't felt in years.

Her hand fell to her waist, which I assumed was where she kept a weapon. No one would come alone after us without a plan for when things turned bad. She took several steps backward, aware this wasn't a fight she'd win if she started one. But it occurred to me that her intention hadn't been about battling us but to gain intelligence.

The urge to sweep her up and spirit her away to the house threatened to blind me to everything else in the world. It was tempting just to say that nothing else was of consequence until I'd gotten my fill of her. But not even her potent allure erased the gravity of other, more pressing issues. My body longed to have its mounting hunger sated by her flesh, and yet I understood that she was no more than a distraction. To acquire her would be to acquire a weak point for my enemies to exploit.

That sobering reality was just enough to snap me out of the dream into which I had fallen. I realized I had been holding Veronica's face as a scholar might hold a sacred relic. Interestingly, she had let me, though the fist persisted at her side. Would she fight if we gave her cause? The prospect of putting her body through its paces threatened to pull me away into fantasy.

"If you aren't going to be forthcoming with me, I will be on my way," she said as Seth started to walk away in the direction of the house. Veronica watched him leave, and a hot spike of jealousy rammed into my chest. I grasped her chin and turned her face back to me. "Don't look at the jester in the presence of his king," I advised her curtly.

Heedless of my words and shoving my hand away, she said, "Who is that?" Her eyes flicked in Logan's general direction. "And that?"

"If you're a good girl, you might find out." The tide of my emotions rose so sharply and unexpectedly, that I struggled to contain them.

"And watch who you're manhandling, clanmaster." If my tone had been short, hers was as thin and taut as piano wire. "I promise you are underestimating me."

"Rich words from a woman who refuses to prove it," I answered quietly.

Her fear was momentarily overshadowed by anger and heat. She was angry too, and curious. Her desires were far less bold than mine, but they were rooted and growing.

I didn't want to turn her loose. It crossed my mind that the cellar was newly vacated of its unfortunate last tenant. She could take up residence there just as easily. The most immediate and complex problem was whether or not she could be convinced to stay put.

And if she was down there, I could count on being driven to distraction every minute by the physical craving gnawing at my insides. It was useless to deny that she held a strange and unforgiving power over me, just by virtue of being a woman capable of catching and holding my attention. My desire was to spend every moment with her, picking her apart, deciphering how and why she'd managed to take up residence in my mind so quickly. And then I ached to devour her until there was no doubt left that she belonged to me.

All of which made Veronica an incredible liability. Though it pained me to admit, there was no way in hell to bring her to the house without compromising everything.

Veronica stepped farther away and looked at me, saying, "Listen, Orion. As much as I appreciate this oh so magnanimous gesture, let's get one thing straight, okay? I don't owe you for this, no matter how much you want me to. You made your choice to not hurt me. Now we're both going to have to deal with the consequences."

The grain of truth in her words stung a little. Precious little had stopped me from flinging her over my shoulder and locking her in the cellar, but I was allowing her to roam free. Maybe it was because I knew in my soul that she wouldn't wander far, that she'd keep returning of her own accord. Even then, perhaps I sensed that the fascination was mutual.

Also, it certainly helped that she wanted to destroy me. I chose not to tell her what a vain aspiration it was. The long span of my life had thus far been marred by countless dangers. One beautiful and eminently fragile human girl posed no threat.

In order to make sure she knew it, I closed the distance she'd put between us and locked an arm around her waist. Her hands braced against my chest to no avail. This time, I leaned down so close that my lips brushed her skin under her earlobe. "I'm not a man to whom consequences normally apply."

A beat of silence passed. Then she faced me, mere inches away. "We both know you aren't a man at all."

I released her like a falconer releases his bird, pushing her off into the waiting embrace of the forest. Veronica hesitated for a fraction of an instant. Her gaze flickered between me and Logan. Then she was gone, her hair a flash among the shadows.

Goodbye for now, Veronica, I thought. *For now...but not forever.*

9

VERONICA

I spent hours in a barely contained rage after finally making it back to the hotel. The floor creaked under my feet as I paced around the suite in my socks, too worked up to sleep or even shower. Every word that sleaze Orion had said stuck in my brain. I wanted to scrub at my skin until I could no longer feel the unnatural coolness of his fingers on my neck.

"Who the fuck does he think he is?" I demanded out loud. Of course it was a rhetorical question, and unfortunately, his concept of self lined up pretty well with his actual status. As clanmaster in Anchorage, his word was pretty much law, as far as the vamps in his clan were concerned. The master said to jump, they asked how high. No doubt he had a legion of henchmen at his beck and call. All he had to do was distribute my face to the troops, and I was doomed to have a very bad time.

It had to be a game to him, a muscle he flexed to try and make a fool out of me, and I hated him for it. I hated the way he so obviously viewed me as prey, and the way he had stared as if he was already entitled to the kill. The memory alone made me shudder.

But most of all, I hated my body's reaction to his presence. Orion was not someone who should have held any appeal for me at all, and yet…some hidden magnetism drew me toward his clutches. I thought I'd done pretty well holding my own this last time, but the potential of the future scared me. What if my resolve weakened for an instant?

He'd gotten so damn close. If I closed my eyes, he might as well have been standing right beside me, his presence lingered so strongly. I'd never met a vamp like him, though I had certainly been warned about the old ones, the ones who seemed able to bend the human psyche to their will. Maybe Orion was used to hapless mortal women falling all over him in the blink of an eye.

Then there were his two accomplices. One with black wings, and the other with smoke wafting from the corners of his mouth and nose. Those two weren't vampires, though what exactly they were, I wasn't too sure yet. Demons? Why was Orion with them anyway and not with more of his own kind?

The next couple of days that followed our accidental rendezvous down by the inlet shore were full of me buckling down on my resolve to get to the bottom of the rash of violent crime Lian called me about. The desk in my room disappeared beneath pages of notes I compiled of my findings, complete with drawings, charts, and diagrams. I listed every conceivable reason I could think of as to why a vampire from Seattle might have been found dead so far from home.

Still, despite my best efforts to explore every angle, there were pieces missing. I just didn't know enough about the way the region had developed in the years since I had last been local. I certainly didn't remember such a robust supernatural presence. Then again, I had a lot of other things to think about.

But I did know someone who was more than happy to fill in the blanks. Lian's huge, rambling house began to feel more and more like home again with each visit. We always ended up on the long, over-stuffed sofa in the den, covered up by blankets, flames crackling in the fireplace. It was kind of strange to be sitting there all cozy, eating fresh baked goods and drinking from steaming mugs of coffee or hot choco-late while we discussed everything hiding in the city's darkest shadows.

"I'm not sure when it started, exactly." Lian sat cross-legged on the sofa, cradling her mug in her lap. She frowned, thinking. "A year ago, or maybe eighteen months. I was helping Dad with the books, and I started to notice all these new names on the payroll. I mean, like a dozen at a time. So I asked him about it and he told me there was an influx of transplants looking for work."

I raised an eyebrow. "Transplants?"

"That's what he called them. I guess I didn't think too hard about it because it's the kind of thing that happens a lot in Alaska, you know? People get wanderlust and they come up here thinking they can go off the grid or live in the wilderness or whatever. I've heard of whole families relocating here to get a fresh start." She shrugged. "So yeah, it was a ton of people, but it just meant more help for Dad, as far as I was concerned."

"Right." I took a sip of my cocoa and stared into the fire. "And it was probably a huge part of why the boats are doing so well now. Not like he's going to turn down an opportunity to expand if he thinks it's viable."

"Exactly. But one day I was running numbers and I kept having to go back and double check. I thought there must have been a mistake—these guys weren't getting paid nearly enough. And usually that's the kind of thing that will start a riot around here, so I called my dad in a panic and told him we were accidentally shorting some of the fishermen." Her frown deepened slightly. "That was when he told me about the arrangement they made and how he was paying them partially in a percentage of their catch."

"Has he ever done that before?" I already knew the answer, but I wanted to hear it from her.

Lian shook her head vehemently. "God, no. He would've laughed anyone who asked right back out the door. I tried to get him to tell me what was going on at the time. He just said this was a special case, not to worry about it, and to get back to work." She chuckled. "I mean, you know Dad. Work is his life. I just did what he asked."

"Was this around when the violence began?" I leaned over to pour more hot cocoa from a massive thermos on the coffee table. The chocolate-scented steam made me think of the couple of holidays I flew back here after I lost Grandma and spent it in the very same place against the quiet backdrop of snow. Those days had never felt more like a dream.

Lian took a deep breath. I could see her sifting through her memories almost like they were physical objects, grains of sand pouring through her fingers. "I think so," she finally said, although the words were reluctant. "I want to say there had been stories about a crime wave on the news before, but this was when it all started exploding. People in Anchorage were kind of shocked. There are a lot of disappearances up here, but not necessarily outright murder."

"And where were the vamps while this was all happening?" I was slowly working my way toward what was, for me, the real heart of the issue. If Lian or her family had had dealings with Orion in the past, she didn't tell me. Would I have done something if I'd known about him sooner?

"I wish I could tell you." She ran her fingers through her hair. "But I didn't put two and two together for a pretty long time. Not until our guys started going missing. And even then, who's to say it had to be vamps? Alaska's like a three-ring supernatural circus. It could've been anything that was just passing through."

She set her cup on the coffee table, stood up, stretched, and went to poke at the fire. A cloud of sparks kicked up behind the screen.

"Has anyone ever mentioned anyone named Orion?" That was, at long last, the million-dollar question, and it hung in the air for a minute. Lian glanced over her shoulder at me, trying to read my face.

"Orion?" She spoke the clanmaster's name like she was trying out a foreign word. "No, I don't think so." She looked me in the eye. "Who is he?"

"Good freaking question," I muttered. "We ran into each other a couple times. He'd like me to assume he's the one in charge around here." My fingers drummed along the side of the mug. "Pretty sure he's murdered at least two people, so…maybe he's not bluffing."

Lian bristled visibly. "Don't tell me he confessed."

I shook my head, also choosing not to tell her about the humanoid hand I'd seen disappearing below the icy surface of the inlet. "Not in so many words. I think something is brewing in Anchorage."

"Yeah. That's what I've been afraid of." We both fell silent for a little while. The grandfather clock in the foyer chimed the hour of six in the evening.

I was the one to speak up first. "How many employees have you lost?"

"Six." Lian answered so readily I knew she had counted over and over. "Only a couple were ever found, though." Her lips pressed into a grim line. "They were dead, of course."

"And was this before or after you found out they were shifters?"

"Most before," she said. "One of them disappeared after and still hasn't turned up. My guess is that they'll probably be recovered after the snow finally melts."

Her theory resonated with my instinct. Orion had definitely seemed to be taking advantage of the unusually cold, brutal weather. Snow and ice could keep a lot of dirty secrets—for a time.

"Did anything change after you caught them shifting?" The absolute last thing I wanted was for the Zhaos to end up in the middle of whatever messed-up bullshit this turned out to be. I felt a great need to protect them at all costs. If that meant throwing myself straight into the fire of yet another turf war, I'd do it happily.

To my relief, Lian said no. "The guy was surprised," she said with a laugh. "But it was at least as much because he turned back stark naked as anything else." Her nose scrunched. "Those dudes are *hairy*, V. How long is it going to take to forget I've seen that?"

"Too long." I smirked. "Way too long. You don't think they'd consider you a liability or anything, since you're technically a witness?"

"Who am I going to tell?" She arched her eyebrows. "Dad already knows; he has to. The only way he'd pay in fish is if he was paying a literal bear. It's not like they're trying to sneak around behind *his* back. Besides, Alaska's like the land of open secrets. Nobody cares what you are as long as you don't bother them with it."

"That's true, I suppose." The forty-ninth state was nothing if not a haven for outcasts and weirdos of all types. Why shouldn't that rule apply to monsters as well as men? "Still, keep your eyes open, okay? Call me if you hear or see anything suspicious. I will hit the ground running."

"I know you will." Lian smiled. "Because you're the best. And because I'm paying for your room." She hesitated. "You know, you could stay here if you wanted."

"Yeah…no thanks." I sucked in a deep breath, imagining the awkwardness of that conversation. *Lian told me you were hiring bear shifters to work on the fishing boats. Well, they're being murdered by a sexy vampire and two of his friends, so I'm here to sort that out. No big deal.* "It's easier to come and go at night if I'm on my own."

"Good call." Lian looked visibly relieved. She sighed. "I had hoped I might be blowing things out of proportion when I first called you. But the more we talk, and the more questions you ask… That's not really the case, is it?"

I chewed my lip and thought of Orion and his two henchmen standing over the half-frozen corpse they'd pitched into the water. I remembered the vampire's eyes raking over my body, cold, piercing, relentless. His voice echoed in my ears as clearly as if he were standing right beside me.

I'm not a man to whom consequences normally apply.

"No," I said quietly. "No, it isn't."

"Think we've talked shop long enough, V. How about I order us take-out and we watch a movie? Dad and Mom are out of town a few days. You can crash here if you want. Will be nice to eat too much food and watch bad movies with you."

Her offer sounded amazing, so how could I knock her back? Especially when she looked at me like she wasn't beyond begging. My mind still churned with everything she'd told me, but I'd also missed spending more time with her where we just had fun.

"Deal." I reclined on the couch, smiling at how good it felt to be at her place. It was rare that I took any time off, my days and nights were usually filled with study and slaying. So this was a nice change of pace.

"Excellent." She started tapping her phone. "There's this new Spanish Tapas place that just opened up and I've been dying to try out their food. I'm going to order a variety of dishes for us."

"I can't wait." Reaching over, I grabbed the remote for the television. "And I'm selecting our movie tonight."

She cut me a serious glare. "Okay, no soppy romances. I want b-grade!"

I scoffed. "I don't do soppy romances."

She fake-laughed, howling loudly. "Says, Ms. I-love-Hallmark movies. You made us watch them each time you returned here for Christmas."

Flicking on the television, I ignored her gloating because clearly Lian never forgot a thing.

10

SETH

The mortal plane was pale compared to hell—pale, desaturated, and painfully boring. I got tired real fast of walking through a miasma of fog every day. Couldn't go a mile without ending up soaked to the skin, freezing rainwater pooling on the ground. I missed the days when flames nipped at my heels, and a trail of smoke heralded my arrival. I was known in my own domain. Hated, maybe. Feared, definitely. But here? Nobody knew who I was.

And I wasn't even allowed to kill anyone yet.

But wandering alone through the damp and dreary night was better than spending hours holed up in the vampire's mausoleum of a house. The more time I spent in his vicinity, the stronger the urge to punch him in his smug, condescending face. Just once, but hard enough that he'd feel it for the rest of his miserable un-life.

Don't get me wrong: it wasn't that I regretted the deal we made where I'd finally gain power over my own realm. To be left the fuck alone so I could do as I wanted without dealing with anyone who pissed me off. To forget my past and start fresh wasn't a big ask, was it?

Contracts had been a way of life for all eternity, and I was used to keeping company I didn't care for. Orion had a singular talent for knowing exactly how to push my buttons—and then doing it all at once. Every day I came within an inch of erupting like some mythical volcano, but I'd gotten very good at reeling back from the edge at the

72

last second. At the end of the day, I understood he offered me a chance to escape my past. He sought me out, asked me to help him, so as much as I wanted to murder him, I remembered the underlying agreement between us wasn't between two enemies. We just didn't see eye to eye on everything.

For the moment, I made do by roaming the streets, picking over the darkest parts of the city shadows in search of something to hurt, eat, or both. The blood in my veins refused to settle. And dammit, I was hungry all the time.

That night, the usual prowl wasn't enough. I had something else on my mind besides idle violent fantasies of raking Orion across the coals. Every time I closed my eyes, even if it was just to blink, the girl flashed in my mind. The one he'd been tormenting on the night we dropped a body in the river, with her shining eyes and annoyingly bright hair. On the outside, she was so much more than another ordinary plain Jane like the rest of the human women in an endless line of 'em.

I could not stop thinking about her, and I didn't know why. Yeah, she was sexy, yeah I was pissed that Orion had kept her to himself the whole time, but what else was new? The bastard never shared anything important with us. He always had to be the center of attention, as sure as the sun rose every day on this godforsaken place. His ego had never bothered me all that much before.

This time, it drove me insane. Whenever I thought about her skin in the moonlight, or the way she stared at me as I walked by, my body demanded more than a sterile memory. I wanted to know what her body looked like under those winter clothes. How perfect she would be pinned under me in bed, or up against a wall, or just naked on the floor. Anything would do. I wasn't about to be picky.

The burning thoughts nagged at me constantly, a crackling hum in the back of my mind. Never before had I met a human who could sate my lustful appetite, and I had no reason to believe she was up to the task. Yet something about her made me think she might be able to deliver. If only there was a way to test the theory without Orion finding out. No doubt he'd throw a shit fit over someone else playing with his toys.

Which, I had to admit, tempted me more. I could easily get off on the idea of making the vampire mad.

I blew out a thick plume of smoke and told myself to cool it. Shoving my sleeves up to the elbow, I let the misty rain turn to steam as it struck my skin. In the dark of the night, my veins glowed faintly, fiery orange and yellow. There was an itch building that demanded to be scratched, one way or another. Some poor son of a bitch was about to have a very bad evening.

Deep down, I kept wishing it was Orion on the other end of my wrath. He annoyed me more after meeting the pink-haired girl than before. Didn't seem fair that a first-class prick like him coasted along on unlimited time. *Someone ought to number his days,* I thought, and not for the first time. Once, months before, I'd almost done it myself.

A smile crept across my face as I slowed down to savor the recollection. He always kept the doors to the several rooms he called his, locked, as if there was anything in his gaudy, antique junk that anyone would want. But there was one night he'd forgotten, and I heard the door creaking on my way by. Sunrise was just getting underway, and he had pulled the drapes tight over the window.

Hell of a weakness, that sunlight.

The casket was sitting in the middle of the room, sealed tight and surrounded by a sprinkling of what turned out to be dirt. Back then, the notion of Mr. High-and-Mighty vampire having to recreate his own grave to sleep in made me choke back a bark of laughter. Of course he couldn't sleep with a blanket and a pillow. What an asshole.

Well, I hadn't been able to resist the urge to snoop around a little bit. Like I said, most of his things were tasteless, gaudy junk, way too overblown and Gothic for anyone in their right mind. A leather couch sat against the back wall with a small table and lamp. It took about five seconds for all of my attention to focus on the one interesting thing in that room: the casket. Heavy and made out of solid ebony wood, it was polished to a shine, lovingly cared for in a way that gave me, a demon, the creeps.

I remembered reaching out and running my fingers across the lid. How easy would it have been to crack that thing open, dump his stupid living corpse on the floor, and drive the closest stake-like object through his corrupted heart? It was strange to recognize that Orion, and all the rest of his kind, were abominations to me, in a way. Creatures like him were outliers on the fringes of our hierarchy of good and evil. They existed in defiance of death, the strongest and most natural force in the universe.

Maybe that was the real reason he pissed me off. Or maybe I just really wanted to devour the sexy human girl he thought he'd claimed.

Either reason worked for me. I did not need to be convinced to despise anything.

The city around me disappeared against the backdrop of my thoughts as I made my way into downtown Anchorage. A cluster of bars remained open, lights weak in the mist. I aimed for them, eyes tracing the sodden pavement. The sound of boots on the sidewalk and my deepening ruminations nearly blocked out all others.

Why hadn't I killed him then? Pragmatism was the answer I liked to give, but cowardice lurked in the realm of uncomfortable truth after he offered me a way out of my problems. The conflict of how I felt toward him drove me crazy.

Somehow, he had convinced me that he was the sole distributor of the prize he had promised—free rein over the mortal realm. He was the one who could loosen my chains and allow me to run amok as I pleased in the land of men. And he ruled over his kind with an iron fist. The other, lesser vampires waited at his beck and call. I could have fought most of them off, but the shadow of a doubt was enough to stay my hand.

At the time, Orion's reasonings, whatever they were, had made sense. And even now, Orion's word was the bond that held me at his side. I was ravenous and restless, but I could also be patient. If he turned out to be a liar, I would simply destroy him. He knew that, too.

But others did not share the same wisdom.

"Hey, freak!"

The taunt snapped me out of my head as quickly as a bone snapped under pressure. I wheeled around in search of its source, reflexive rage rising in my chest. The heat surged from my body; I felt the lowest layer of clothes begin to smolder on my skin.

A low whistle cut through the gloom. "Over here, Smokey."

This time I pinpointed the voice right away. The cluster of vamps leaned up against the walls at the end of an alley, their dead eyes flat in the dusky light. They were not the same maddeningly elegant breed as the bloodsucker I loved to hate. No, these were mongrels, mangy and feral. No scruples at all.

No one would miss them.

They grinned at me as I turned to face them down the narrow passage, mouths stretching to expose hungrily pointed teeth. The ravenousness I could understand, but I wasn't about to give up my own blood.

"Sorry." I rubbed my chin, eyes narrowed. "You talking to me?" All of us were obviously itching for a fight. The air crackled with thinly veiled tension.

"What if we are?" The vamps straightened up, tall and thin and gangly. Two of them cracked their necks and knuckles in anticipation. They thought this was going to be as straightforward a beatdown as they were ever likely to get. A gift from the gods of the street.

But that would make me the sacrificial lamb, and if there was anything I had never been, it was meek and compliant. "Well, then you'd better be ready to have something to show for that bad attitude." Again I pushed up my sleeves. The veins in my forearms burned hot, and I wondered if I should just let the sons of bitches drink my blood. Call it an experiment, see what that would do to them.

The vamp in the lead laughed and spat on the ground. He spoke like his throat had been packed full of gravel. Eyes that should have been bloodshot were spidered with gray capillaries. "You think you're on the high ground, all cozied up with the clanmaster, don't you? Think you're safe in this town?" Their advancing circle began to pull in tighter around me. "Think again."

My least favorite thing about vampires was the inherent difficulty in gauging their strength. Every one of those assholes looked like he had walked straight out of the crypt he'd died in, but experience taught me how easily they could be underestimated. If there was anything I did not want, it was to be shown up by the local stiffs.

"Are we gonna do this, or what?" I sucked in a deep breath, churned it into smoke, and as the first one lunged toward me, blew the whole cloud out in his face. He reeled back and came up choking as I grabbed for his throat through the smoke screen. "Never mind. Guess I answered my own question."

"You cocky son of a bitch!" The vampires leaped on me from either side, clawing at my arms and shoulders with ragged nails like an angry, grotesque flock of birds. I used the one flailing in my grip to shove them off. My hand tightened around his neck. He gagged. His tongue lolled from his mouth. Someone threw a punch into the side of my face, causing stars to briefly explode behind that eye.

I dropped him and swung around to face a different attacker. This one wasn't much more than a scrawny punk, probably a kid struck down and turned out of pity. For all he lacked in muscle mass, he knew how to fight in the way a caged animal fights: with desperate, wild strength. I clenched my fist until it glowed white hot and drove it into the center of his sternum. He howled in pain, and when he staggered back, the imprint of my knuckles was branded on his skin.

The leader of this pathetic little club still writhed on the concrete, holding his throat. The two who remained knelt at his side. I turned to stare down at them. Blinding heat radiated off my fist. I lifted it and snapped my fingers.

"Want me to burn it all down?" I demanded. "Because I will." All I had to do was apply a little pressure, and he'd be in prolonged agony at the very least.

Then I remembered how I'd have to return to that damn house and face up to Orion about killing some of his men. Didn't matter that they were like plague rats, weak and disgusting. Their beloved clanmaster would have my head. And I couldn't count on Logan for shit.

The realization was a downer, to say the least. Instantly, I felt the adrenaline ebbing, its high spiraling down into an immediate depression. A black cloud formed in my head as I forced myself to step away.

"Where you going?" the vamp croaked from the ground. He pried one hand off his neck and used it to flip me off.

"Hey." I glanced back at him. "A word of advice? Don't press your fucking luck."

VERONICA

I gripped the stake at my belt having just watched Seth battle a handful of vamps. Who started the fight was questionable as I stumbled upon them mere seconds earlier. Though that was enough time to reveal Seth as a man who never backed down and let his rage rule him. Not to mention his ego. Except, he wasn't really a man, was he? With every punch and kick he had delivered, thin threads of dark smoke curled out from the corners of his mouth and nostrils.

I'd seen my fair share of supernaturals, so what was a demon doing out of Hell and in Anchorage of all places?

They were known for their berserker-like fighting tendencies.

Unrelenting.

Ferocious.

Unstoppable.

They were the warriors of the supernatural world and no one

volunteered to battle them. Well, unless you were a tribe of idiotic vampires who had no clue.

Fury filled his eyes as he had reached for the throat of another vampire, then dropped him to the ground. It intrigued me that he worked with the clanmaster, yet openly destroyed vamps. Maybe these were Orion's clan enemies? It was hard to tell in all honesty.

Though it was difficult to ignore Seth's strength and power. Something tightened in my chest at seeing how easily he dealt with the vampires, at the way his muscles flexed. One thing was for sure, he was having a blast taking down these fiends.

After a small exchange with the vamp still on the ground, Seth whipped around and walked away from him, his face twisted into a frustrated expression. He was headed right in my direction.

Our gazes locked, and I quickly retreated down the narrow street lined with storefronts. Lowering my hand from the stake, I licked the cold from my lips, and stood tall as he rounded the corner. Of course I expected him to come this way.

"Have you taken to spying just on me now?" he asked, looming over me, wearing all black from his boots to the heavy coat that fell to his waist. The tone in his voice didn't belong to someone angry but carried a playful tone.

"I have better things to do with my time. If you happen to be in my path, then that's not my problem."

He arched a brow and gave a slight shake of his head as if unsure if he liked my answer. As much as I reminded myself who stood in front of me, my body betrayed me in response to the eye-candy studying me from head to toe.

Never in a million years would I have expected myself to think *that* about a demon, but Seth was unlike any of the beasts I'd encountered. He was built to be a fighter, broad and powerful, yet those solemn eyes and damn perfect lips undid me. The darkness behind his gaze told of heartache, or a broken past. It called to me, drew me to him, and for a short pause, I let myself believe someone like him and me could have something in common. All the hurt and guilt that chewed me up on the inside reflected from his eyes.

"If you keep looking at me that way, I'm going to take that as an invitation, little girl."

My thoughts evaporated, bringing me back to the present and under the watchful eye of a demon.

"That's not happening. Anyway, what was all that about?" I stuck my chin out in the direction he'd just come from. I reminded myself who I dealt with and the danger he posed, the unpredictability. He wasn't a man to let myself lust over.

"Just a small altercation I'm sorting out very soon. So, are we going back to your place or mine?"

I laughed at his presumption. "Keep dreaming. If that's how you come onto women, I bet you strike out a lot."

He drew in a sharp breath and raked a hand through his hair. "I like you. You don't back down. I admire feisty women. And you don't want to know how many women flock to me." That deviously sexy grin split his lips, revealing a white row of perfect teeth.

The air between us thickened, my heart thumping into my ribcage. His yellowing eyes caught the light of the bright sun.

"How about you tell me what you're doing working with Orion?"

"We're business partners," he answered me, smirking through his lie.

Before I knew it, his arm swept around my back, pulling me to him, our bodies pressing together.

My hands snapped up to push against his chest. His rock hard muscles flexed under my touch.

He inhaled the air, then narrowed his gaze on me. "There's something different about you than the other humans, isn't there? But what is it?"

I refused to tell him anything about myself, and I instinctually shoved him, but it was too late to stop losing myself to him or end the feelings he roused deep inside me. He gripped me with enough to strength to know escaping wouldn't be easy, though at the same time, his sheer size and power sent an explosion of butterflies through my stomach.

One touch and I forgot the danger he posed. His hand stroked across my lower back, leaving a streak of fire in its wake.

His face was inches from mine, and I was breathless. I should knee him in the balls and turn away, yet I let myself stay in his arms a bit longer.

"Tell me when to stop," he teased, and his words lit me up from the inside. "I promise to go slow at first."

A flush flared over my body, and as much as I wanted him to do the things he promised in his eyes, it wasn't going to happen.

I drove strength behind my hands and pushed against his chest. "Let me go!"

His hand fell away, and I stumbled from his grasp. Gasping for air, my whole body tingled with a need I refused to acknowledge.

I clenched my hands by my side. "You can't just go around taking what you want."

"That's where you're wrong."

I shook my head. "Just keep out of my way, okay." I swung away, trembling from how easily he affected me, just as a small gust of warm air rushed across my back.

I glanced over my shoulder and Seth was gone. Yet the earlier arousal still pulsed deep in my core. *What was wrong with me?*

Turning around, I headed down the street and kicked myself for letting Seth get under my skin. He knew exactly what he was doing, and I fell royally for his tricks.

Asshole.

11

ORION

lack coffee was the only mortal indulgence I entertained on a regular basis. Its caffeinated bitterness ran through bloodless veins like a small electric shock, giving everything an edge that was just a little bit sharper. I liked to think it helped me see the world through human eyes.

The brewing and drinking of my coffee had become almost ritualistic in a sense. I had gotten the process down to an art, designed to produce a cup exactly the way I liked it. I was in the middle of pouring the water over a mound of fresh grounds when the front door of the house slammed open. In moments, the pleasantly cutting scent of my coffee was overwhelmed by acrid brimstone.

"We need to talk," Seth snarled from the kitchen doorway. "You and me. Right now."

"Nothing's stopping you." I chose not to turn around. Though it was essential to his very demonic nature and had been from the start, Seth's uncouth manner grated on my nerves more than anything else had in centuries. He knew nothing of respect, nor how to address his superior.

"A pack of your dirty little psychopaths tried to take me out just now." He slammed his fist into the doorframe. The house quaked. "You got anything to say about that?"

"Surely you didn't allow them to think they stood a chance?" He wore the minor marks of a skirmish, not least of which was the purple bruise under his left eye. Its hue contrasted nicely with his reddish skin. "Don't tell me—that one was free, right?"

He stormed across the threshold toward me. "Listen up, Supreme Leader. If you don't get your worthless pack of miscreants under control, I'll call off our arrangement. And then you'd better watch your back."

That was enough to capture all of my attention. I set the empty kettle on the countertop and met his furious gaze. A matching rage had begun to simmer inside of me, but I held it down. The scaffolding of future plans hung in the balance.

"Are you insinuating that I sent them after you?" I asked calmly. "As if I've forgotten who my allies are? I apologize if they didn't observe proper etiquette toward you. Sometimes the clan's manners come up lacking."

It was his chance to back down and defuse the ticking time bomb sitting between us. But I could see he had worked himself up into a fervor during the walk home, and he refused to be mollified.

"Don't feed me that fancy bullshit," Seth snapped. "Excuse me for thinking a leader ought to be able to control his minions. Let me know if I'm wrong about that."

I bristled. His words were thoughtless, born from a bubbling cauldron of spite, and yet they struck true. I'd already had enough of my authority being questioned in recent weeks. Any more could turn dangerous, especially if the source of dissent was so close. And, as I well knew, letting the demon have his freedom wasn't really an option. I needed to secure his allegiance.

"You're not. But I would caution you to choose your words carefully from this point forward." Even I was able to hear how drastically my tone had cooled in the past twenty seconds. He had thrown down an unspoken gauntlet, knowing I was not one to back down from such a challenge. The audacity of his boldness failed to endear him to me. We were rapidly approaching a standoff.

"Yeah?" He leaned close to my face. This close, it seemed that the monstrosity of his true nature strained at the seams of his human likeness. "I'd caution you to think about who you really want on your side." He paused to let the words sink in. "Next time, every last one of them will end up dead." A beat of silence passed. He decided to double down. "And I'll take the girl too, just because I know it'll burn your ass."

The world went white. I whipped toward him, lips curling up over fully extended fangs. "You wouldn't dare!" The mere mention of the girl —for I understood exactly which girl he meant—awakened a force of primal jealousy. I had come to think of her as *mine*, and mine alone.

He might disrespect my clan or call my leadership into doubt. But the pink-haired girl? I owned her.

"There it is." He grinned. "I've struck a nerve. Can't wait until she gets sick of you and starts looking around for something better." The grin widened. "I'll be waiting, I can tell you that much."

"Hold your tongue," I growled. "Or lose it. Your choice."

Now the demon had started to enjoy himself. He took a step back, reveling in my momentary loss of control. "You know, I can't blame you for being scared. You filthy rats are a dime a dozen. I don't think I would've known the difference between your boys and the other ones, come to think of it."

I wished there was someone, anyone, present to appreciate the sheer willpower I exercised in deciding not to screw our agreement and destroy him completely. He was toying with me, an intolerable feeling. I saw myself reaching out and tearing into him so clearly it might have been a vision of the future.

By some miracle of self-discipline, I refrained. The tiny voice whispering that he was still worth more alive than dead prevailed against all odds. My teeth shrank back into my mouth. I managed to put an extra sliver of distance between us. The black tide of destruction slowly ebbed.

"Your ignorance is not my concern," I declared.

He laughed. "Not yet. But I could turn from your solution into your problem real goddamn fast, Orion. Don't forget it."

A lot of Seth's claims could be chalked up to passionate bluster, but this was not an idle threat. His glare held a deadly, solemn seriousness that belied all his melodramatic antics. I knew better than to assume he wouldn't take drastic actions, either to preserve himself or get revenge.

For once, he had managed to trap me in a corner. The fact that the fault lay with my own reckless followers did not escape my notice. I pressed my lips together, focused on a point over his shoulder. My hidden anger spiked and threatened to boil over for an instant, but I quashed it as quickly as possible. He must have sensed the tide of my emotions, however; I saw him smirk out of the corner of my eye.

How dearly I desired to snap his arrogant neck, right where he stood. But sacrifices had to be made in the interest of diplomacy.

Taking pains to appear incredibly long-suffering, I let out my breath, ran my fingers through my hair. Behind me on the kitchen counter, the coffee finished percolating. I took the opportunity to swivel away from him.

"Very well," I agreed, somewhat tightly. "I will make sure to speak with the clan about this. Rest assured there will be no more trouble."

"That's right," he agreed. "Even if I need to take matters into my own hands."

He left, and I poured a blistering hot serving of coffee. The side of the mug seared my palm—I clutched it harder, leaning into the pain. My knuckles had gone white. The first sip led me to close my eyes and imagine bounding after him up the stairs, ripping him limb from limb and throwing the pieces out the window onto the lawn below. The ever-coiling spring inside me longed for that sort of macabre catharsis.

But alas, the neighbors wouldn't like displays of dismemberment, would they? And neither would the police. As much as I hated to admit it, I felt the net closing in. There had already been sightings of those West Coast cretins sniffing around the property in search of the one we had so unceremoniously sent off to sea. If only they knew he had probably reached halfway down the Knik Arm by now. Soon, he'd be lost for good.

Unfortunately, as far as the Seattle clan was concerned, the suspicion would only deepen. They were a hundred times more tenacious than the blessedly clueless Anchorage police. To my annoyance, the Seattle vampires were my kin in a very distasteful way. My tricks couldn't fool them forever. After all, not much on the mortal plane could do away with a vampire so effectively that he disappeared into thin air.

Not much, except another of his kind. In that way, I was dreadfully exposed. Who else could it have been?

The coffee was gone in the blink of an eye. I poured another mug and drank it through clenched teeth. The thick, fragrant steam poured into my nose. I let the smell surround me. Then I took my cup and retreated to the sanctuary of my personal chambers. As soon as the door closed at my back, I made sure it was locked. Seth's fury never dissipated right away. And he was not to be trusted in a rage.

The eye of the moon glowed mutely from behind the curtains. I reached over and shut them, closing out every whisp of light. Sitting on the end of the couch in complete darkness, guarding the mug from no one, I allowed myself some minutes of self-pity. How far had I fallen as clanmaster to be held to the whims of a tempestuous, ugly being of fire and lust?

"He is a necessary evil," I murmured aloud, for perhaps the hundredth time since summoning him forth from his cursed realm. "When the work is finished, we will be free of each other, and I'll never be afflicted with the sight of his face again." Usually, that affirmation cleared my mood at least a bit, but not this time. The notion that power had begun to shift, however imperceptibly, clung to the back of my mind. I sat back, placed the cup on the floor, and shut my eyes, letting all thoughts pass away.

The next day came and passed.

Dreams of shadowy figures and indistinct violence crept through my mind, carrying me up into consciousness. I woke with a singular purpose at sunset: to reassert my dominance and draw a line in the sand. This territory belonged to one clan alone. And we would hold it to our deaths.

The moon was rising by the time I stepped out into the quiet house. Logan and Seth were both near; their energies spoke easily to mine. Seth had cooled considerably, to the point where I thought he might almost be cordial. Such a window of opportunity would not last long. I went down to the den and called them like a shaman summoning bonded spirits.

Despite our earlier clash, Seth was the first to appear. He stopped just inside the doorway, regarding me warily. "What's this about?"

"Wait for Logan," I said. "You'll see."

He rolled his eyes, forever the petulant child. "Can you make him move faster?"

"Not any more than you can."

He grumbled, but that was all. A moment later, Logan appeared silently. He glanced between us. "It's all right," Seth stated brusquely. "We decided not to kill each other."

The comment fell on willfully deaf ears. I looked at Logan. "There will be a meeting with the intruders tonight. I'll need you and Seth to cover me."

He nodded. No questions asked. It was a refreshing change of pace.

"Since when?" Seth demanded. "This is the first I've heard about it." He eyed me keenly.

"Maybe you would have known yesterday, had things gone a little differently." Our eyes met. I gave him no ground. Wisely, he chose to pick his battles.

"Fine. Let's go." Without waiting for an answer, he brushed past Logan and stomped out of the house. Logan allowed me to precede him. I had never been able to tell if his cold grace had anything to do with actual respect. He averted his eyes as I passed.

Why did his polite submission feel more like a subtle insult? I wondered if I might catch him laughing behind my back, were I to turn around at just the right moment.

Of course I didn't. I had other, more pressing matters on my mind. Then he and Seth scattered into the night, and I was left to make my way into the heart of the city alone, trusting that their eyes would be watching.

12

VERONICA

It was a good thing I'd gotten so used to being tired. A week into running nonstop, firing on all cylinders to try and get to the bottom of this great Alaskan mystery, I had made the switch from coffee and tea to undiluted energy drinks. My mind and body teetered on the edge of total collapse, but I pushed through the haze of fatigue. There was too much ground to cover.

Even though I had lived here before, it never occurred to me that Anchorage might be an unsleeping city. And yet, every night I stepped out of my hotel room into a different world, one teeming with supernatural oddities. The police reports on television and radio were constantly sprinkled with strange stories of monster sightings, "paranormal activity," sounds of wolves howling at the moon. Most of it ended up being categorized as quintessential Alaskan weirdness, filed away, and only spoken of again in whispers. The city was growing its own mythos right in front of my eyes.

But I knew those reports were more than a bunch of residents with wild imaginations. For some reason, it seemed like the barrier between planes had thinned considerably while I was away pursuing a higher education in Seattle. The more I thought about it, the more it made sense. Alaska's mortal population was already highly transient; why shouldn't vamps and shifters and other reality-defying entities pass through too?

I didn't realize just how many there were. Once I started paying attention to more than the latest vampire drama on the street, I could barely tap into my slayer senses without being inundated by information. The trails of magic and energies overlapped and intertwined to create a constantly changing maze in which a person could get lost if she wasn't careful. It was sometimes hard to separate the chaotic noise of Anchorage's regular paranormal community with the conflict between the vamps.

Still, I did my best to tune everything else out—not that it was always easy. The weave of intrigue hidden in Anchorage's dark side had way too many intricacies to ignore completely. I walked by a dozen shady encounters: people whispering at the back corner tables of clubs and restaurants, huddling under a lamp in the park, slinking around corners to meet up and discuss secret matters. Everywhere I looked was something else to pique my interest.

But focus was everything. Vampires permeated the city like cockroaches in an abandoned building. Blink, and you could miss them, but they were everywhere. It only took a couple stakeouts to start identifying all the major players. As it turned out, Orion's clan was thriving in its numbers—and its backroom dealings. At least, that was what the meetings looked like to an outsider. But then the few times I managed to eavesdrop, I only ever heard them talking in nebulous terms about "negotiations."

My experience with the vamps in Seattle taught me that usually meant some kind of organized crime. And everything about Anchorage —its remoteness, its rustic mystique, its inherent subtext of oddity— lent itself to the development of fertile gangland. I sat in the clubs and bars, my hair tucked carefully away underneath a hat and a hood, and I watched a rotating cast of characters walk in and out of the doors.

Some were great at blending in and only my slayer senses betrayed their true nature. Others, not so much. I saw people shuffling along the walls of the room with skin so pale they almost glowed. One guy had a bald head like a cue ball, its curvature painted with bluish veins. After enough time in the industry, I had learned to spot vamps from miles away. These days, Anchorage was infested with them.

They weren't all locals, either. My first good look at a guy from my own neck of the woods sent an electric shock of surprise down my spine. Of course, I remembered that one of the dead had been a Seattle vamp, but until the moment I saw another, I'd assumed he was an outlier, maybe some vagabond wanderer outcast by his clan. It happened sometimes. Now, however, things looked different. And as the night wore on into the wee hours of the next morning, I counted more and more Pacific Northwestern ghouls roaming the streets.

It was obvious that Seattle's vamp outfit had an away team deployed —to the very place I had been called to, no less. Thinking there was no way these events could be the world's biggest coincidence, I made an extra effort to be unassuming, just in case one of them should recognize me. In Alaska I was a nobody, but my name had begun to make the rounds down south. I knew the vamps in the Emerald City whispered about me.

What the hell were they doing two thousand miles north, trudging into shabby dives out of the slushy, miserable cold? Seattle had plenty of gray days and half-frozen nights; the weather wasn't worth traveling for. Yet, there they were, congregating in scummy droves. Their words, spoken low and often directly into each other's ears, were nothing but a murmur in the distance to me. But every now and then, I got lucky and caught a word or two.

"Clanmaster...disgrace...remove him." This statement was met by a solemn nod of every head bowed around the table.

I studied the surface of my drink, which I'd been nursing at a snail's pace for the last forty minutes. Were they talking about Orion?

"...missing...dead."

The hair stood up on the back of my neck. They had to be talking about the owner of the hand I'd spotted disappearing into the inlet. Unless it was a brand new, undiscovered body. Leaning forward slightly, I gripped the sides of my glass hard. My fingertips and knuckles went white. If this thread of conversation ended in a viable lead, it would be my lucky day.

But luck wasn't on my side. My focus on the vamp gathering was interrupted by the arrival of a secondary figure striding into the barroom. Tall and brawny, the man looked like he could snap three vampires in half at once. A full beard cloaked his face, and through the open collar of his dirty work shirt, I saw coarse tufts of chest hair exploding outward.

The whiff of salty fish stench following him into the space sealed the deal. The guy was undoubtedly a shifter—and I suspected he worked for Mr. Zhao, at that. His entrance made the air crackle with brand new tension, even as he did nothing except stand there and scan the room.

The moment his flinty gaze landed on the table of vamps, he glanced back over his shoulder and whistled, jerking his head.

What followed was a veritable parade of people I could only assume were his brethren. The men came in all shapes and sizes, but they had their aggressive hairiness in common. All moved with the sauntering, self-assured gait of a genuine bear, ignoring the curious glances of other patrons. And they all stank like the daily catch.

I sucked in my breath, shifting in my seat.

My ability to sense danger, inherent in any good slayer, was going off like fireworks in my head. There had been meetings before, but never so well-attended in a place like this. My gut told me something was getting ready to go down.

The first shifter laid a meaty hand on the tabletop between the vamps. He leaned in conspiratorially, as if a man of his size could do anything on the down-low. Nor did he really have any concept of a whisper; where I had strained to hear the vampires talking, his husky voice came across loud and clear.

"Any sign of him?"

The vamp, clearly annoyed by his companion's indiscretion, shook his head and motioned for him to be quiet. Offended, the shifter grunted and turned away. He and his men took up residence at the nearest empty table and proceeded about the business of getting hammered. Some ordered strong spirits, but the vast majority seemed to prefer the economical approach—veritable gallons of shitty beer.

The spectacle of it all would've been funny if it hadn't filled me with such foreboding. I felt my pulse slowly rising as I wracked my brain in an attempt to figure out why they were obviously loitering. Was I about to bear witness to a hit?

And if so, could I stop it in time?

The seconds began to crawl. Each minute felt like an hour there in that stuffy, poorly lit hovel. I'd forgotten all about anyone who wasn't at those two tables.

At least until the door opened again. By now, the place was starting to get a little packed, and for a moment, I couldn't get a good look at whoever had just come in. Then a wave of energy smacked me in the face. More vamps, but not from Seattle.

The natives were in the house. Their presence appeared to change the game; all the players knew it. Every head at the tables locked within my sight turned toward the front of the bar. The shifters stopped their half-drunken carousing. The air in the bar grew thick with something other than cigarette smoke and booze.

One of the vamps from Seattle spoke first, sneering at the newcomers. "What do you want? Come to cry about being forced off your own turf?" He laughed mockingly. "Save it, you hillbilly assholes. We've got other things to worry about. Like, say, what we're going to do with all your land once we finish smoking you out."

"Big words from a shrimpy little man," the Alaskan growled. He was, in fact, not so much taller on his own, but his words lit a match in a room full of gasoline. "Why don't you back 'em up with some power?" For emphasis, he beat a fist against his chest. His cohorts drew up around him like a starving pack of wolves. I could see the bare bloodlust in their eyes. "Oh, right. You don't have any here."

Instantly, everyone was on their feet. Several chairs toppled over, and the sound of a heavy glass mug shattering cut through the noise. Around me, the bar's other denizens also stood up, some heading for the exit, some vying for a better vantage point to see the action. My view had been blocked by a few of the burliest shifters, but the rapidly raising voices left little to the imagination.

My pulse spiked, the tension close to bursting.

"Come on, dickhead!" shouted someone with a shrill, nasal tone. "I'll make a goddamn rug out of you!"

I rolled my eyes. Then a primal roar ripped through the air. Behind me, a woman screamed. I saw the dark, rugged form of a gigantic grizzly loom up on two legs in the middle of the crowd, claws out, fangs glistening. It smashed one of the downed chairs with one great paw, sending the wooden frame soaring. I had just enough time to duck out of the way before it crashed into my table and sent splinters everywhere.

"You think you're tough?" the Alaskans jeered. "You ain't shit! Who's getting their asses run out now?"

It only took a few seconds for the barroom to dissolve into utter chaos. Soon, chairs weren't the only things flying around. I dodged a table, a heavy serving tray, and a barrage of glasses. My heart pounded in the chest at being caught in here, but I made no effort to leave. If a fight was going down, then why not take the chance to eliminate some of the foe.

The floor sparkled with shards of broken cups. My footsteps

crunched as I crouch-ran for cover. All of a sudden, I found myself in the middle of a warzone, and a shiver raced down my spine.

Still, I couldn't resist the urge to sneak a look. A frenzy of sounds threatened to overwhelm my senses. As I peered over the top of an overturned booth, the scene in front of me didn't make much more sense. Shifters and vamps clashed together in one horrific, writhing mass, slashing, biting, striking at each other. At least one vamp lay sprawled on the floor, stunned. The bears had already shed a ton of blood.

Telling anyone apart had become impossible. All of the energy churned together into a dizzying miasma of signatures. I couldn't have said who was coming out on top if my life depended on it. Nor was I aware that the bar had emptied of its previous crowd. Survival instinct had driven every single person into the streets.

Everyone but me.

13

SETH

There's not much I hate more than showing up late to a good party. That's how you miss all the fun. And that was almost what happened when we got to the heart of the city. I was itching for some real action, something more fun and visceral than carting around a guy who was already dead. I wanted to be part of the process this time. To be there when it mattered.

And I was the one who smelled the fight first. It was the animal half-bloods that led me there; they reeked for miles. That, and the scent of spilled blood. Once I got a whiff, I was on it like a hound. For once, Orion and I had ended up on the same page. We tracked the trail all the way to the door of that hole in the wall. Stepping across that beat-up threshold was like stepping into my own personal paradise.

But like I said, we were late, and the battleground was messy. Looked like some vamps had taken a serious, no-joke beating. In fact, it looked like most of them were still in the process of getting their asses whooped. The shadows seethed with the huge, menacing silhouettes of the bear-hybrids, glaring from the dark like rabid monsters.

"Come on," I muttered to Orion. We were side by side at the front of the room, staring down this catastrophe of a scene. "Let me put 'em down. It'll only take a second." I wasn't exaggerating. The hybrids were all bark and no bite. Not much more than teddies, as far as I was concerned.

But Orion held up his hand. "Wait."

I could've strangled him and staked his heart with one of the chair legs scattered on the floor, and I'd have been lying if I said the thought didn't occur to me. Every nerve and muscle in my body was alive and twitching. I was born for this kind of carnage, and yet he had the audacity to deny me? A blazing hunger for violence gnawed at the pit of my stomach. How could he expect me to stand idly by?

Near the back of the room, a bear and a vampire hadn't quit duking it out. I watched the bear-man tear a gash the width of the vamp's whole chest, with barely any payoff. Not much blood either, meaning this vamp was starved so he didn't bleed as much as he should from such a deep cut. The flesh hung ragged—but goreless—from its frame. Still, the vamp screeched in pain, a sound like music to my ears. He bolted away from the bear, vaulting haphazardly over a minefield of ruined furniture. As he disappeared behind an overturned booth in the opposite corner, I caught a flash of movement and a short, involuntary shriek.

As if attuned to that specific noise, Orion's head snapped around. He stared hard at the booth, and I realized he had been searching for something all along. We were both watching as the wounded vamp popped back up and tossed something—someone—out into the open. The girl kept her balance just barely, the floor squealing under her feet.

She straightened up, and a lock of bright pink hair tumbled out from under her hat. Orion's gaze sharpened.

"God damn it," I mumbled. Whatever our original mission had been, I knew enough to consider it derailed once he'd positively identified her. The bitch was priority one in his mind, judging by the way he eyed her up like he could see every inch of her skin. But he had to act fast, because he wasn't the only interested party. The bears and the remaining vamps had all congregated around her.

Everything in the place wanted a piece of her ass. And if she didn't do something about it quick, there was going to be trouble. The circle had already begun to close in around her.

"Never mind," Orion said abruptly. His voice was frigid and hard. "Go get her."

I had never been so happy to do anything he said. A surge of searing heat leapt from my body as I charged through the barricade of vamps and shifters. The sudden hot glow from my skin sent the vamps scurrying backwards, hissing, teeth bared. From the sheath on my belt, I pulled out my knife, brandishing it with a flourish.

"Get close. I dare you." The challenge was real and made in earnest. There was nothing I wanted more than to obliterate all of them in as delightfully cruel a manner as possible. Thankfully, a vampire obliged me. He was scrawny, all sinew and bones, his eyes bulging out of his face. Starving, probably so not much blood in his system. The madness of bloodlust was written all over him.

He didn't see the knife coming, didn't even try to turn away. It felt like cheating, the way the blade sank between his ribs with almost no resistance. I yanked it out and watched him drop, wheezing through a lung that was now most likely punctured. Goggle-eyed, he stared straight ahead like a fish that had been dragged from the water.

I turned back briefly to Orion. "Don't you guys regenerate?"

He was shielding his eyes and facing away from me. "Not in the light. Hurry up."

"Oh." I looked down at the glow from my skin, which was rapidly approaching white hot. "Right. My bad." To the rest of the vamps, I said, "Who's next?"

Some of them scattered, the cowardly rats. A few of the braver vermin leapt toward me. It was fun to watch them try to protect themselves from the scorch of hellfire even as they reached to tear at my face and arms. Long, unkempt nails raked over my skin. I reveled in their screams of pain. The scent of roasting meat filled the air, although vamp flesh always smelled a little rotten. I would have happily stayed there until they'd all burnt to piles of char, but alas, the bear-hybrids were on the move, and so was Orion's little girlfriend.

She disappeared from my sight as the vamps got up their courage and piled on. It felt like a dozen clammy hands grasping, scratching, gouging at all the places they might hurt me the most. Sheer terror, for a mortal. For me, the sensation was closer to nostalgia. A sea of desperate, ravenous hands reminded me of a place where I was revered and free to do whatever the hell I wanted—like tear those hands clean off.

The vampires did not react well to being relieved of their appendages. Harsh shrieks of pain and outrage colored the air that only intensified as I started to fling the assailants off of me, one by one. They hit the floor scrambling for purchase. The first one I staked hadn't quite regained his feet. He fell back instantly into a flaccid heap. The snarl on his lips melted down into a blank stare. I lunged forward, loving every moment.

VERONICA

The back of a meaty hand clipped the side of my head, so suddenly, so fast, I saw stars as I was sent crashing into a wall.

In a flash, I pushed back into the chaos in the bar, my heart pumping furiously, my gaze settling on the bear shifter in my way. He might not have transformed yet, but the smirking asshole was as big as one in human form.

"Don't waste your time, girl," he snarled, his gaze leering over my body. "Only one thing you're good for, and it ain't fighting." He reached down and groped his dick over his jeans, and I gagged.

Fury burned through my veins. I licked the blood from the corner of my lip, closing the distance between me and the brute. He didn't budge but took his eyes off me and focused on the battle around us. That was a mistake.

I threw a roundhouse kick, my heel slamming into his chest. The idiot stumbled backward, but chortled like a pig. Little did he know, my intention wasn't to make him fall... not right away. But rather nudge his huge mass.

The back of his knees suddenly bashed into a fallen chair, and his eyes widened as he tumbled backward, arms flailing outward for purchase.

All that went through my mind were Lian's words about the dead girls found in town since the arrival of the bear shifters.

Not wasting a second, I leaped toward him, fingers gripping the hilt of my blade.

The chair snapped under him, breaking and he hit the ground hard.

Crash landing on his chest, I shoved my knee into the curve of his throat, my blade pointed at his eye.

"Just imagine if I was a decent fighter, asshole."

His fist came flying for my head. In haste, I slashed my knife outward, the blade biting across his forearm. Blood bubbled instantly.

He roared, bucking his hips, his other arm latching onto me around the neck.

I cracked the end of the hilt right into the side of his head, so hard, I was certain I heard a snap.

Eyes rolling upward, he collapsed onto his back, the tension from his body melting beneath me.

Suddenly, someone grabbed my hair and wrenched me backward. I cried out from the sharp pain zigzagging across my skull, while I flung my blade over my shoulder. The knife sang threw the air, not hitting the mark.

Moments later, the grasp on my hair disappeared, and I fell. Rushing to get up, I whipped around, weapon raised. I came face to face with Orion. He was driving a fist into a bear shifter's gut. So powerful, his attack sent the assailant soaring into a group of vamps.

As they fell, Seth, who'd been in the middle of the vampire circle, came into view. He punched two of the scum at once, pivoted around and kicked another aside, sending him across the room. His strength was phenomenal, and a tingle zipped up my spine at watching the way he fought with such brutal ease. There was definitely something captivating to watch a powerful man like him and Orion fight. I suspected Logan would be similar, if he were in our company.

The whole time Seth smiled like he was on a rollercoaster having the time of his life. The pits of hell burned in his eyes, and the fight was where he came alive. I started to understand why Orion kept him so close. Seth was the muscle for the clanmaster, though I still didn't understand why a demon would partner with a master vampire.

"You're welcome," Orion's voice drew my attention to him as he looked my way with a grin. "Now, get out of here."

I cocked an eyebrow. "Firstly, I was fine without you, and secondly, fuck off."

He tsked and reached over so fast, I had no chance to react. He gripped me by the side of my head as his thumb wiped the blood from my lower lip. "While I love you talking so filthy, now is not the time for dirty talk. I don't want you hurt."

I shoved his hand off me. "I don't need to be wrapped in cotton." Everything about him infuriated me, drove me insane, and more than anything, I hated myself for still finding him attractive. Yet, even as he stood tall before me, blood splashed on his cheek and the blue of his shirt, that tempting tingle curled in the pit of my gut. Strong cheekbones, a captivating gaze against waves of thick hair, and the body of sinner, he was everything I shouldn't have wanted yet craved insatiably.

I swung away from him as two huge men stepped forward, one of them partially transformed, his arms furry and clawed. A shiver gripped my spine. One swipe and he'd tear my head off.

I tensed, tightening my hold on my knife, legs slightly bent as I readied to dive out of the way.

Sneering, the big guy with bear arms unleashed a roar, spittle flying in every direction from his mouth. His buddy heaved each breath, his chest rising and falling faster.

A shadow fell in alongside me, and Orion's arm pressed against mine. "I take the furball. You can handle the smaller one, right?"

I cut him a glare. "You can be such a prick."

"I don't want you harmed and you think I'm the bad guy here?"

The bears came at us, and I pivoted in their direction. In haste, I hurled my weapon at the furry one, hitting him dead square in the center of his chest.

He staggered, growling, pawing at the knife in his chest frantically.

"You're welcome." I tossed the words at Orion as he studied me with a look I couldn't decipher. A cross between anger and admiration. I doubted the clanmaster understood the meaning of that word, but I still smirked at him.

I charged toward the so-called smaller man. Except, there was nothing freaking small about him.

My hand fell to my belt, and I grabbed the staff. One flick and it extended two feet. I ducked from the monstrous punch flying my way. While low, I grasped the weapon with two hands and bashed it madly at the side of his shins. Enough force smacked into him that he collided into his friend being punched to hell and back by Orion.

Swinging back up, I whacked the staff against the brute's back, then another to the side of his face.

Fury burned across his cheeks, and my skin pricked with the energy of his transformation.

Shit! I didn't want him in animal form... these bears were stronger, more resilient that way.

I flicked my staff to retract and collected the stake from my belt instead. The sharp end would do enough damage while I was short a knife.

In that same second I pushed forward to finish this, Orion veered in our direction and thrust himself at the transforming bear. The explosion of growls, arms and legs boomed, and I sighed that he stole that from me.

The sounds of war encased me, vampire against vampire against bear. Goddamnit, how many of them were there.

Orion climbed to his feet, the two bears at his feet, bleeding all over the place. "Now where were we," he said, eyes locked on me, smiling deliciously.

"You were leaving me the hell alone," I answered, despite the fire he ignited in me when he stared at me that way.

In two long strides, he reached my side and scooped an arm around my waist, dragging me against his side. The movement took me by surprise, and my stake slipped out of my hand, cluttering to the floorboards.

Fury surged through me, and I bucked against him. "Get off me, or I'll drive my stake so deep in your heart, it'll—"

"Not happening." He kicked my weapon into the tangle of legs where others fought.

The reality was painfully embarrassing to say the least, that he treated me like a doll.

I drove my fist into his side, but he didn't so much as flinch, his grip squeezing me to his side, his fingers like iron digging into my ribcage.

"You know you're pissing me off even more by pulling this caveman shit!"

"I adore you too sweetheart, but this is our battle, not yours. Now, where the fuck is Seth?"

SETH

I pulled out a chair leg from one nearby and spun around with it outstretched. The vamps who'd advanced upon me drew back, hissing. The fire oozing from my palm ate lazily away at the dry wood. A thin reed of smoke curled up from my grip.

I grinned. "Didn't like that, did you?" If the angry silence was any indication, I had the vamps all out of action. Furious eyes flicked from the blunt end of the stake to my face, as if weighing the pros and cons of another direct attack.

"Intruder!" The biggest vampire snatched for the stake.

I jerked it away and jabbed it at him, playfully.

He glowered. "Infidel! How dare you trespass on our ground!"

"Well, from the sounds of it," I replied, "I'm not the only trespasser here, am I?"

"Seth." Orion laid his hand on my shoulder, subtly easing me backward.

I looked at him at the same time that I shrugged his hand away. "What?" The first time I'd gotten the opportunity to have a little fun, and he was already ruining it. Then I noticed he had the girl with the pink hair tucked under his arm. She was clearly pissed about the arrangement. I snorted.

Orion pushed her firmly at me. "Take her out of here. I'll deal with these cretins." Over his shoulder, I spotted what appeared to be the dead carcasses of several bear-hybrids in an ever-expanding pool of blood. Evidently, the boss had put on a horror show while I was busy.

But now I resented being yanked out of the midst of a good time. He was the one who liked her so much, so why couldn't he escort her himself? Better yet, she could simply be killed on the spot or left at the mercy of the enemy.

"Are you serious?" My temper got the best of me before anything else. "I'm the best fighter you've got and you're going to sideline me to be her bodyguard?"

"Hey!" Mortal danger hadn't dampened the girl's natural spice. She glared at me. "I'm perfectly capable of holding my own, thank you very much. Now release me." She swung her gaze up to Orion then at me. That was when I saw she too was splattered in blood. A streak of it crested her cheekbone like a stripe of rusty warpaint.

I had to admit, blood looked good on her. Next thing I knew, dual desires fought for dominance within me. The stubborn, authority-despising part of me wanted Orion to fuck off forever and let me do my thing in peace. But I also knew I could make good use of a little time alone with this girl. And that made playing the role of a dutiful lackey seem not so bad.

"Do as I say," Orion warned. "Or else." The guy could be so damn dramatic.

I shrugged. "If you're sure, fine. I just figured you might want to take care of her yourself." I wasn't wrong about that—his disdain for handing her over to me was plain as day. In that light, I was happy to take possession of her. The muscles in her arm tensed as we made the transfer. Coiling for a punch, maybe? "Settle down, sweetheart," I told her. "No amount of piss and vinegar is going to get you anywhere at this point."

"Fuck you!" The expression on her face was completely impassive, betraying nothing. When I walked, she walked, but it wasn't the restrained gait of a prisoner. She kept her head held high, chin up, eyes defiant.

That attitude made me want her so bad. And I could sense Orion's eyes on us while we moved farther and farther out of his reach. It was killing the smug bastard to see his prize entrusted to someone else. I knew he wanted to chase after me and threaten to wring my neck until my head spun all the way around if I so much as glanced at her the wrong way. But he had other concerns, such as the small herd of vamps and a few bears still occupying the bar. To them, Orion was no one's friend. He had no choice but to let us go.

I rode the high of that satisfaction for minutes, leading the girl in the same way a farmer leads a stubborn mule.

"You can let me go, now," she snapped, tugging from my grip, but I held her tighter. She remained rigid and unyielding the whole way away from the bar. I admired her strength.

"Tell me how you ended up in the middle of that brawl, or were you following me again?" I asked, after a long pause of silence. "That was no place for a mortal."

The girl frowned. She flicked her pink forelock back from her face. "Who said I was just a mortal?" Her gaze stayed fixed directly ahead, but I wanted her to look at me when we spoke. I remembered she had jewels for eyes.

"Maybe I jumped to conclusions." I doubted, but I played her game. I reached under her chin and turned her face toward me, just hard enough that she wasn't able to resist. It was not my intention to hurt or destroy her. The more time I spent in her uniquely other-worldly presence, the more I came to understand that she was a trophy of some real value, to be handled with care. Why, I couldn't quite say.

"I'd say so, yeah." She tugged against my hold, and her resistance showed no signs of lessening, which only increase my desire exponentially. "Look, do us both a favor and don't try to connect with me, okay? It's not going to work."

"At all?" I tugged her a little closer, into the sphere of heat from my body. Her breath caught slightly in her throat, which made me smile. I loved having that kind of effect on her. "How about if the connection is purely physical?" My hand slid down her arm until I reached the bare skin of her wrist. She shuddered slightly as we touched skin to skin for the first time. It was then that I gave her a little taste of warmth. A preview.

She tried not to react, but I saw the way her eyes widened for a fraction of a second. She might not have admitted it, but the girl was hooked. As I moved in to kiss her soft, full lips, I thought about how infuriated Orion was going to be. I thought about how he might actually try to kill me.

And then I put my mouth on hers. Consequences could come later. It was time for pleasure.

14

VERONICA

Seth tasted like sharp, acrid smoke that left a sweet burn on my tongue. I didn't want to want him. The moment the shock of his boldness had left my system, I shoved him back, breaking us apart. Still, he lingered for longer than I liked, and his eyes held mine unfalteringly.

I wished he was hideous, like I had grown up believing all demons were. If only this hellish creature's vicious, brutal reality were reflected in his face. But no; he was cruelly handsome, his sharp features somehow only enhanced by his simmering rage. Short dark hair sat messed up from the breeze, eyes that never left me seemed to slide right through my soul. Behind them, I was certain I saw a flame that most likely connected him with the pit of Hell where he came from.

"Excuse me," I protested, a little too breathlessly. "I barely know your name."

The demon smirked. "But you *do* know it." The tip of his index finger curled under my chin, propping my face up so I couldn't avert my eyes. "Say it. Out loud."

His demand felt like sacrilege, but I wasn't able to articulate why. My brain, which I tried to keep so calm and collected under these exact circumstances, had been totally turned on its end, all the thoughts inside churning and flustered. Did I even remember my *own* name?

I clamped my lips shut tight and shook my head. He threw his head

103

back and laughed. The sheer power in his joy chilled my bones. There was a distinct, yet unspoken acknowledgement that everything he did or said was at my expense, an express intent to exploit me for his own gain. I shouldn't have been into it. Not even a little bit. But I was. Each time I'd crossed paths with him, that intensity and curiosity inside me heightened even more. Whatever was going on between us, I craved to let myself fall, to see what it would be like to have such a dangerously gorgeous demon show me a different kind of attention.

When he kissed me again, so fiercely I felt his heat radiate through my whole body, I failed to stop him.

Looking back on the moment later, I had no excuse. Maybe I would've tried to justify my consent by pointing out that I hadn't gotten laid in months, that schoolwork and vamp slaying left no time for any kind of relationship, including a one-night stand, and my body was starved for physical attention. I might have admitted that despite being the embodiment of true evil—or perhaps because of it—he knew exactly what to do with his tongue.

By the time he'd made his way to my neck and shoulder, I was weak at the knees, stifling a moan. The way he touched me made me want to fall to the floor in his arms. My fight or flight senses tingled through every rough kiss and demanding caress. His hands began to roam over every inch of skin he could uncover.

"C'mon," he murmured. His lips brushed the skin just below my right ear. "Say my name." One hand snaked around my waist and planted its palm firmly on my ass. He squeezed. "Take any longer and I won't ask so nicely."

I huffed and glared at him, determined to give up no hint of satisfaction. "What, Seth? That what you want?"

He narrowed his eyes. "I'll give you credit for your guts and your tits."

Another kiss stole my breath. My fingers clenched around the front of his shirt. I was starting to get used to the near-bitter way he tasted; frankly, I was starting to enjoy it somewhat. And I knew he had the ability to work out what my body didn't want him to know.

"Why don't we make the most of our little unsupervised visit?" he suggested. His bright, keen eyes leered at me, and for a moment, the unabashed eeriness of his gaze was enough to snap me out of my trance of desire. Smart, rational, no-screwing-demons Veronica prevailed.

"One, no." I shoved him backward hard enough to catch him by surprise. He came within a hair's breadth of losing his balance and sprawling backward onto the ground. "Two, fuck off. We are *not* doing this today. For any reason."

Seth recovered himself quickly. He straightened his clothes, ran a hand through his hair, and stared at me with a coldness in his expression that cut like a knife. I knew by his face that running would be useless. He'd catch me, and after that, who knew what would happen? Would he tear me limb from limb and devour my organs? Would he chain me to a radiator and force me to fulfill his every command? My battles usually consisted of facing off vampires, sometimes shifters. But demons…that was a first.

All I understood for sure was that nothing could be put past him. He was ruthless, and he'd made it clear that I had something he wanted.

My only option left was to fight. To that end, before he had the chance to move another muscle, I put my head down and rushed him. On the face of it, the effort was pretty futile. He stood at least a foot taller than me, built like a brick wall forged in hellfire. My shoulder drove no higher than the base of his sternum. I didn't have to check to know the impact was almost nonexistent.

"Seriously?" He caught me by the shoulders in a bruising grip. "Cut it out." The irritated, condescending tone of his words pushed my blood to the boiling point.

"All you have to do is let me go." I had not gone through a year of grueling slayer training to be patronized by an example of the very abomination I was taught to take down. That was why I hauled off and punched him in the face. His head snapped back. I saw his eyes roll. But then he countered so fast there wasn't time to see it. Next thing I knew, his hands had locked around my wrists and pulled them together above my head.

The jolt of pain through my shoulders hurt so much my eyes teared up. I refused to let those tears spill over. If I had anything to say about it, he would never know he hurt me.

"I admire your idiocy," Seth admitted. He licked his lips as he looked at my body. "And now you're going to pay for acting up. You're lucky I believe in rewarding acts of bravery."

Immediately, he tossed me over his shoulder and strode off. His arm locked around my legs, ensuring I wasn't going anywhere.

Anger bubbled in my chest, and I thrashed against him. "You prick. Put me down."

"Keep sweet talking me."

No one was around to spot us, and not that I'd drag any innocents into facing a demon. I had to watch the lights of downtown recede farther and farther into the distance. What replaced them was an endless army of trees and the foreboding voice of the river.

Okay, V, I thought. *How long can you hold your breath? Oh yeah, and survive in water that's full of ice?* A few times, I struggled, but the demon simply held me tighter. He spanked me, hard, and ordered me to "Behave."

I flinched that he did that. I thanked everything holy that he couldn't see me biting my lip. Why did it feel so deliciously enticing to let him manhandle me? Why wasn't I just mad as hell about it, instead of mad and vaguely intrigued?

Seth carried me into a house, up some stairs, and into a bedroom on the second floor. I studied everything and the path he brought me through the house for an easy escape. There, he unloaded me onto the bed. In the same swift motion, he pulled the hat off my head. My hair went flying everywhere, bouncing off the mattress. He tossed it aside.

"So what happens now?" I made sure to be extra snarky-sounding, lest he get any ideas about what I thought of him. It wasn't that my overall opinion was changing—a demon from hell with a six-pack was still a demon from hell. I just happened to be turned on by his particular brand of bad attitude. Did I regret that? Yes. Was it preventing me from teetering on the edge of some truly awful decisions? Nope.

I pushed to get up, but he kneeled next to me, claiming my mouth once more. My lips stung from where the bear shifter had punched me. Though, I easily forgot that as Seth kissed me with hunger, with a desperation like he might lose me, which was surprising. I should have shoved my hands into his chest, but my body had other ideas. There was no denying the attraction I felt for him.

Following my desire over my logic, I cupped his face, returning the passion, giving into my whims. My head screamed to get the hell out of there, but my body and excitement took charge. That moment when I craved someone so intensely, nothing else made sense. I cursed him for being so sexy, and well, I was a big girl and knew exactly what I was getting myself into. Even if it was with the enemy. A one-night stand with a hunk I'd regret later, but in that moment, I wanted what he offered. Call me crazy, but I craved more. Life ended too fast, and I promised myself to never hold back on what I wanted. Plus, at the back of my mind, I kept thinking that getting closer to a demon came with benefits, like getting him on my side, gaining insider information, and playing with his thoughts. He might be turning me on, but I intended to have the exact same impact on him…ongoing.

He broke our kiss and reached down beside the bed, then came back up with a length of hefty rope in his hands, which he snapped like a belt. My heart skipped a beat. "Don't take this personally," he said, tying my wrists to the top two bedposts. "Call it insurance for when I'm at my most distracted, and you sweetheart are unpredictable."

"You have no idea," I answered.

The pull of the rope was just shy of uncomfortable. If I shifted too much, I could feel the rasp of the cord on my exposed skin. In a strange way, I enjoyed hearing he tied me up because he feared me.

With my legs free, I clenched my knees tightly together, but he pulled them apart with ease. I saw how easily my body betrayed me. I did find it interesting that he didn't tie up my ankles, giving me the option to still hurt him. Guess he liked to play with danger as much as me.

But when Seth traced his fingers up the inside of my thigh, I forgot everything.

A moan rolled over my throat as heat flared through me, collecting specifically over the apex between my legs.

He examined my face for a reaction, and I swear I did my best not to let him see one. But my cheeks burned, no matter what. He liked that by the look of his grin.

"More of a devil than an angel, aren't you?" he murmured.

"I'm going to kill you for teasing me." I craned my neck to stare him dead in the eye. "Maybe not today or tomorrow, but someday you'll pay tenfold."

He leaned down over me, our lips once again mere inches apart. "I look forward to it, slayer."

Of course he had worked it out. Whatever my preconceptions might have been about evil demon sex, Seth defied most of them. He was not a romantic, tender lover, but he was full of passion and power. I found an undeniable thrill in the way he had so effortlessly rendered me at his mercy. Unbuttoning my thick jacket, he drove the fabric of my shirt up. I gasped as his hungry, hot mouth roamed across the pale plain of my chest and stomach. Tugging down on the fabric of my lace bra, he lingered with rapt attention on each nipple.

I couldn't help but squirm, my desire melting my panties. Licking my lips, I moaned, eager to not feel anything but blissful pleasure.

How could a demon's tongue be so dexterous? My hands, suspended by the rope, clenched automatically. And it was incredible to feel this way. He undid the waistband of my jeans and pulled them down. To my annoyance, my panties were visibly still on me.

Seth smiled wickedly. He pulled the crotch of the underwear aside and teased me with one long finger. My hips rocked up to meet his attentiveness. The feel of his touch had every inch of my body igniting. My heart raced, my nipples hardened. I had no intention to stop when he promised me so much more.

"Hell, I fucking hate you," I breathed, already writhing for more.

"Yeah?" The smile stretched into a cocky grin. "Prove it." Without waiting for an answer, he kissed and licked a sensual trail down to my pelvis. I half expected him to torment me with interminable teasing, but there was no pause before he was ravenously devouring me. Stunned by the sudden shock of pleasure, I gasped. He responded by gripping my ass with both hands and delving deeper into my folds. I shoved my hips into him.

"Oh my God. I want to kill you..." The threat came out in a moan of ecstasy. Every muscle in my legs and abdomen tightened as I strained to get the most out of what he was doing to me. His tongue danced around my clit, and then he sucked it greedily, growling into me. The sound I made wasn't quite human. "*Fuck!*"

A river of arousal flooded through me, the pressure building and building, the sensation of his tongue unbearably insane. But if I thought his mouth was relentless, I had no idea what was in store. He pulled me to the edge of a wild orgasm, only to back off at the last second. I was writhing and trembling in my restraints, dripping wet, covered in sweat. He traced the outer edge of my entrance. I squirmed some more.

"Beg for it," he ordered.

I would rather have died on the spot. "Fuck you," I managed between heavy breaths. "Shut up and fuck me."

Annoyed, Seth leaned back between my legs, his lips on my inner thigh, and suddenly, sharp teeth bit into my skin. Not hard enough to tear skin, but enough to leave a bruise.

"Hey!" I bucked to throw him off, even if his form of punishing me only intensified my already building arousal. He had not appreciated my flippant reply, and I felt his displeasure in the way he climbed over me, his hand wrapped nonchalantly around my neck. Pleasure, pain, and panic surged through me, as they each vied for dominance over my body.

Unbearable desire seemed to win out as I leaned back, eager for this, unable to stop myself if I tried. That was the problem, wasn't it? I should have stopped myself and him but I craved this as much as him. An upspoken lure pulled me to him, and all I could think was, fuck it! Was it so wrong to follow my instincts, my lust for a change?

He pushed into me slowly at first, then filled me up and rode me hard. The bedposts creaked and swayed as if they'd come crashing down on me at any second.

His hands rapidly went from hot to burning. He released my throat and groped my breast. Every thrust brought a new, pounding wave of incredible pleasure, the kind I knew would leave me sore in a few hours. It was so wrong in all ways, but still so amazing. We climbed toward a dizzying peak, my body arching, my pelvis rocking to meet his every thrust, and then he started to back off, to deny me that climax.

His strokes alternated between roughly wild and long and slow, a pattern that kept me on the very edge for an agonizing amount of time. I threw my head back in frustration. If this was a game, two could play. Whatever rise he was trying to get from me stayed firmly under wraps. My torture became his as well as his lips tightened, his chest rising and falling faster, waiting for me to back down first to beg for it.

The demon held out for as long as his innate indulgence would allow. Eventually, as I knew he would, he finally snapped and mounted me with renewed vigor. The sensation of being fucked so hard and deeply filled all my senses to bursting. I gripped the rope and let out a carnal, orgasmic scream. Seth's answer was to reach down and rub directly on my clit.

And I came so hard I saw stars. The force of it left rope burn on both contact points as my body spasmed and bucked underneath him. One of the ties snapped in the throes of my pleasure. I almost punched him again. I clenched his cock inside me, causing him to hiss with undeniable pleasure.

Still deep inside me, Seth roared his satisfaction, pulsing within me. He was like an earthquake—one big tremor followed by waves of aftershocks. It wasn't clear how long we lay in the mess we had made of the bed, dazed. At some point, he roused himself long enough to cut my other arm down as I clung to him, my hands grasping strong, round shoulders.

I collapsed on the rumpled bedspread.

"That's what you get for talking back," he told me casually.

"Well, joke's on you." I sat up, breathing heavily, swooning in the most incredible sex, and made an attempt to fix my disheveled hair. "Because now I kinda want to do it even more." There was no lie. I've never had a man take me this way before.

He arched his eyebrows. "I keep thinking I've got humans figured out," he said, "but then you say some crazy shit like that, and I have to second guess."

Inspecting the chafe marks on my wrists, I replied, "Isn't it part of my job to keep you on your toes? At least until I lay you out."

"So I show you a real good time, and you still want to off me? That's how it is?" The questions had the lightness of humor behind them, but also a dark edge. He was sizing me up as a threat. We both knew it.

I lifted my gaze to meet his. "That's how it's always going to be."

15

ORION

The hardest part of my current situation was pretending not to think about Seth and Veronica alone together. The demon was, as I knew him, the consummate predator. In every other context, it had served me well. Now that I saw him directing his animal charm toward something of mine, I despised him for it.

As much as my mind wanted to dwell, however, Seth's intentions toward my gorgeous prize were neither here nor there. A significant percentage of the bear tribe lay dead, dying, or otherwise incapacitated in the other half of the bar, but my main targets, the vampires, had by and large regained themselves and were closing in around me. Keeping my wits sharp had never been more vital.

"What's the matter, old man?" I turned to the vampire brave enough to taunt me through a mouthful of broken teeth. He had obviously been a casualty of one of Seth's uninhibited pummelings, and yet his spirit seemed undaunted. "You look bothered. Couldn't be because your henchman ran off with the bitch, could it?"

"Watch your tongue, whelp." I enunciated each syllable with sharp precision, just to make it clear that the metaphorical ice beneath his feet was very thin. "If it's true my mood is less than charitable, then you ought to tread very lightly."

"Ha!" He coughed and spat on the floor. "Listen to yourself, *clanmaster*. As if you really think we're the ones who need to worry." He glanced

111

to the left and right, at the unbecoming faces of his cohorts. Their circle around me drew ever tighter. "But that isn't the case, now is it?"

"I wouldn't be so sure." Logan had disappeared from sight, as was his wont, but I perceived him there, his frosted aura leaving a bite in the air. On my subtle signal, he stepped back into being at my side. The shadow of his fallen wings glimmered. Indulgently, I smiled at the intruders from Seattle. "What do you say we settle this? Right here, right now."

The answer did not come immediately. We stared each other down, unblinking. Droplets of blood fell from the vampire's chin to the filthy floor. Why they chose to hang out in such hovels, I had never understood.

At long last, he muttered, "Fine." The uneasy truce endured a few moments longer. Then, at the same time, we leapt forward. I struck him first, knocking his punch off its trajectory. His closed fist, quick, but smaller than mine, swooshed harmlessly past my face. Meanwhile, the cartilage in his nose shifted audibly beneath my knuckles.

He grunted and backpedaled, weaving. His left hand rose to cover his ruined features. A tooth bounced from his lower jaw off the ground.

"Cheap shot, you bastard." The narrowed eyes were yellowed and mean. "Should have known you wouldn't know how to fight fair."

"Come now." I offered my most infuriatingly ingratiating smile. "I won't apologize for your inability to hit me. That's ridiculous."

The eyes darkened with anger. He whirled on his back foot and charged forward again. This time, I side-stepped, allowing Logan to extend a deceptively impenetrable arm and clothesline him to the floor. The vamp lay flat on his back, all spirit drained from him. His gaze went glassy as he stared into Logan's face.

"Man, screw this!" a young, dark-skinned vamp cried out impatiently, galvanizing the small crowd. They surged forward to immerse us in hand-to-hand combat. Logan's first move was to open his ethereal wings, sending at least two enemies flying. He followed their flight arc all the way to where they hit the walls and fell.

While I admired the theatrics and the style of the fallen angel's method, mine stayed utilitarian. Quite a contrast to the usual flair for the dramatic, inherent in most of the more elegant creatures of the night, but try as I might, I couldn't scrub Seth and Veronica from my mind. Imagining my last glimpse of them as he led her off into the night made my insides churn.

I had to rejoin them as soon as possible. And that meant these weaklings were no more than useless obstacles.

But they had their own agenda on which they refused to give up, and they fought like madmen. I started off genuinely trying not to hurt them if I could help it, for as maddening as they were, the scope of the Seattle clan they came from far exceeded that of Anchorage. I needed to step carefully as clanmaster to avoid sinking my people into a trap we could not escape. Thus, the first vamp to stop cooperating in any fashion had his neck snapped.

A bold statement, but one that carried. The chaos around me paused in its intensity, long enough for the doomed vamp's associates to process what was going on. The downed vamp struggled to get away, but his body couldn't heal the damage I had done fast enough to save him. A broom handle taken from the closet and wielded with proper malintent spelled his doom.

Logan gave me an inscrutable, quiet look. If he had been a man of words, I figured he might have expressed some form of his differing opinion.

I understood at the same time that I didn't want to hear it. "Don't," I warned him, holding up a hand. "Now is not the time." More Seattleites seemed to be pouring out of the woodwork, rising up one behind the other like a shark's infinite rows of teeth. And they were not shy about attacking, trying to eliminate me for their own clanmaster to claim my territory.

At previous times in my life, there were some days when I absolutely felt the full centuries of my age. Some evenings, I woke up exhausted of it all. Why couldn't my miserable, jackass rivals let me rule my slice of North America's wildest wilderness in peace? There was nothing up here that they could want except fish, real bears, and cold winters.

But the greed of a vampire knows no bounds. This was a truth I understood far too well. I, too, had fallen prey to extreme greed in my early days, back when I thought the game of survival in this wretched world was much more complicated.

Now I knew better. Our fight was beautiful in its cruel simplicity. It only had one rule, with no exceptions. And that was to survive.

The enemy flew at me, teeth gnashing, striking at the air with their unimpressive fists. Rarely did a punch connect, and when it did, I barely felt it. The only strength they had was in numbers. For some minutes, I could hardly see the room directly around me due to all the vamps advancing on my position. It should have been at least a fair fight, if not stacked against me and Logan. But the vamps held their ground with the same tenacity as paper dolls.

All too quickly, it became apparent that I could delegate the majority of the work to Logan. And so, I stood back, watching him throw them around as if they weren't beings of flesh at all. The oddity of the spectacle made me furrow my brow and think hard about the man who sent them—because he was not a stupid man.

Why were these the ones he had chosen to flock to Anchorage? Those who weren't weak were newcomers who stood no chance against any member of my clan. These unwelcome guests felt eerily dispensable, a whole army composed entirely of cannon fodder.

It was too easy. I had heard too many tales of the Seattle clanmaster to be fooled by a ruse of incompetence. Instinct warned me that he was using the bottom of his resources to gauge our strength. Not knowing the extent of his plans was enough to drive me mad.

"Tell me something." I had another vamp on his knees before me, glistening eyes wide and slowly filling with terror. This one was pitiable rather than detestable—not that that would buy him mercy. "Will your leader miss you when you have been ground to dust beneath my heel?"

The vamp's eyes darted unsteadily around the room. Anywhere but meeting my gaze. I palmed the broom handle that I had used to kill several of his associates and nailed him in the head with it. The noise it made on impact with his skull suggested hollowness between his ears.

"Speak," I told him calmly. "Now."

The vampire started to laugh nervously. The high pitched, atonal melody of his manic giggles cut through the air. Logan frowned in his direction, and so did I.

"The boss is coming for you," he declared. "No matter what. We're only the beginning. And when he gets here..." The laughter reached a fever pitch. He wrapped his sinewy arms around himself and rocked back and forth. "I'd leave it empty for him if I were you. Otherwise..." He shook his head. "Boss has no problem scorching the earth. He knows he can always rebuild."

I clenched my teeth. "I'll scorch it myself before I let him take it."

"Doesn't matter," said the vampire again. "He'll be happy to take it anyway." Once more, the laughter swelled, as did the rage inside me. I blinked, and when I opened my eyes, the broom handle was embedded in the center of the vamp's chest. He fell backwards, nearly in half. His eyes had become fixed on death.

But his last words stuck with me unpleasantly.

He'll be happy to take it anyway.

Well, I was more than ready to see him try.

The shrill wail of sirens cut through the air: our signal that time was running short. Logan caught my eye across the room, and we both headed for the closest exit. Not all the vamps and bears were dead, but that was all right. They'd look like humans again by the time the cops busted their way in, and we'd be long gone.

On my way out the back, I glanced toward the splashing of red and blue as it tore down the street behind me. At first, only one patrol unit showed up to the scene, and I contemplated sticking around for a while to keep an eye on their activities. Then a whole caravan of others materialized at the end of the road.

Quietly, I melted into the shadows. Observation would have to be another day. Secretly, I was relieved, because it meant I could separate Seth and Veronica faster.

But that relief didn't last beyond the first step through the door. I smelled it immediately, that unique aroma I knew so well. Musk, and sweat, and the scent of a woman, mixed with the demon's sickening stench of brimstone.

At that moment, he appeared at the top of the staircase. I knew I was too late. He had already done that for which I had privately sworn to destroy him. And Veronica was somewhere up there—even still in his bed—tainted. Deflowered by a demon.

"You are a dead man, Seth," I whispered.

16

LOGAN

I could hear Orion and Seth shouting up on the next floor. Nothing new about that—it hardly ever took long for them to be at each other's throats. But this was a new record even for them. Orion had barely been inside the front door before the chaos began. And from the sounds of it, the show wasn't stopping anytime soon.

"Why don't you kill me, then?" Seth roared. "Seems like you want to, so come on! You know I never turn down a fight!" He laughed, and then a shattering crash shook the house's frame. I wondered what kind of scene I might find the next time I walked through the upper floor. It wouldn't be the first time one of their skirmishes had torn the place apart.

If Orion was dignifying Seth's outbursts with responses, I couldn't hear them. His anger took a different shape than the demon's, perhaps unsurprisingly. Orion's rage was more like mine: quiet, seething, and running deep. Though the two were temporary allies, they had never been friends. I thought the likelihood of them eventually parting on benevolent terms was slim to none.

Another crash rattled the window. Seth laughed again. I could see him in my mind's eye, head thrown back, grinning mouth ajar. He delighted in this type of discord for discord's sake. Never was he happier than when Orion was pissed. And this time, Orion was *pissed*.

I knew why, of course. Anyone with eyes in their head could have deduced the way he felt about the girl with the pink hair. Before that night, he hadn't ever struck me as the type to keep those kinds of trophies, but there was no denying that he saw something in her.

Was it the same hazy familiarity I had seen in the moments prior to bringing her forward? The thought that Orion and I might have more in common never crossed my mind. I was uninterested in him, aside from our working relationship, and as far as I knew, the feeling was mutual. But we had this mutual curiosity about the girl.

Normally, if push came to shove, I'd be the one to back down without question. It was rarely a good idea to get on Orion's bad side, and after all the time and effort I'd already invested in his endeavors, I was committed to seeing things through. A moment of hollow triumph simply wasn't worth the risk of loss.

The entrance of the mysterious girl had changed my perspective, however. Her presence awakened a long-dormant curiosity the likes of which I had long since assumed I would never feel again. She made me dive reluctantly down into my past and bring up memories from those depths. Memories of a time less dark and barren.

Ironically, they were the same memories Orion had tapped to secure my pledge of temporary loyalty. Now they both seized upon that hidden longing, the ache of regret. In her bright, pretty face, I saw the life I had lost in order to gain the burden of the wings upon my back.

It was stupid to believe she could grant me a wish that I'd already taken on an enormous debt to fulfill. And yet I couldn't seem to help myself. I wanted to see her again. Her aura haunted me.

Out of the corner of my eye, I caught a blur of movement out in the hallway and turned to see the door to the room I was in swinging wider. There she stood, as if a vision manifested by the call of my desires. Skin-tight pants, thick coat that remained unbuttoned to reveal a gray simple top, and unruly pink hair draped over her shoulders. But those gorgeous eyes carried so many emotions. Fear. Confusion. Anger.

I blinked. She blinked. We stared dumbly into each other's eyes for a few moments longer than necessary.

"Oh my God. I didn't see you in here." She spoke suddenly. The puzzled clouds in her eyes cleared. She shook her head. "I'm sorry. I thought this was...actually, I don't know what I thought this was. The bathroom?" An apologetic little smile tilted her lip, then immediately faded in the face of another booming impact from upstairs of our large home. The ceiling trembled.

"The bathroom is there." I nodded to the opposite wall, where another door led out. "If that's what you need."

It wasn't what she had been looking for. We both knew that. My best assumption was that she had really been searching for a way out that might protect her from Orion's keen perception. Her gaze darted toward the window, more or less confirming my thoughts.

"Come on!" Seth bellowed again from the floor above. He guffawed. The sound was becoming a regular refrain that I expected to keep up for some time yet. When those two really got going, they could trade hits for hours. And still, no matter how hard I listened, Orion remained inaudible. His anger, on the other hand, seeped through the entire house. It was almost tangible, a smothering haze.

The girl rolled her eyes. "I can't believe them. Honestly, I can't believe *this*." She opened her mouth to continue, changed her mind, and closed it again, pressing her lips into a thin line. Then she just looked at me.

I said, "You can hide out in here until they're done. I don't care. But it might be a while." The silvery splintering of glass supported my statement. I shrugged. "See?"

She took a deep breath. I watched her lungs fill and deflate, her heartbeat slowing. One hand wandered through her mane of messy pink waves, the other wrapped like a security blanket around her own waist. "I guess this happens pretty often, huh?"

"They were getting better," I admitted. "Don't think that's the case anymore."

"Ugh." She sat down heavily on the end of the couch and balled her fists up in the cushion. "I'm sorry. I don't know how you stand living here."

"You say that like you don't assume this is where I belong." I kept my eyes on her. How much was she able to work out about me, about who I was? How far could she see into the nature of my spirit? These were questions I hadn't bothered to ask about anyone before. None had mattered before her. But suddenly I was hungry for—what? Gratification, perhaps. Or in a strange, abhorrent way…approval?

She paused long enough to take another breath and weigh her response. "My name is Veronica," she said at last. "In case you forgot from the last time we met."

Somehow it made sense to me that she'd been given a devoutly religious name, despite, or maybe because of, the utter profanity of her chosen profession. She had the look of a modern saint, inner strength cloaked in a shroud of innocence. The hue of her hair was a strange, befitting touch. Highlighted by gentle beams of moonlight, it held a pale glow.

"I'm Logan," I told her. "Orion calls me Logan."

"And what about Seth?" she asked dryly.

I chuckled. "He doesn't call me anything." Not quite true. He had a whole repertoire of irritating nicknames. The only one I had ever heard him consistently calling by name was Orion, and then only because he knew he was required to show a modicum of respect in order to get what he had been promised.

"I like Logan," Veronica responded, glancing up to the shaking ceiling. "It suits you." She turned to face me. Her shoes were untied, the laces dragging along the floor. Clearly she'd dressed in a hurry. "What are you doing here, Logan?" she asked now. "To answer your question, no. I don't think you really belong here. If you did, you'd be upstairs slugging it out with Beavis and Butthead."

"I could be." I caught her uncertain gaze and held it.

"But...?" I asked. Her tenacious personality shone through in every exchange. Veronica thought I had secrets she might want or need to know which explained why she hadn't turned and walked out of the house. And she was determined to get answers out of me, I saw it in her narrowing gaze. That was annoying, but for reasons I didn't quite understand, I decided to indulge her. To push her away would be to stunt the growth of a tempting connection.

"Not worth my time." I frowned and glanced at the ceiling. Another rattling blow shook the building to its foundation. A hint of brimstone smoke filtered down to us through the staircase. Apparently Seth had doubled down, as he often did.

Veronica noticed the smoke as well. "Is everything okay up there?" For a brief moment, nervousness flashed across her face. "He's not going to send this place up, is he?" She laid a hand on the wall, feeling for heat.

I shook my head. "There's too much at stake for that."

"Good to know, I think." She stepped toward me until we were less than a few feet apart. Her presence had a tangible warmth, in stark contrast to mine. She was the sun on the surface of a frozen lake too deep and cold to melt. But she was trying. And I had to admit it was making more difference than none at all. "Tell me what Orion's got on you. Maybe I can help. Why else would you be working with him, right?"

I frowned once more. "No, and no. You can't."

She folded her arms. Stubbornness radiated off of her in waves. Veronica wasn't going anywhere. "Try me," she declared flatly. "Really. I dare you. I'm stronger than you all seem to think."

"Are you?" I rounded on her then. Not to hurt or scare her so much as to teach her a lesson. She was correct about her strength; that much I could feel. But for all her potential, all her current capability, the girl was stunningly naïve. There were occasions in which her forthright, persistent manner might get her somewhere.

More often than not, it would come back to bite her. Hard.

"You're mistaken to think there's always going to be a place for you in these conflicts." My voice was calm, but dark. "We don't have the patience to entertain the meaningless designs of mortals." Quick as a flash, I reached out and grasped her slender wrist.

She tensed.

I turned her arm over, tracing the blue lines of her veins with my finger and pressing down until her pulse thrummed beneath my touch. "Do you know what this is?" I asked her.

She stared at me in silence. Her large, luminous eyes stayed impressively inscrutable. Eventually, she moved her head the tiniest amount left and right.

I didn't let her look away. "It's a timer. And it's counting down."

VERONICA

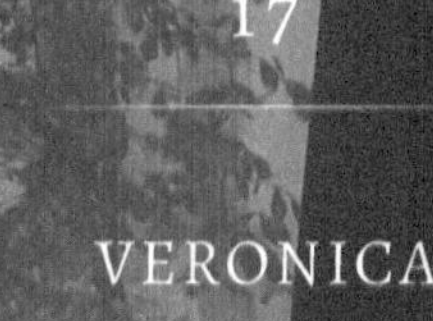

ogan's hands were cold, but his touch was softer than I expected. His silver-blue eyes, eerily light, bored into mine, his ash-gray hair sitting on his shoulders. Part of me wanted to back away and free myself from the otherworldly grip he had on me, but another, larger part remained a somewhat willing captive. Besides, I didn't think he really meant to hurt me—not in the moment, at least. No doubt he could have removed himself from service with Orion and Seth just as he claimed. And he'd even caught me off guard.

I knew I was being reckless as hell, trying to coax him into opening up. And I knew it was cliché to think he wasn't like the other supernaturals I had seen. The voice of reason inside my head did her best to persuade me otherwise. *Are you nuts, Veronica? Can you hear yourself thinking right now? This guy is not a neglected puppy locked up in a back room. He's strong, and he's smart, and he's definitely more dangerous than he looks!*

All true. I understood it in my heart. Still, Logan was the only one I had found myself able to talk to as if we were almost equals. He was moody, sure, and obviously capable of great cruelty. But he lacked the arrogance of his compatriots. He spoke without their repulsive smugness. I nearly believed he thought he might not actually be better than me.

Though, there was so much to him I had to uncover. I wanted to know about that secret core, lurking like the shadow of a leviathan below the surface of the water. There were so many mysteries I had yet to unlock. And he was one I understood the least.

"Talking about death isn't going to scare me," I informed him now. "Look, I don't know how much experience you really have with vamps, but they're not very nice. I'm…" I hesitated on the brink of spilling that I was from the Pacific Northwest—in fact, the very same city that harbored Orion's rivals. What he'd do with that knowledge was utterly unpredictable. He could use it against me. He could throw me to the wolves. "I've seen some pretty awful shit."

Dylan's face, a guy I'd been dating and lost to a vamp assault when I was seventeen, floated up into the back of my mind, and I tried to keep my face as neutral as possible. Logan paused and looked at me, suddenly curious. His fingertips moved lightly along the inside of my arm, as if he was reading the path of my veins.

"Who is that?" he asked quietly. The intensity of his stare chilled me deeply. I knew he had to be talking about Dylan, even though it didn't make sense. Had he seen my recollections of him? "Lost," Logan added, more or less to himself.

I chewed on my lower lip. Abruptly, the situation in this room had turned intimate in a weird, intangible way. I felt like the tables were turning on me; I was no longer the one doing the prying. And on one hand, that made me extremely uncomfortable. Dylan was, to me, a rather sacred subject, though I haven't thought of him in a while. I pushed the tragedy to the farthest recesses of my mind. Even thinking about him for too long made my eyes sting.

"He died." Those two words were all I could manage at first. I had no idea why they felt so different to say in front of this silent stranger. "They killed him," I finished at length. "The vamps. Okay? Is that what you wanted?"

Why was I the one being interrogated now, and how had he done it without saying more than a few words? He was still gazing at me with that X-ray vision, his eyes like marble glaciers.

"You hold it against them," he murmured. "I see."

"Yeah. Yeah, of course I do," I blurted. "They fucking murdered my friend!" A slow wave of heat crept up through my chest and neck, coloring my cheeks. This was a pain I had not expected to revisit when I stepped through the door, and for a minute, I truly regretted it. Dylan was my secret, my own private knot of pain to carry, and suddenly it was all out in the open again. The wounds that had not fully healed squeezed out a few drops of fresh blood.

"So you hunt them for what? Vengeance?" The twist of amusement in his smooth, cool voice raised my hackles.

I curled my fingers into a fist against his palm and yanked my hand away.

He let me go easily, unperturbed. I'd have been lying if I said I didn't think about hitting him right in his perfectly chiseled, Adonis-y face. Then the white-hot flash of anger died down.

Breathe, girl. I tossed my hair defiantly. Taking my wrist back made me realize that it was numb and freezing. Alarmed, I tried to shake some feeling back into my extremities. "Hey, what the hell did you do to my hand?"

"Sorry," he remarked nonchalantly. "Side effect. It will go away."

"Ugh." I scowled at him. "You know, I didn't give you permission. For any of that."

Logan remained totally unconcerned. He leaned back against the wall of the window alcove where he was sitting, propping one foot up on the edge of the window seat. "Death is public domain," he said.

"But my memories aren't. And before you go denying anything, I know you saw something, because that's the only way you could've known about Dylan. Thanks for bringing him up, by the way. That's exactly what I needed today." As I finished the last sentence, I realized with a start how panicked I was. Both my heart and my thoughts raced a million miles a minute as I attempted to collect myself. Tears gathered at the corners of my eyes. "Don't ever do that again."

Logan observed me without a word. Then he reached out. "Give me back your hand."

"No." I shook my head. My hair fell into my face, and I pushed it fiercely back. Distraught or not, there was not going to be any hiding. I was just trying not to remember the way Dylan looked when I found him. "Don't touch me."

He gave me a slightly impatient look, as if I were simply being diffi-cult instead of having a panic attack. "Is that why you think you can 'help' me?" His tone was disarmingly conversational. "Because you think your vendetta against Orion and his kind means we have some-thing in common? Or is it that something else stirs in your veins?"

"It's not a vendetta, and what do you mean?" Having a point to argue forced me to focus and cleared some of the fog from my brain. "They have no place here among mortals. All they do is spread chaos and kill." A lump rose in my throat. I swallowed hard. "I'm not the only one who thinks they're a plague. Therefore, not a vendetta."

"If you say so." He caught my eye once more, and I was startled to see that he'd reclaimed my hand without me noticing. His fingertips resumed their delicate, precise track over my skin. "You never answered the first question."

"Do I have to? You never answered mine either." I was unapologetically sullen. He had gotten me more out of sorts than I wanted to admit.

"I would appreciate if you answered. And there's nothing for me to reveal about you, other than I sense something unusual. But I don't know what it is." The way he talked was so bafflingly unassuming, for a man who kept the company he did. Upstairs, the battle raged on between his two untamed associates. Every now and then I caught another whiff of Seth's smoke, usually right around the same time as another thing hit the ceiling. The house trembled intermittently at the center of its own personal earthquake.

"Fine." I tugged at my arm, but he held fast. "Move over, then," I grumbled. "If you're going to keep me trapped, the least you can do is give me a seat." Logan moved his foot, and I sat down in the newly available space on the couch. "I don't know why I offered to help you. Not like you're asking for any. I think I just…thought you were different in some way."

Hearing the words leave my mouth made me cringe internally. What was I still doing in this room, talking to this guy? Being near him was like being hypnotized but self-aware. I knew full well that he was having an unanticipated effect on me, and that my efforts to resist weren't entirely successful. The source of Logan's allure wasn't as readily apparent as with Orion or Seth, either, although he was just as handsome.

I had always been drawn harder to men whose first instincts were to issue orders or start fights. Logan exuded a different type of power and charisma. He preferred to bide his time, waiting patiently in the shadows for the right moment to strike.

He ran the side of his index finger along the length of my forearm, smiling slightly as goosebumps raised on my skin. "I am…unique," he said slowly. "But it doesn't matter. There is no help for the fallen."

I furrowed my brow. "Fallen from where?"

"Grace." He shrugged his shoulders. "Paradise. Whatever you want to call it. I was there, and now I'm here, and there is nothing to be done."

I froze, my mouth dropping open at first. "No way." Throughout my time in the field, I'd heard of certain forsaken beings, but not in any concrete sense. The rumors of things like cursed angels held the quality of urban legends, so rare were the shreds of proof. Up until I realized that Logan was very serious, I wasn't sure I believed them at all.

Logan, for his part, could not have cared less whether I subscribed to his reality or not. He idly spread my fingers apart, traced over the lines in my palm, and let me go. "I'm not going to convince you." The trace of irritation crept back into his tone. "You're too raw and idealistic. I would suggest you come back to discuss your experiences in a hundred years, but you'll be dead by then."

"Wow, okay. Sorry I asked." Now he was the one acting sullen and difficult, and some of his mysterious charm was wearing off. "I was just trying to…" I trailed off. "Actually, I have no idea what I was trying to do."

Just then, Logan held a finger to his lips. "Shh." I shut my mouth and we both listened together—to brand new, total quiet. The cacophony in the background had faded to a dull roar the longer it had gone on. It was a mild shock to recognize that I heard nothing.

"They're done," Logan said. "You have to go. Unless you want Orion to find you in here."

"No thanks," I retorted wryly. "Sounds like he's already trashed the place. I don't need him to snap me in half for good measure."

Logan studied me closely. "You shouldn't have come here," he said. The sentiment was both sudden and unprompted.

"I didn't. Seth brought me because Orion told him to."

"No," he said. "To Anchorage."

"Oh." I laughed. "Well, it's too late for that. I only had a one-way ticket." I thought I was being funny, but Logan's face remained unmoved. He was so stoic, so carefully measured in all ways. The unnatural perfection of his features made him seem like a living statue, framed by the arch of the window.

Shit, maybe he was an angel after all. The shock rattled through me. I was used to bumping into different supernatural creatures, but an angel was a first. Fallen angel for that, still as startling. So, what was he doing down on Earth?

A sudden sharp bang yanked me back into the real world, and I glanced into the hall, toward the stairwell. One last thin current of smoke drifted in through the open door.

"Seth is leaving," Logan remarked. He pointed down from our vantage point in the window, to where Seth was just being swallowed up by the thick trees. Watery footprints marked his trail from the house to the edge of the wood. "Fight's over."

"I guess that's my cue to get moving." I stood up, moved away from the window seat, paused, and glanced back at him. "Can't say I blame you staying away from Seth, though. I don't really want to fight him either."

"The fighting isn't the problem." Logan's face masked over into stony resolve. "I don't want to kill him. Yet."

I was out of the living room pretty quickly after that. The more I learned about this house, the more it seemed like a constant power struggle between three personalities that were each dominant in their own way. Orion, the ironclad leader, Seth, the wild enforcer, and Logan, the patient strategist. It was a house of cards, built precariously on the foundation of impermanent loyalties.

And I had arrived just in time to watch it all start to give way.

18

ORION

*E*very fight with Seth forced me to remember two things. One, he was not like the vampires I had bullied into loyalty to me, and to mentally categorize him as such was a mistake. Two, the surrender of mortal life did not necessarily mean the absence of pain. I stood under the showerhead, wincing as the burns on my arms and chest shed off and began the process of healing over. A process I was simultaneously thankful for and disgusted by.

In the end, I stepped out from under the water without permanent wounds. By the next nightfall, there would be no sign of an altercation. This was hardly the first time our tempers had risen to their flashpoint. I knew it wouldn't be the last. The encounters had taken on their own ritualistic vibe, a way for us to release the constantly mounting pressure day by day. If Seth respected anything, I liked to think it was my willingness to engage with him in my arena.

He wanted to fight, so we fought. And I let him think he could get the better of me, that he was calling the shots. These battles always ended on one side of a very thin line, and I didn't expect to see hide nor hair of the demon for a while. But Seth was greedy above all else, and I had promised too rich a reward. The siren song of wealth and freedom always drew him back.

But after each battle we engaged, something changed with us... only minuscule, but the wall between us always thinned. By meeting him on his grounds of how he dealt with problems, I believed he started to come around to working closer with me.

So, I embraced our encounters, knowing it aided us both to deal with the shit between us. I didn't want to constantly argue with him or to have him endlessly piss me off. These small steps were progress as far as I was concerned.

As I toweled myself dry, I glanced in the mirror, briefly contemplating the figure I saw there. An old soul corralled into a comparatively young body for eternity...if all went according to plan. I barely remembered what it was like to be mortal in this suit of flesh, to feel the warm blood running through my veins. Had I lived more richly due to the impermanence of it all?

My reflection and I smiled at each other. No, of course not. What a foolish notion. The two greatest enemies of the mortal man were time and death. I had conquered both. Now my foes were strictly tangible, not concepts hiding out in the furthest corners of my mind. And that meant they could all be soundly defeated.

The house, being old and drafty, had a distinct, salty chill when the sun was down. I preferred it, personally, and on occasion I retired entirely devoid of clothing. The sensation of settling into cool, grainy soil was one I had taken a long time to embrace—it was hard to process how much the meaning of a grave had changed after turning. But on this night, rest had to wait. I slipped into some clothes—wincing at the sting of newly forming raw skin rubbing against cloth—and retraced my steps downstairs.

The aftermath of our latest brawl was impressive, in its own uncivilized way. The floor was littered with shards of glass, some of which had melted into iridescent disks on the floor. Most of the cabinet doors in the kitchen hung open, their contents either strewn about or simply broken. The refrigerator, which none of us used much anyway, no longer hummed; it and the stove had been marred by a scorch mark that splashed across the back wall as well.

I couldn't help but be amused. Were we no better than a pair of squabbling children fighting over a toy? But even as I had the thought, I understood the depth of my investment. However much I indulged Seth's wildness normally, my anger had been a lot more real than usual. I had found a flower, and he had plucked off the bloom.

Not that it mattered at the moment. He had gone off alone, and the house was still a mess. If not for my attention to image, I might have been happy to leave the second floor in ruins. But the Seattle clan still had their eyes on me. It wouldn't do to have my personal dwelling fall to pieces.

The footfalls pattered down the corridor behind me as I swept up the debris on the tile. I recognized her before she spoke a word; in fact, I had felt her moving toward me.

"Orion?" She said my name cautiously, as if she thought it might summon someone other than me. Or perhaps bearing partial witness to my dust-up with Seth had convinced her to fear me.

"What do you want?" I asked her tersely. "Did Seth leave you wanting?"

She frowned at my back when I glanced behind me. "Don't be a prick. I just came to check on you."

I shot her a derisive glance, but she was already examining the state of the kitchen and the living room beyond. "Feel free to atone for your pleasure in any way you see fit." As a tactful suggestion, I took a washrag from the sink and tossed it over my shoulder at her.

She stepped toward me. "I'm sorry. I didn't realize we had any kind of deal at all, let alone an exclusive one." There was a pause. "I also didn't realize I'd be cleaning your house for free." On her way past me, she looked me over in what I assumed was supposed to be a disdainful way. Then her eyes flicked over the exposed burns on my neck and arms, and she stopped. "Hey, wait. You're hurt."

"And you expect me to believe this concerns you?" I laughed. "Don't mock me, Veronica. I have no need for your pity."

"Ugh. Let me see your arm."

I eyed her closely. "Most kidnapping victims wouldn't go out of their way to aid their captor."

"Well, you haven't killed me yet," she quipped. Then she said, "Judging by the dents you made in the sheetrock here, I figure you're not just mad at Seth."

Hearing his name in her voice made me bristle. Veronica felt the tension and paused. "You should wrap that."

"It's unnecessary," I told her. "In a matter of hours, these injuries will be gone. They mean nothing."

"Yes, I'm aware of how vampire regeneration works, thank you." She raised an eyebrow. "That's why it's so goddamn hard to get one of you to stay down for good."

Her hands were warm on my skin, life radiating from her touch. I let the faint drum of her heartbeat invade my ears and thought about how perfect she would be if I could wrest her from the unforgiving clutches of time, as I had been. Her pale skin, a shade paler. Her beauty preserved for all eternity. And of course, the mark of her sire somewhere on her body.

She had retrieved a rag, wet it under the faucet, and brought it back to me. I blinked, suddenly aware of how near she was. She moved up my arm toward the cutoff of my shirtsleeve. The cool water was, admittedly, quite soothing on the burn. "But then again," she continued, "here you are in a bachelor pad with two other guys. That's not what I would've expected out of a clanmaster either."

Had the words come from anyone else, I might have been offended, perhaps deeply. But Veronica spoke with such open candor that I found it impossible to rebuke her. She barely entertained the thought of a lie.

"I would be interested to know whoever you thought you were going to meet by coming here," I said. "And what you hoped to accomplish? Anchorage is not a city for outsiders."

Veronica gave me a look, her eyes sparkling. "Who said I was an outsider, Orion? Maybe you just didn't know me before."

I shook my head. "No. I would remember you." An insolent beauty like hers would never have left me until I captured it for good.

She scoffed. "Well, whatever I thought I was looking for, it sure wasn't..." She gestured vaguely around at the house. "This."

Once more we lapsed into a comfortable silence. Veronica pulled the shirt from my shoulder to apply the next compress, I hissed a breath through my teeth as the cloth made contact. "Infernal demonic mutt," I muttered.

"Says the guy regularly putting up with him." Veronica gave me a sidelong glance. "Honestly, help me if I'm missing something. You *despise* this guy, don't you?"

"It's none of your business, but since you are currently providing a service, I might be inclined to entertain your questions." Running a hand through my hair, I sighed. *What are you doing, Orion? She's just a nosy little girl. She could use this against you.* In my soul, I knew I was letting a foolish, blinding desire get the better of my common sense.

Nevertheless, an unquenchable yearning smoldered within me. Her gaze flicked to mine, igniting the endless fuse. She smirked. "You vamps always look so tortured. Must be hard, living forever and trying not to get stabbed through the heart."

It was my turn to scowl. I grunted out a reply. "The demon is helping me protect my clan, and despite how it looks, not to mention how much he does piss me off, underneath his fiery demeanor, I see someone who reminds me of myself."

His admission surprised me. "How so?"

"That's something you can work out on your own."

She eyed me with narrowing eyes. "That I will. And to answer your earlier comment about exclusivity, I don't belong to you, Orion. I belong to whom I give permission to, be it one or three men." She held my gaze to drive her point across.

Her words swirled on my mind, and I stiffened in my seat, unsure how to respond. She'd been eyeing Logan too? I bit back my initial response to counter her comment. Sharing wasn't in my nature, but I also suspected her being forced into anything wasn't in hers.

"What exactly are you hoping to achieve in town then?" I asked.

She finished up with the last of the compresses, returned to the sink, and washed her hands. "We both know I'm not here to protect you or your people." Her slender arms folded sternly across her chest, changing the topic. "Quite the opposite, actually."

I glowered at her. "Your intentions are a thorn in my side, and yet, you're far from the biggest threat. There are others attempting to invade the territory and steal it from its rightful heirs." I stared at her. "I will kill anyone who tries."

"Like the guy you threw in the river," she said.

I shrugged. "Casualties are an inevitable possibility. He knew where he could end up once he set foot in my city. I make no apologies for defending the clan's right to our land."

The expression on Veronica's exquisite face shifted between exasperation and something else that I couldn't quite pinpoint. Eventually, the frustration won, and she pinched the bridge of her nose, squeezing her eyes shut. "That may be…but you're still murdering people, Orion. Violence always brings about collateral damage sooner or later. Someone totally innocent is going to die because of this."

"So be it." I let my gaze roam over her body. "Your kind was meant to be sacrificed."

"You just lost all the points I was willing to give you for sparing my life." She tossed her hair. "I'm gonna go ahead and say you broke even at a big, fat zero."

I grinned. "A harsh judgment, but perhaps it is fair." One of the compresses threatened to slide off my arm, and when she turned her attention to straightening it, I reached out with the other arm and caught her by the waist. Immediately, her knuckles dug into my chest, close to another hidden spot where Seth had left burns.

The pain I would have felt was completely overshadowed by the thrill of touching her. She braced against me, her taut muscles coiled. "Let go."

"I will." I spoke in a low, almost gentle voice, directly into her ear. "What's more, I won't even harm a hair on your gorgeous head. But if you think you'll be out of my sight for long ever again from this point forward, I have bad news for you, my darling."

"Watch yourself," she warned. Her fingers curled into a fist. "I'm not afraid of you."

"Maybe not now," I murmured. "But I think you could learn."

19

LOGAN

$\mathcal{A}$s unabashedly bitter as I had become, I had never learned to revel in the brutal glories of conflict quite like Seth and Orion. Their latest fight cast a heavy pall over the house, the air thick with unspoken tension that made my skin crawl. For perhaps the first time, I started to feel the restraints of the mortal plane quite acutely.

When my allies were fighting like a pair of spoiled children, it was hard to know if I had truly made the best choice. The days remained largely unchanged, as Orion lay dormant in his makeshift grave during the day and either dealing with the enemies or watching over Veronica at night, while Seth disappeared somewhere. But each emerged fully reinvigorated, self-righteous tempers ready to flare.

I sat by the window and listened for the sound of one or both of them leaving. Only then would I be able to recapture an echo of the serenity I'd grown accustomed to. And even still, the threat of their return cast an enormous shadow over any hope of peace. How foolish I had been to take the quiet, uneventful days for granted!

We were all on edge. Seth in particular seemed to sense my displeasure—and held it against me. On the rare occasion that our paths happened to cross in the house, he stared me down, eyes narrow. I bore the brunt of his suspicious passive aggression for a matter of days, maybe a week. Then I couldn't take it anymore.

The demon shouldered past me in the upstairs hallway. His gaze clashed with mine. "What?" I snapped, almost before I had the chance to realize what I was saying. We stopped at the same time, turning to face each other. "Do you have a problem, Seth? Because now is the time to air your grievances."

He looked at me and arched an eyebrow. "Well, well, well, Logan. And here I thought you didn't have an ounce of fire in you." A condescending smirk lifted his lip. "I've gotta say, I'm impressed."

"Don't be. I don't care." I glared steadily into his face. "Are we going to talk, or is this a waste of time?"

"Listen, angel boy." His retort was sharp and immediate. "No idea what the fuck's gotten into you, but since we're already here, I'll lay it out. This little Three Musketeers act Orion thinks he has going isn't gonna hold up too much longer, so you need to decide what side of the line you'll be on when the shit hits the fan."

I chuckled. "I guess you think you're going to kill him."

Seth glowered. "Who's going to stop me if I do?" He stepped closer. "I won't pretend I know anything about what's going on in your head. But I'm telling you right now, you're not a match for me. Not even close."

"That's not true," I said calmly. "You're kidding yourself if you don't think one of the reasons I'm here is because Orion knows I can put you down." I didn't say it would be a tall order to do so, or that I knew better than to imagine I'd come out unscathed.

Seth's composure slipped just long enough to expose the bubbling chasm of rage within. His irises blackened, his expression hardening into a mask of dark fury. The air around his body shimmered with a searing burst of heat that I could feel from where I stood. In the next moment, he was inches from my face. "Watch your step, Logan," he growled. "It's a fucking long way down."

This close, he reeked of hell and alcohol, and the veins in his face and neck threatened to pop. Despite the way in which he constantly sought to pave a pathway to ruin, by any means necessary, I found his existence grotesquely fascinating. A being made of little more than self-indulgent passions, barely contained in corporeal form. Really, we were lucky he hadn't self-destructed long ago.

I laughed at him. "Look at you, presuming to talk to me about falling. That's very funny, Seth." I paused. "I recommend you save your breath. Someday soon you might not have any more to waste."

If looks could kill, I would have dropped right where I stood. He turned and stormed away toward his room down the hall, leaving me to be washed over by his searing wake. The slamming of his door sent a tremor down through the foundation.

Technically, by standing firm, I had come out on top. But I didn't wait around to see if he'd reemerge looking for a second round. It was my turn to retreat into my own modest sanctuary—not that a closed door provided much protection from Seth's ire. Still, I made sure to engage the lock.

It was all becoming too much to handle. Homesickness wasn't an emotion I'd ever felt in regard to the underworld, the cold, cruel side of the veil between dimensions, and yet I longed to step back into that blessedly serene realm for a little while. The barren plains of stone and ice would be a balm to my senses.

Orion wouldn't like it; that much I understood implicitly. He wouldn't like it, but he lacked the authority to prevent me from returning to my place of origin. And I was coming back. I just needed a respite from this chaotic space and the people with whom I had to share it.

A floor above, Orion slept in his modern crypt, dead to the world. I had learned from experience how difficult it was to rouse him from that state, but I kept my guard up nonetheless. If he should happen upon me while I was transitioning back and forth between realms, I'd be too vulnerable for comfort.

But as it turned out, none of that mattered. After I settled down to begin the rite of passage, I was quickly met by a strange sense of emptiness, as if looking off the edge of a broken-down road into nothingness. Where the path to the underworld should have manifested before me, I instead saw nothing more than dense, immaterial fog. And when I attempted to walk forward through the veil between dimensions, the haze cleared to reveal a solid barrier.

Something wasn't right. Confused, I walked along the wall, running a hand over its smooth, unyielding surface. No door opened to admit me, no gateway broke free to let me through. Not even my wings could carry me over.

I was locked out. In disbelief, I stared at the cursed obstacle, mulling it over in my mind for much longer than was necessary. There had to be a way through, or around, or behind. Not once in the considerable time I'd spent moving between realms had the path ever closed without my knowledge. I felt a stone forming in the pit of my stomach.

Could it be that the paths had been altered somehow? The thought of some rogue supernatural tampering with gates between the planes filled me with unease. I knew of no one with the audacity, let alone the power. And worse, the only other person who might have more information was the very individual I'd intended to avoid for the foreseeable future—Seth.

I closed my eyes, and when I opened them, I was sitting on the side of my bed in Orion's house. The light vertigo that always accompanied any planar shifting caused the world to rock gently for a few seconds. I shook it off and pushed to my feet. Best to get this conversation over with while Orion was still unconscious. No doubt he would want to be consulted, but these were not matters to be presided over by an ex-mortal.

I walked down the long hall, focusing my gaze straight ahead on the entrance to Seth's room. At first, my knock received no answer. Then he was standing in the doorway, leaning on the frame, staring at me.

"Screw off," he said. He took a deep breath and the next words he spoke were heavy with sullen resentment. "What do you want?"

I chose not to mince words. "I can't go back."

"Huh?" The momentary confusion in his expression morphed quickly into amusement at my expense. "So they changed the locks on you, huh? And what, you want me to see if I can get you in my way?"

I shook my head. "The way is blocked. I think there's something wrong." My assumption was, of course, that Seth would both understand and care about how a problem beyond the veil might affect him. In hindsight, I should have known better. He was a creature of almost pure impulse, for whom the past and the future meant equally little.

Seth shrugged. "Sounds like you've been kicked out," he remarked. "Hate to be the bearer of bad news, but you know how it is in those shitholes. You start the wrong fight, you commit the wrong murder, you get on the wrong bad side, and that's it. You're out until you can weasel your way back in." He stepped back into his room, preparing to close the door. "Tough luck, angel boy. Maybe you can try again in a couple hundred years."

"No." I caught the door and held it. "This is different."

"Could be." Seth frowned. "Either way, not my problem. You said you're tough, so figure it out." With that, he forced the door shut. I heard the lock click into place. Once more, silence reigned in the house. And I was on my own.

Having been denied my preferred method of escape, I decided to take the next best option: a walk around the city. Anchorage's unique blend of desolation and wild beauty often helped to clear my mind, and I needed the fresh air. But as I made my way down the winding drive toward the road, all illusion of the peaceful, meditative walk I had envisioned rushed from my mind.

Something else took up residence there—an explosion of bloody violence, a primal scream of unsophisticated rage. Almost unconsciously, I turned toward the source and broke into a run, wings unfurling. Seconds later, the wind caught their edge, and I began to ascend.

20

VERONICA

I was back in my room at the Anchorage Grand Hotel before the night's events really hit me. Suddenly drained, and more than a little sore, I stepped into a long, hot shower to scrub off my sins and think about what I'd just done. As wild as I'd expected my night to get, screwing a demon was one thing that had absolutely not been on my radar. And yet…there I was, steamy water pouring over me, flashbacks from that night filling my mind's eye.

"God damn it, Veronica," I muttered. Ever since Dylan's death, my cardinal rule had been not to get involved with the subjects of my investigations. Such emotional investment was just asking for trouble. Hell, I'd seen it happen to other people in front of my eyes and openly criticized them for it.

Dylan and I first fell for each other when I was sixteen and he was nineteen. It happened at the height of the vamp wars in Seattle, when he fought to keep streets safe, to cease the constant battles between vampire clans. I adored his dedication, his ferociousness. Vamp slaying ran in his family bloodline and he followed in his dad's footsteps, but to me this battle was new. For years, I never knew there were people who took up the good fight to balance the dark. Dylan introduced me to that side, trained me to defeat the monsters in the shadows.

Then on a routine night he took me out with him, he was killed in action.

Ice wrapped around my heart, and when I closed my eyes, I still saw him ambushed by three vamps as he tried to save me from another. His screams bled in my ears, those huge green eyes flooded with fear, arms reaching for me. He knew that his end had come. It was written all over his terrified face. Then the fuckers took his body with them, maybe as a trophy or to gain favor with a vampire higher up.

I didn't know but I tried to help, charging after them, but failed miserably. They were gone in the blink of an eye. Ripped him from my life, and I was left to mourn and attend his funeral with no body. Weeks turned into months of sorrow, and I never wanted to experience that agony ever again, to lament the death of anyone close.

My heart was racing, my eyes pricking with tears at the memory that haunted my dreams.

After that night, I picked up the slayer mantle in his place and vowed to fight for him. As it turned out, I had a talent for eliminating vamps. I was stronger than I should have been, and coupled with my ability to sense supernatural and death, well it turned out I was made for this profession.

But Dylan's loss still bled through me at not being able to save him. Just like I couldn't protect my parents.

Nevertheless, somehow since arriving in Anchorage, I'd allowed myself to be overtaken by...what? Plain old curiosity? A starved libido? The allure of forbidden attraction? Or some insidious combination of all of the above? The answer wasn't rocket science. Not all monsters came in hideous packages, and I had given in to a moment of weakness —albeit an extended one.

The rational side of my brain was furious. These guys weren't just my enemies; they were supposed to be my prey. In a perfect world, I would have neutralized them already and been on my way back to Seattle. Instead, I was fresh out of bed with one of them, and grappling with the shameful knowledge that I wasn't about to say no to either of the others.

What kind of slayer did that make me? If I was employed with the organization of slayers that resided in New York, I could expect to be fired at best, skinned alive at worst. Did this one admittedly monumental indiscretion make me a traitor? Had I just betrayed Dylan's memory?

Those were the thoughts that plagued me as I finally lay down to get some rest in the king-sized bed. I'd have loved to say they kept me up all night, but physical fatigue worked in conjunction with a fortress of extremely fluffy pillows to put me right out. The next time I opened my eyes, it was aggressively bright outside. The sun's rays pried through a gap in the drapes.

I sat up and yawned. My whole body ached with varying degrees of intensity. I could still feel Seth all over me. Ghosts of vague, erotic dreams haunted my recent memory. I shook my head to clear it.

Then the phone on the nightstand next to the bed jangled loudly. I nearly jumped out of my skin.

"Hello?" I had intended to pretend as if I didn't just wake up from ten or eleven hours of much needed sleep, but the thickness in my voice gave me away instantly.

"Sorry to disturb you, miss," said the cheerful voice on the other end of the line. "We're just calling to notify you of a personal delivery waiting for you here in the lobby. You'll need to show ID in order to collect it."

"Uh, okay. I'll be down soon. Thanks." She hung up, and I held the receiver in my hand, looking at it. A delivery from whom? Fifty-fifty chance it was some kind of grisly warning, as historically utilized by the vast majority of organized crime.

Great. Just what I needed, to be on the vamp mafia's certified shit list. I reprimanded myself for my poor life decisions as I threw on some clothes and ran a brush through my hair. All I needed was an ounce of self-control, and I wouldn't be neck deep in this mess. It wasn't until I picked up my cell phone and saw the half dozen texts from Lian that it even crossed my mind the package might be something else entirely.

"Hey, are you up? I can hook you up with a scanner if you need one," she'd written. Then a couple hours later, "Hello? Figures you'd be sleeping the one time I've got something really useful for you, haha. Call me when you get up!" The most recent one said, "Ugh, never mind. I'm too impatient to wait for you. I'll just send it to the front desk at the Grand, okay? Let me know when you have it!"

My heart jumped in my chest. A police scanner was the one thing my arsenal of skills and tools was missing in Alaska, because of course it was the one thing I hadn't stuffed into my luggage at the last minute. I gargled some mouthwash and ran down to the receptionist, my grogginess forgotten in the face of this new development.

Maybe now I stood a better chance of staying out of trouble. At least for a while.

I had the nondescript box open on my bed inside of six minutes. The model inside was new and fancy, leagues better than the dinosaur sitting on my desk at home. While I fiddled around setting it up, I dictated a text back to Lian.

"Sorry! No sleep finally caught up to me. I crashed out super hard. But love you for this, thank you so much. Let's talk soon?" Right as my phone chimed to let me know the message sent, the speakers on the scanner crackled to life. I grinned. "Now we're talking!"

The mid-afternoon sun poured through the window onto the long desk against that wall as I integrated the scanner into my workstation setup. The audio was crystal clear—the calls might as well have been addressed to me. I wondered if maybe it wasn't worth it to upgrade my equipment after all. Yeah, I loved my trusty old scanner, but this one I could actually hear.

I was ecstatic, so much so, that I called Lian.

Lian answered, "Hey babe, how's the scanner?"

"Insanely amazing. I can't believe you got it for me, but I love you for it."

She giggled over the phone, which made me smile. "Wanted to make sure you had everything you needed to clean up this town."

I could almost see her smile at her sarcasm. Places like Anchorage were so heavily infested with supernaturals, I doubted it was ever possible to eradicate them all. "Well, right now I'm intrigued more and more about the partnership between the clanmaster, Orion and a demon and an angel."

A small gasp come over the phone. "He's the clanmaster? Shit. Why is he hanging out with a demon and angel?"

"There's a lot more going on here than I first thought, so I need to spend more time studying them. I think I've got one of them on my side who might talk."

She didn't respond at first, then asked in a stern voice, "V, please don't tell me this intrigue is turning into personal interest?"

I scoffed. "As if. You know me well enough. I'm here to stop them." I was worried I didn't know myself that well, seeing I just lied to my friend after she hit the nail on the head.

"Okay, just keep me posted, but I gotta go, someone's calling me. Please stay safe. Bye." She hung up.

I hated the growing unease in my gut that I was letting myself get too close to the enemy on a personal level.

After that, I stepped out of the hotel just long enough to grab some food and snacks, and then I parked my ass right in front of the snazzy new scanner, settling in for a quiet afternoon of eavesdropping on Anchorage's finest. And I had to admit, sitting all cozy in the room beat the hell out of cold, rainy nighttime stakeouts. It was probably a good idea to cool it on those for a while anyway, given that the last one had ended with me literally in bed underneath a demon.

Most of the police calls were pretty standard fare for daytime in a small city. Noise complaints, public disturbances, traffic stops, the usual. I spent a little time familiarizing myself with the local codes, and then comfortably let the stream of calls drone on in the background while I organized my notes. As the afternoon moved on toward evening, the reports became a little more serious. Breaking-and-entering, a few thefts, an assault following a fight at a gas station downtown.

"Dispatch to all units in the downtown area, we've got an 11-1 called in just now. All available units, please respond. 11-1, all units please respond."

I snapped to attention, my pen freezing above the page. Dispatch rattled off an address not too far from the Grand Hotel. 11-1 was the Anchorage PD's code for homicide. In progress or not, I wasn't able to tell. As I sat stock still at the desk, waiting for details, all other sound in the world drained away. My senses focused on the words coming out of the scanner.

Within seconds, the airwaves were briefly choked by squad cars calling in their responses. I held my breath, fingers clenched tightly around the pen. One mention of a strange-looking corpse and I'd be on my way. Gray skin, no blood, neck wound—didn't matter what it was. Every muscle in my body was primed and ready.

But clarification didn't come easily, even after the first cops arrived on the scene. The first thing they did was start to report discovery of bodies. More than one. By the time the officer had counted to four, I was up and grabbing my hunter's belt. They were already far out of their depth. Fortunately, it wouldn't take long to get there.

The sun hovered just above the horizon as I left the hotel, sitting low in a blood-red sky. I was never a big believer in mystical omens, but it was hard not to take it as an ominous sign of things to come. I wondered what I would find on scene, and whether or not the police had managed to cordon things off already. I picked up my pace; if I moved fast, I might be able to beat them to investigating the scene.

The road leading up to the crime scene headed right into the woods, and it was in the process of being blocked off. A line of police cars formed a temporary barricade, their lights casting the dirty snow and darkening day in intermittent reds and blues. On the approach, I saw an officer with a huge roll of yellow tape starting to establish a perimeter, and I thought better of advancing. No way would a supposed citizen be allowed anywhere near multiple fatalities. The more I peered around, the curved street and houses revealed nothing. That told me the incident happened perhaps at the end of the street, closer to woods... or perhaps just beyond the edge of the forest.

But maybe I could trick a little extra information out of them. The best investigators were extremely tight-lipped, but they were also not usually the first ones on site. I wove a long path around until it looked like I was coming from the other side of the road, heading toward the hotel. Twenty yards from the police barricade, I stopped and looked confused. An officer came up to me, waving his hand.

"Sorry, miss. You can't come through here. Road's closed."

I blinked innocently. "But I just came through here a couple hours ago and everything was fine."

He scrutinized me. "It's a recent development, and I'm afraid it's very serious. Where are you trying to go?"

I frowned. "I'm staying at the hotel over there. Are you sure you can't just let me under the tape real quick?" These were abhorrent, annoying questions to ask any law enforcement officer in the middle of securing a violent scene, but I wanted to know if he'd let anything slip.

He shook his head. "I'm sorry, ma'am. A crime has been committed. I can't let you across this line." Still wanting to help, he turned in the direction of the Grand Hotel and pointed out a detour. "If you cross here and head that way a few blocks, it'll take you down near where you want to be."

I sighed. "Okay. Thank you, sir."

A voice came across the cop's radio and summoned him away, which was perfect timing. The moment his back was turned, I got the hell out of there. The beginnings of a crowd of rubberneckers was forming outside the tape. I disappeared among them, transitioning from the small sea of interested faces into the protection of the trees that surrounded this town. I'd go the long way around to reach the scene. The going was a little tough, as well as being wet, slushy, and icy in the woodland, but I picked my way along parallel to the scene. With any luck, there'd be an adjoining clearing or some other space I might use as a vantage point to an unobstructed view.

Every ten seconds or so, I shut my eyes and let my senses lead me toward the epicenter of the incident. I had known from minute one that vamps were not likely to be involved, based on time of day alone. But I also knew at that point that ruling out vampires didn't exactly narrow down my options. Anchorage had become a teeming petri dish of supernatural energy, ever shifting, ever evolving.

There was no way to tell what I'd encounter, so I was loaded for anything at all. The closer I got, the more confusing my intuition became. The prime energy signature was nothing I had ever seen before, and it was splashed all over. I could practically see it in my mind's eye, like blood detected under Luminol at crime scenes. The auras of its victims were shattered like glass, spread in a huge radius around the bodies. I know for certain these victims I sensed were humans...innocents. None of them were supernaturals, which told me two things.

First, the attacks weren't a result of the vampire clan fights.

Second, I was certain something else was hunting humans in Anchorage.

"What the fuck happened here?" I whispered. "What could do this?"

In my pocket, my phone vibrated. I ducked behind a tree to check it, just in case.

"I thought you'd never answer," Lian said. "Whenever works for you."

"Give me a rain check," I told her. "Something came up."

And then, at the same moment that I tucked my phone away again, I became abruptly aware of a presence nearby—a living one.

I had company.

21

LOGAN

I followed Veronica at a distance, the falling night concealing me as I puzzled over her actions. As a slayer in close contact with any number of supernaturals, including us, why was she speaking to the police? She knew firsthand that Orion's relationship with law enforcement couldn't be great—not if he was disposing of victims off the bank of an icy river. It seemed like an unnecessary flirtation with trouble to be interacting with the officers at all.

But they didn't think of detaining her, and she managed to slip away unnoticed by anyone other than me. I tracked her deep into the trees, closer and closer to the imprint of death that stained the atmosphere. Could she feel that heavy shroud? I sensed the unusual energy from her back in Orion's house. There was something very different about her, but I couldn't pinpoint it. Which was strange in itself.

If she had any misgivings, they weren't reflected in her smooth, confident stride. She appeared to be a woman on a mission.

I didn't have to speculate about how grisly the scene would be. I could smell the thick, metallic stench of blood on the cold breeze. Currents of violent energy whipped around me, strong enough to rival Seth's demonic rage. At first, I thought it could have been him visiting destruction on whoever happened to cross his path. It wouldn't have been the first time a random stranger bore the brunt of his fury.

This time, however, the aura that remained was foreign to me. I

144

paused for a minute to try and identify its distinctive signature, without success. When I looked up to resume tailing Veronica, she was gone. Softly, I cursed myself for looking away in the first place. She might have been mortal, but she was crafty. She knew better than most how to disappear.

I stepped forward along the same trajectory she'd been traveling, all senses open. Unless she had used some type of magic, she couldn't have gotten far. Sure enough, in a matter of yards, I saw her pop back out in front of me. Then she stopped in her tracks and glanced around.

I'd gotten too close. The game was up. Veronica turned.

"Logan?" Her tone registered more surprise than anything; maybe I'd caught her more off guard than I thought. She stared at me with bald curiosity. "What are you doing here?"

"I could ask you the same," I replied. "Do you know where you're going?" What I really wanted to say was, *Do you know what you're about to see?* Intuition told me it wasn't going to be pretty.

"Sort of." She shrugged. "Something tells me it won't exactly be hard to miss." Her gaze sharpened and turned searching. "You know something about this, don't you?" Immediately, all of her walls went up. I saw her body tense, flight or fight response kicking into gear. It was funny, in a way, that she was so prepared to fight me. As if she stood a chance.

"Not as much as you think I do." I held up my hand, moving forward so that we were almost standing beside one another. "Relax. Let's go."

Veronica hesitated initially. She didn't want to fall into step with me, which was fine. Once she saw me proceeding forward without her, she changed her mind very quickly. "Wait. Is this you helping me?"

I laughed. "No. This is me not hurting you." If she thought I was going to void my bargain with Orion for her sake, she was quite wrong. But I had never been a strong advocate of baseless cruelty. She could, as far as I was concerned, do whatever she wanted. Provided that she stayed out of my way.

She walked beside me in complicated silence for half a minute before speaking up again. "I don't understand you, Logan."

"I am sure that's true," I agreed. "Our kind is rare."

She twisted a bright lock of hair around her finger. "Forgive me if this is an insensitive thing to ask, but how is it that you become...what you are?"

When was the last time someone—anyone—had asked me for forgiveness? Against my better judgment, I felt myself warming to her.

"What do you know about angels?" The question was sincere, and slightly playful.

She smiled a little. "I admit there is a lot I don't know. Even the ones who are, um…pre-fall."

I carried with me the spirit of exile, a lonely shadow. The mark of no true belonging.

"I'm sorry," she said. "Don't talk about it if you don't want to. I'm just interested."

I cast her a sidelong glance. She kept her gaze fixed directly ahead, avoiding mine. The apples of her cheeks glowed with the hint of a blush. In my very soul, I knew I could be removed for following in Seth's footsteps with regard to Veronica. There was no need at all to make my own life immeasurably more difficult.

Yet the creeping tendrils of temptation threatened to take root. Had we not been steps from the edge of a murder scene, I might have been in trouble. But the trees were beginning to thin out in the preamble to a small clearing that backed onto a residential street. My mind's eye showed me the dead in various states of repose. Their blood coated the surrounding vegetation in dark, rusty splashes.

"Here," I said to Veronica, our previous conversation all but forgotten. It was a word of warning.

She stopped and sucked in her breath, locking the air into her lungs for a long time. When she finally exhaled, it was with a single word. "Wow."

The far side of the clearing crawled with uniformed officers. A series of searingly bright flashbulbs detonated in the night, illuminating the carnage strewn across the frosted ground. The light reflected off of dull, dead eyes, splayed hands and fingers, wounds ripped into torsos. Some of the men were more stoic than I might have anticipated—others, not so much. One patrolman staggered off into the opposite line of woods. I saw him bend over with his hands on his knees, retching.

"Is it what you expected?" I asked Veronica softly, leaning in closer to her.

"I don't know." Her voice was flat, drained of nuance. "What happened?" Once more, she pivoted toward me. "I don't believe you're totally clueless about this, Logan. And honestly, I'm not going to push you on your reasons, because I am telling the truth when I say I'm only here to help. Okay? So it would be incredibly generous of you to clue me in on what you do know." Her eyes were earnest and imploring.

"Maybe I can help you, too. With whatever it is you're trying to accomplish."

I smiled at her, tucking that stray lock of hair behind her ear. "I wouldn't say that if I were you."

Veronica rolled her eyes. "I take back some of what I said before. You do have some common ground with the other two; you're all *dramatic*." Her gaze shifted from me back to the activity in the clearing, impatiently surveying our surroundings. "I wish there was a way to get closer."

Her resolve impressed me. Other than a fleeting moment of shock and awe, this woman had displayed no reluctance to investigate, no fear. If anything, she seemed annoyed by the continuing presence of the police. That surprised me.

"That would be difficult at present. I suspect they'd have questions for you."

"I know." She pressed her lips together. "Damn it. I should have waited. I don't even know what I'll be able to find over there. Maybe this one is out of my depth." The frustration was written largely on her pretty face. She folded her arms over her chest and huffed quietly.

I'm not sure what made me do it, but I was suddenly possessed by an almost visceral urge to aid her. She was straining to reach beyond her boundaries and into uncharted territory. Was that what I admired about her? Or was it the full curve of her lips, the tantalizing hollow between her neck and her collarbone, the way her long, dark eyelashes dusted her cheeks when she blinked?

Perhaps I'd never know. And perhaps it didn't matter. The next thing I knew, I heard my voice offering to join our efforts.

"It's possible I could be of some assistance." I spoke casually, as if this whole exchange meant little in my eyes. "With your permission, that is."

"You *are* helping me." A little smirk tugged at the corner of her mouth. I wanted to be insulted, but the outrage refused to manifest. "Fine, I'll bite. What have you got?"

"You'll find out." I may have plunged into the deep end, but I wasn't about to give every secret away. "Tell me when you want to meet again."

"Here?" She raised an eyebrow.

"Where else?"

"Right." She glanced at the whirlwind of officers marching on and off the scene, their boots leaving a mess of prints in the snow. "Well, I don't see them finding much of anything here. Nothing they can use, anyway. Why don't we give it forty-eight hours, and then we can come back and scope things out again?"

I nodded. "Sounds reasonable."

She regarded me closely. "Promise you're not going to ditch and make me look like an idiot for trusting you. Because that's what I'm doing right now, Logan. I'm trusting you."

As if I could parse her motivations any better. "Forty-eight hours," I said. "I'll be here. That will have to be good enough."

Veronica held out her hand. "All right. Shake on it, then, and let's get the hell out of here before they see us."

We shook hands. On the way back out, I let her go ahead of me, and then I veered off her path, looping through the forest.

If she stopped, or if she looked for me, I didn't see her, nor would she see me. And that was exactly how I wanted it to be.

22

ORION

Whether or not she thought I was ancient, Veronica had forced me to realize how much of my life had gotten stale. Seeing her was like taking a shot of adrenaline directly into a vein. It was a small relief to know that her liaison with Seth had not diminished my desire for her. If anything, my passion soared to new heights, fueled by seething jealousy. Coupled with that, her words about her not being necessarily just exclusive with me played on my mind a lot. I still hadn't worked out how to overcome the jealousy inside me, but the thought percolated.

In turn, I began to brainstorm ways in which I might successfully turn her. Before she came into my sphere of awareness, I would've considered the very notion unconscionable. Veronica was far from the first enticing, attractive young woman I had sired into a vampire, but it had been decades since the last attempt.

And there were several good reasons for that. Whenever those memories threatened to creep to the surface of my consciousness, I shoved them down deep. She would be different. She had to be.

And what if your precious, beautiful Veronica goes rogue, like the others? What if you have to put her down?

The possibility, however remote, was agonizing. Part of me wanted so much to push her away and save us both from the suffering that often seemed inevitable. But another, larger part figured that if we were going to be dragged into an eternal hell, we might as well go together.

It was too late for anything else, really. I already thought of Veronica as mine.

The sound of the house phone ringing was so foreign to my ears that it barely registered. I doubted anyone has called us on it since we moved in here. Annoyed, I grabbed it blindly off the cradle on the table where he sat, prepared to either ignore the call or deliver a blistering criticism.

I answered the phone, "Hello."

"It's me," she said. Veronica's voice was low and furtive, as if she thought the line might be tapped. "Got a minute?"

The moment I heard her voice, my entire perspective shifted. "Maybe." The answer was yes, but I wasn't about to give her the satisfaction of knowing it. "What for? And how did you get our number?" I didn't even know the number.

"It's very easy to track down house phone numbers if you know where to search on the web. Anyway, there was an incident earlier tonight. Like an hour ago. I couldn't get too close, but there were a bunch of people dead, from what I saw. And…Logan showed up."

"Oh?" I leaned forward. "Now you have my attention. Are you sure it was him?"

"Couldn't misidentify him if I tried," she answered. "We talked face to face."

Automatically, my fist clenched in my lap. A hot flare of temper flushed my vision red. How could it be that both of the henchmen I had so judiciously hired were spending more time with my prize than I was? "And what did he want to discuss?"

"Not much. I was hoping you'd be able to give me a little more insight on him." She paused. "That is, if it's convenient for you."

I hesitated, considering. The possibility of a trap was not lost on me. I suspected Veronica was as skilled as she was gorgeous, and she'd already shown her nerves of steel. It took a lot of guts to come waltzing into a vamp territory as tightly knit as Anchorage. She may have decided to turn some of that admirable boldness against me.

"There must be some give and take involved. Surely you understand my unwillingness to take a blind risk without compensation." There. The line had been drawn. I sat back and waited for her return fire.

"I thought you might say that," she responded without missing a beat. "Come to my room at the Grand Hotel. We can work something out."

I didn't need much more convincing. "I'll hold you to that, Veronica." If she tried to back out after I got there, I was fully prepared to negotiate by any means necessary.

"Of course you will," she answered. "See you soon."

I was still on high alert, as always, but not going to seek out trouble. With any luck, there would be no violence tonight. I could only hope Veronica felt the same. I set the phone down and headed out. It was strange but refreshing to be walking in downtown Anchorage without an ulterior motive.

The lobby of the Grand Hotel was empty at that hour, and I bypassed it entirely. Veronica's energy shone like a beacon, as easy to follow as if the way had been marked with signs. I tracked her up to the fifth floor—room 502—and knocked gently. She made me wait approximately fifteen seconds.

"Well, look who's here." Veronica leaned in the doorway, eyeing me through her long lashes. Her pink hair had been swept over one shoulder as though she'd been playing with it. She wore casual blue jeans, tight mesh top over a white sleeveless top with thin straps. And white socks, adding to that casual but sexy vixen look. "I have to admit, I kind of thought you wouldn't show."

"And miss an opportunity to spend time with you?" I smirked. "Perish the thought." She stepped back from the threshold and started to turn around. I stopped her. "Veronica."

"What?" She looked at me quizzically.

"You're forgetting something." I glanced at the floor and back at her.

"Am I?" She smiled slightly.

I sighed. Okay, so maybe she had some traditions to learn. But she was smart, and I had no doubt she'd be able to keep up. "You need to invite me inside."

"Ohhh." Veronica looked me up and down. She chuckled, putting a slender hand to her mouth. "I'm sorry. I didn't know that was a real thing."

I furrowed my brow. "You've been a slayer for how long without knowing that?"

She rolled her pale blue eyes. "Sue me if I don't typically invite my enemies into my house." Tossing her hair, she waved me on. "Here. Would you like to come inside?"

"Thank you," I said wryly. She led me down the short hall into the main common area of her suite. Positioned against the wall underneath the window, a desk sat piled high with papers, photographs, files, and a very new police scanner.

"Don't look over there," Veronica urged as soon as she caught me. "Just because we're in talks doesn't mean the treaty's been signed."

"Noted." I sat down in one of the two armchairs that afforded the best view of her. She stayed on her feet. "Now, let's talk. You want to know about Logan."

"Do you think he's a double agent?" Veronica pulled no punches with her line of questioning.

"Of course not," I scoffed. "I have foolproof ways of ensuring his allegiance. He wouldn't dare try anything…unwise." It was a scenario I'd wondered about on my own, more times than I wanted to admit. To me, Seth read like an open book, all his volatile moods on full display. Logan was closely guarded, brimming with more secrets than I was able to ferret out of him.

I never truly knew what he was thinking, a reality I found deeply unsettling.

"Then what would you guess he was doing there?" she pressed. "Just happened to be in the neighborhood?"

"Hold on a moment." I stared at her sternly. "Before I consent to any more of this interrogation, I was told there was a bargain to be made." My gaze raked over her immaculate form. I licked my lips. "What do you have to say about that?"

Veronica's eyes bored into mine, full of intensity and yearning. "I am prepared to make a fair trade." Her lips lingered on the word "fair."

I reached out, stroking the side of her clothed thigh with my palm. Her jeans felt like a second skin under my touch. She was so warm and alive. My hunger rose like the tide. I could no longer help myself. My fingers tightened around the back of her leg, just below her right buttock. Veronica gave a tiny gasp.

"Stop me if this isn't what you want," I told her bluntly.

She didn't.

23

VERONICA

It would probably have killed Orion to know that the first thing I thought of when he touched me was Seth, but I couldn't control raw thought association. Nor could I help making the comparison—Orion's smooth, deep-running power versus the force and excitement of the demon. When Orion drew me close as he sat in the chair, there was none of the wild heat that constantly emanated off of Seth's person. But still, an electric thrill shot up my spine.

I didn't even think about stopping him. His right hand moved to grip my ass, the other arm snaking its way around my waist. In one swift motion, Orion pulled me down into his lap. We were inches apart, our faces almost touching. My hands came to rest on his chest.

"You don't have a heartbeat," I observed, like the smartest person in the world. Never would have thought a vampire had the ability to get me flustered, but there we were. I made a plan to do what was needed to get insider information, but deep in my mind I was also secretly excited about exploring the unusual attraction I held for my enemy. I slayed vampires, not slept with them. Yet, I was prepared to make an exception for the sake of gaining intelligence. I almost laughed at myself at how transparent I'd become. He'd been on my mind since first crossing paths with him and left me lusting over him, so this was me getting him out of my system once and for all, I kept telling myself.

153

"Does that bother you?" He caressed my cheek with the back of one cool hand.

"Not as much as it should," I admitted.

His hand flipped to cup my face, and then our lips met. They were cold to the touch. He kissed me slowly at first, but then the gates of passion crashed wide open. I moaned as he slipped his tongue into my mouth. My legs wrapped around him, straddling him, pressed tightly to him.

"I should have guessed you'd be so eager to get in bed with your adversaries," Orion murmured. The points of his teeth grazed my neck just enough that I felt them on my skin. "How far are you willing to go?"

"Don't push your luck," I warned.

He grinned and pulled my top over my head. I shook my hair out of my face and went for his buttons, my fingers clumsy with excitement. I ran my palms over his strong planes of muscles... everything about this vampire was deliriously gorgeous. The way he stared at me made me feel confident, stunning, and sexy as hell. I met his gaze, and there was something I didn't expect behind his those spectacular eyes. Tenderness. I thought his main reason for accepting would come down to pure lust. I'd seen the way he studied me before, but I didn't anticipate something this soft in the clanmaster's gaze.

If someone had told me I'd be getting it on with both a demon and a vampire within a week, I wouldn't have believed them for a second. And yet, he was taking my bra off, running his long tongue along the curve of my breast.

I trembled with desire in response, breathing heavily, my panties soaking wet.

I couldn't believe how badly I wanted him. When he lifted me deftly into his arms and carried me to the bed, I let him. I even let him toss me down onto the mattress. He ran his hands over my whole upper body, tracing the contours of my waist, kissing the tip of each nipple. Then he pushed down my pants. He yanked them off before tossing them behind him. He unbuttoned his own pants and dropped them, kicking them aside.

My gaze settled on his erection, so hard and thick, the tip coated in pre-cum. Elation swept through me at the promise of what was coming for me. My core ached for his touch, for this vampire to show me what he had planned for me. The thought left me quivering, but I couldn't forget that at the end of the day, he was still a monster.

An incredibly handsome monster, but still deadly.

"Let me be clear about one thing, Orion," I said between deep, hungry kisses. "If I feel so much as the ghost of one of your eyeteeth anywhere near my jugular, I'm shutting the whole thing down. And then I will kick your ass into next fucking year before you even get your clothes back on."

Orion pushed his mouth down against mine, growling into my lips, "I love it when you talk dirty."

He was a dominant lover, even more so than Seth had been. It was obvious that he got a real kick out of dictating my pleasure. Without hesitation, he pushed open my bent legs, lowering his gaze and himself onto the bed. I caught the smirk curling on his mouth, sending delicious tingles down my spine. His mouth sealed over my heat, and I arched with pleasure. The strange sensation of something cold against my fiery offering turned me on ridiculously. He teased my clit with the tip of his tongue until I gasped and trembled, my hands balled into fists around the sheets. Desperate, I braced my feet on the bedspread and pushed up against his tongue, throwing back my head in anticipation of ecstasy.

"Give it to me," I moaned.

He drew a tantalizing circle around my clit. "Tell me you want it, Veronica."

"You son of a bitch." I glared at him, panting. "This isn't fair." But he wouldn't budge, so I relented. "I want it so bad. Please."

"That's a good girl." I felt him smile as he sucked me hard, slipping his fingers inside me at the same time. My body writhed on its own. I grabbed his wrist with both my hands. I think I howled.

What happened after that, took place in a red haze of primal desire. He made his way up my body, leaving a trail of kisses and licks around my budding nipples, taking one into his mouth, sucking hard, then bestowing the same attention to the other. Sweeping his mouth over my collarbone and neck, I stiffened at him lingering just below my earlobe. I sensed him tensing as his hardness teased my entrance. He caged me in with his arms on either side of my shoulders, and I bucked up against him, but he refused to give me what I wanted. After I had come to the point of rigid shaking, I flipped him over without any pause. He grunted, surprised, but didn't fight back. I shuffled down his body and maintained eye contact as I took his cock in my hand and slipped my mouth over it. Orion clenched his jaw, breath hissing between his teeth.

"You're perfect," he whispered.

As payment for the compliment, I worked him over hard, exploring his shaft and balls with my tongue, moaning as I licked and sucked him. He tasted salty and sweet at the same time. It wasn't long before he was throbbing, his eyes blazing with lust. Instead of allowing me to finish him off with my mouth, he pulled me up to straddle him. I lifted my hips and let him guide them back down onto his waiting cock.

I gnawed on my lower lip as he slid into me, stretching me wider, and I loved every fucking ache.

"I want to watch you," he mused.

I gasped as he pushed deeper into me, and I shifted to spread myself wider to accommodate his size. Pushing myself to sit upright on him, I took a deep breath, settling over his hardness, letting him fully fill me.

"You are stunning."

Then I rode him as hard as my body would allow, bouncing up and down on him, his eyes searing over my jiggling breasts. The whole world melted away for a few minutes, leaving only our bodies gyrating together, the sensation of him filling me with every thrust. Every so often, he'd pull me up higher, maximizing his depth. In those moments, he often hit a spot deep inside that made me see stars.

"Shit," I moaned. "Shit!" Frantic and on the edge, I leaned forward over him, grasping the headboard in both hands. I floated on the edge of ecstasy, desperate for that release.

As if sensing my need, Orion grasped my hips, fingers digging into flesh as he hissed his arousal.

With his help, my hips worked in a frenzy on top of him until I finally went sailing over the crest of that wave. It crashed into me so fast, it consumed me whole. The sounds I made were guttural, pulled from my chest. As long as he was in me, I could not stop coming.

Orion tangled a hand in my hair and pulled my head back, kissing my throat and chest. He growled against my lips, his body tensing, and he pulsed inside me. We were one, locked together and the moment was so perfect.

I gasped. Every inch of my body trembled. My legs were weak, and I didn't remember how long I rode him when I finally came down from the clouds. I moaned gently as I slowed down.

When he disentangled us at last, I sort of collapsed in the bed beside him on my stomach. "Holy fuck."

Orion stretched out beside me like the god he was. His fingers, blessedly cool, traced a delicate pattern along my spine. He wasn't flushed like I was, but I noticed with some gratification that he was sweating somehow. He had a look on his face that reminded me of a contented predator toying with his prey.

"You are unlike anyone else I've ever been with." His fingers never stopped stroking down my back, luring me into a relaxed state. "I think that will do for now," he said, his voice colored by a hint of smugness. "I must say, I'm blown away with your performance, darling. It's an image that will never leave me."

"Mm-hmm." I was so worn out, half drunk on endorphins, that all the questions I still wanted to ask simply leaked from my brain. I let my face sink into the pillow. My eyelids wanted to drop closed and stay that way indefinitely. "Thanks."

He leaned over and kissed the crown of my head. "Sweet dreams, Veronica. We'll talk about the angel some other time."

"Wait." I shook my head, making a vain attempt to rouse myself. "No, we should discuss him now. That was part of the deal."

In response, Orion kissed me once more. He eased me back down and massaged my scalp with his fingertips until I was back to teetering on the edge of oblivion. "Don't worry about it for now," he murmured. "I'm a man of my word. I won't forget."

That was the last thing I heard before sleep claimed me.

Upon waking, I found the bed beside me empty. No sign of the vampire clanmaster remained, other than the sexy musky smell of him in the sheets and the sweet ache between my legs.

"Ah, damn it." I rolled onto my back and stared at the dark ceiling, hugging a pillow to my chest. I cursed myself for proposing such a deal in the first place. I knew the answer, though. His presence had unleashed something inside me, and I stupidly let myself follow my lust instead of my head. I'd let myself fall for a vampire and demon, and now they were both engraved on my thoughts. They were enemies, yet I craved them madly.

"What the hell am I doing?"

There was no answer, except for the faint whine of an eerie Alaskan wind on the other side of the window.

24

SETH

I couldn't tell exactly when it had happened, but at some point in the very recent past, my feelings about our little three-person enterprise had begun to change. Specifically, I wasn't sure if Orion's silver-tongued promises were worth the suffering anymore. To bite my tongue and hold my fists in the face of endless harassment from outsiders was bitter agony for me.

With every passing minute, the urge to unleash this pent-up anger mounted dangerously. It boiled just below the surface of my outward veneer of calm. At any moment, I felt I could snap and transform into the monster I wanted to be. The one with the freedom to rampage until I was spent and could be calm again.

It wasn't often that my fights with Orion left me sour. Usually, one destructive outburst was all I needed to set me back on an even keel for a while. But this time, I wasn't so lucky. Instead of being relieved, I cultivated resentment. Who was he, a dead man, a walking corpse, to tell me what I could and couldn't do?

Besides, the girl had clearly enjoyed herself. My mouth watered just thinking about her. Man, she was delicious. There was something to be said about forbidden fruits—they always turned out to be the sweetest. But then, why was Orion the one who got to determine what was and wasn't forbidden? I shoved my hands into my pockets and glowered heavily as I marched down the hall of our house. I needed air.

Orion stepped out of the living room as I walked past. I should have just kept going, but instead I stopped. Veronica refused to leave my mind, along with Orion's insistence she was his, and it would burn me up if I remained silent. "Listen, I don't normally care what you do with your personal life and all that shit, but when it comes to Veronica—"

"She's open to several men in her life," he interrupted me.

I flinched, taken aback by his comment. "Say again? She said this to you, and you're okay with sharing?"

Orion snorted. "That wasn't what I said. But before you got all ballistic, I wanted you to know her opinion."

I eyed him as he stood there, hands deep in the pockets of his black pants, and I searched his face for the truth. "It must have killed you to hear her say that."

"I always get what I want, Seth. But I'm not a fucking monster and am open minded." Tightness crowded around the corners of his lips. "Thought you should know and maybe we can try to mend whatever's the hell's going on between us."

Again, I wasn't sure where his sudden caring nature came from. Maybe guilt, or maybe in realizing that if he wanted Veronica, he might have to concede to what she wanted. For once I was lost for words.

Part of me respected Orion more in that moment more than I had in forever. Though, I fought the urge to burst out laughing to see the grand vampire leader showing a softer side because of a mortal. That was fascinating.

"Is that all?" I asked, struck by a strange awkwardness between us.

He nodded and turned down the hallway, putting distance between us.

Outside, I couldn't come to terms with what Orion just dropped on me. I cruised along the sidewalk, going over it again and again.

I get he had been pissed that I claimed her first. The bastard didn't want my sloppy seconds. I grinned wickedly at that. Except, V's reveal stunned me as much as it clearly had Orion.

"Hey!" The shout jerked me out of my funk, and I came to a stop on the sidewalk, looking around like I'd just snapped out of hypnosis. "Watch where you're fucking going, asshole!"

"Who are you calling an asshole?!"

The voices filtered back to me from their origin point at the end of an alley up ahead. I turned toward them out of a mix of curiosity and a need for distraction. The closer I got, the more voices I heard, until the words had devolved into a jumble of thickly layered interactions. Most of them were shouting, words ringing through the air like stray bullets from a gun.

"What don't you get about this, man?" A young man stood blocking the mouth of the alley, poised in a fighting stance. "We don't want you city rats around here anymore. Consider your welcome overstayed." The last sentence was punctuated by cheers, clapping, a lone shrill whistle. His boys pulled in tight around him.

A fight was brewing. I craned my neck, peering through the blackness to try and get a look at the other side. They were bunched up at the alley's dead end. Disadvantaged, maybe, but nothing close to defeated. I had seen the looks on their faces before from cornered animals making a desperate bid for freedom.

"And what don't *you* get, assclown? We're not going anywhere anytime soon!" The vamp on the far end had no discernible accent, but he moved with the practiced aggression of a city dweller, a man who made a habit of squaring off with rival gangs at least once a night. He was a foreigner, an out-of-towner. One of Orion's enemies from the Seattle clan, I guessed.

I should have called him right then. Except these pricks had pushed me far enough. Rather than calming down and walking away from a situation that had very little to do with me, I stepped forward, shoving through the small crowd.

"How about this?" I raised my voice so it would carry. "You're all douchebags and this ain't nothing more than a mediocre circle-jerk. Can we agree on that?"

They all turned and looked at me, their eyes glowing dully. The resulting effect was eerie enough to raise goosebumps on my skin, which I promptly shook off. "Get the fuck out of here," I ordered. "All of you. Now."

They looked at each other. "Says you and what army?" the first vamp demanded snidely. "We were here first. If anyone should be getting lost, it's you."

"Butt out, will you?" the Seattle vamp added. "Things are complicated enough without your ugly ass trying to interfere. Go back to the circus or whatever hole you crawled out of, you freak."

"Nah." I advanced into the alleyway, spreading my arms in the universal challenge-issuing gesture. "I'd rather we settle this here and now, wouldn't you?" The faster I plummeted headlong toward a bad decision, the less bad it seemed. My knuckles burned with unused heat. I wanted to brand one of these wise guys right across the cheek.

The vamps exchanged looks. A murmur swept through their ranks. If I had been paying even slightly closer attention, I might have picked up on some clues that would've helped me avert the crisis that was seconds from occurring. But of course I missed every sign. I was too wrapped up in imagining the glory of fighting.

"C'mon, boys and girls." The Seattle vamp cracked his neck. "Let's show him what we've got." With a sweeping motion of his arm, he led the charge straight down the center of the alley. I braced myself and met him with my shoulder. He reeled back, dazed. His nose looked off center after the collision. I felt a little bad about it, but not enough to reevaluate my attack strategy.

Good thing, too. They came in from all sides, swarming like a horde of insects. I didn't get a chance to see where every one of them came from, nor how they kept arriving. The first couple waves were bearable, almost routine. I threw all kinds of vamps in all kinds of directions, sending them sprawling and scattering. Massive tongues of flame singed the brick walls on either side.

Then, as the numbers refused to diminish, I realized I might have a problem. There was no stemming the endless tide of the undead fuckers. And they were relentless, jumping right back after I'd brush them off. It took a long time, but I started to get tired. My punches turned sluggish. I didn't want to move.

How could there be so many?

I fought as long as I was physically able, but in the end, they managed to restrain me. The hard ground underneath my face was almost a relief. I didn't even care that they seemed to be celebrating my downfall.

"What should we do with him?" A circle of vampiric faces crowded around me. It was interesting to note that the crowd had chosen at some point to desegregate. Alaskan and Seattle vamps glared at me in unison.

"Throw him to the cops," one said gruffly. "Tell them he's the one behind that killing a mile from here. It doesn't matter if he's not. They're looking for someone to blame, and it'll get them off our backs."

"Hmm. That's not a bad idea." A dozen heads gazed down at me. I felt like some dead stiff right before the autopsy.

"Screw off," I muttered, somewhat less impressively than I meant it.

It was dawning on me, slowly and unpleasantly, that I had been drained from the fight. I could barely lift my arms. The side of my face melted into the floor.

"Will he die if we leave him?" someone asked. It would've been touching if not for the hard edge of practicality around every syllable.

"If he does, he's no good as a patsy," came the reply. The vamps concurred, and a few of the strongest stepped forward. They grabbed me around the armpits and dragged me to my feet. "Don't make trouble," they warned. One of them tied a blindfold around my eyes. "And don't peek. This is classified information."

That was how I ended up in the back of a moving vampire caravan, being packed off to some secret hideaway in Anchorage. I sat staring at the jet black dark on the inside of the blindfold, cursing my own conceit. It would've been so easy just to keep my big mouth shut. As a last act of defiance, I rattled my restraints.

"Shut it," snapped a vamp. "Just sit there and look ugly, will you?"

I wanted to kill him. But exhaustion made my body seem like it was filled with sand. For the moment, all I could do was obey.

That alone damn near killed me.

25

VERONICA

The next forty-eight hours passed at an agonizing crawl. I couldn't focus on anything other than the three men who had suddenly swept in and taken over so much of my world. Orion had not been in contact since the visit he had paid me at the hotel, and I knew when not to push an issue. Besides, much like my tryst with Seth, I still wasn't sure how I felt about it. That wasn't what I came to Anchorage for, yet I found myself tangled with them. My mission was always to observe, learn what was going on first, then jump into battle. But that was seeming less possible with each passing day.

But standing around in my hotel room was driving me crazy, and the police scanner offered no insight into anything potentially super-natural, so I got dressed, added my stake, extendable staff, and blade to my belt, then covered it with my thick jacket. Stepping into my boots, I made the call that my watching time was over. I needed to get involved and end the battle that would eventually spill into killing innocents if not stopped.

Dressed warmly, I went into my bag of weapons.

I slid the blade on the sheath on my belt, a stake, both of which I carried backups. Then I grabbed my extendable silver cylinder and hung it off my pocket which worked best as a long stake.

An icy wind greeted me at the sliding doors of the hotel. Chin tugged low, I folded my hands over my stomach and rushed out to the sidewalk. Fresh snow crunched underfoot, and I hurried onward.

Over the day and a half that followed, I spent a lot of time shaking my head and wrestling with complicated emotions. The problems I faced in the moment could not have looked more different than the ones I left behind in Seattle. Who had time to worry about schoolwork and rescheduling exams? I was caught in the quagmire of a potential love rectangle, between lovers who lived together even as they struggled to tolerate each other.

My head spun with the feelings that searing feeling inside I held for the three men. Three enemies... and whatever was going on between us was different. I'd never felt this way before. Other slayers had fallen prey to the allure of vampires, and I'd seen it personally myself. I never understood the attraction, the dynamics... until now. Well, in truth, I still didn't understand how I could be so drawn to them when I had one mission. Find and stop the vampire killings. I'd done the first part and found the killings, but the second part was a lot more complicated. There was a clan war going on, and if Orion was wiped out, was the next monster to step into his shoes going to start butchering humans more openly? Orion's followers didn't seem to practice this or there would be more innocents killed.

Then my thoughts swung to the gruesome scene from earlier... who was responsible for that?

I had more questions than answers to understand what was going on here. There was something I still remembered Dylan would say to me often. He'd compare vampire actions to the ice berg principle. The attacks they carry out were only ten percent of the real story that explained their behavior. It was so much more than feeding, he had said. But I wasn't sure I believed him. The assholes who killed my parents seemed to be there for the purpose of feeding. Not to mention the two in the alleyway attacking the young boy shortly after I arrived in Anchorage.

Dylan taught me a lot of new things, and I followed his approach as I only got into slaying after he passed, after watching him kill the wicked, after I needed to do something to put out the inferno burning me up from the inside out. That came in the form of eliminating vamps.

I shook away those thoughts because it felt like I was going in circles. There was so much I needed to uncover. Plus, would it really hurt if I scoured the streets and took out any fiends who got in my way?

Bright lights lit up the dark street. People strolled from one store to the next quickly, carrying grocery bags, or heading into the local bar. Normal life, but how did they feel about living so close to the supernatural? Most didn't know about them, or turned a blind eye to anything strange happening. But in a place like this, how could they really not see how many creatures lived right under their noses.

The thought brought me to Orion, Seth, and Logan. How exactly had the trio found each other? They were an odd bunch, and yet somehow they'd made it work so far. Along with having me attracted to them and already succumbed to my urges with two of them. I don't regret a single thing. Life was too short to not take what I wanted when it offered itself.

The only one who wasn't directly involved yet was Logan. As inconceivable as the whole thing really was, I couldn't help wondering if I'd be able to, um, *connect* with Logan in the same way. I liked to think that he and I had a different sort of affinity, a little more profound. He was the one who didn't mind baring some of his soul when we talked. He didn't walk around behind a shield of arrogance.

Orion and Seth I would happily have slept with again out of pure pleasure and getting to know them better as I felt they showed more of their real selves when in the clutches of desire. I almost laughed at myself with that thought. But Logan I wanted to get to know better emotionally. And I was genuinely looking forward to getting that chance.

Assuming he even showed up later at the crime scene.

I wandered along downtown Anchorage, and the farther I went into the residential area, the quieter the streets grew. Smoke billowed from chimneys, kids crying in houses I passed, the television loud enough to hear the game show one family watched.

At the next corner, I swung right where lofty trees lining the streets stood heavy with snow. Lamp posts lit up the sidewalk, and I moved faster to keep warm, figuring I might as well make my way toward the edge of the woods where I'd meet Logan at the crime scene.

A sudden scream had me flinching, my gaze lifting to several houses up ahead. I rushed closer, only for it to be followed up by laughing from inside.

I groaned with frustration at the lack of vamps and tuned into my ability once more. I took a deep breath to calm myself, then the energy flowed. My body vibrated like I was a struck tuning fork.

Except, there was not a single sensation of any vamps nearby. Not a goddamn thing.

It was as though all the vampires had withdrawn. Usually, I sensed them here and there, but now nothing. Were they having the weekly vampire neighborhood meeting? I laughed to myself and hurried toward the explosion of snow covered forest at the end of this street.

I had my doubts as I made my way to the meeting spot with Logan. By the time I stepped off the side of the road to head into the woods, it seemed safer to bet he wouldn't make an appearance. I retraced my steps from two nights earlier, eyes and ears open to the surrounding night. The crisp air raked its fingers through my hair and along my neck.

Then I saw him standing in the exact spot we had promised to meet. He was silent and still, looking through the heavily shadowed tree trunks into the clearing beyond. For some reason I couldn't quite pinpoint, I hesitated, just watching him.

"You're here," I said finally as I walked up.

He glanced at me. "Yeah. Are you ready?"

That was, I was learning, very much like Logan. No preamble, no wasting time, no beating around the bush. We were both there to do a job, first and foremost. His dispassionate commitment to maximum efficiency was something I ought to admire. But I couldn't deny the pang of disappointment that settled in my chest.

Had I really been hoping he might try and seduce me? Clearly, my priorities needed to be reexamined.

I shook my head to reset my thoughts. "Okay. Let's go."

Logan's gaze lingered on me for a moment or two, as if he wasn't sure I meant what I said. I refused to acknowledge him further, and he eventually stepped out from the tree line. The tape still clung in a yellow line to the perimeter, but it was wet and sagging from two nights of half frozen rain. The clearing itself sparkled with crystal droplets that soaked through my shins as I waded toward the center.

The bodies weren't there anymore, having been carted away for examination by the coroner. In some places, I could still pick out where torsos and limbs had left imprints in bloodstained grass. The ethereal stain of violence marred every inch of this quiet clearing—the silent mark of a ruthless predator.

There was no sign of the officers who had swarmed the vicinity on the night of the killings. Except for the yellow tape and the mess of bent grass and boot prints in the soggy ground, the area might as well have been abandoned. Mildly shocking, given what had transpired here, but understandable. I knew as well as anyone that this was not a case for mortal cops to solve.

Unfortunately, it wasn't shaping up to be all that easy for me, either. The energy swirling in the air was like nothing I had ever encountered before, and nothing I found on the empty site of its transgressions gave me any further clues to its identity. Stumped, I stopped in my tracks and appealed to Logan for help.

The scary part was that based on Logan's surprise about this gruesome scene earlier, I doubted Orion and his men knew anything about what was killing humans. That part terrified me because if I could see a monster, I could deal with it.

An invisible enemy was lethal.

"Didn't you say you had something for this?" I asked Logan.

He regarded me evenly. I had the distinct impression that he found my confusion amusing. "I can help," he agreed. "But it's going to be a matter of personal trust."

I gave him a skeptical look. "As in, I have to trust you? I thought I was already doing that." I shrugged, holding out my hands. "That's why I'm here."

Logan dropped his gaze for an instant. He stood motionless, lost in thought. Then, at the same time I took a step toward him, he grabbed my hand and pulled me in. One lean, strong arm wrapped around my waist.

"If you say so." His lips were on mine before I could truly say anything.

Is this real life? My thoughts scattered in a million directions, head spinning. The love quadrangle thing had been an amusing idea, too preposterous for reality. Nonetheless, here we were, embracing like star-crossed lovers or something. In the middle of a violent crime scene, no less!

But that was where I drew the line. If he tried to get a home run right here, right now, I'd shut it down and lock the building. As it was, he might not escape a verbal lashing. Hot as he was, I hadn't shown up to have a makeout session.

The minute I opened my eyes, however, I forgot everything I was just about to say. It was like the world had been desaturated while I wasn't looking, veiled over with shades that were more light and shadow than color. I turned to Logan, and he was *glowing*. I flinched at his appearance… it freaked me out.

"What happened?" I pushed hard on his chest. "What did you do?"

He eased up just enough to get me to stop struggling. "You're fine. You can talk to them now. Look."

"What?" I forced myself to focus. He pointed toward the spot where the majority of the bodies had lain, and I gasped. A small crowd of bright, ghostly figures stood in the grass, watching us. Their faces were uncanny, features blurred and indistinct. I felt my body snap into fight or flight mode—and so did Logan, because he finally let go.

"Relax," he said flatly. "They're just spirits. If you want information, go get it." Having said his piece, he withdrew and put his hands in his pockets. I stared between him and the ghosts, dumbfounded.

"*This* is what happens when you kiss people?"

Logan shrugged. "Sometimes. And it doesn't last forever, so hurry up." He nodded toward the silent observers. "They're waiting for you."

I frowned. "Okay, but we're going to talk about this later."

"The clock is ticking," he said.

The spirits shifted restlessly as I approached them. The eye sockets on their blank faces were empty and heavily shadowed. I could barely make out noses and mouths. A couple had flowing, ethereal hair. I paused. Would they answer if I spoke to them?

There was no time to waste worrying about it. Although Logan hadn't specified a time frame, the pressure mounted steadily. Five feet away from the nearest ghost, I stopped. It pivoted toward me, its movements eerily mechanical.

"Were you killed here two nights ago?" I asked. The question seemed to grab the attention of the others, and before I knew it, they had crowded around me. The air chilled by about ten degrees. I tried to look for Logan, but the spirits blocked my view.

One of them attempted to speak. A dark void opened up on its countenance, morphing and changing with each garbled word.

"Yes," it mumbled. "I am…sad."

"I'm sorry to hear that." I took a deep breath and did my best to calm the tension in my nerves. Pure instinct had me prepped for the worst; I'd heard tales of ghosts looking to reclaim the souls of the living and things like that. What if the rest were angry rather than sad? Or spiteful? "I want to help you," I added, "but I need you to tell me what you know. Did you see who caused your death? Any of you?"

A low murmur made its way around the circle.

"I was the first," declared a different ghost. "But I only saw a large shadow behind me. It happened…too fast."

My heart started to sink a little as I saw a ripple of agreeing nods. So, whatever it had been, there was only one monster and could be anything kind of creature in reality. Many beasts hunted alone.

"All I saw…were the dead," said the next specter gloomily. "Fresh corpses…lined up so neatly." It paused, apparently thinking. "And then…I became one of them."

"Nothing?" I gazed in a slow circle at each androgynous face. "None of you saw a single thing that could help identify a murderer? What it looked like? Did it make any sounds?"

They shook their heads in unison. "Death is…funny. Our memories…like fog in rain."

It's been two days! I wanted to grab their noncorporeal shoulders and shake them. But already, I could feel whatever sense Logan had given me was beginning to fade. The ghosts flickered unsteadily. They started to back away. Within moments, they were completely gone, and colors were seeping back into the world.

I ran back to Logan. "No good. Any way I could get an extension?" He gazed down at me as if he'd spent the last few minutes under heavy hypnosis. "Hello? Logan? Can you do that again?"

"What? Kiss you?" He ran his finger underneath my chin, stroking my bottom lip with his thumb. "I guess so, if you wanted."

I rolled my eyes. "What I want is to see dead people for like five more minutes. Yes or no?" The second kiss was a welcome fringe benefit, but I wasn't about to let him know that.

"Let's find out." This time, he held my face in his hands and unexpectedly kissed me so deeply I was almost lifted off my feet. The sparks that shot from my lips to my toes were pure electricity. I tingled all over.

Nothing else happened. The forest was the same afterward, if a little hazy. We stared at each other.

"Damn." The word came out soft and awestruck. "It didn't work."

"Then it won't, for a while." Logan gave up a small, apologetic smile. "Sorry."

"I mean…" I chewed my lip. "Maybe there's a placebo effect?"

Instead of waiting for him to respond, I stood on my toes and kissed him once more. He drew my body close against his. The intrinsic coolness of his energy slowly turned to low heat.

There was no placebo effect, as it turned out. But I didn't pull away as his hands moved to explore. And I didn't stop him.

26

ORION

I had known from the start that Veronica was not about to be an easy conquest—that was part of her appeal. But the reality of not being able to access her whenever I wanted needled at me, especially with the thought of sharing her. That still sat on my mind like a mountain. Where was she? What was she doing? Who was she with?

That last unknown was the worst.

When the knock came at the door, I practically flew to answer it, craving a distraction from my own one-track mind. But the face that greeted me wasn't any better than Veronica's maddening beauty. The vamp sneered at me, his thin lip curling over jagged teeth. "Good evening, Clanmaster." The words had a mocking lilt that I did not like at all.

"What do you want? Out with it." I didn't bother asking him inside; whatever business he had could be conducted here in the twilight.

He glanced around, shifty eyes darting back and forth. "I've been sent to deliver a message on behalf of all my brethren." The lips pulled back into a sickly grin. "We've stumbled upon something of yours. I believe you call him Seth."

I clenched my jaw hard. "Is he dead? He must be, to have gotten captured by the likes of you."

The vamp giggled with macabre delight. "Oh, no, no. He is very much alive. And angry." The grin dropped into a split second of worry.

171

"We'd like to return him to you as soon as possible, frankly." Regathering his composure, he cleared his throat. "So, your *honorable* presence is being requested for the purpose of negotiations. You may come alone, or bring your…associate."

The mention of Logan, however indirect, made him nervous. He took another quick look around and shifted his feet.

"What's stopping me from rolling up and putting an end to this entire charade?" I asked. My voice stayed calm, but inside I was boiling. I should have known better than to trust that fire-breathing idiot. His anger had compromised us all.

"With all due respect, Clanmaster…" The shit-eating grin was back. "We hardly think you'd keep the devil around if you didn't need him for *something.*"

Annoyed by my inability to deny their logic, I capitulated. "Fine. Where is he?" The address was deeper into the city than usual, and I wondered at their brazenness. Hiding in plain sight. "Tell them I won't be long, and they'd better not waste any more of my time." Without further ado, I stepped back and slammed the door.

Had Seth been standing in front of me, I might have wrung his neck, snapped it, and throttled him again. This was far from his first blunder, but absolutely his most serious. The repercussions would have to be severe.

After I got him back, of course. I closed my eyes and sent a summons out into the world, intended for Logan.

"Seth got caught. Convene immediately at my location. Recovery operation."

Typically, it took him no longer than seconds to reply, but Logan wasn't in the mood to acknowledge me either. From him, a certain measure of aloofness was expected, and yet his coldness only blackened my mood further. Perhaps there was something in the air tonight, some golden, tantalizing whiff of mutiny.

Not that insubordination mattered so much at the moment. I had bigger problems on my hands. If Logan chose not to show up entirely, he'd regret it.

I arrived downtown in record time, brimming with utter dissatisfaction. Everyone I passed on the street gave me a double-wide berth. Haunted whispers followed my every step. This sort of passive intimidation was one of the greatest assets of a vampire's nature. A weapon I desired Veronica to hone to its sharpest edge.

Seth's prison turned out to be a semi-derelict warehouse, all but abandoned by its former owners at the edge of the city's heart. Several of its windows were boarded up or broken; the front doors stood ominously open like the slack mouth of a dead man. I showed no hesitation in striding through them, straight into the pitch dark.

"Bold as usual, I see." The voice was low and silky, gliding through the air like water. I searched in the shadows for its owner and found the glowing circles of a vampire's pale irises trained on me, unblinking. He stepped into the weak spill of light from one of the windows, and I saw the contours of a gaunt, cruel face, long and hard like a jackal's. The pallor of his skin contrasted with the intensity of his gaze.

How old was he? And how long had it been since I'd last encountered a vampire near my age? I held his stare.

"Where is the demon? Show him to me."

The vampire smiled. "As you wish." Someone flipped an invisible switch, and a light blazed on in the far back of the room. Seth sat propped against the bare concrete, affixed to the wall by thick iron chains. The cuts and bruises in stark relief on his face and body confirmed that he had not submitted quietly. He squinted at me through the sudden brightness, his expression contorted into a glowering mask.

My stomach turned. He was mine and when we fought that was what we did, but to have anyone else harm him seared through me like hot pokers. Seth was under my protection, part of my tribe. I turned back to his captor. "Your terms?" I sneered.

"Well..." The vampire cast his eyes to the side. The hairs rose on the back of my neck. Belatedly, I wondered if I had fallen into a trap. "Firstly, I would like you to know that I am not alone in this." He gestured, and a veritable army emerged from the shadows—including many of my own people. Fire burned through my veins.

"What kind of reckoning is this?" I hissed. "You think you can make your leader bow?"

"No, Clanmaster." A small contingent of Alaskans stepped forward to face me. "Hear us out before passing your judgment." They paused, glancing at each other for courage. "We want the demon to leave our territory."

"I'm listening," I grumbled. "For now." Admittedly, it was an idea that appealed to me as well for a plethora of reasons.

"He's reckless," they continued. "He's unpredictable, and he shows no loyalty to anyone other than you. He could tear this city apart if he were ever to go unchecked."

"And what makes you think that will happen?" I demanded.

"What makes them think it won't?" The vampire who had met me cut in smoothly, redirecting my rising temper toward himself. "With all due respect, Clanmaster, your iron grip on the territory is weakening. We *are* occupying you, after all." He smiled, as if he'd made a harmless little joke.

"Let it be said that your welcome is fast running out," I answered.

"Then allow me to propose a solution." He folded his hands, steepling the tips of his fingers, and smiled. "We will relieve you of this hellish burden, take him back with us, and consider a truce brokered."

"No." I didn't even have to think about it. Like hell was I ever going to give up a mercenary, no matter how frustrating and bullish he could be. I didn't give up on one of my own. That was just a needless advantage for them.

"Not even a counter-offer?" The city vamp raised his eyebrows. "You aren't much of a businessman, are you, Orion?"

"Maybe I would be if you posed more of a threat." I shook my head. "No. You have finally missed a step. This dance we've been doing is over." I held his eyes. "Get your cronies and get out. Now!"

"And what if we refuse?" came the reply.

I bared my teeth. "Then I'd be happy to assist you."

One of the lackies from the enemy clan lunged at me, followed by others. Those loyal to me were quick to remember who their clanmaster was and took their side alongside me to fight.

I lashed out and grabbed the oncoming attacker by the neck, twisted it with ease and tossed him aside. Then I threw myself into battle, eager to spill blood and break bodies. Punching my fist right into another's chest, I kicked him aside and turned to two others. Fury licked at my insides, and with everything of late, I craved to destroy all those who stood in my way.

The battle grew brutal, and I threw punches, headbutted the enemy, and I wasn't below ripping out hearts. Blood splashed on my face as I tore out a vamp's throat, and I reveled in it.

One slammed into my back, an arm latched around my throat. I swung an arm over my shoulder and loped it over his head. I crouched forward suddenly and wrenched the asshole forward as he lost his footing, then I made quick work of snapping his neck. Shoving him off my back, I straightened and glanced to the back of the warehouse, the chains binding Seth grated heavily across the floor, igniting showers of sparks. The demon strained against his shackles. He couldn't stand to sit by and watch volley after volley of frenzied blows fly back and forth. To be denied even a small sliver of the excitement was worse than any torture for him.

But Seth's strength had been spent during the futile struggle to avoid captivity, and now he stood no chance of an unaided escape. He watched, his anger rising, as the vampire clans tore into each other. Shrieks of fury and pain echoed off the walls.

I was too preoccupied with the onslaught of enemies to spare him too much more attention. Had I been able to, I would have loosed him from his chains with my own hands so he could take his place by my side. As it was, the urban rats purported to overwhelm me. I lost sight of Seth in the ensuing frenzy.

Perhaps fittingly, my thoughts were consumed with someone else.

Logan, where the fuck are you?

VERONICA

*L*ogan had me up against a tree, my legs around his waist, arms encircling his neck. Immediately, the rough bark of the trunk bit into my back and shoulders through my clothes. I felt my skin and clothes threaten to tear with the slightest friction.

"Wait." I tore away from his kiss breathlessly. "I can't do it like this. The tree will shred me."

Half of me expected him to shrug it off and keep going. I could feel his hardness pressing between my legs after all. To my surprise, he paused long enough to lift me away from the trunk and wrap his huge black wings around my body. The feathers were cool and soft. I sank gratefully into them.

"Better?" he murmured.

"Yeah." I ran my fingers up into his shoulder-length hair and pressed my mouth urgently to his. "Thanks."

He responded by cupping a breast and pinching my hardened nipple through the fabric of my top and bra. I moaned against his lips, lifted my hips to grind myself against him. The way in which we were positioned made it easy to be as close to him as possible; every muscle in his body seemed to ripple against me.

I dug my fingers into his back and shoulders, savoring the intense, unyielding pleasure. Logan's grip tightened on the back of my thighs. He kissed me until I couldn't breathe. My back arched against the tree trunk. The moan that left my throat turned into a kind of carnal growl.

His mouth caressed my neck greedily. The tremor of his arousal traveled all the way through to the tips of his wings. The feathers flared around me. For a moment, we were wrapped up entirely in each other. We'd only kissed, but I knew if we didn't stop, this would end up leading into something else completely.

I broke from our kiss, needing to remember my mission and not the desire I couldn't shake. "Maybe we shouldn't do this."

Then he was letting me down carefully onto legs that were still shaking. I clung to him and laughed sheepishly. "I didn't mean for that to happen."

"Do you regret it?" He brushed the hair from my eyes.

I looked up at him and noticed that it had started to snow, very lightly. Delicate crystals adorned his ash-gray hair and eyelashes. I let myself sink into those ice blue eyes and how incredibly gorgeous Logan was. But there was so much more to him than he allowed me to see.

"No." I told the truth.

Logan smiled, then frowned. His demeanor changed completely. "Orion is calling."

I sighed. "Of course he is." I pulled out my phone to check it. Surprise—a bunch of messages from everyone's favorite clanmaster. "He tried to get in touch with me too…"

"Seth is in trouble." Logan spoke dispassionately, but I heard the resignation in his words. "We need to recover him."

"That makes it sound like he's dead," I said, unable to hide my alarm.

Logan showed no emotion. "Maybe he is."

---

*L*ogan traced Orion to the outer edge of downtown. The place looked abandoned, a squatter's dream hovel. On the approach, we could already see a whirlwind of activity inside. "What the fuck is going on in there?" I muttered, mostly to myself.

"Let's go." Logan broke into a full run and sprinted straight for the doors. I kept hot on his heels. My trusty knife hung in its permanent place on my belt, but the closer we got, the more serious things appeared to be. My dire assessment was only confirmed when a body came smashing through one of the windowpanes. I dodged just in time to watch it hit the ground and sprawl grotesquely, held up at an awkward angle by the jagged end of an improvised stake.

"Yeah, okay. Some shit is really going down." I leaned into my run, reaching for a palm-sized silver cylinder hanging next to my pocket. "Time to bring out the big guns."

Inside, the warehouse was a chaotic mess. Vampires ripped at each other in the near-total darkness, snarling, hissing, shrieking. I saw thatches of hair and skin littered around the floor, even severed limbs and chunks of bone. *You know,* I thought, *in case I forgot they were fucking monsters.*

Logan darted into the chaos.

As soon as the vamps smelled living blood, a group turned toward me and came in a maddening rush. My skin crawled, but I pressed a button on the side of my metal staff, and it telescoped neatly into a staff. I intended to put it through its paces and prayed I hadn't gotten too rusty with this weapon. I cut a clean swing at the coming assault. I admired the trueness of its strikes, and I struck several in one go. Then I swung around and jabbed one end into a fiend with wild black hair. The vampire dropped dead, a hole through his undead heart. In seconds, another followed suit. Then another. I stabbed three more, and whacked another in the head hard enough to knock him off his feet.

Boots slapped the concrete floor, closer and closer they came.

One of them snatched my shirt from behind me and heaved.

"Bastard," I growled and threw my elbow into his face, dislodging him from me.

I fought, everything becoming one big blur, which came with such a crowd, with being outnumbered. This wasn't what I expected. I couldn't see Logan from the crowd of vampires encroaching.

And then someone grabbed me by the hair and yanked backward. I stumbled on my feet, the searing pain through my scalp made me cry out in shock. An icy chill raced down my spine.

I kicked and punched at everything, trying desperately to get free. The last thing I needed was to get dragged down off my feet into a death orgy of these guys.

The hand brutally pulled my head viciously downward.

I cried out but lashed outward with my staff, my other hand retrieving the stake at my belt and I struck something hard enough to elicit a grunt of pain. I wound up and took a strike, and another, while kicking. Fear bucked inside me but the numbers around me had thinned, and I would finish them.

"Fresh blood," the vampire tugging on my hair behind me said, and I flinched at the venom in his voice.

His fingers in my hair abruptly relaxed. I pulled free and slammed my stake into the heart of a huge bastard who lunged at me. I shoved him off me, and he fell to the ground with most of the others. The few that remained seemed to recoil now.

Behind me, I heard a snap and a soft tearing sound.

The next hands that touched me were strong and familiar. I whipped around to see his face, my heart in my throat. "Orion!"

He gave me a quick inspection. "Are you hurt?"

I rubbed the back of my head. "No, I'm fine. What—"

He put his fingers to my lips. "Not now. Go find Seth, and I won't ask you why you're here." The firm, almost paternal way he said that made a flame flicker inside me, but I pushed it down. He was right. *Not now.*

"Have you seen him?" I asked.

Orion pointed, just before a new assailant attempted to leap onto his back. I pulled away as quickly as possible and began to beat my way through the pandemonium. I sliced my way through the mess, hard to tell half the time which vampire was on Orion's side. But those who stood in my way, I lashed out at.

A direct hit to the side of my face had me staggering sideways, the pain cutting along my cheekbone. I snapped around and without thought, thrust out my stake into the monster. I caught him right in the throat, blood spurting out. He gurgled, eyes wide with shock at my retaliation as he stumbled.

"Oops. Wrong spot." I wrenched the weapon back, and in a heartbeat, thrust it directly for his heart.

Slammed in there, I smirked. "There you go, all good now."

The moment any sign of life evaporated from his eyes and he started to fall, I pulled free my stake and kept going across the warehouse.

Soon, my staff was filthy, slick with the aftermath of killing undead.

By the time I pushed through the back of the fight, I looked like I had fought my way through a warzone. My shirt and jeans had been torn in several places, and I thought I could feel the sticky trickle of blood mixing with sweat. The adrenaline pumping through my veins doubled when I laid eyes on an incredibly angry hell-demon railing against the largest set of chains I'd ever seen.

A tremor jolted through my body, and under the rush of adrenaline came pity at seeing Seth in this state. It pained me to watch him fight for escape. Every inch of me screamed to save him.

"Seth!" I ran toward him. He looked at me, the haze of rage clearing as I met his eyes. Everything else fell away as I choked on the dread splashed across his face. Nothing scared Seth, yet seeing him this panicked left me trembling.

I was suffocating.

Gasping for air to see him like this.

"Seth!" I cried out.

His expression twisted with agony.

But I had only taken a few steps before I knew something was wrong. The heat pouring off of him rivaled a nuclear reactor in crisis. His veins glowed iridescent through the reddish tan of his skin. I stopped short as the light began to pour from his eyes, mouth, even his nose.

"Oh, shit," I whispered.

"Veronica, stay away from me," he begged, his voice more scared than threatening.

A split second later, Seth erupted. That was the best way to describe it. I caught little more than a glimpse of his body shaking violently, panic scribbled over his face. His body stiffened, his shock palpable by the force of his expelling energy.

My stomach dropped through me as fear collided into me. I knew then, something bad had happened to Seth. Something so horrendous, that it terrified him.

Then in a flash, everything disappeared in a white explosion. Sparks danced in front of my eyes, blinding me for seconds.

The shockwave that came next crashed into me, throwing me to the ground. I covered my head, curling in on myself, part of me wandering if he'd bring down the whole warehouse. Moments later, I opened my eyes to see the warehouse ceiling above me remained intact, and a tangled mess of confused vampires all still scrambling to regain the upper hand. Frantically, I glanced over to the wall where Seth had been fixed into the wall. The chains were still there, but their heavy black links lay scorched and empty. There was no sign of Seth. He'd simply vanished into thin air.

My chest tightened and I reached out a hand, a chill encasing me. "Seth?" I whispered.

Footsteps pounded toward me across the concrete floor, and Orion grabbed me by the arms, lifting me to my feet. "Are you alright?" he asked.

I shoved him as far away as he would allow. "I'm okay. But Seth is..." We both looked back to the wall. I took a slow breath in. "The fuck?" Coldness licked over my skin as worry made me sick to my stomach.

"Fuck." Orion grimaced, and a wave of worry washed over his face. Despite all their shit, he truly cared for losing his friend. "Where the hell did he go?" Fear gripped his voice.

No sooner had I come to realize how much harder this has hit Orion than I ever suspected, than a hand fell onto his shoulder from behind. I backed off as Orion turned around to face his newest challenger. There was something oddly familiar about this vamp, but it wasn't until I got a good look at his face that I realized I'd seen him before—in Seattle, coming and going around the vamp gangs' favorite haunts.

Didn't know his name, but I didn't have to. All I knew was that the guy was a prick. And apparently, Orion thought so too.

Now I had seen plenty of vamp-on-vamp infighting in Seattle; pretty much the only thing they fought was each other. And I rarely got involved. If they wanted to thin their numbers, I let them. But this was different. Orion didn't engage the way I was accustomed to seeing vampires moving. The ones back in the city had become somewhat tamed by their modern, urban surroundings. They had less of a connection to the wild, bestial part of their nature. It was like fighting suped-up humans.

Orion tapped into a much more ferocious, animalistic style. He moved almost catlike, low to the ground, each motion executed with deadly precision. His eyes never left his opponent for a second. I watched him scan for weak points as he waited for the opportune moment to strike. The Seattle vamps could be deadly in their own right, but something told me this one wouldn't stand half a chance against Orion.

Orion was like nothing I had ever seen. The air hummed with his concentrated power. I felt him coiling to attack. And when he sprang at last, it seemed I barely saw it. Just a flash of darkness and death. The city vamp sidestepped nimbly, but not quite in time. Orion caught his shoulder, leaving behind a heavy tear through clothes and flesh. Orion pivoted and attacked, bringing with him his full force. He moved so fast, I struggled to make sense of what was happening. The enemy shrieked and blood splattered to the ground. Soon followed by the vamp.

That was the beginning of the end. As I suspected, the Seattle vampire was ill-prepared to handle a "wild" creature like Orion. He was never given a chance to react properly. His jacket and shirt were shredded to rags, to say nothing of the skin beneath them. When he fell, the weak light glanced off an exposed bit of bone.

Orion pinned the enemy under his knee, glaring down into his eyes. "This act of disrespect," he growled, "will be the last thing you ever do." Without looking up, he reached his hand out toward me, palm open.

He wanted the metal staff. And I knew exactly what for.

I threw it to him.

Orion raised the weapon with one hand, the pointy end aimed to his enemy. In a flash, he struck down hard and fast. The sound of the vampire's last breath rushing from his lungs filled the whole space. His arms and legs went limp, and his head lolled to the side, eyes open and rapidly dulling. Orion didn't move until he was sure the guy was dead.

"Thank you, Veronica," he said quietly.

"I'm really worried about Seth," I admitted.

"I can tell. I'll find Seth, no matter what it takes. And you're a lot stronger than I initially thought." He put the staff into my hand, turned my face up, and kissed me. I couldn't stop myself from melting a little.

"Gross," I told him. "You smell like dead vamp."

"I'm not the only one who needs a shower," he fired back. His expression quickly sobered. "Come home with me. We don't have much time."

Behind him, the window showed a horizon just starting to lighten toward dawn. But I couldn't leave yet. "What about Logan? And…" I turned to look at the wall with the chains, unable to stop the ache growing in my chest at Seth taken. "He's not dead, is he?"

"Logan will be fine," Orion said coolly. "As for Seth…Demons don't die that easily. He annoyed the shit out of me, but I never wanted him hurt. I'll track him down one way or another, I give you my word." He took me by the hand, and while he didn't say it, I saw the worry in his eyes that maybe Seth was in more danger than he let on, and it troubled

Orion. "We have to go, Veronica. Unless you want to keep me on the mantle in an urn."

I hated leaving the warehouse without any sense of where Seth was or what had happened. Fragments of pain struck through my chest at the possibility that he might be in horrible danger. The brief image of him disintegrating into light was seared into the back of my mind. I shouldn't care, and the one time we shared was just that... a one off. Yet I never wanted to see him hurt or killed, no matter how much of an ass he was. One last time, I scanned the scorched wall where he'd been earlier, my hands trembling. Anger and guilt floated to the surface. And with it came something feral surging through me that I never got a chance to help Seth. Goosebumps danced along my arms.

I twisted away, my emotions melting into one another, until they sat like a knot in my chest. This wasn't how I should feel about a demon, yet there I was feeling empty at the loss.

It was only a mild consolation to see Logan emerge from the front of the building, wings folded on his back, looking no worse for wear. He nodded to Orion. The majority of the enemy vampires had run or lay on the floor. The ones that remained bowed their heads at Orion.

"Seth is gone," Orion said softly.

Logan's brows pulled together, and he lowered his gaze momentarily as though he experienced his own moment of loss. "We need to find him." The darkness in his voice surprised me.

"We will," Orion answered curtly, and the hunger for revenge rose in his tone. "I'll destroy anyone who stands in my way."

"And I'll help," I added.

The smile from both Orion and Logan brought with it a strange union I felt with them, with us being a team, working toward one goal.

While I swallowed the lump in my throat at Seth being gone, as a demon was he really gone somewhere else or just to hell? Whatever had been done to him had to involve a summoning or a curse. Didn't it? Or he self-combusted from rage? God, I didn't know, but I had to find out. I had only spent a short time with him, but I wasn't ready to just watch him vanish as though he never existed.

Dawn broke as we walked through the huge open room toward the door. Orion ducked behind a support pillar, covering his skin. Logan and I glanced around at the corpses of the fallen as they turned to ash, slowly at first as the sunlight found them through the windows and door, and then rapidly. A hard breeze swept through the broken windows and bore most of the ashes away.

Orion reemerged, now safely obscured by remaining in the shadows, his hood over his head, his body covered.

"What's next?" I wondered out loud. In the wake of this massive destruction, the investigation I had taken on was a favor to an old friend, now seemed too large to truly comprehend. We were standing at the tip of an iceberg whose shadow loomed deep underwater. There was something strange and mystical about this untamed northern city, this frozen, lonely place. A killer taking out innocents that I couldn't help but think it wasn't vampire or shifter related. Then there was the warring battle between the Seattle clanmaster and Orion.

With Seth gone, I had to find him. As crazy as it sounded, that ache in my chest from seeing him vanish deepened. What the hell happened to him?

Which brought me to my final dilemma...my attraction to these men. Somewhere along the way, the whole slayer and monsters being enemies had turned on its head. I had to correct that.

"The word will travel fast that the Seattle detachment is dead," Orion answered solemnly. "We will need to prepare for the worst—all of us. Because when it reaches home..." He turned his gaze to me, staring defiantly. "A storm is coming."

Yet my thoughts kept swinging back to the odd energy I'd sensed at the gruesome scene of all those butchered humans. Something was really wrong here beyond all the other shit. A darkness slid through the shadows undetected in Anchorage, and everything was about to get a whole lot worse very soon if I didn't find out who was hunting humans.

I had come to Anchorage to stop a war amid vampires. But instead, I found myself dragged into a battle zone.

And I had no plans to walk away.

MOON KISSED

CHOSEN VAMPIRE SLAYER

BOOK TWO

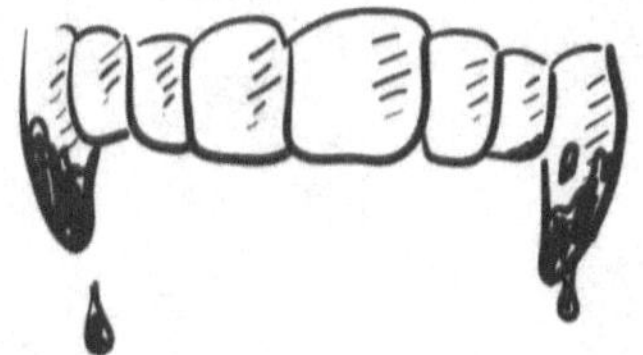

There's a war on...

...and we're on the losing side.

But that's not the only problem I've got. Someone or something is killing off the humans in Anchorage... and the fallout is landing right on our shoulders.

Or at least on those of us left.

Seth has vanished. I refuse to believe he's gone for good. I won't. If I have to go through heaven and hell to find him, that's just what I'll do. I owe him that.

And I'm on it as hot and heavy as the growing attraction between me and the monsters I've fallen for. Which is more than complicated. And could use some of my time...

But I've got none.

Another monster, one hidden in the shadows, is making it his business to get in my way. Which means the boys and I have our hands full just surviving another day. And things are only getting worse.

There's something coming for me, and it won't stop until I'm dead.

PROLOGUE

SETH

I woke with my back to hard stone, the acidic air all but singeing the skin on my face. The first thing I felt, on pure instinct, was elation. That burning smell meant only one thing to me. I was finally back home.

Or so I thought. After opening my eyes and getting to my feet, brushing the dust off my clothes, I realized a few things. One, it was still frigidly cold—my breath steamed at every exhale. And two, the light was a matching, frozen blue. Nothing like the shimmering red heat of my regular domain. I looked around at the vaulted, heavily shadowed walls. Vague silhouettes, specked with pinpricks that could've been eyes, skittered through the darkness.

"Shit." I ran a hand over my face. "Looks like I'm not home after all." The cold seeped through my clothes like water. I could already feel it battling with the heat in my veins. "I gotta get out of here."

The last thing I remember was being shackled to the wall by those mother-fucking Seattle vampires. It wasn't an easy thing to admit defeat against the fanged bastards, but they overpowered me with sheer numbers. Add to that the iron fetters they used were no ordinary hand-cuffs. I felt their magic the moment they snapped around my wrists, a spell that had me literally burning up to the point of combustion. It takes a hell of a lot more to kill a demon like me, but they did what they'd intended. Got me out of their way. So, where in the fuck was I now?

Great blue-gray slabs of stone stretched up to a cavernous ceiling that I couldn't quite see. I kicked at the ground, tossing up little clouds of ice and dirt. Every sound produced an echo. If I stayed perfectly still, it seemed even my heartbeat reverberated.

The whole damn place made me paranoid. The dark was so deep that determining a direction was more or less impossible, except for faint traces of some cold, ethereal glow. When I moved to take a step, my skin crackled, and I realized a thin coating of ice crystals had already begun to form. The implication was clear, and I didn't like it.

Time to move or be frozen forever.

As I walked forward into a looming abyss, my vision began to adjust very slowly. Still, I almost missed the first moving shape that darted across my path. The sensation of eyes on me grew heavy, a nearly tangible weight. With each blink, I imagined these unseen enemies inching closer. Waiting for the perfect opportunity to strike.

It wasn't long before they found it. One moment I was heading deeper into the unknown, and the next, the unknown had come to me. The freezing darkness coalesced around my body, ensnaring each limb in its tendrils. I gasped, unable to keep the air in my lungs. A billion tiny pinpricks seemed to perforate my skin. Not enough to wound—just enough to torture. I hissed at the deepening pain swallowing me.

But then the old, familiar fighting instinct welled up, ignited by an ever-smoldering instinct for violence. As a demon born of fire and avarice, the answer to such a brazen attack was simple.

Fight back.

The tide of adrenaline flooded through me, bringing a surge of searing heat. I clenched my hands into rock-hard fists. Steam poured off my skin where that thin veneer of ice had channeled instantly. The dark, indistinct aggressors flinched back from the blazing warmth pouring out from my body, as if it hurt them.

I laughed. "What, are you having second thoughts? Come on! I'll go easy on you this time."

No one was there to tell me how fucking dumb it looked to be taunting sentient shadows as I stood fully entrenched in their realm. Would've been just as smart to antagonize a lion in its den, or a dragon in its lair. But I was nothing if not bold. Wasn't that the reason I had teamed up with a prideful, power-hungry vampire in the first place?

Constantly hungry, looking for the next thrill... not to mention he made me an offer I couldn't resist. The thought of Orion, also brought back my last images of Veronica. Of her running toward me while I was tied up to the wall, fear crowded in her eyes. The beautiful slayer worried for me, which was a complete surprise. That memory struck me the hardest... No one truly cared about me without wanting something back, but what I'd seen in her eyes in the warehouse was unadulterated sympathy and care. Where did that come from?

Shaking off the memory that haunted me and made me soft, I refocused on my current problem.

The shadows regrouped, blinking the same brilliant, jewel-like eyes I had seen earlier. Everywhere they touched, a fractal of ice formed and spread. The temperature seemed to be plummeting by the minute. If I let them stall for too much longer, they'd freeze me out. And what a humiliating end that would be.

Long story short, I was the one who lunged for the first strike. The dark, shifting creatures appeared almost incorporeal, but there was something there for my hands to seize upon, and they hissed and warbled in pain at my grasp. It was an eerie cry, uncomfortably distinct from the human screams that were so often music to my ears.

Still, a fight was a fight. I thrived on them, and as I tore into the odd, ethereal flesh of an enemy, I realized how badly I'd been itching to do some damage. After all, I had gotten my ass dumped in this forsaken place in the middle of a brawl I wasn't allowed into. This little skirmish, if nothing else, was a good place to offload some simmering aggression.

Then I happened to glance over my shoulder and see a whole advancing platoon of these things, eyes glimmering in the dim light. The skirmish was fast growing into a full-on battle: me against the underlings of darkness. Not that I minded; it was practically a relief to be doing something on my own instead of waiting for Orion to sneer orders down his nose.

The problem was that as their numbers grew, the temperature shrank. Only a few minutes passed before I thought I could feel my eyeballs starting to ice over. Their needly teeth and claws pulled at every inch they could grab, exposing red-hot blood to the air in gouts of blistering vapor.

"Fuck off!" I snarled through gritted teeth. The human oath had no effect, and so I repeated it in every demonic tongue that I knew, building in intensity alongside my frustration. The air had grown thick with a metallic steam. Behind me, a trail of bloodstains gradually lengthened. The pain was nothing. I just didn't appreciate being detained by a bunch of nagging Underworld gremlins.

Another fifty feet of struggle, and my anger hit its boiling point. Throwing back my head, I let out an earthshaking bellow of rage. Jets of white-hot flame erupted from my eyes and mouth. The veins glowed under my skin. All creatures climbing and hanging on to me vanished in smoke and ash, incinerated.

Temporarily free from their burden, I bolted down a dark passage. The wind stabbed into my face and neck, a different, less tolerable kind of pain than the lacerations leaking red drops onto the floor. That deep, bone-piercing ache was the pain that might have scared me if I'd ever chosen to acknowledge things like fear. It gnawed at the sharp edges of my ordinarily unchallenged vitality.

I did not want to admit weakness—of any kind, for any reason.

The cavern yawned on endlessly, as far as I could see, for minutes at a time. Just when I was beginning to think I had either been tricked or would be trapped forever in a barren stone tundra full of things that wanted me dead, an archway rose up out of the shadows. My heart leapt in anticipation. Then I saw there was no doorway beneath.

"What the *fuck?*" I slid to a stop. At my back, the growing ranks of my enemies advanced, but I had momentarily forgotten about them. All that mattered was the door, or lack thereof. "You can't be serious," I muttered to the empty air. "There's got to be a way through."

The wall proved to be both unyielding and so cold I could barely touch it without feeding some of my power through my hands. A closer inspection revealed the outline of a portal, what was undoubtedly supposed to be a way through. I tried everything I could think of to force it open, but the bitter surface just wouldn't give. I beat my fists against the stone, to little avail. A few chips scattered across the ground.

Finally defeated, I let my shoulders slump. The thoughts in my head spun a million miles a minute as I attempted to make some sense of the current predicament. The onslaught behind me continued to mount. I could hear and feel the gap closing between me and that glittering sea of shadows. I closed my eyes and took a deep, sub-zero breath.

Suddenly, a recollection surfaced in my mind. Something angel-boy had said not too long before everything went south. I scowled, trying to remember the words I had carelessly brushed off at the time. Hadn't he tried to pass between the veil from there to somewhere else...and failed?

I groaned. "Don't tell me I'm on his turf now." It was one more annoyance on top of a mountain of others, and yet it made sense the more I considered. That winged, pretty-boy bastard sure did love the cold.

And if I was here, and he was still there, did that mean we could help each other? Maybe. But first, I had to figure out a way to get through. If the sealed doorway was any indication, that was not going to be the kind of simple task I wanted. Not to mention there were some other things left to handle before I could even think about it. A whole horde of them, in fact.

I had to get out of this frozen shithole, and somebody needed to pay.

Plus, the promise Orion had made me of an unfettered dominion over the mortal realm tantalized me even now. Whether or not the vamp could deliver remained to be seen, but on the off chance he came through, I wasn't about to miss the chance.

And hey, if I found myself back on the mortal side, maybe I'd get another taste of the sweet little pet slayer, maybe try to understand why she looked at me like it pained her to lose me. I licked my lips.

I took another breath, held it for a second, and let it out in a plume of white vapor. Lifting my head, I turned back the way I'd come, toward an oncoming storm of darkness. The shadows surged forward. I cracked my knuckles and grinned.

"All right, you fuckers. Bring it on. I got places to be."

1

VERONICA

The rain poured down in sheets from a concrete sky, filling my long-term suite at the Anchorage Grand Hotel with the soothing din of a storm. I lay on my stomach atop the bedspread, head resting on folded arms, staring out the water-blurred window. Evidence of my latest efforts to study littered every surface of the room, from the made-up king bed to the table beside the TV.

Deep down, I knew I had to put my nose to the academic grindstone. The dates of my deferred midterms were fast approaching. And I really did feel the pressure on the rare occasions I could spare a few minutes to think about them. But in the wake of the time I had spent in Alaska so far, what with the murders and all, schoolwork seemed low on the list of priorities.

In truth, I'd been struggling to concentrate on anything after the recent events in Alaska, the battle with the Seattle vampire clan, the three men who'd invaded my life, and especially Seth. He'd self-combusted! That image still remained imprinted on my brain and left me shaken. While Orion insisted he'd work on finding the demon, I had so many questions on where Seth had gone and if he'd even return. Maybe I shouldn't care if he did or didn't.

Except, my chest clenched at the question, and I sighed. Who was I kidding? I cared too damn much, and since when did I worry so much about these men… these monsters who were meant to be my quarry?

Instead, I should've been taking full advantage of these rare quiet nights, and I knew it. Things had changed since Orion had ousted the Seattle faction of vamps and an unknown third party was running rampant in the city. There had been more murders surfacing rapidly, sometimes every day for as much as a week. Many of the corpses were old, frozen under hard-packed drifts of snow, but unquestionable victims of violence. I'd attended every crime scene and tried to listen in on the authorities' conversations, but they were just as clueless as me as to who was killing these humans. Orion and Logan insisted they knew nothing after asking around.

And as the mystery grew, it occupied an increasing amount of space inside my head. No matter how much I tried to focus on my textbooks, which were genuinely fascinating in their own right, I couldn't shake thoughts of the case. It haunted me at all hours of the night and day. It followed me into dreams when I got the opportunity to sleep.

If I wasn't a detective in title yet, I was definitely behaving like a veteran on the force. Dark circles under my eyes, spent coffee cups filling the trash, neck-deep in an investigation that wasn't the reason I'd come to Alaska in the first place.

I also knew Orion thought of me as belonging to him, and only him. I may have been in lust, but I wasn't stupid. The guy had some serious jealousy issues.

And yet, as much as he pissed me off sometimes, I wasn't able to tear myself away or forget how we fought side by side against the Seattle vamps like somehow he considered me an equal. But I also knew who I was dealing with. Orion was arrogant and dramatic, and his temper could be black as night.

It wasn't just him who affected me so much, either. There was Logan, and there was Seth. I might still be able to pretend it wasn't becoming a part of my identity. Veronica, the slayer and scholar, was turning into the slayer, the scholar, and the...slut craving three men?

"Oh God," I groaned out loud, digging my fingers into my scalp. "Note to self: never think that again." Sighing deeply, I turned my face to the side and went limp, staring blankly out the rain-washed window. The bleak colors of the streetscape outside ran together in a solemn picture. At times like this, I felt alone. Too damn alone.

Maybe I ought to call Lian, go and spend more time with her, stop falling so deep into the darkness that swallowed Anchorage.

The loneliness was a reminder of growing up in this town, when everything seemed perfect. Until the vampire attack in the alleyway that took my mom and dad from me. My chest still tightened, even after all this time.

If that attack had never happened, where would I be now? Married, maybe still studying, or joining the police force? I doubt it mattered as long as I had my parents back. I drew in a hiccupped breath.

The sound of my vibrating phone jerked me out of that sorrowful lull. I groped blindly for it over the duvet and squinted into the lock screen. The familiar notification of a message from Lian stared back.

Seriously, V. Call me before I send out a search party.

I hadn't talked to her in at least three days. She was too smart not to be getting suspicious. Wracking my brain for an excuse that wouldn't sound totally lame, I swiped to call her. "Please don't answer," I whispered, half into the phone, half to the powers that be.

My appeal didn't work; she answered on the second ring. "There you are. I was starting to think you'd gotten into real trouble." The lighthearted bend of her voice masked an undertone of real concern.

I grimaced, feeling even more like shit. "Trouble? Me? Perish the thought." I sat up and raked the hair out of my face. "No, I'm sorry. Just been real busy trying to wrap up the semester while I have a chance."

"Shoot," she said. "I forgot about that." She paused, and I braced myself. Lian had always been a great master of communication—she only hesitated when she was about to say something I wouldn't like. "Do you want me to call James to come in and back you up for a while? I'm sure he'd do it."

I winced, remembering him from primary school. The guy I'd had a massive crush on and the last face I saw on the sidewalk after my parents and I were ambushed by vampires. He'd always ignored me, which was fine by me as I moved to Seattle shortly after the attack. Years later, Lian had told me he'd gone into the vampire hunting gig to help clean up the streets and trained with Lian's ex, also in the business. Apparently, he'd witnessed my attack and been the one to call the police once the vampires fled.

"I heard he only does jobs if you paid him. With money," I said.

"Come on." She became gently admonishing. "He doesn't hate you, V. I don't know how many times I have to tell you that he was dealing with guilt from not helping you and your parents, but I won't stop until you believe me."

"Ugh." I could picture James so clearly in my mind, how he sneered at me, even shoved his shoulder into mine each time he walked past at school before the attack. He'd hated me for no reason, so I struggled to believe he'd change his mind because I almost died. Sure, we were kids but I didn't want to bring up more of my past if I could help it. "Don't call him. I'm fine."

"He might come through regardless in the near future," Lian warned tactfully. "If that happens, I'll give you a heads-up."

"I appreciate that."

"Any news? Or are you just up to your eyes in school bullshit?"

"I'll take 'school bullshit' for five hundred, please." I wasn't being completely truthful, but the yawn I stifled at the end of the sentence was authentic. "It's like I don't want to quit on my degree, you know? I just feel like I'm pulling overtime on life. I bet I could sleep for a thousand years."

"What's going on?" I heard the frown in Lian's voice. "They're not hassling you about having to leave, are they? I'd like to think I'm above bribing a school board into giving you a pass for one semester, but let's be real."

I laughed and shook my head. "No, it's not that. Let's just say I've gotten a little more embroiled in the situation here than I intended to be." Understatement of the century, if not the millennium. And if I had anything to say about it, she'd never find out. How could I expect her to understand my illogical desire for three supernaturals?

"You know you don't have to stay at the hotel if you'd rather be at our house," she said. "You're always welcome here. I bet my parents would be thrilled to see you."

"Me too," I replied sadly. It had been years since I'd seen Mr. and Mrs. Zhao. I missed them with the same intensity as an unwillingly estranged child. But the notion of putting them in danger via my very presence in their lives was unbearable. I was already walking a fine line with Lian. "It's too dangerous, though. I need to stay away. Once this is all over, we'll have a major reunion."

"God, I can't wait for this to be over…whatever 'this' is." Lian spoke with the silent certainty that told me she understood I was keeping secrets, but that she trusted me to reveal them when the time was right. Meanwhile, I sat cross-legged on the bedspread, second-guessing the hell out of myself.

"No kidding," was all I said in the end. "I'll be in touch the second I've got anything new, okay? Promise."

"Okay. I'll hold you to that. Good luck with your exams, lady. Hopefully the vampires will let you get a good night's sleep soon."

"Actually, could you tell James to ask them for me?" I joked. "That would be great." Then, fearing she'd take me a little too seriously, I backpedaled. "Just kidding. Please do not call him on my behalf."

"I swear I won't," she answered. "Don't worry. Hit those books, girl."

We hung up, and I started the arduous task of pretending to hit the books. Every word on every page blurred together, even my meticulously color-coded notes. Before coming to Anchorage, I had been an exceptional, almost obsessive student. Now I could not get my head in the game.

And unfortunately for me, the distractions did not stop arriving. This time, it was in the form of a soft, distinctive knock on the room door. Out of reflex, I glanced at the window to see if night had fallen. It hadn't quite yet, which was puzzling. Curious, I hopped off the bed and went to peer through the peephole.

His broad-shouldered, imposing build couldn't be disguised well even underneath the bulky ensemble he'd put on in order to venture out before full dark. In the wide lens of the peephole, I picked out dark jeans and a hoodie underneath a long coat. His hands were deep in his pockets, and he had pulled up both hoods as extra protection against any errant sunbeams.

I locked my expression against the urge to groan as I opened the door. "Isn't it a little early for a vampire to be outside?"

"Close the drapes," he demanded. Then he glanced at me, his eyes obscured behind dark glasses. "Are you not pleased to see me?"

"Should I be?" I asked, rolling my eyes and crossed the room to the windows. I knew in the pit of my stomach that having him over was a bad idea. Each time he visited, my body morphed into a desperate teenager, and the struggle between my libido and mind was an unfair match.

The thick hotel curtains swished shut, tossing us both into artificial darkness. Orion watched me, and then, appeased, he began to remove his layers.

"What are you doing here?" Ever since we'd become battle buddies, he made it his business to pop over to my hotel with some reason or another, which of course intrigued me beyond words.

"I have news," he announced. The jacket and hoodie both came off, and I did my best not to stare at the way his tight black shirt clung to his chest and shoulders. Waves of thick, dark hair framed his handsome face, his intense eyes never leaving mine. It was easy to get lost in his gaze, to forget that this incredibly beautiful man was also a monster. Something I forget easily in his presence. He noticed anyway and reached for me, smiling slightly. "But first, I must ask for a proper greeting."

"Oh? And what does that entail?" *Hell, don't flirt with him.*

He stepped close enough to draw me into his strong embrace. Electricity sparked between us, and let's be real, his body and mine should never touch if I ever intended on holding any semblance of control over it.

Orion studied me for a few moments the way he always did, his piercing metallic eyes roaming over every feature. They lingered on my lips.

Then he suddenly kissed me deeply, and I forgot about every other damn thing in the universe.

2

ORION

J savored every moment of her warmth in my arms, the weight of her body against mine. There was something so tantalizing about the living in general, but particularly Veronica. Her potential was an as-yet unkindled fire, waiting to light within.

"Is that the way you greet everyone you meet?" She kept her hands flat against my chest as if undecided yet on whether she'd push me away or curl her fists around my top and drag me back for another kiss.

"I don't make a habit of visiting others."

Her gaze narrowed, studying me, while the corners of her delicious mouth twitched like they might break into a smile. "Must be serious, if you came all this way before the sun went down." Her perceptions annoyed as much as they impressed me. I liked to be the one in charge, whose authority was never questioned. As clanmaster, I hadn't needed reasons for my actions in a very long time.

To be challenged so boldly, and by her of all people, caused an altogether new type of friction within me. I wanted to quell her impudence as I would any insurgency among my clan. But the thrill of resistance was impossible to deny. I felt her straining against my will, much like she strained against my body.

I was intoxicated by every aspect of this woman. And I loved and hated her for it.

"I'm hardly as fragile as you're implying," I told her now, somewhat brusquely. She bit her lip to keep from smiling, but I saw amusement dash across her exquisite features. "The night is a preference as well as a precautionary measure."

Veronica rolled her eyes. "It is not. I was there when those other vamps turned to dust, remember? I saw it myself." She paused, looking keenly at my face. "Unless you're saying that wouldn't happen to you." Her words turned slightly pointed, sharp with the curiosity I often wished she did not have in quite as much abundance.

I frowned. "Don't treat me like one of your specimens, slayer." My fingers ran upward along the curve of her hip and waist, over the delicate ridges of her spine. How easy it would have been to claim her forever in that deceptively gentle moment. I could've ended her human life with one quick, brutal snap.

Afterward, of course, her body would be mended. She would never feel pain again. Not the way she felt it now.

She arched her brows. "So really, what's going on?" She paused. An odd recognition dawned in her gorgeous pale eyes. "Have you found Seth?"

The frown I wore immediately deepened into a scowl. I thought of the sight of them together at the top of the stairs in my home, cloaked in the smell of intimacy. The urge to chastise her was nearly overwhelming, but at the very last moment I bit my tongue. Seth made me livid, but I never wanted him dead or taken from my side. Despite us clashing at every turn, Seth wore the burden of a wounded past like the rest of us. Him jumping into any fight without thinking was to avoid the pain he carried with him. In battle, emotions are cast aside, and he'd mastered that.

Long ago, Seth's own legion turned on him due to a lie from another demon who sought his rank and position. But Seth being Seth, he fought back as rage overcame him. He took down everyone who betrayed him… friends and even a brother alike. He knew as well as the rest of us that a rat among your crew will be quicker to stab you in the back than your enemy.

Guilt tore him apart for so long, though he'd never show it, and I was sure he buried the memories. This was one of the reasons I picked him to work with me. He wasn't going to betray me if I showed him loyalty, and if I didn't hold back when he pissed me the hell off. He craved someone he could trust again, so I held nothing back.

Plus, I made him a promise, and I sure as fuck was going to keep my word by giving him a new start. And that meant finding where the hell he had vanished to.

"No. He remains missing," I answered.

She studied me. "Right." We locked eyes. I dared her silently to push the issue, a challenge she chose to decline. Instead, she touched her fingers to my lips. "So…the news thing was a cover and you're just here to see me?"

Just as quickly as my temper had risen, it fell in the face of her sensuous charm. "You would be so lucky," I replied. She smiled. "But again, no. I've received word from a credible source that the Seattle clan is withdrawing to regroup and alter their strategy."

She nodded. Her soft, candy-colored curls bounced lightly. "That's why the streets have been so quiet. They're retreating."

"That's right." I spoke with a touch of clannish pride. "It seems their master may have finally bitten off more than he could chew." There were, however, two sides to every coin. Our successful rebuffing of this first onslaught from the south meant that I had effectively bought us time to mount a defense—or a counterattack. But I knew better than to underestimate my enemies. They were capable of learning from their mistakes, of innovating upon new knowledge.

I had every reason to believe that when the Seattle faction returned, we would be facing an entirely different, more potent threat. And *that* was the reason I had come to Veronica's hotel room in the gray glare of twilight. Because of a certain impatient, hardheaded demon, my army was missing a general. Someone had to fill that empty spot until I found Seth.

Unfortunately, there were few who could take his place; in fact, Veronica was the only one who came to mind. I knew she was able to fight like hell. I'd seen it on more than one occasion. Nonetheless, I didn't like having to ask her for help. Given a choice, I would've kept her as a plaything, a sublime trophy. She would be an acolyte, my first thrall in years.

Alas, such a luxury was hardly possible. I could not tolerate the mere possibility of losing a single stone of my territory to those blood-hungry Washington interlopers. That meant my lovely little slayer needed to earn her keep in more utilitarian, less blatantly carnal ways.

"They'll return," I told her. "As soon as they can. And the bastards will be ready to wage war."

"Why do they want Anchorage so badly?" Veronica chuckled to

herself. "No offense. It's just…you'd think it would be easier to stick to the contiguous states. They could roll down to Portland, or even into California if they wanted…although it is very sunny and dry there."

I brushed a lock of hair back from her forehead. "History. I have been in the seat of power here for a very long time. My brethren to the south do not approve." The root of the conflict was ravenous greed. For decades, I had watched others yearn to possess my land from afar. The rise and fall of vampire dynasties had taken place beneath my watch, and really greed has no limits. "Of course they want all I have. Envy is a powerful force."

"No kidding." She watched me expectantly. "Okay, so where do I come in?"

The time had come for me to swallow my pride. I knew it was necessary, and yet each word had to be drawn out on its own. How many times in my long, long life had I been forced to bend the knee and ask for aid? Not many, and certainly not of someone like Veronica. The whole situation struck me as vaguely sacrilegious, but I knew I had little choice.

I tried not to grimace as I said the words. "Will you help the clan? The conflict is mounting behind the scenes. Your assistance will benefit us greatly."

Perhaps it was foolish of me to expect a woman of her shrewd intelligence to throw herself upon the chance for selfless concern. She gazed straight into my eyes, the wheels turning behind them. I resisted the powerful compulsion to show my hand by asking her thoughts. If there was a psychological game being played, I needed to have a competitive edge. I said nothing more, and for several moments, neither did she.

Then she asked, "What's in it for me, clanmaster?" Her playful tone matched the subtle smirk on her lips. I felt the heat of her palms pressing into my chest as she leaned closer, yet the sharpness in her gaze came with a warning. She was playing with me, testing the water, but little did she know I never played the mouse in these games. I always did the hunting and won.

"I assume you'll make it worth my while," she whispered, teasing, and I quite enjoyed watching her.

That was when the thought occurred to me that I might be able to have the best of both worlds, in a way. There was no real reason Veronica couldn't work in her official capacity as a fighter alongside the clan, while also serving me in all the ways I desired. And given the patterns established by her past behavior, I had the distinct feeling she wouldn't truly mind, even if she pretended to.

My true aspirations for her had not been crossed off, only deferred. For now, I could think of a few good ways to keep her satisfied.

I wrapped a hand around the back of her neck gingerly and held her in place as I moved in close. She tensed, well aware that I called her bluff but that I had every intention of taking this all the way.

"Something wrong?" I asked, placating her.

"Do you always assume everything between us comes down to desire?"

My mouth split into a smile, and I adored the way she stared at me with challenge in her eyes.

"I'm never mistaken." I kissed her parted lips, softly at first, and then fiercely. The air left her lungs in a sweet, warm draft. So many other mortals left humanity seeming like a pox upon the earth. But Veronica was—to me—a sort of twisted blessing. She responded hungrily to my embrace, and in the next moments, we fell back on the bed together. She pushed the books off the mattress, and I aided her to clear the bed.

Then I flipped her over, causing a cascade of silky pink locks. She pulled her hair back and grinned at me. "You know, I was talking about money, but if you have other means of payment in mind, I think we could come to an agreement."

In lieu of an answer, I pressed my mouth to her throat, breathing her in, her delicious scent layered with a sharp smell I couldn't identify. There was something so different about her and I had yet to find out what it was.

Just below the surface of her smooth skin, fresh blood coursed through her veins. I longed to taste it on my tongue, even just barely. The dark, constantly simmering primal lust in the depths of my soul told me to throw all caution to the wind and sink my teeth into her now, while she was vulnerable and unaware. It would have been easy to quell any last-minute struggle she put up. And afterward, she would be mine for eternity.

I nipped at her. Testing the waters. Her taut muscles tensed, but then she relaxed again. She offered no resistance to me sliding off her top and bra, nor did she make any attempt to hide herself. She lay on the bed like a goddess, her bright pink hair spread around her head like a halo, except she had fire inside her.

I let my tongue wander over the pale, rolling curves of her breasts, visiting each rosy nipple, taking them into my mouth. They firmed against my tongue as I flicked them. Her moans drove my own carnal desires, my cock hardening in my pants.

Now was the golden opportunity I had told myself I was waiting for. A quick glance upward told me her eyes were closed. Her body shifted and arched with the rise and fall of pleasure. When I slipped my fingers between her thighs and under her skirt, she gasped and clutched at the bedspread. A shudder of pure anticipation ran beneath my hands.

I imagined stroking her, caressing her, moving inside her until the peak of her climax disguised what she would doubtless consider a great moment of betrayal. Her cries of pain and ecstasy would harmonize as I consumed her life force. But she'd be helpless, utterly powerless to stop my will. And that made me ache with arousal.

She spread her legs the moment I slid my fingers under the elastic of her underwear to find her wet and so ready for me. Her hand sank into my hair, grasping eagerly. I drank in her beauty, her arching body beneath my touch, and I relished every moan, every push of her hips against my hand. Lust sparked in her blue eyes as her hips rose, wanting more of me. I pushed two fingers into her as I leaned in to kiss her shoulder, taking small mock bites until I reached her mouth. She cupped my face, her tongue spearing into my mouth as I drove my fingers into her unrelentingly fast.

I ignited a fire in my little slayer, her breaths racing, her hips rocking back and forth. Fuck she was beautiful. She held my gaze the whole time, never saying a word, but teasing me each time she let out small gasps. Her lips are swollen from our rough kiss, like the ones between her thighs.

I kissed her possessively. Part of me toyed with the idea of ripping the rest of her clothes off, spreading her legs and fucking her until her throat ran raspy from screaming. But I realized this wasn't about me, now was it. I had to show her I could put her first, that somehow she'd crawled into my very soul and while I didn't want to take her by my side with force, I'd first endeavor to win her over.

She belonged to me, and as she lay beside me, her body convulsed and her sweet pussy sucked at my fingers. My cock twitched, aching with need to sink into her.

"Orion," she moaned, and I felt her legs shaking. I stole her orgasmic screams greedily with my mouth, our tongues tangling together, my fingers never stopping until she was completely soaked and satisfied.

She had a unique ability to make me appreciate vitality in a way I hadn't since leaving the ranks of mortal men. Veronica's life fed my restless spirit. I longed to take it from her and bind our souls together forever.

Would she let me? It didn't matter. From the moment she had first come into my sight, I'd staked my claim. As far as I was concerned, this beautiful woman who had come to my city to kill me was now in my possession.

As soon as the Seattle clan was taken care of, I intended to make our arrangement official—whether Veronica liked it or not. It pained me to admit she could still be unwilling, but her turning into a vampire was non-negotiable, even if she didn't know it yet.

The truth was, I refused to exist without her by my side. And I was going to do everything in my power to ensure that I didn't have to.

VERONICA

For all his aggression, Orion was a generous lover—and he knew exactly what he was doing. I lay in his arms for a long time after we had finished, too blissed-out on endorphins to do much other than bask in the afterglow. He held me close, which was nice except for the fact that if I let myself think about it too much, it was easy to get freaked out about his lack of a real heartbeat.

"I love the way you enjoy yourself," he murmured. His long fingers played along my spine like the keys to a piano. My forensic training told me his fingertips were cooler than they should have been, but I'd come to find it sort of soothing, in a strange, macabre way. Orion was different—that much was inescapable. I was just getting good at rationalizing those differences in a way that didn't make me look like a hypocrite.

"There's a lot to enjoy," I told him, nuzzling my head against his chest. He laughed and squeezed me a little tighter. I took a deep, slow breath and let it out. "But what about your pleasure?"

"Being with you is all the satisfaction I need."

I half laughed at him. "Hold on, that sounds romantic and so not like you."

"Maybe you just don't know me well enough yet."

Pressing myself against him, I cradled my head to his chest, wanting to somehow believe that Orion was just a normal guy. One could hope.

"How did you end up in the slayer business?" he asked me nonchalantly.

"I guess like most, trauma from death, from losing someone to vampires."

His hold squeezed around me slightly. "Who did you lose, if you don't mind me asking?"

I hesitated at first as I disliked talking about the past at the best of times, but I also appreciated Orion showing interest. "My parents," I answered. "It's why I ended up living in Seattle to move in with my grandma."

He kissed the top of my head and his leg slid over mine, like somehow he tried to wrap me up in his body. There was no instinct to push him away, nothing but settling against him as it had been a long time since someone just held me in their arms with no intention other than care. That confused me because this was Orion I was dealing with.

"Earlier when I said why the Seattle clanmaster was so intent on taking over my Anchorage, I wasn't completely honest," he admitted, which piqued my curiosity.

"Oh, yeah?"

"The asshole killed someone close to me. A new vampire needing guidance, and I foolishly let my guard down, so I missed the clues of the enemy entering my territory. All that bastard left for me was her head." His spoke so quietly, though I still picked up on the uneven tone in his voice, and how much that still affected him.

"Fuck, I'm sorry."

We didn't exchange words for a long moment, even if my mind billowed with questions about who this vampire was and if he had been the one to turn her into a vamp in the first place. And was it wrong of me to feel a thread of jealousy that another woman held his interest so much that it lead to a war between two clans?

"Sometimes when someone close is taken from you so unexpectedly and harshly, all you can use to fill the hole in your soul with is anger, and sometimes even revenge. But that path will not save you in the end."

I wasn't sure what to say as those deep words were not what I expected from Orion, which tells me so much about the hurt he must have felt from losing her. How he still held onto the past, how he struggles to let it go.

Orion's arms loosened around me and he sat up suddenly. He stayed still in the dusky shadows for a few moments, gazing down at me. Then he leaned over and kissed me on the mouth one more time. I pushed up onto my elbow. His strong hand cupped the back of my head, looking down at me like he was about to say something, but he never did. But as he climbed out of bed, I watched him leave my hotel room, something unwelcoming flickered in my chest.

He would've been so perfect if he wasn't my archenemy. I loved his strength, his passion, even his dominance, to an extent. He kept me on my toes, and of course, I couldn't get enough of his body. But as things stood, an emotional involvement with a vampiric clanmaster was the worst idea I'd ever had, to put it lightly.

Recently, I'd found myself facing down an unexpected problem: Maybe there were strings attached after all between us. Or if they hadn't yet attached, maybe the strings were weaving themselves tighter. I had the nagging sense that I was headed for big, big trouble.

"No." I covered my face and groaned. "No, no, no. We're colleagues at *best*. And at worst, one of us is going to kill the other. This absolutely cannot go any further than it already has." Nonetheless, I knew I was beginning to care about him against all of my better judgment, and probably against the better judgment of everyone I had ever known.

Squeezing my eyes shut tight, I tried to conjure up the face Lian would make if I ever told her the whole truth about what had been happening since I came to Alaska. Equal parts bewilderment, annoyance, frustration, and *Are you fucking kidding me, Veronica?* She rarely used a curse word worse than hell, but I bet she'd have some choice expletives for this special occasion.

Nope. I could never tell her—not about this. Not only would she mightily disapprove, Lian also knew too much about what had happened the last time I got too involved with someone. A vampire slayer. That person was my ex, Dylan. And Dylan was dead. I'd told her everything from the beginning when Dylan and I were dating, about him taking out fanged monsters, and him teaching me how to fight vampires. It was at this time when she shared with me that her then boyfriend, also a vampire slayer, knew Dylan well.

It was such a small world. And because Lian and I were both going through something similar, even though we lived in different towns, it somehow normalised it all for us.

All at once with the memory, my pleasant, post-orgasm haze was replaced by crushing sadness and cold, heavy dread. No longer comfortable, I rolled out of the bed and into the bathroom, where the shower waited to help me drown my sorrows. I turned the water up as hot as I could stand it until drafts of steam billowed from the gap in the curtain. Then I stepped into the tub and stood under the scorching jets.

"God, I'm so fucking stupid." I poured a dollop of shampoo in my hand, scrubbing my scalp with more force than necessary. In the wake of Dylan's death, I had struggled to honor him in the way I lived my life. He was the reason for the textbooks strewn about the room. Books Orion and I had unceremoniously shoved onto the floor in the throes of desire.

The heat of shame and guilt almost overpowered the hot water. I rinsed the cloud of suds from my hair, remembering all the time I'd spent languishing alone after his funeral, wondering if he was still connected to me. Now I hoped he didn't.

"One of these days, I'll learn to go five minutes without screwing up my own damn life," I muttered. Which wasn't to say that I regretted getting closer with Orion, because I didn't. At all. I just knew he wasn't good for me, and the deeper I wandered down this particular path, the harder it would be to get out again.

Plus...I felt strangely guilty about him sharing something so close and personal, for opening up to me like I encouraged him to do so.

I had to keep my head straight and focused on finding who or what killed those humans. Add to that list, tracking down Seth. I shouldn't care about him either, but until I knew he was somewhere relatively safe, I doubted I'd stop worrying. Hell, since when had I grown so weak around monsters anyway?

The problem was that I got along with them too well, enjoyed their company more than I should. I called them monsters, but what if I connected to the same part of them that lay inside me? After all, didn't everyone have darkness inside of them?

My skin was pink by the time I finally stepped out from under the water. A film of vapor coated every surface in the bathroom, and when I opened the door, the steam puffed out into the room air that felt as cold as if it'd come from outside. Shivering, I ran naked across the carpet and dove into the rumpled bed. The sheets smelled like us, and like traces of Orion's cologne. On the nightstand, my phone sat ignored. I felt another pang of guilt as I checked it.

This time, there were no messages from Lian. Granted, it had only been a matter of hours since I'd last talked to her, and she was probably in bed, like a normal person who did not cavort with vampires in the night. But I still briefly debated calling her, just to have someone to talk to. A sounding board for the maelstrom of thoughts and emotions swirling in my head.

Then again, what would I say? *Do you know how to find a demon from Hell who may or may not have transcended the boundaries of time and space? He was with us, but we lost him in the shuffle, and now we don't know where he is. Also, I just had the best orgasm, and it wasn't with a human man.*

"Yeah, that'd go over real well." I sighed and turned on the TV for some background noise. All a confessional would do at this point was get her to call James immediately. And if I thought she was the one who wouldn't understand... Well, the guy who never liked me would judge me to hell and back.

What I wanted was to get on Seth's trail without Lian's help. He was, however, one of the first beings of his kind that I had ever met at all, let alone so personally, and I wasn't sure where to start. Other slayers might know, but it wasn't reasonable to expect them to share data without accusing me of going against the very fabric of slayer ethics.

No. The only two people who could truly be of any use in locating Seth were Orion and Logan. I drew my knees up to my chest under the blankets and frowned, thinking. With Orion insisting he hadn't found anything, maybe it was possible to sway Logan into searching for him beyond this plane of existence.

I just really wanted to know where Seth was, what he was doing, and if he was okay.

Mulling things over, I flipped through the television channels without really seeing what was on. The familiar red and blue flash of police lights on a local news station caught my attention. I stopped there and watched an anchorwoman speak emotionlessly about the discovery of yet more bodies in Anchorage.

"The latest victims were recovered on the inland outskirts of the city, just inside the perimeter of a densely forested area of Chugach State Park. Their identities have yet to be confirmed, but law enforcement says the investigation is ongoing. Anyone with tips or information should contact the Anchorage police."

The report was accompanied by air footage of the enormous, sprawling park, acres upon acres of true wilderness. Looking at the sheer scale made my heart sink down into my stomach. I had decent survival and tracking skills, what with my trusty slayer sense, but tackling an area like Chugach was uncharted territory for me. If there was something lurking in there, it would definitely have the upper hand.

Still, I pulled out my notes and marked the crime scene in the park down as a point of interest anyway as I may find some clues if I search in the vicinity. At the very least, it could function as a reasonable excuse to see Logan again.

"Someone else has to be missing him, right? It's not just me?" Talking to no one was a habit I had picked up as a way of dealing with the mounting trauma that followed Dylan's death. It had morphed from a coping mechanism into a quirk, the method I used for sorting out my jumbled brain. Usually, the one-sided dialogue was comforting, the sound of my own voice a steady hand on my shoulder. But at the moment, it only made me feel even more on my own. Lian had once told me that it was better to be alone, than to be with someone who made you feel alone. I suspected at the time she had been talking about her relationship with her then boyfriend, Trent, but there was a point to be taken from her words.

I shook my head to clear it of all other thoughts. The fact was, Seth remained missing and a killer still remained at large, in my eyes, those were huge problems. If nobody was mobilizing to find a solution, I would. I had an iron will, so there had to be a way. Sitting there on the bed, all wrapped up in the comforter, I began to formulate the skeleton of a plan.

Step one: Talk to Logan—without Orion around.

4

———

LOGAN

I liked the house better when it was empty. No heavy footsteps on creaky floorboards, no passive-aggressive slamming of doors. Even though I was more or less on even terms with Orion, his presence always filled the space—and of course, Seth had been a never-ending storm. The serenity left in their absence was a welcome change of pace.

Still, it was odd to think of Seth in past tense only. And it would have been dishonest of me to pretend I never thought of him or wondered where he'd ended up. My assumption had been that the demon's recovery was going to be top priority once Orion's rivals were out of the way. But hours were morphing into days since the end of our last major conflict, and Seth remained conspicuous in his absence.

Given the contentious state of affairs between Orion and Seth pre-disappearance, I supposed the vampire's lack of motivation wasn't a great surprise. He seemed distracted lately with something else.

Every now and then, as my eyes searched for the hidden line of the shore, I thought I saw the withered shape of a hand reaching out from the dense underbrush. The notion that there were corpse bones scattered around Orion's property was more than a paranoid delusion. Sometimes the memories of our most recent victim flashed unbidden through my mind. It was his hand disappearing beneath the broken layer of ice.

But why was he the one who chose to haunt me? There were others —too many to count. In a way, it was my obligation as a guardian, a messenger, a sentinel, to facilitate the transition between the living and the dead. Had I lived a different life, it might have been a romantic duty, a fulfilling role. My own inherent tragedy made such a thing impossible.

I was not the angel who waited with outstretched hands to escort a dying grandmother to her place in the afterlife. I was never allowed the privilege of protecting the souls of the blessed on their way to eternal life. Those like me, who were born of dark and barren sorrow, witnessed unbearable agony and listened to the screams of the damned. When I stepped across dimensions into the mortal plane, I questioned if these banal horrors would follow me through.

So far, they hadn't—until recently.

The visions happened randomly, without any kind of discernible pattern. I'd be walking down the road and see a man in the middle of the street whose face was mashed into a gruesome pile. Once in the morning I had opened my eyes to the sight of a fang-toothed monstrosity with vertical black slits for eyes, wrenching a hole in reality and screaming through. The shrill, piercing sound of its shriek stayed with me for days.

Soon after that, they began to arrive in a steady stream, passing through in a rush of often unintelligible whispers. Most looked relatively normal, betrayed only by vague hints at the nature of their deaths. A young lady with the brutal scarlet lines of strangulation across her throat. A boy with a drowned and bloated face. In the early days, the macabre parade had nearly driven me to madness.

Now, I hardly saw. Even when they seeped into my dreams, I remained ambivalent. I moved through the motions of my day in willful ignorance, because I served another now, at least for the time being. This sudden influx of free time did not signify an openness to becoming a spirit magnet.

But the tide of ghosts seeking attention only swelled, to the point where I felt a surge of strange relief whenever I heard Orion walking through the door. The vampire clanmaster was like a curse to spirits, even angry ones. *Perhaps,* I thought, *they don't like being reminded of what could have been.* The moment Orion entered the vicinity, any phantoms dissipated like wisps of smoke.

It was a quality I rapidly learned to appreciate. But of course, my need for his unique anti-charms came at a time when alone in the house with me was the last place Orion wanted to be. Sometimes we hit the streets together, cleaning up Seattle's last dregs. More often, he struck out alone.

"Stand by," he would say. "You're my backup." The calls for reinforcement rarely reached me.

Not that I really wondered what he was doing as he prowled his own city by night. Orion's nonchalant arrogance tended to blind him to certain details, such as the fact that he was saturated with Veronica's aura after many of his excursions. I could practically taste her on him.

Who does he think he's fooling?

The answer was probably no one. Orion's jealousy made him a boaster. No doubt he wanted me and everyone else in the city to know that he had claimed her as his own. More than once, I fought the rising urge to ask him how she was. I knew he wouldn't like knowing his girl was on anyone else's mind, and the last thing I needed or wanted was to take Seth's place as the mercurial vampire's punching bag.

Orion kept an eye on Veronica. And I kept seeing ghosts. For days at a time, they would escalate from portraits of simple death into portraits of violence and torture. But it wasn't until I started to recognize certain wound patterns that I really paid attention. There was no mistaking the distinctive tearing slashes through necks and stomachs and chest walls. I had seen them before—with Veronica, ironically—at the murder scene in the woods.

A scene Orion had not witnessed. I doubted he knew about those killings at all, or else he would have brought himself along every time thereafter. Nor could he be the killer; the marks indicated a rough, classless hand. Everything Orion did was meant to be a form of art. The clanmaster would never have killed so savagely, like an animal, even at the height of his bloodlust. I couldn't imagine it.

Then again, nor could I imagine the beast that had left those marks upon its victims.

We crossed paths in the upper hallway one midnight, and he stopped to look closely at me.

"Tell me something, Logan," he said. "Are you not immortal?"

I deflected the query with a wry smile. "Spoken like a man who is plotting my demise."

He laughed. "Perish the thought, my friend. You are far too valuable to me." A slight frown shaded his features. "You look...thin, is all. Faded, perhaps?" He shook his head, as if the correct word truly eluded his grasp.

I debated for a moment over whether or not to tell him the truth, and how much. A full confession would certainly arouse suspicion that was bound to turn bitter. Veronica's involvement had to stay a tightly guarded secret in order to avoid civil war. I had no desire to fight, but Orion's possession of her was like nothing I'd seen, even from him.

It piqued my curiosity over what he was up to. He was not a man prone to the whims of love as far as I understood. I had learned to tell when Orion was scheming. And although I couldn't say precisely why, his investment in Veronica reeked of motive.

"The spirits are walking," I told him at length. "Through the house. Is there a graveyard in the cellar that you may have forgotten to warn me about?"

Again, the vampire laughed, showing his gleaming, subtly pointed canines. "Spare me, Logan. I'm not a highly superstitious being, but you won't see me treading on burial grounds, either. The rival clans are more than enough complication for me." As if to emphasize his point, he rolled his eerie, metallic eyes and sighed.

"Well..." I paused. He looked at me expectantly. "They don't like you very much."

He smiled. "Is that so? You can let the spirits know the feeling is mutual." Then he clapped me on the shoulder and brushed by. "Take care of yourself, Logan. My cursed brethren to the south will be back for another fight before we know it. And they will be stronger next time."

I watched his back recede into the shadows. The door to the master bedroom opened and closed, and the lock slid into place. If I'd had a goal in sharing that information, it hadn't been realized. Sometimes there grew a sneaking suspicion in the back of my mind that Orion was playing dumb as a way to maintain the upper hand, conceal the extent of his knowledge.

If so, the tactic was proving to be as effective as he needed, and frustrating as well. I stalked sullenly down the stairs, hands in pockets. Now I was left to ruminate over how much he might already know. Was it possible that Orion *did* know of the anonymous maiming victims spread out around the city?

He wasn't the killer. But could he have orchestrated so many murders? The man had an entire clan of vampires at his disposal, after all.

At the bottom of the staircase, I turned and gazed up at the mouth of the dark, still corridor. The click of the door lock was the last sound Orion had made. Silence reigned, almost louder than my thoughts.

No. The conclusion I had started to come to was preposterous. Why would he have to hide his identity? I had witnessed him killing in the street, making sordid examples of his enemies. As clanmaster, he had the right and the privilege to execute at his discretion, and he did.

The night air embraced me as I stepped onto the porch. I closed my eyes as it ran its thin, frigid fingers through my hair and stretched my power outward. Anchorage teemed with souls, living and dead. I sifted through the city's wild energy, searching for anything that could be considered an anomaly. Anything simmering with rage, hunting for victims, about to explode outward.

And as it had in many nights past, my patient search bore fruit. One of the first things I had learned to recognize as a harbinger of death was the way a mortal soul looked and felt as it prepared to make its transition from one realm to the next. On the outskirts of the city's sprawl, I found what I was looking for. A life on the verge of ending.

In a dense line of trees. Facing down a killer too strong to defy.

Just like all the others.

SETH

The barren caverns went on forever, shrouded in shadows so thick I couldn't see beyond them. It was all icy blue rock, and so cold I felt my blood slowly turning to sludge in my veins. All sense of time and distance was lost to me as I trudged toward the next path. There were only two ways to mark my progress: the assholes who leapt into my path every now and then, and the goddamned mirrors.

Ugly fuckers looking for a fight I could deal with no problem. I'd already left a plum-colored trail stretching far into the distance at my back that was punctuated by half-frozen corpses and scattered bones. But the mirrors were what really put me off the place. For starters, a lot of them refused to reflect, no matter how close I stood. I told myself the ice caked over the glass probably had something to do with it—until I walked past the next one and caught my own eye.

After the second time that happened, I'd made up my mind. I had to get the fuck out of this place. That, or find a way to burn it to the ground. A smirk crossed my face as I wondered what it would look like without all the ice. Just a boring cave. An abandoned mine, maybe. So much for the allure of the Underworld.

Still, what it lacked in excitement, the labyrinth of halls made up for in complexity. I had no idea how many times I'd stopped, looked at some frosted rock, and thought, *I've seen that fucking rock before.* As I walked, I kept my head down and contemplated how long it might take for a fire demon to freeze to death.

Then it occurred to me that if I did die in this godforsaken abyss, angel boy would probably be the one in charge of dealing with my soul. Or at least someone who looked kind of like him.

"Oh, fuck that," I muttered under my breath. Suddenly my determination was renewed. A shot of adrenaline sizzled through my veins. I melted the thin layer of ice on my nose with one strong exhale. "This place has to end somewhere."

"Come on, come on…" I grimaced against the stinging temperature. "There's no way in hell I'm dying like this." I paused. "No, really. I'll never hear the end of it."

My one-sided conversation was cut short by a floor-shaking blow to the wall on my left. A small avalanche of rock and ice crumbled from the brand-new hole, out of which poured a swarm of weird little ice gremlins. I didn't have time to count them before they threw themselves headfirst at my body. All I saw were the claws and teeth, outstretched and glittering.

The searing pain on impact surprised me enough that I stumbled backward, narrowly avoiding the drop to one knee. Glancing down, I saw the creatures clinging to me like grotesque little ornaments, their long talons hooked deep into my flesh. They hissed and bared mouthfuls of needly teeth.

"Mind your own damn business!" I grabbed one by the back of its head and pulled it off, ignoring the sting of claws extracting from my skin. It trailed a piercing, squeal in a high, hard arc across the chamber. I grinned as it was transformed into a smear of blackish red on the floor yards away.

"You see that?" I asked the others. A handful more of the little monsters followed their comrade in short order. "That'll be you, right about now!"

At first, tossing them was fun. Therapeutic, in a way. The motion of my arm stretched out my frozen muscles at least on one side, and it was easy to channel my frustration into every throw. Not to mention the satisfaction I got from seeing the floor change color.

But the flood of gremlins from the hole in the wall grew from a steady stream to a rising tide. And I could see bigger things pushing their way through the wall, widening the cracks. The tiny ones had begun to climb up my legs, scratching and biting their way toward bare skin.

I growled and smashed at them with my fists. They fell away with crushed skulls and broken legs. If I took a step, the ground crunched beneath my boot. The scene had gone from 'iced-over catacomb' to 'twisted horror' in the space of a few minutes.

It was not going to get better, as far as I was concerned. The weight of a much larger hand fell around the bottom of my calf. I caught my breath as claws wound around me, threatening to snap shut in what seemed like it could be a viselike grip.

"Fuck off!" I kicked viciously. The toe of my boot connected with something surprisingly soft and heavy. I turned my head to see a fat, grublike creature squirming on the ground. My boot had cut a crescent-shaped wound in its side, out of which poured a glut of pale, slimy fluid.

"I did not sign up for this," I muttered, clenching my teeth. "Someone tell me how to get out of here!" I hadn't realized I was shouting until I stopped and listened to my own voice reverberating. Momentarily, the horde of monsters attempting to strip my skeleton of flesh paused too. Seeing an opportunity, I grabbed it and ran.

Literally. While all enemies were distracted, I took off down the length of the room, swatting at myself.

Instead of looking back to confirm the exact amount of shit I was in, I looked forward and bent into my run. My arms and legs were covered in all kinds of blood that was already coagulating in ropes from the cold. I felt like I was running through mud up to my knees. My vision blurred at the edges.

"Shit!" I slowed down, gasping. "Shit." It shouldn't have been so diffi-cult, and yet there I was, slowly running down. Just as I forced my way back into a pace resembling a run, something weighty hit me between the shoulder blades. I dropped and rolled, crushing it beneath my weight and pummeling it with my fists.

My shoulders ached. My ribs ached. The open lacerations stung, and the cold air bit at me through a hundred new holes in my clothes. I was running off of survival instinct more than energy by then. It was like my fuel source had been sapped.

"Come on," I hissed again through gritted teeth. "Give me some-thing!" With a painful burst of strength, I propelled forward, back into a run. The open maw of a doorway loomed suddenly out of the shadows.

It came up so fast I nearly smashed into the door itself, but I didn't even care. Slipping through to the other side, I braced my shoulder against the massive slab of stone and shoved it into place.

Then I sank down onto the floor.

The first thing I noticed after my lungs stopped screaming was that the air in this chamber was significantly warmer. Compared to the wasteland I had trudged through for who the hell knew how long, the blazing torches might as well have been dripping pools of lava. I relaxed, leaned my head back on the door, and shut my eyes for a while.

"Screw it," I whispered. "Screw everything about this."

Slowly, the sensation crept back into my extremities. "From here on out, it's all forward, baby."

Immediately after saying that, I wished I could take it back. The room appeared long and narrow, and one side was adorned with a cluster of five mirrors. They were arranged in the shape of a diamond, the four smaller encircling one large, round center mirror.

I squinted at them from where I sat, unwilling to end my rest just yet. The steady, blazing glow of the torches lit the glass in reds and oranges, washing its surface with fiery colors. I couldn't tell if I was looking at my face or not. It was this uncertainty that finally forced me to my feet.

"I can already tell this is going to be some bullshit," I grumbled. Upon closer inspection, I saw that each mirror showed something different. Only one was clouded over. Three of the others showed still house interiors. I studied them for a minute or two. "Why the fuck do I...?" My face morphed into a mask of confusion. "That's the house."

It had to be the house. I recognized the stuck-up furniture, the useless paintings on the walls. And it was perfectly lifeless, as usual. No sign of Orion or Logan at all. "Maybe they've got a search party out for me," I said. Then I laughed. "Nah."

As I stood there looking into the glass, a fleeting, curious notion crossed my mind. "Hey, maybe..." I stepped forward, reaching out almost unconsciously until my fingertips touched the surface. It rippled. My hand began to sink in. "That's what I'm talking about!" The way out I'd been looking for had presented itself at last.

But before I could take advantage, the big mirror in the middle caught my attention as it shifted into motion. My eyes moved to the image cascading across the glass. A forest path flanked by huge, dark trees, gnarled roots reaching across the forest floor. Trees and ground both flew past under the view, which was traveling fast. Every stride caused the camera to bob as though attached to the head of a galloping creature.

I took a step closer, leaning down. The picture veered off to the side, taking a jarring plunge through the tree line. There was no sound, but I could almost feel the thin, whiplike branches and rough brush cutting into skin. But whoever was moving so fast did not stop.

Not until a tiny, claustrophobic clearing came into view. There was only one path in or out, and it was massively overgrown, to the point of near-invisibility. Briefly, the image went dark. As it cleared again, I saw a lone figure standing in the center of this clearing.

A human man, obviously lost and disoriented. There was no time for anything more than the barest glimpse of his face as the picture crept up behind him.

At the last possible moment, he turned around. His expression went from shock to horror, just before huge, long hands with brutal claws for fingers plunged into his chest. He gasped. Gurgled a little. Red began to seep out around the fingers still firmly planted deep into his torso. Then the lifeless body slumped to the ground, leaving that pair of enormous, monstrous hands in plain sight, bloodied halfway up the wrist.

The unseen killer let out a noise that was a haunting mixture between a howl and a roar. It made the hair on the back of my neck stand on end.

"Well, I'll be damned," I said to the image in the mirror. "Who the hell are you?"

6

———

VERONICA

I glanced over my shoulder at the bathroom door as I flicked the switch on my police scanner. An initial burst of static crackled out of the speaker, and I inhaled sharply, jerking the volume dial down. "Shit." With one eye still on the closed door, I fiddled with the tuning bar until the low, measured murmur of voices broke through.

In the bathroom, the shower went on, and I breathed a sigh of relief. It was a small miracle he hadn't insisted we shower together. Mostly because I had things I wanted to do, but also because I didn't trust myself to be able to say no to anything he wanted. It was a big enough struggle to think of something other than his body under the water.

This was the third night in a row that he had stayed over in my room at the hotel, and to be honest, I was starting to get a little claustrophobic. We had spent almost every minute of the last seventy-two hours attached to each other, often literally. It shouldn't have come as any surprise to learn that vampires came with raging, voracious libidos. Orion would've kept me in bed all the time if I let him.

Sitting down in the chair, I scooted close to the desktop and bent my head to hear the scanner. The tired voices of third-shift Anchorage patrol cops mumbled out routine updates.

I held my breath, waiting for something big. It had been three days since I'd had the chance to tap into the Anchorage cop scene, and I couldn't shake the sense of guilt that I'd been slipping off my duties. The more time I spent with Orion, the more my priorities seemed to change. What if I missed something critical that ended up putting Lian or someone else in danger?

I needed to get my head back on straight. And maybe that meant asking Orion what his deal was. Ever since the Seattle vamps started clearing out, he'd become increasingly possessive and jealous of me. He didn't like when I went out without him, or for me to get an assignment from anyone other than him. The only slayer work I did that he approved of was rounding up stragglers who were on their way out of town. And he was almost always there, lurking in the shadows.

It was starting to make me uncomfortable.

Don't get me wrong—I actually did enjoy being with him, but I was used to being a free agent, physically and emotionally. I'd spent years telling myself there wasn't time or space to be catching feelings. Especially not for the master of a vampire clan who might have just gotten himself embroiled neck deep in a turf war.

And yet there I was, playing boyfriend-girlfriend with him. I imagined him coming out of the bathroom in a few minutes, naked from the waist up, wrapping his arm around me and kissing me on the neck. Just the thought of it put butterflies in my stomach. But I also knew he'd hold me a little too tight, his grasp a little too demanding.

"408 calling in a flag-down out at 46th and Fairchild."

I snapped to attention, my shallower worries shifting into the background. This was the most exciting thing I'd heard on the scanner so far. Odds were that some tourist had broken down on the side of the road and needed help, but something in my gut told me that flagging down a cop in the middle of the night was more likely to mean trouble than usual.

Dispatch came through. "10-4, 408, can you clarify? Do you need assistance?"

A few seconds of tense silence slipped by. Then the reply, "Motorist is reporting a possible 11-29 in the woods just north of Sixmile Lake. We're investigating. Can you run this guy's plate for me?"

The code made my heartbeat kick into overdrive. One of the first things I had done upon arrival in Anchorage was refamiliarize myself with the local police lingo, including their incident codes. 11-29 was one I had made sure to etch into my memory—dead on arrival.

"Another one," I whispered.

"Sure thing," dispatch was saying. "Go ahead."

More than anything in the moment, I wanted to hear that plate number, just in case. Did I think a homicidal, slash-wound-inflicting monster was just casually driving around at night, looking for authorities to alert of its presence? Not really. But weird shit was happening all over Anchorage. For all I knew, this could be just a regular human serial killer thinking he'd outsmart the cops.

What a fucked-up thought that was, *just a regular serial killer*. But hey, Ted Bundy had been regular, hadn't he? More information was always better. And if it *was* a serial killer, I could sleep easy leaving it in the hands of the Anchorage police. Static cut across the radio and I groaned. It had been doing this lately, but I waited, and when it finally faded away, so had the conversation. Hell.

I turned off the scanner and put it back into place on the desk for now.

The bathroom door opened in a flood of hot steam. He didn't say anything, but I could feel his presence coming up behind me as surely as if he'd called my name. Standing over my chair, he pulled my hair back off my neck and kissed the soft skin below my ear. I shivered. His lips turned upward.

"I was rather expecting you to join me," he remarked. Despite the nonchalance of his tone, I detected an edge of displeasure underneath his words.

I laughed it off. "If I spent all my time in the shower with you, I'd never get anything else done. You know they actually do want me to take these tests at some point, right?" In fact, I had several emails currently in my inbox asking me to confirm final test dates for the exams I had deferred.

Orion frowned. "Why should you need to provide such arbitrary proof of your intelligence? Haven't you demonstrated an adequate level of skill?"

"Spoken like a true centuries-old vampire lord," I replied. "In case you haven't noticed, my college professors don't give out credit for unsanctioned field work. And somehow I doubt they'd be comfortable including me killing werewolves in the accepted curriculum."

His frown deepened. "Werewolves? In Anchorage? Do you know something I don't?"

I rolled my eyes. "No. You know what I mean." Actually, I had almost said 'killing vampires' instead of werewolves, and managed to catch myself at the last minute, so I really hoped he didn't know what I meant. Then I glanced at him. "*Are* there werewolves here?" Now that I thought about it, an angry beast shifter could account for the mauling wounds on the mystery corpses. Was it possible one of the bear shifter tribe decided to stay behind?

"There were," Orion said. "A long time ago." He smiled cryptically, an expression that I took to mean he had personally eradicated the population, or at least had a hand in it.

"But not anymore," I prodded.

It was almost a step too far. He looked at me sharply, his eyes narrowing. "Not as far as I know." His gaze flicked to the open book in front of me. "Is this on one of your tests?"

"It's cute that you think vampires are the only things I like to kill," I said acidly, wondering if he was in rare form tonight, or if this was just the way things were with him. Because if he didn't learn to lay off at least a little, we were going to have to have a talk. And I didn't need to be told how he'd feel about that.

Orion kept his eyes on me for a long time. I turned away from him, but I could feel his gaze boring a hole through the back of my head. Not for the first time, I secretly hoped I wasn't in over my head with him. To be cared about so intensely was nice—to be obsessed over, not so much.

"I'm leaving," he announced at length. "The clan has business to attend to."

"Okay." I barely looked up. "Should I not wait up for you, then?" The question came out with more of a bite than I intended, and I pursed my lips. *All right, Veronica, maybe don't send your vampire boyfriend into a frothing rage.*

"You should," Orion answered. "But you don't have to." He turned the chair around and pulled me to my feet, gripping my chin in his hand as he kissed me hard. I bit back a moan. Literally all he had to do was touch me, and I was falling all over him. "Soon you'll come back to my home," he murmured. "To be with me. There's no need to stay here."

I shook my head. "Thanks, but I'll stay where I am." I knew better than to rush into cohabitating with him, no matter how alluring he could be. And there was no way to explain a change of residence to Lian, who was still very generously footing my bill. The thought reminded me that I owed her a call yet again, and the old guilt settled in my stomach. "Don't let me keep you, Orion," I said, letting him go.

He kissed me one more time. "You are delightful, but endlessly frustrating." Real irritation smoldered on his face, but he backed up and left, closing the door softly. I listened for his footsteps to recede down the hall before I went back to the desk.

"Of course he's crazy," I muttered to no one. "I know how they are. What the hell did I expect?" The wisest thing to do would have been to get the fuck away from him while I still could. But even as I flicked the police scanner back on and turned the volume up to see if I could catch more information on the dead person, I understood in my soul that it wasn't going to happen.

Against my better judgment, I'd already gotten addicted to his body, his voice, the feel of his hands on me. Wherever the point of no return had been, I feared I was long past it.

I almost didn't expect Orion to return that night. But he did; I felt him slip into the bed beside me. His hands were startlingly warm as he wrapped his arms around my body from behind. A sure sign that he had eaten recently.

Half asleep, I tried not to think about that too much. Facing the truth of Orion's nature was the most difficult part for me, and I wasn't very good at it. I leaned back into his chest and let my eyes close again. He gave me a little squeeze.

See? He can be sweet when he wants to be.

My dreams were murky and indistinct, dark shapes floating in a misty world of shadows. Muffled voices called out to me from somewhere beyond, over great expanses of space. If I looked down at my feet, I could see a line where the ground changed from dirt and grass to icy gray rock.

And if I looked up again, I saw a figure standing in the distance, facing me. The face had no distinguishable features, but I swore I recognized him somehow, just like I knew instinctively he was a man. One of his hands lifted from his side, reaching in my direction.

I tried to take a step. The world began to tremble. I took another. It began to crack. And just as the ground gave out beneath me, before I tipped forward into a yawning abyss, the fog around that mysterious man cleared for half a second and I saw, clear as day, who it was.

In the dream, I gasped. "Seth!"

7

ORION

There were many ways in which I had always been my own worst enemy. Perhaps chief among these was the way in which I selected those who would become my thralls. As a younger vampire, the prospect of turning someone had heated the borrowed blood in my veins. I wanted nothing so much as to amass private ranks of devotees.

Well, the hubris of youth soon revealed itself, and by the time Veronica entered the scene, my ambitions had massively cooled. I no longer had any delusions about the glamor of thralls, nor any desire to cultivate my own. Instead of the fulfillment I had craved, that path had brought me little more than tragedy.

And I had been perfectly content to reign alone over the clan for generations—until Veronica. Suddenly, that old spark of yearning was rekindled. I needed to possess her in every way possible. I had to make her mine. The craving overwhelmed me most days.

Despite my clan of vampires and countless lovers, it was surprising how alone one could feel. My time as clanmaster had been long and fruitful, but what if I shared the future with someone by my side?

I grew up as an orphan in my human life. I was born in 1437 in Wallachia. I had been abandoned as a newborn and taken in under the wing of the army. On the day I turned twenty-five, the Ottoman empire attacked our land. So many were butchered on both sides, and unfortunately I was one of the casualties slaughtered on the battlefield. Bitter sweet birthday really. But perhaps that day wasn't meant to be my demise as I awakened a creature of the night. Like my first birth, I was alone again with no sign of who had turned me. It was a pattern in my life and I wanted to put an end to it. This was a history I didn't talk about to anyone about... a past that I loathed. I let others believe what they want about my age and past.

Coming back to reality, I walked through a night that was even darker than usual, on account of a thick layer of blue-gray clouds cushioning the stars. I kept all my senses open to the surrounding dark, just in case some overconfident rogue got the idea of a coup in his head. My authority in Anchorage hadn't been tested in quite some time among my own people, but there were always fools and outsiders among us.

The recent upheaval from the Pacific Northwest hadn't helped matters either. And when it came to the Seattle clan, I chose the possibility of eternal death over surrender. The odd coincidence of Veronica's arrival only cemented my determination.

The clan met in a massive, round clearing deep in the forests north of Anchorage, near where Mud River fed into Sixmile Lake. The vampires were already gathering as I drew near; their energy saturated the air between the dense, dark trees. They flitted in and out of shadows, passing unseen along the path toward the gathering point. A soft rush of ethereal voices gathered on the wind.

I paused just outside the border of the clearing to watch my clan assemble. As a result of the lethal clashes between us and the Seattle clan, our numbers had fallen. The emptiness was more apparent than I had expected in the space of the wide, open clearing. I clenched my jaw, nurturing the smoldering coals of resentment in my chest. A loss so significant demanded retribution, and I was going to make sure I reaped my pound of flesh.

The others quieted down as I emerged from the trees. Hundreds of eyes glittered in the dim light. I surveyed them in silence, back and forth across the rapt throng.

"My brothers and sisters." My voice carried effortlessly over the clan. "I have called you here to our sacred grove, on this night, to make an announcement. At the next Convocation of the New Moon, we will be adding one more to our numbers."

A murmur traveled through the crowd. I waited for it to run its course. Then I continued. "It is my hope that this new potential youngblood will be welcomed with every hospitality. I know that one body cannot possibly atone for the losses we have suffered in recent months, but this one displays great potential, should she be accepted into our clan."

The host of upturned faces began nodding. Their whispers intensified and coalesced into a single voice that rose into the cool, evergreen air.

"As the Clanmaster wills," they murmured reverently. "As the Clanmaster wills."

I smiled. The sound of worship never wore out its welcome.

"That is all in terms of news," I said. "Our enemies continue to retreat further to the south, like rats scurrying back to their nest. They will regroup, and they will come back stronger. We must remain vigilant. Keep your ears to the ground. Watch out for one another." I paused. "This land is ours. It will not be taken from us."

This declaration was met by a rumble of agreement. Then a lone vampire separated herself from the others. I looked down on her slim, hooded figure, skin so pale it seemed to reflect every last bit of light. She turned her face to me and raised her hands.

"Clanmaster Orion, what about the devil that stalks us through the forests?"

I stared at her. "What devil is this?" Instantly, my mind flashed back to Veronica's offhanded mention of werewolves. Could she have known more than she let on?

The vampress glanced back at her friends. "We do not know its nature," she admitted. "Only that it hunts for flesh and bone. So far, it has taken only mortal humans, but we fear its hunger grows."

I looked to the rest of the clan. "Does your sister speak the truth? Who else has seen her devil? Come forward."

A beat of tension passed. The woman stood very still, eyes fixed upon her kinsmen. One by one, they began to emerge, forming up beside her.

"See, Clanmaster?" She gestured broadly. "The devil seeks us all."

I frowned. This was the first I had heard of any such thing, and for some reason, it irritated me. My people weren't overly prone to superstitions because I was not. I had not trained them to jump at shadows, and they all knew better than to lie to me. Pure logic would suggest that they were telling the truth, this nervous handful of followers.

And again, I thought of werewolves.

"Stay sharp," I told them. "Keep your guard up. If this devil you speak of is a true threat, we will find it, and we will strike it down. You have my word."

"Thank you, Clanmaster." They melted back in with the rest of their brethren, and soon after, the meeting was adjourned. I observed as Anchorage's vampires scattered to the winds. My mind churned. In addition to Veronica's ceaseless presence, I'd acquired another thing to think about.

What do they mean by 'devil'?

And what did Veronica know?

---

*T*he Grand Hotel was quickly becoming as known to me as the house on the inlet. I would've vastly preferred to keep her at the house instead, but in true Veronica fashion, she refused to move. It was certainly a hurdle, but one I expected to overcome eventually. For now, I'd have to tolerate her whims, rather than the other way around.

The arrangement was unheard of and vaguely insulting. Were she anyone else, I wouldn't have given it a second thought. Veronica, however, had a strange hold on me. I couldn't let her go, even if it meant making concessions I had never imagined.

At this hour, I elected not to trifle with the lobby doors. The light was on in Veronica's window, and as I climbed up the side of the building toward its ledge, I could see her through the glass, still working at her desk. The glow of her laptop screen cast her gorgeous face in an eerie bluish light which did nothing to diminish her beauty.

Just as I reached the window, she stopped and rubbed her eyes. I tapped the glass; she jerked them open again. A look of sardonic amusement crossed her face. She got up and unlocked the window.

"Really?" she said, gripping one hand on the open window and the other on her hip. She wore jeans and a oversized, off the shoulder sweatshirt with a love heart and penguin on it. Rather adorable.

"I see you waited up for me," I answered.

Veronica leaned up and kissed me, then she glanced at the clock. "It's not that late." She moved to sit back down at the desk, but I caught her by the arm. "What?" The mood between us shifted rapidly. Her guard went up.

I didn't like that very much. What did she think she could hide from me? "I want to talk to you about something."

"Okay." Veronica followed me to the bed, but she didn't sit down, and she eyed me warily.

I decided to cut directly to the chase. "The clan told me they've seen a creature in the forest. They call it a devil, and they say it's killing humans." I studied her closely. "Do you know anything about this? They are afraid it will move on to killing them next."

Veronica furrowed her brow. "Honestly, Seth is the closest thing I know to a devil. You don't think it might be him, do you?"

"Not if I'm lucky," I muttered. "Are you sure? I'm placing a lot of my trust in you, Veronica."

"Well, I appreciate that, but I can't draw a conclusion without more information." She shrugged. "I think if it really was Seth, we would've seen him by now. I don't need to tell you that Anchorage is a dangerous place, Orion. There's all kinds of shit crawling out from under rocks here these days. Maybe some new monster moved in while no one was looking. Maybe it's a serial killer. Normal humans can be monsters too."

That much I already knew. I had the distinct feeling that she was holding back on me yet again, and I had to bite my tongue to keep from commanding her to tell me the truth. The line I walked with Veronica was very, very fine—my desire to turn her successfully gave her more leverage than she would have had otherwise.

"I suppose so." I folded my arms, mimicking the illusion of deep thought. "A human would be little threat. But..." As if struck by a sudden bolt of inspiration, I glanced quickly at her. "Will you attend the next clan meeting with me? I fear the others are correct and this beast's behavior will escalate. We can't afford to make assumptions about our safety when we're all gathering in one place."

Veronica blinked. "You want *me* to come to your clan meeting?"

"Why not?" I asked casually.

"You know why not!" It was her turn to cross her arms. "They'll tear me to shreds if they figure out who I am and what I do."

"Of course not." I touched her face, stroked her cheek. "You'll be with me. No one will touch you."

Some of her trepidation remained. She gazed searchingly into my face. "You're serious about this, aren't you?"

"Why wouldn't I be?" I put my hands on her shoulders. "I promise, within the clan you are perfectly safe. I have never once been defied." After a moment I added, "This is just to ensure the safety of the clan, because I've witnessed your strength. There is no one better."

Veronica sighed and smiled. "Fine. But flattery will only get you so far."

I chuckled. "It's gotten me far enough for now."

And just like that, my makeshift plan had been set into motion. Now that Veronica's presence at the Convocation of the New Moon was all but assured, it was time to move on to the next order of business— preparing her for the turning.

8

——————

VERONICA

Orion was up to something. I could tell he thought he was being slick, but maybe years of unchallenged power as the master of his clan had made him forget that not all humans are idiots, especially not slayers. He might've had many years on me, but I knew when someone—anyone—had an agenda.

And to be honest, I'd kind of been expecting it. He was about as pure a vampire as I had ever seen, and they didn't exactly reek of integrity. Orion was a slightly different breed than the seedy, shifty creatures prowling the back streets of Seattle, but not even my white-hot attraction to him could fully blind me from the reality of past experience.

He was always going to be working an angle, and I was a fool if I got blindsided. It was a risk I took every time I fell into his arms.

For all of Orion's faults, he knew how to keep my suspicions at bay. My brain screamed not to trust him, but my heart and body preferred to go along for the ride, so to speak. I fell asleep secure in the choices I had made, if not especially proud. I was starting to think about Orion the way an addict thought about their substance of choice. *This is just for fun. I can quit anytime I want.*

Still, it sucked to wake up alone in the bed, his spot cold and abandoned beside me. I rolled my eyes and flipped over onto my back. "What an asshole." But even as I cursed him out loud, I understood that whatever twisted thing we had was supposed to be the epitome of no-strings-attached. No feelings—and definitely no commitment. How could I be pissed about him ducking out when I already knew we were fundamentally incompatible?

Not to mention I had two other guys waiting in the wings, neither of whom were any better for me.

"Wow," I muttered. "I'm really killing it, aren't I?" The longer I spent staring into the darkness, the further sleep slipped from my mind, until I finally just gave up and got out of bed. There were still a few more hours of night to go, but I resigned myself to bad hotel-room coffee and some study time before the sun came up. As the little coffee machine in the kitchenette gurgled away, I put my hair up in the messiest of messy buns and sat down in front of my books.

"Okay, where was I?" I flipped through pages of highlighted text, searching for the place where I'd left off. The rustling of glossy text-book paper filled the room.

Then I heard something else, a strange, muffled shuffling. I stopped turning pages and glanced reflexively toward the kitchenette. The light was on, and it was obviously empty. Only the coffeemaker made any noise at all. *Am I hallucinating?* I wondered wryly. *Side effect of fucking a vampire?*

But the sound came again, and this time I recognized it as slow, uneven footsteps. The hair stood up on the back of my neck. It was coming from outside, from the other side of the shut window. I stood up, my books all but forgotten, and crept up to the curtains.

The footsteps grew louder as I neared the window. Very carefully, I inched the drapes open just enough to peer through with one eye. The street below lay bathed in pools of light from the arched lamps along the sidewalk. A lone figure struggled along the pavement, one foot dragging uselessly behind. From my vantage point above, I couldn't see a face.

I replaced the edge of the curtain and closed my eyes, focusing all my senses down onto the sidewalk. There were broken bones and unhealed wounds, but no bloodshed. And no heartbeat, either.

I let out my breath. "So much for studying." Although I had to admit that the thrill of the hunt held way more allure, even in the face of looming exams. *Note to self,* I thought as I threw on some clothes and grabbed my weapons, *you actually do need to schedule those.*

Less than ten minutes later, I stepped out from the entryway of the Grand Hotel and looked both ways up and down the street. The shambling figure had disappeared, but there was no way it could've gone far. Once again, I reached out my slayer senses. A mottled path of energy led erratically out to the corner, then zigzagged down toward a narrow alley.

I took off running, determined to catch up before anyone saw the guy limping down a city street at night. "Why is it always alleys with these guys?" Yellow lamplight reflected off wet pavement, wavering in puddles as I ran. I rounded the corner of the last building on the block and dove into the alley where the trail disappeared.

A dark, hunched shape stood unsteadily against the back wall. One pale, bony hand had been braced on the side of a huge dumpster, thin fingers hooked over the edge like claws. The figure's clothes hung off its gaunt frame.

I thought I could hear it chewing.

"Hey." My right hand slipped into the pocket of my coat, gripping the staff that lay hidden inside. I hit the button on the end with my thumb, and it sprang to its full length, moonlight glinting off steel. "Break time's over. Let's go."

The figure paused. I didn't like how still it seemed, or that I still couldn't see its face. Then it turned haltingly toward me, wobbling on its bad leg. This close, I could see that the ankle joint had been torn through and was now resting grotesquely on its side.

The right hand clutched the carcass of a large rat. Its feet and tail hung limp. There was no head to speak of.

"Begone, slayer." The face was that of a shriveled old hag, her beady eyes glaring from sunken sockets. Thin, waxy skin stretched across the angles of her skull. Her complexion, sickly white in places, had darkened to purple and blue in others, particularly around the withered lips. "What quarrel do you have with me? I am already close to my end."

"The same as I have with those who left you behind," I told the hag. My grip on the staff tightened. "You don't belong here." I could only assume she had gotten injured in some scuffle and couldn't keep up with her vampire compatriots any longer. And because there was no loyalty among monsters, they had abandoned her.

"Left me behind?" She cackled. Her voice grated, like nails on a chalkboard. "Oh, child. How little you know of this old place." The hag's murky, dark eyes lit with a sudden sinister glow. She smiled and reached out a skeletal hand. "But you've come to kill me. I understand. Perhaps this is truly how my days come to an end."

Acceptance slid behind her dark eyes, almost a gleeful acceptance to escape her fate in this world.

I advanced on her, slowly, keeping one eye on the outstretched fingers of her hand. "Yes," I said. "It is."

She shifted her weight. The broken ankle dragged over concrete. I was expecting her to grab for me, but not the speed with which she managed to do so. Her fingers grasped onto a fistful of my coat and pulled at me. She smelled like mold and rotting flowers.

"Perhaps I'll take you with me!" she rasped gleefully. "You might find what you're really looking for there, beyond the pale." Her eerily bright eyes narrowed into slits. "Or should I say…whom you're looking for?"

I paused. It was only for a fraction of a second, but no hesitation escaped the hag's deceptively sharp perception. She laughed again, scant frame shaking.

Does she mean Seth? I knew the trickeries of hags, and yet my curiosity was piqued. Could she help me find him before I dispatched her? No, it was too risky. No telling what kind of trouble I'd get into if I dealt with the old witch.

I shook my head. "Sorry, Grandma. One-way trip, and you're going alone." In one swift motion, I pressed the end of my staff to her sternum and prepared to drive it home.

She was too frail to put up more than a token amount of resistance. But her icy fingers circled around my forearm, and she stared into my face as her nails made tiny gouges in my flesh. "So be it, slayer," she said. "I welcome my last breath with open arms. But Death is following you, too. You'll see it soon."

I had seen more than my share of strange shit as a slayer, and I'd heard hundreds of cryptic deathbed comments. This one sent a legitimate chill down my spine, despite the fact that in my time in Anchorage, death had been present at every turn so far. I glanced at the hand clutching onto my arm, at the thin lines of blood running down my skin.

"I'll take my chances," I told her. The sound of her bones cracking underneath the force of my staff seemed to echo in the cramped quarters of the alley. Her eyes went dark and hollow, and her broken body crumbled into a pile of dusty clothing.

I almost didn't notice how that hand maintained its death grip on me. I pried it off, disgusted. The marks from her nails stung in the cold air. By the time the disembodied hand hit the ground, it was stiff and a barren vessel, just like all vampires I eliminate.

I backed the hell out of the alleyway and headed for home. Maybe for the first time in my life, I kind of wished that I'd just run into a regular old vampire. There were stragglers still filtering out of Anchorage, making their way back to Seattle. Why couldn't this have been one of those encounters? Kill it, brush off the vamp blood, go home and study. Easy.

But no. Instead, I had a hundred new thoughts spinning through my mind, and the extra ominous weight of her prediction to carry.

Death is following you too. You'll see it soon.

The idea that I hadn't yet scratched the surface needled at me. I shoved my hands in my pockets and picked up the pace. How much more death could there be?

It was a rhetorical question. I was not eager to find out the answer.

9

———

VERONICA

I stayed up for the next sixteen hours with my schoolbooks and police scanner, pretending everything was totally fine. But the vampire hag's last words kept haunting me, and I did not want to know what might happen if I dared to fall asleep and dream. I'd already had one weird vision of Seth, wherever he was. I didn't need another.

All day, the scanner spit out information I had come to think of as routine: burglaries, other thefts, carjackings, minor assaults. Days spent tuned into the crime beat in the city had made me realize just how dicey Anchorage could get on a day-to-day basis. Was it any surprise that such an already chaotic place was teeming with supernaturals?

By afternoon, boredom had temporarily usurped my desire to study. I had my feet tucked up on the edge of the desk chair and was spinning slowly back and forth, hugging my knees, listening to the steady drone of the scanner.

"This is unit 341, reporting discovery of human remains in the northwestern quadrant of Chugach. Repeat, that's 11-29, possible 11-1 in northwest Chugach. Requesting support at the scene."

The officer gave the coordinates of the body, which I scribbled down on the nearest scrap of paper. When I punched them into the GPS on my phone, I was surprised to see how close it was to Glenn Highway, the major route that ran locally through the state. Seemed like a pretty bold place to leave a corpse, given that the others had been buried in the forest under mounds of debris-laden snow.

Then again, maybe the randomness was part of the point. The lack of a discernible pattern had made for a slew of crimes that were proving very difficult to solve. If it was only one perpetrator, I had to hand it to them; even in Alaska, not many got away with a body count half as high.

The sun was slipping down below the horizon as I made my way out to the scene of the latest discovery. I looked at the brightly painted clouds.

The car I had called let me out about a quarter mile from the scene. For half that distance, I followed a trailhead, then slipped off the path for the last six hundred feet. There was a police truck wedged in among the trees, its red and blue light flashing over lines of yellow tape. I hunkered down in a spot behind a large, mossy boulder where I could peek over the top and see the perimeter.

The site was crawling with officers. They scurried around like ants across the forest floor, placing markers down and taking pictures. I picked the CSIs out right away, all decked out in gloves and masks and boots made for handling remains. They came in with a stretcher and carried it down to the shallow gully where the body lay. A moment later, I saw one turn, run up the gentle slope, yank his mask down, and puke into the underbrush.

That told me everything I needed to know. Well, not *everything*, but it sure did substantiate my hunch that these killings were being perpetuated by the same ruthless being. As more and more corpses turned up in all kinds of places—unearthed from massive, months-old snowdrifts, washing up on the shores of lakes and rivers, found in fields and drainage ditches—I went around to countless similar scenes and watched the same dramas play out.

What struck me the most was the atmosphere in those places and how indescribably bleak and heavy it was. In the beginning, there had been an air of confusion, even intrigue. But now the morgue was nearing full capacity, and good leads were nowhere to be found. The police were sick and tired of tagging and bagging John and Jane Does, most of whom had yet to be identified. They were tired of being summoned to remote areas on the outskirts of Alaskan civilization to comb through someone else's makeshift gravesite.

The frustration was palpable. I couldn't blame them, honestly. This string of unsolved murder cases was fast becoming the longest in state history according to the news, and it showed no signs of letting up. All the crews that came out during the long and often inclement nights looked exhausted. They started slipping up when it came to securing their perimeters. I went from skulking around in the dark to waltzing directly onto the scene after the last cop car pulled away.

It made my job simple as hell, but I did feel for them. The sheer number of bodies overwhelmed the standard police force. Anchorage had always been a dangerous city, but never like this. For now, I enjoyed lax police surveillance, but that was only due to depletion of resources. Recently, I had overheard officers talking about bringing in the FBI and the Alaska Bureau of Investigation.

When the suits arrived, I'd have to watch my step. There was no telling what they would or wouldn't know about slayers in general—or how they'd feel about me if I were to be discovered. Something told me I couldn't expect to be left alone by federal agents.

To that end, I savored all the uninterrupted quiet time I could get in these grisly locations, somber and lonely as they were. My chances to get a real good look at undisturbed remains were few and far between, but there were always copious amounts of energy left behind, which I used to reconstruct body sites from the ground up.

It was hard, depressing work. After a while, I found myself growing even more desensitized. More than once on my macabre and never-ending tour, I thought about the hag in the alleyway, and what she had said about death. Had this been what she meant, this relentless resurfacing of the dead who were not just dead, but slain?

In a weird way, I kind of hoped so. The necessary numbing of my emotions was something I knew how to take, from years of experience. An angry storm, but one I could weather.

By the time I'd hit my fourth or fifth recovery scene in as many days, I had learned to drift in and out of a trancelike state of rest during downtime; at least, I told myself it was an intentional transition. It might have had more to do with sleep deprivation and lack of proper food than I wanted to admit. But whatever the cause, it gave me a precious opportunity to conserve some of my energy.

And that was what I was doing, my back against a thick, sturdy tree, when I sensed someone approaching from a direction other than the bustling scene behind me. Alarmed, I turned one ear toward the cops. Everything on their end seemed normal—no emergency was being called, no alarm being raised. I furrowed my brow, eyes still lightly closed.

A brisk drought of cool, crisp air washed over me. Then the presence was right there, casting me in its shadow. I opened my eyes, tilted my head up, muscles tensed and poised for a defensive strike. Like a snake, camouflaged but deadly.

Logan looked down at me. His bright blue eyes, gleaming in the dark, could not have been less impressed. "What are you doing?" he asked. His voice was soft, but I flinched.

I put a finger to my lips, indicating the nearby cops with a flick of my head. He glanced briefly in their direction before extending his hand to me. I took it and let him pull me to my feet. My joints were stiff and sore from sitting cross-legged for so long.

"What are *you* doing here?" I whispered, turning the question around on him. "You're going to blow my cover."

He remained completely nonplussed. "I doubt it." Again, his calm gaze moved to the police, and back to me. "They have other things to worry about right now." That much was true, but it wasn't addressing the real heart of my question. He shrugged. "I noticed that something was wrong."

Tilting my head, I eyed him closely. "And what does that mean?"

"It doesn't really concern you," Logan responded bluntly, "but the paths between realms are impassable. Something came here and caused a lot of damage on its way through." He paused. "I think that's what happened to Seth."

My ears perked up. "Have you heard from him?"

"Not him specifically." Logan's eyes gained a faraway, dreamlike expression. "As a matter of fact, I wanted to ask if you might help me retrieve him."

"Yes." I replied instantly, without thinking twice. "I can't really tell if Orion gives a shit, but I do. We can't just leave him stranded. Do you know where he is?"

"I can find out," he murmured. He then fell in beside me, both of us staring out to the cops and watching. There was something comforting having him with me, almost like a partner in crime to bounce theories against. Logan was nothing like Orion or Seth. He carried a softer demeanor in comparison, something I rather enjoyed.

The rest of that night's stakeout crawled by with how slow the investigation and clean up went. Logan, by far the most patient of the three supernaturals I had somehow adopted, stayed with me the whole time, hovering on the edge of the police perimeter. We watched the ambulance depart with the body, lights dark and siren silent. As the temperature dropped, he wrapped me in his wings to keep me warm.

I tried to keep focus on the problem at hand, but Logan's mention of Seth had my thoughts spinning in a hundred different directions. That, and standing so close to his body was a huge distraction all by itself. Unlike Orion, I could feel him breathing, sense his strong heartbeat at my back. He carried himself with an authority that was quieter than Orion's, but just as absolute.

I kept staring out at the place where the latest set of remains had lain, but all I really wanted to do was turn around and kiss Logan right on his gorgeous mouth, press myself against him, feel his hands on my skin.

Settle down there, V. Take it slow. The logical, non-thirsty side of my brain struggled to prevail. It was a losing battle. Suddenly the prospect of sitting there any longer struck me as completely unbearable. I just wanted to be somewhere quiet with Logan, scheming over how to spring Seth from the ethereal prison he was trapped in, and to bring him back.

We both knew the bodies weren't going anywhere. They could wait a few days.

"Come on." I reached over and took Logan's hand. "Let's go somewhere private to figure this out."

Logan looked at me, and I thought he might refuse. But then he smiled slightly. I allowed him to lead me deeper into the trees, far away from the lingering contingent of officers. Then he scooped me into his arms.

"Hold on tight," he advised.

The next thing I knew, the ground was dropping away beneath us as we soared up high toward the thick blanket of clouds. Chugach State Park spread out below us like a blanket, fringed by the lights that denoted civilization.

"Wow." I leaned my head back on Logan's shoulder, simultaneously awestruck and a little terrified. He held me close, winging silently on toward the inlet shore.

10

LOGAN

I had known Veronica would be at the scene of the body in Chugach, although I didn't tell her so. As of late, I'd taken to asking the spirits who turned up at the house where they came from and what they wanted, mostly because the questions got them to stop their constant harassment. That night, I was told about a place off the highway, a corpse left reclining among the gnarled roots of trees.

And about a woman watching from the shadows. A woman with bright pink hair.

Lo and behold, she was there, and now I had her in my arms, pressed against me. Her body soft, her breaths speeding up. I enjoyed the way she felt against me. But when we began the descent to the house and she recognized it from the air, she balked.

"Uh, Logan? We're not going in there, are we?"

"Why not?" I asked. The place was as dark as it had been when I left it. I saw no reason to think we wouldn't be completely alone.

"Well...is Orion home?" She looked down at the house as if she thought he could already hear her—which, knowing him, wouldn't have surprised me all that much. Somewhat apologetically, she added, "You know how he is. I would just really prefer not to make this a whole thing."

"I see." I nodded wisely but didn't stop easing down over the lawn. "Don't worry about it. I can take him."

She sighed. "That's not really what I meant." As soon as her feet touched the grass, she stood up and took a step back. "Listen, Logan. Don't take this personally, okay? I'd love to spend some more time with you. I think you're…" Veronica paused. Her hand had landed on my chest, and she left it there while she chose her words. "I think you're different from the others, and not in a weird way. But I don't want to cause problems between you and Orion."

I chuckled. If being with her meant problems between me and Orion, I had fully committed to them. "That bridge is mine to cross, if I ever even come to it," I told her. Then I took her hand and kissed the back of her fingers. The grin spreading over her lips left me more determined to spend time with her, to listen to her voice, to discuss anything she wanted.

"He's not in there. Let's go," I reassured her, rather impressed that she worried about Orion and I getting into a fight. It told me she cared a lot more than she admitted… she cared about us both.

Despite obvious doubt, Veronica followed me. She slowed down as we approached the door, but I didn't allow her to stop. The door shut at her back, and she stood nervously in the front entryway. I nudged her toward the kitchen, letting her soak in the weight of the silence around us.

After a few moments, she exhaled, her shoulders dropping. "I guess you're right. Sorry."

"I understand your concern. He's very…interested in you." That was a grave understatement, which she seemed to acknowledge.

"Yeah. Let's not talk about it." She gave a little half-smile. "We have other things to discuss."

My first instinct was to lead her straight up the stairs to be locked into the private sanctity of my bedroom. But while she was there in the house, I had this strange desire to ease her mind, to indulge in some of the human rituals I just barely remembered from a different life.

"Do you want a drink?" I asked. "Or something to eat?" The latter was sort of a bluff—there hadn't been much regular food around since Seth's surprise eviction. He was the perpetually hungry one who had consumed anything other than coffee or tea.

Veronica side-eyed me, still smiling. She knew I was faking it, but apparently decided to humor my good intentions. "I want to say coffee, but I'm going to exercise self-control and ask for water."

"I can make you coffee." I had no idea why I was going to such lengths to accommodate her. Other than her exceptional beauty, she had little right to be so fascinating. But she was, for me, unexpected brightness in a world long composed of grays.

In short, I couldn't help myself. And after she'd gotten a drink and preceded me up the stairs, I couldn't keep my eyes off her, either. Standing out in the open, whipped by Alaskan night air and dampened by fog, it was a little easier to stay stoic and unaffected by her presence. Having the girl sitting on the edge of my mattress, looking at me with her luminous eyes, was a different matter entirely.

But she insisted on talking about Seth, to my mild annoyance. I wanted to find him, too...but not as much as I wanted to kiss her. Then I wanted to push her down into the blankets, strip off her clothes and taste her sweetness with an eager tongue. All the things our first encounter in the woods had not allowed for.

"I think I had a dream about him," she was saying. "It seemed like he might be trapped somewhere." She paused. "We should try to help him."

I should have been gratified to hear those words coming from her. Although I might have framed it less charitably, locating Seth and returning him to the mortal realm was the main reason I had sought her out in the first place. And here she was, giving me the perfect opportunity to advance my agenda without pushing the point.

Instead, I stood by the bed and watched her lips move, examining how they curved to form words when she talked. She was right—Seth did need help. If he could have done the job himself, he would've been back by now. But try as I might, I couldn't focus on anything other than the way the moonlight silvered her skin and ran mercury highlights through her hair.

Veronica cocked her head to the side. "Logan. Hello? Are you listening to me, like at all?" She reached out and took my hand, tugging me toward her. "I know he's not your favorite person in the world, but I'm kinda worried about him. And I feel like Orion's just going to leave him to die as he tells me he'll find him, but I haven't seen any progress." She made a nonspecific gesture with her other hand.

I sat down close to her on the bed. She glanced at me, laced her fingers through mine.

"He might be dead," I said, for no real reason other than possible plausibility.

She pressed her lips into a grim line. "I know."

"Do you?" It was my turn to look at her with an expression other than muted awe.

"Well, no," she admitted. "Not for sure. But in the dream I was *trying* to tell you about, he felt like he was..." She trailed off. "Oh, I don't know. Beyond some kind of veil. That sounds stupid as hell, but you know what I mean."

In fact, I did. The veil to which she referred was the very thing I had been trying to pierce myself. And if the sudden surge of spirits in the house was any indication, it was growing thin as of late. Which might explain why someone like her was suddenly able to see past it. Veronica may have been remarkable, but she was still ultimately human.

I paused. *Wasn't she?*

"What?" She reached out and playfully nudged me in the chest. "You're looking at me like I just sprouted another head."

I had thought I was looking at her like I wanted to kiss her, because I did. I thought about telling her so, but ultimately decided to let actions speak for themselves. She kept that mildly bemused expression right up until our lips met. Then she just melted against me.

The kiss only lasted for a few seconds, but we were both quickly in over our heads. Veronica moaned as I pulled back and stared at me with bare lust in her eyes.

I touched my forehead to hers. "Tell me if this isn't okay."

She grabbed my face, drew me to her again. "Oh, fuck yeah it is."

We barely came up for air after that. Her clothes, and then mine, came off fast, and she seemed desperate for body heat, for skin-to-skin contact. I knew that in this particular scenario, moving together in the unique intimacy of a bedroom, I would struggle to stay in the moment.

For so long, I'd survived by disconnecting from the base of mortal emotion, viewing its peaks and valleys from afar. There was something about Veronica, however, that lured me from the safety of a comfortable distance, right up into the point-blank trenches of pleasure. I focused on the silky planes of her stomach and thighs, her soft curves, the contrast of rosy nipples against white skin.

This time, she was eager, almost frustrated, and I admired how she took what she wanted. There was nothing shy about her. She squirmed impatiently as I kissed her everywhere other than the places she especially wanted to be kissed, and when I finally ventured down between her legs, prying them wider as she laid back on the bed for me, she was already wet with anticipation. Veronica opened herself wide to me, rubbing her fingers over her clit. I breathed in her delicious scent, watching how much she glistened with slick. My cock hardened to the point of pain.

"Please," she said, "I want you so bad, Logan." I stroked her with the back of my finger, and she gasped. The tone of her pleading, more forceful than submissive, aroused me further.

I leaned down and ran my tongue over her, tasted her slowly at first, then deeply. She tossed her head back and thrust her hips against my mouth, her clit rigid against my tongue. The air rushed out of her lungs all at once, only to be drawn back in and released as an uncontrolled, near-feral moan.

"Fuck. Oh, fuck. Don't stop."

I didn't. Her hands moved restlessly in and out of my hair, gripping the bedspread, winding around the posts on the headboard. The rhythm of her body gyrating underneath me was hypnotic and surreal. My tongue found its way deeper, and then so did my fingers. Veronica lifted off the mattress in her ecstasy. If she was saying something, it had moved beyond articulated language. She suddenly screamed, her legs shaking, her body shivering with her orgasm. Fuck, she was beautiful.

She squeezed around me as she fell back to the bed, panting and shuddering. "Oh God. Oh my God. Holy shit." Her hands roamed blindly until they found my face. I kissed her trembling body, making my way up to her mouth.

"I need you inside me," she whispered, once we were face to face.

"Now?" I admired her stamina.

"Right now." She turned me over so she was on top and pushed my knees apart where she kneeled. I leaned back and felt her hands and then her inquisitive, exploring mouth tracing down my chest, licking and kissing me. The sensation of her tongue on me drove all other thoughts from my head. I was barely aware of myself anymore as my heart raced, my balls tightening with an aching need.

Everything about Veronica made me crave her intensely. She climbed up and over my hips, then lowered herself onto me. I hissed as she pushed herself over my cock, the tightness of her walls drove me over the edge. She smirked, loving that she had the upper hand, and she rode me vigorously, hands braced against my chest. Again, she threw her head back, and I joined her dancing rhythm, my hips rising to meet hers, moving faster and faster. My attention locked on the most gorgeous breasts bouncing up and down. I felt her coming intensely from deep inside.

That was what pushed me over the thinnest edge. Resting one hand in the small of her back, I let her grab the other and press my fingers frantically to her clit. Then, rubbing her hard, I bent her back and thrust as far as I could at my own climax.

Veronica's fingers dug into the back of my neck and shoulders. She rode me through the entire tide of her orgasm before collapsing on my chest, her breaths heavy. We were both sheened in sweat, breathless, spent. It was the most intensely physical experience I'd had in a long time. And I wanted more.

"That was amazing." Veronica gently disentangled us, pressing her mouth to the side of my neck. She curled up next to me. I pulled the blanket halfway up her gorgeous, naked body. "I really needed that," she said.

I smiled, liking how well our bodies fit together. "It was my plea-sure." I resisted the urge to ask if Orion wasn't taking care of her the way he should. Though unspoken, the thought stayed in my mind. Or maybe it was more about understanding why he had taken to being so obsessed over her lately. She got under my skin, in my nostrils, in my mind.

She smiled into my shoulder. If I hadn't been looking at her in that moment, I might have missed seeing her eyes tracing patterns around the empty room. She said, "Can I ask you a question?"

"Yes." My thumb ran down the path of her spine. I was ready to tell her anything—cosmic secrets, if she wanted them.

She lifted her head. "Who the hell are all these people?" Suddenly, she recoiled, then burst out laughing. "Oh my God."

My eyes, which had drifted closed, snapped open to reveal a host of spirits standing around the bed, observing us. The expressions on their faces varied from delight to disgust. I rolled my eyes, realizing her connection with me had opened her up to the view the dead who lingered, as I did every day. Just as I had on the first bloody murder scene in the woods where I opened up her sight to speak with the dead. "They are just the nosy dead. They can't hurt you."

She was still laughing, half sounding embarrassed, the edge of the blanket drawn up to her eyes. "I think I saw Seth," she told me. "Like, just now. He got out of here *so* fast."

"Huh." I searched the small audience for his distinctive glowering form and didn't find him. "I might've thought he would be into it." It seemed unlike a demon as proud as Seth not to embrace a thing like voyeurism. "Does it bother you?"

"No." She shook her head, raking her vibrant curls out of her face. "I'm just glad I didn't make eye contact with him while you were making me come so hard I almost passed out." A little smirk crossed her lips. "I think he was jealous."

"I'll make sure to apologize in person," I said dryly.

"So they watch you all the time?" she asked.

"You learn to ignore them after a while."

"Still must be strange to know you are never ever alone."

Her words hit very close to home, but there was nothing I could do to change my situation whether I wanted to or not. Maybe I'd become so used to it that it was more of a nuisance.

Veronica hesitated. "I guess this is a weird time to bring it up, but I really do think we need to get him back over here. In the dream I had, he..." She trailed off, staring pensively out the far window. "He seemed like he wasn't doing so well. We need to get him out now that we know for certain where he is."

"He probably wasn't," I agreed. "And probably still isn't. Demons have specific environments. If he isn't in one where he can thrive, he's in trouble."

"How much trouble?" She chewed her lip. "A lot?"

"Potentially." I shrugged. "The kind of cold in some of those places could put him out for good." This appeared to upset her, her mouth parting, her face slightly losing color, so I tightened my arm around her waist and let her snuggle close. "But we'll find him. And we'll bring him back."

She glanced at me. "I hope so." Neither of us made mention of the brooding vampire, but I thought about him as she fell off to sleep. Did he know, right this moment, that I had his precious slayer in my bed?

I wasn't sure, but the thought of his anger made me smile.

11

ORION

I roamed the dark streets of the city, glaring into the unpleasant brightness of my phone screen. I had meant to comb every last nook and cranny of Anchorage for clan members who were hiding or injured or were simply too pragmatic to do anything other than wait out the storm that had recently passed. But I hadn't been able to reach Veronica in hours, and her conspicuous absence was now consuming my thoughts.

Growling, I shoved the phone into my pocket. None of my messages had merited even a one-word answer from her. The calls I made went to her voicemail, which I doubted she was currently checking. Wherever Veronica had run off to, it was inaccessible to me. I had the needling suspicion that she'd slipped under my radar on purpose.

And that stoked the fires of my fury into a blazing inferno. It was not a secret that I preferred to keep my close associates, especially lovers, on a short leash. Veronica in particular was a prize I wasn't willing to lose. The connection I felt to her was too rare to let go.

Of course, I didn't fully expect a mortal slayer, ages younger than me, to understand her own significance. She needed me to make her into a legacy; without the turning, she'd be more like a cherry blossom, her life beautiful and heartbreakingly brief. I was already determined not to let her fade into a fate as demeaning as obscurity.

But she had churned me into a rage, whether she knew it or not. For reasons I admittedly could not pinpoint, I hadn't expected to ever be ignored by her. Perhaps it was no more than a foolish assumption on my part that she knew my mind, that she would understand the depth and uniqueness of my feelings and respect them.

Foolish, indeed. At the end of the night, she was raw and untaught, a clay figurine ripe for molding. After years of experience with this very scenario, I should have known to lower my expectations until she had a chance to learn, clearly, what they were. But what could I say? I was at least infatuated with her.

I walked until the sky began to lighten in the east, warning of the day about to dawn. Burning inside, I took the next right turn and headed in the general direction of home. The undercurrent of paranoia in my thoughts told me that Veronica was using the sun as a shield, hiding from me in daylight.

While I wrestled with my temper, the phone in my pocket went off. Like a starved and wild animal, I snatched it. Veronica's name titled the message she'd finally sent.

Sorry I was MIA. Working on a case.

I frowned deeply. *Unacceptable. You cannot cut me off that way.*

I didn't cut you off, Orion. I was busy.

My frown stayed put. *Too busy for me?*

At the moment, yes. But I'm here now.

The woman's sheer audacity made me livid, as much as it made me long for her. Immediately, I redirected my course toward the Grand Hotel. I was tired, and I'd be cutting dangerously close to high levels of light exposure, but I had to see her.

I'm on my way. You'd better be there, I wrote.

Once more, she didn't answer. I put the phone away and ran the rest of the distance, buildings and pavement flashing by. Without slowing, I scaled the exterior of the hotel in seconds. Her window was open a crack. I leapt into the room.

"Where were you?" In theory, I understood that the first words out of my mouth to her should not have been a demand. But my emotions were high, unchained. I couldn't remember the last time anyone had had such a profound effect on my state of being. She was the soaring high and crushing low of a potent drug, experienced simultaneously.

Sitting on the bed, she looked at me as if I'd gone insane. "I told you where I was." Her voice was maddeningly calm, undisturbed. "I was out, working a case. You're not the only thing I have to do in Anchorage."

I glowered at her. Something different lingered in the air around her, a foreign strain shot through her aura. "All night? I should never be out of touch with you for so long."

"Is that so?" Veronica put her pen down and closed the book she was reading with a heavy snap. A thrill ran through my bones and raised the hair on the nape of my neck. Electricity crackled in the air the same way it did before a brawl in the street. If she wanted to fight, I wouldn't hurt her—but it was possible to be merciless without being outright violent.

"Do not ignore me, Veronica. I won't stand for that type of flagrant disrespect." I pulled myself up to my full height so that I towered over her. True to her nature and her vocation, Veronica did not back down.

"And why is that, Orion?" She spat my name as if it were poison on her tongue. "I don't know what's been going on in your head lately, but let me remind you of something. You don't fucking own me. I don't care what you think."

The force behind her words was almost tangible. I stood my ground, but the urge to step back took me by surprise. For the second time since meeting Veronica, I wondered if I had gravely underestimated her. "Forgive me for caring about you," I said acidly. "I need to know where you are."

"Oh, bullshit." She folded her arms. "What you need is to control me, and I really don't have to put up with it. You can get your shit together, or you can get out." To emphasize her point, she nodded toward the window. "Curtain's still open, by the way. And it's getting pretty close to dawn. I'd be careful if I were you."

The realization that she was actually threatening me hit like a point-blank explosion. However defiant I already thought she was, Veronica kept raising the standard. I wanted to grab her and shake out the insubordination. But I also admired her intensely. Her convictions weren't just strong; they were unbreakable.

And I needed her to be willing if she was going to join the clan. Any resistance, no matter how subtle, put her at risk of rejecting the turning, an event which I had seen end in disaster many times. With her, that sort of catastrophic failure simply was not an option, so much so that I was willing to swallow my pride in order to prevent it from happening.

"Fine," I said brusquely. The task of softening my tone required a concentrated effort, but I managed. "I'm sorry. It is unreasonable of me to expect you to allow your freedoms to be curtailed. I'll...be more considerate in the future."

"It's a start." She came over to me, stood on her toes, and pressed her lips to my cheek. "I don't know what other women have let you down in the past, but I'm not going to let you treat me like shit, Orion. I think you're better than that; we wouldn't be standing here like this if I didn't."

"That's fair," I admitted. "I appreciate your—" I stopped talking as that whiff of intrusion struck my senses again. This time, close to her as I was, I recognized it. "You were with Logan." My anger flared again before I had a chance to control it.

"For fuck's sake, Orion." Veronica drew back, scowling. "Listen. First of all, it's none of your business where I spend my time, or who's there with me. Second, you're on thin ice, so you'd better watch your fucking step. We don't have to fuck. We don't even have to be friends. You and I could be on opposite ends of this war that's brewing, easily." Her stony gaze bored straight through me. "If you want me to stick around, you're gonna have to learn to share. That's just the way it is."

Her unvarnished honesty was agonizing. Briefly, I wanted to go back to pacing the streets, scrounging in dismal corners for the dregs of my clan. To be told by the object of my undivided attention that I couldn't be the planet to her moon was a blade that plunged deep.

But I knew what choice had to be made—she'd been cruelly, brutally clear. I could either accept her dalliances with Logan, or I could lose my hold on her forever. And if I thought I'd be able to intimidate her into submission, a reevaluation was in order.

Never in my life had I been put into this position. Somehow, I was the one in the corner, my back against the wall. Trapped by my own all-encompassing desire for the one person who could force me to agree with her, rather than the other way around. I wasn't used to making concessions, especially not to those beneath my power.

Veronica was nothing to me. And yet she was everything. I had allowed myself to be played like an instrument. She had grasped the upper hand, and as yet, I had little recourse.

"No one has ever made such frivolous demands of me," I told her, sounding somewhat sullen. Up to now, there had been no place for resignation in my life. It was an adjustment I resented having to make.

"There's a first time for everything," she responded. "You'll be okay."

I watched her climb back onto the bed and pull her heavy book into her lap. She caught my eye and sighed. "Come over here and stop looking like I locked you out in the rain. All I'm asking is for you not to be so damn selfish, that's all."

Those words stung too, but I could see the merit in them. She was still a human, and she operated by a moral compass that was stronger than most. When I walked over to her, she made room for me beside her on the mattress. I sat down, and she leaned into my body. Her living warmth was comforting, intoxicating in a way.

I had the fleeting thought that I would miss it.

"Are you ready for the clan meeting?" I asked after a few moments of silence. The meeting was mere days away. I decided not to ask if she had mentioned it to Logan.

Veronica glanced at me. "And here I thought you were going to ask me about my exams," she quipped. "Yes, I'm ready. Whatever that means. But I want to know what you're up to with this. We both know I shouldn't be welcome at a thing like that."

I kissed the exposed skin between her shoulder and collarbone. "It's nothing special. Consider your presence a breaking of the ancient mold. Maybe the landscape of slayer-vampire relations is on the verge of change." The sentiment wasn't truth or lie. Historically, dealings between our people had always been complicated, always in flux. Slayers had been converted. Vampires and others had gone rogue.

There were no hard and fast rules. We existed in a mural of gray areas. But I knew Veronica wasn't convinced by the answer I had given. "You really won't tell me, huh?"

I kissed her again, nipping gently. "There's nothing to tell."

"Uh huh." She stretched against me. My right hand slipped to her breast. "Keep your hands to yourself," she said playfully. "At least for right now. I can't put this stuff off another night."

In keeping with the spirit of compromise, I obliged her request—for a while.

12

VERONICA

I looked at myself in the mirror, half amused, half quietly uneasy. It wasn't that I looked bad. Far from it; I hadn't had occasion to be this hot in years. I just knew in my goddamn bones that Orion was planning something, and it drove me nuts that I couldn't work out what it was.

His nonspecific denials meant nothing to me. Why else would he be so insistent that I attend? I was familiar enough with vampire clan customs to know that an invitation like that was rare, especially to outsiders. Yeah, sure, maybe I had 'girlfriend privileges' in his eyes, but even then, there was absolutely no way this level of access was unconditional.

But of course, he wouldn't tell me what he was playing at. He thought he was so clever with all the easy denials glossed over by great sex. Maybe Orion didn't fully understand that the afterglow haze never lasted forever. And as soon as the endorphins had faded, I was right back to being suspicious of his motives.

Still, it was just too good an opportunity to pass up; I was sure he knew that, too. And I wasn't scared. If shit hit the fan, I could hold my own—or bail, in a worst-case scenario. Didn't feel good to think he might double-cross me hard enough to make that possible, but I had to be realistic. The truth was, I really had no idea what I was walking into.

Hope for the best, prepare for the worst.

Stepping away from the mirror, I patted myself down for the essentials: phone, keys, money, and ID. My staff was there too, of course, craftily hidden away in a little holster way up on my thigh. The skirt I was wearing was so tight Orion would be able to feel it as soon as he touched me, but I didn't care too much. He was not delusional enough to think I'd be coming to a vampire clan meeting unarmed.

As I gave myself one final glance-over, I walked to the window and cracked it open. The air that burst in was cool and wet, but it smelled new, like spring. Not two minutes later, a shadow fell across the table underneath the sill.

"That was fast," I said, without looking at him right away. "You haven't microchipped me or anything, have you?" The thought of him putting some kind of tracking device on me had crossed my mind before. I swore to myself that if I ever found him doing bullshit like that, I'd be done.

He gave me a look. His gaze roved over my body, barely disguising his carnal interest. "I don't need to do that." He seemed a little on edge, impatient. Instead of coming all the way into the room, he lingered in the window. His energy felt restless. I wondered if he was worried about how the meeting would go. Or maybe he thought someone was going to fuck up his mysterious plans.

"That is not the answer I wanted," I told him, "but we should get going." Sometimes I cringed at the way he got me talking to him. How could I enforce the "no attachment" rule I knew we needed when I was busy indulging in petty bickering? I motioned for him to go out the way he'd come.

He obliged, but not before pulling me into his arms and giving me the kind of kiss that might have led to sex right there in the open window if we hadn't had somewhere important to go.

"Tonight is proof of my trust in you," he murmured. "In case that's what this is about." Then he tipped backward out of the window. I closed my eyes, feeling the dizzy rush of the fall, the cold air cutting straight through my clothes. How we ended up right-side-up on the sidewalk, I wasn't sure. Orion set me on my feet.

"I'm guessing that was supposed to prove *my* trust in *you*," I said sardonically. Up over his shoulder, I could see the pane still open. "I'll have you know I did not buy insurance on those books. You'll be getting a collections call from Seattle University if anything happens to them."

"It won't," he answered. "I'd know."

Again, not exactly a comforting answer, but I kept my mouth shut this time. For now, there were bigger fish to fry, and it wouldn't be smart to risk alienating him literally minutes before gaining access to potentially valuable intel. *Business before pleasure, V. Always.*

"Where is this place, anyway?" I asked as we set off down the lamplit road.

"I'm escorting you there so I don't need to tell you," he replied, quirking his lips into a wry smirk.

"Are you going to blindfold me?" The question came out before I really had a chance to assess how it sounded, and realized quickly how easily it could be misconstrued.

His smile widened. "Would you like that?"

I kicked myself. Why did I always lose the ability to think first, *then* speak around him? It was like most of my sense periodically went out the damn window whenever he looked in my general direction. "Very funny," I said now, rolling my eyes. "I'm just asking because I know you like to keep your secrets, that's all."

"Of all the secrets I possess, I think I can spare you one." He reached back and took my hand in his. "Come on. Time won't wait, and the clan doesn't like to either."

Looking back on it, I wasn't able to determine whether he'd cast some kind of spell as soon as he touched me or not. But the entire rest of the journey there was a blur, despite the fact that he had just implied he wasn't keeping secrets from me. As he led me up a lightless path flanked with the densest trees I'd ever seen, I found myself wondering where the hell we actually were.

The forest floor was carpeted thickly with fallen needles that cushioned our steps nearly into soundlessness. I could barely see a foot in front of my face. All I sensed for sure was Orion's hand still holding mine, leading me forward. I had no choice at this point but to trust him completely.

Was that his plan all along? Too late, I realized just how vulnerable he'd made me.

Then the darkness began to give way to a soft, ethereal glow. Started by the sudden illumination, I paused for a second, inadvertently tugging on Orion's hand. He turned back to me, his eyes incandescent in the shadows.

"We're almost there," he said. "There's no backing out anymore." The deep hush of the forest seemed to amplify his words.

I nodded. He led me forward again.

By the time we reached the mouth of the clearing, the light was almost as bright as day. Torches with strange blue flames blazed along the perimeter, casting everything in an eerie, icy glow. One end of the crescent-shaped space held a raised stone platform adorned with what looked like an altar and a tablet inscribed with runes.

In front of the platform, Orion's clan assembled, bathed in the blue torchlight. The way they stared with the same metallic eyes as he had was very cultlike, but I understood at once why he'd instructed me to wear tight, irreverent clothes. Beneath their dark cloaks, the vampires themselves weren't very clothed at all.

For a moment, my thoroughly human brain thought, *Aren't they cold?* Then I remembered, of course they weren't. Because they were all technically dead. And that was what made it all sink in. I took a deep, steadying breath. Orion was right. I had officially reached the point of no return.

He gave me a moment to take everything in, then brought me to a spot a little ways away from the others, which seemed to have been specially prepared for me. I could feel the weight of their eyes boring into me. Nobody said a word, not even a murmur of curiosity.

"Face forward," Orion whispered. "Wait for me to call you." He held my chin in his fingers just long enough to stare into my face himself, and then he turned and approached the platform.

The clearing was absolutely silent. No one coughed—because no one breathed. The only sound was of Orion climbing the steps carved into the side of the platform. He stood there for a moment, surveying his throng of devotees. It was obvious that this was where he was most in his element. The center of attention, being revered by a crowd. Typical vamp shit.

"Brothers and sisters." The note of total authority in his voice made me tingle in a way I both loved and despised. My weak spot for men in power was never more evident anywhere than it was with Orion. "Tonight, I want to make an introduction," he continued. "There is, as promised, someone new among us."

I raised an eyebrow. He'd told them about me already?

He glanced at me. "Her mortal name is inadmissible within our ranks. Henceforth, she will be known only as V."

I kept my poker face flat, but a sudden flood of apprehension welled in my gut. In the interest of not making him suspicious, I'd refrained from peppering Orion with too many questions, and I was beginning to think of that as a tactical error. He was using language that sounded as though we were about to enter into a long-term arrangement.

I had not agreed to anything like that. As much as I could learn by being immersed in the inner sanctum of vamp culture, I knew the longer I stuck around, the more dangerous things could get. Eventually, something would have to give. The fact that he was ready to throw me into the deep end kind of pissed me off.

But then he was beckoning me to come forward. "Step up, V. Let them see your face."

Silently swearing some form of vengeance, I did as I was told. There were too many of them for me to even think about raising a stink. Orion had effectively backed me into a goddamn corner—and I'd let him! Definitely not my finest moment.

He motioned for me to join him on the platform, where he placed his hand in the bare small of my back and pivoted me to face the clan. That was when I noticed just how large the clearing was, and how the clan's membership didn't fill it. My stomach sank even further. Was the decline in population all casualties from the recent turf wars?

Or was the mysterious Anchorage killer picking vampires off too?

Orion was speaking again, but I didn't hear him over the racing maelstrom of my thoughts. I was too busy trying to recall the details of every crime scene I'd been to since the Seattle contingent retreated. Some of them had been bloody for sure, the snow and ice all splashed dark crimson. But others—

Orion's hand slid around to my hip. His grip tightened. Inhaling sharply, I straightened my posture, gazing straight ahead. If he had asked me a question or expected me to say something, I had no idea what was going to come out of my mouth. All of those hypnotic eyes were trained on me. Yeah, it sure looked like everyone wanted me to talk. I opened my mouth.

In the next instant, I thought the earth had broken open, so loud was the boom reverberating through the clearing. Orion snapped to attention. Another huge crash shook the ground. The vampires began to scatter.

"Get down!" Orion leapt in front of me, shielding everything, including my view, with his body. But he wasn't fast enough to keep me from seeing the giant tree at the back of the grove that had abruptly been reduced to little more than a towering, jagged stump. And in the space where it used to be, a wild, ethereal creature loomed way up into the shadows.

With one long arm, it reached forward and snatched up a fleeing vamp in its taloned fingers. I forced my way around Orion just in time to see that vampire lose his head to jaws made of bleached white bone. The black antlers protruding from either side of the bare skull ended in brutal points.

"What the hell is that thing?" I whispered, awestruck.

Orion grimaced. "Soon," he growled, "it will be dead."

13

SETH

I had made the room with the cluster of mirrors into my unofficial home away from home. The cold still dug its claws into my bones if I stayed too still for too long, but for some reason, as long as I hung out near the mirrors, the other creatures in the Underworld didn't want to bother with me. I could still see them hanging out in the darkness, waiting for me to come out and play.

I did keep an eye on Orion and angel boy through my mirrors. It wasn't them I wanted to see as much as the sexy slayer. I could tell Orion was being surly with her, trying to keep her all to himself, so it gratified me to look in one day and see her and Logan going at it hard while Orion was out of the house.

She might have seen me then, but I didn't really care. If I ever found a way to return, my number one goal was to get her on her back again anyway. From my vantage point in the room full of mirrors, it sure looked like she could use a stress reliever. I'd watched her visit body scene after body scene and struggle to put the murder pieces together.

It was during times like these that her newness and inexperience really showed. She was younger than all of us by generations; the girl had a lot of ground to make up for. And Orion's constant hovering didn't help her do it. Whenever I happened to catch them together, I willed Veronica to haul off and punch him in the face—or the dick. On more than one occasion, she'd looked like she was thinking about it.

I paced around the chamber, trying to get the blood pumping through my veins again. Too much time in the cold made it all feel like mud in there. Everything got sluggish and weird, like I was trapped in an underwater swamp. As I moved, I kept my eye on the mirrors. Veronica and Orion had been active for a while. I'd appreciated her skimpy, racy little outfit until I realized it was all for him.

"Greedy bastard," I muttered to no one. Who the fuck did he think he was, keeping her all to himself? In my opinion, she'd been enjoying herself way more when it was Logan on top of, behind, and underneath her. Obviously Orion wasn't the only one who had carnal needs demanding to be met.

But he was the one dragging her through the forest on some bull-shit vampire vision quest. I'd stopped watching as soon as they reached the meeting grounds in the grove. That was a place I knew, and not one I remembered fondly. His fucking race had hated me from day one.

My gaze was somewhere else at the exact moment the shit hit the fan—but I still heard and felt the impact of that tree getting snapped in half like a twig. The scene that immediately followed, of vampires scurrying like roaches under a bright light, gave me an almost visceral satisfaction that was undercut by furious jealousy.

I wanted to be the one turning and fighting that ugly thing, swinging from its antlers as I snapped its neck and lit a literal fire in its skull. Just watching it tear into Orion's precious sycophants made my blood boil with violent glee. He had already sustained considerable losses following the invasion from the south. Part of me hoped this attack would be the last straw, that he and his cult would break and fall apart under the onslaught. I'd be out of a job then, but what did it matter? He'd be too weak to keep me from running amok.

The grin started to slip off my face as the ocean of vamps continued to part and scatter. None of them seemed to be any match for whatever hellspawn had been visited upon them. They fell like paper dolls at its brutally clawed hands. I watched the borrowed life drain from their eyes. More than one head rolled across the clearing after an unceremonious removal from its body.

"Hey!" The shout startled me. Mirroring my reaction, the creature whipped around, searching for the source of the sound. I saw her before it did; her pink cotton-candy hair whirled by. She had a long, thin weapon in her hand, slicing through the air. She brandished it fiercely. Not an ounce of fear showed in her eyes. "Over here, ugly," she called.

The creature moved to focus on her. It bounded forward, its stride long and loping. A gust of wind blew Veronica's mane of curls across her face, but she didn't flinch. The point of her staff stayed aiming true at her target.

"Veronica!"

I recognized Orion's voice, slightly unhinged from panic and rage. He showed up at the edge of the creature's field of vision, and for a second, I couldn't comprehend his physical form. He had gone full vamp: eyes blazing, fangs jutting from his mouth, bloodless veins raised on his skin. Looking at him, I thought I kind of preferred him that way. He was more authentic, more intimidating. This version of him helped me understand how he'd gotten to be clanmaster.

Veronica, however, was completely unfazed. "Shut up, Orion!" she shot back. "Do you want to get out of here or not?" Her eyes, clearly annoyed, darted to the side. "Either help me take this thing down or get out of the way!"

I had never wanted her more.

Provoked by all the shouting, the creature took a heavy swing at Veronica. She dodged nimbly out of the way, using her staff to deflect the blow. I could see that it was sharpened on one end, almost like an oversized needle. Then the design finally clicked in my head. She was wielding a massive silver stake.

Did Orion have a death wish, or what? No wonder he was so obsessed with her. She walked around with the very thing that could ruin him. Maybe that was what he really wanted to control. As I tracked her leaps and flips around the clearing, I smirked. No matter the size of his engorged ego, he couldn't control *that* if his un-life depended on it.

It was a small consolation that I didn't have to see him for most of the fight. Veronica moved with the grace and strength of a tiger, occasionally darting in like a bullfighter to bleed her quarry. She was lightning-fast, and she had an uncanny clairvoyance toward the creature's next move. Everything it did appeared to be half a second too late.

Only once did Veronica get caught moving too slow, and it cost her a thick lock of her hair. She saw it lying on the ground as she came up from her duck, and her face darkened like an oncoming storm. The next time the creature had the audacity to reach for her, she flourished her staff. One of the bony, pointed fingers fell limply to the dirt.

The creature howled, recoiling. I saw a dark, wine-colored water sprout erupt into existence, joining the rest of the splattered blood. All the thrashing that ensued in the aftermath of an impromptu amputation meant I only caught glimpses of her cocking her arm back, aiming with the point of her staff.

Then the creature's viewpoint was pulled and pinned to the night sky—no doubt held there by Orion. I heard the singing of the staff as it cut through the air. The image in the mirror shook. It grew fuzzy around the edges. I thought she had this thing in the bag.

I was wrong.

The surface of the mirror flashed a sudden, blinding white, so bright I had to look away. A piercing roar ripped through the cavern. When I was able to see again, I caught sight of Orion being wrenched from the behemoth's back, crushed in its grasp. The pressure made his eyes widen and turned his skin grayer than usual. In the background, Veronica was screaming.

There was a sickening crack. Orion went too limp too fast. He was tossed aside, out of view. The sound of his body landing made the hair stand up on the back of my neck. Under other circumstances, I might have enjoyed the moment. But if he had just gotten his ass kicked, then Veronica was likely alone. Orion's underlings had already proven their cowardice.

It advanced on her. She was standing, but a patch of dark blood had bloomed on the front of her clothes; whose blood that was, I didn't know. This time, her gaze did not stay steady; she kept trying to steal glances at Orion. Probably thought he was dead as a doornail, like the others. I couldn't really blame her, but I hated that her focus was split. That was a recipe for disaster.

Unless I found a way to help. I turned to Logan's mirror. The glass was dark, inert. Impatient, I knocked hard on the surface, generating silver ripples. An image began to form, but it wasn't clear enough. I could only see him, not where he was or what he was doing.

"Logan!" Again, I knocked on the glass. "Hey, asshole! Can you hear me?" No response. I tried again. "I'm sorry I called you an asshole just now. Orion just got his shit rocked, and Veronica's in trouble. You gotta go help her out!"

He looked up, and I felt a rush of excited adrenaline. But it was something else that caught his eye. I might as well have been shouting at a brick wall.

"Logan, she's gonna die!" I pounded the icy walls with my fist. The mirrors swayed precariously. One mirror over, Veronica parried the creature's strike. But she was getting tired—sooner or later, she'd falter. Normally, I delighted in scenarios of brutality, but I didn't want to think about what would happen to her.

"Logan! You fucking—" I let out a growl of pure frustration. It wasn't working even a little bit. Wherever I'd been locked up, it wasn't the place he could see all the time. "Of course not," I muttered. "Why would it be that fucking easy?"

Stepping back from the wall, I tried to collect myself. The mirrors mocked me. Orion's was pitch black, completely unmoving. Veronica narrowly landed her next block. Her back foot slid on the ground, and I held my breath, waiting to see if she'd fall. Her face contorted from exertion, she managed to force her adversary back.

But it took her too long to get back into fighting position. Her adrenaline high was beginning to wear off. She was exhausted.

My hands balled up into fists so tight the nails drew blood from my palms. Then, suddenly, my field of view swung completely around, past Orion's crumpled body. Someone brand new had come barreling into the clearing. He charged, raising a gleaming, mean-looking blade.

The blue light glinted off its sharpest edge as it came arcing down.

14

LOGAN

I raced above the tree line, face numbed by the cruel edge of the wind. The agitated chatter of spirits rang in my ears. Minutes ago, they had started to become even more restless than usual, like wild animals before a storm. But I didn't need them to tell me when the impact hit—because Orion and Veronica had both been caught in it. A sour sense of duty propelled me on toward Orion's location.

For Veronica, however, the feeling was much closer to real fear. She was strong, fast, more than capable. But I cared about her so…differently.

As soon as I homed in on the chaotic cluster of energy surrounding her, I knew exactly where they were. Winging my way over the dark mass of the forest, I wondered what Orion's motivation for bringing her to the clearing really was. In all the time I had known him, he'd never opened the clan's meeting grounds to anyone else. Veronica seemed to always be the exception.

But my train of thought was interrupted upon arriving at the grove. From the air, I could see what looked like bodies strewn across the dirt. The massive, broken trunk of a destroyed tree carved a trench where it lay, and in its shadow, two figures squared off. One was a towering monster with claws for fingers and a bare skull for a head, two branching antlers protruding from the bone. The hollows of its eyes glowed with a pale, baleful light.

The other was a human man wielding a long, sharp sword. He had a body slung over his shoulder. Veronica's face was out of sight, but I recognized her hair instantly. One of her arms hung limply over the man's shoulder, but she was still alive—even in the midst of all the white noise, I picked out the faint hum of her energy. The human was saving her from the monster.

The skull-headed monster swayed on its massive hind feet. It was bleeding profusely from a deep wound slashed across the front of its gaunt torso, presumably by the sword in the human's hand. Great drops of black blood splashed onto the forest floor beneath it. The creature's movements were hesitant, unsure. Then the man glanced to the side. The creature lunged as soon as he looked away.

The man's sword jabbed forward, a quick lance of moonlight. I heard the crack of the monster's ribs as clear as a gunshot on a silent night, followed by a hoarse howl of anguish. It recoiled, clutching at the new gash as yet more blood flooded through its fingers.

The man slipped into the trees so quickly and quietly that I might have missed his exit if I hadn't been watching him already. He took both his weapon and Veronica with him, and in little more than a second, he had passed out of sight. I darted after them to the edge of the woods to where they were no longer in sight. Briefly, I could still hear him moving through the foliage, but soon, even that trace of him had faded away.

Just as I was about to abandon the grove that was now a vampire graveyard in favor of tracking Veronica's captor back to wherever he was taking her, I noticed Orion lying motionless in the dirt like so many of his clan members. Like Veronica, however, I felt his energy fighting to stay stable. He was severely injured.

"Shit," I muttered. Although my desire to pursue Veronica hadn't lessened, I understood the man who took her would care for her injuries, and seeing as he protected her, I guessed he was a friend and not enemy an her. I also understood implicitly where my duty lay. She'd been my lover once, my confidante a couple times as well. But he was master of the Anchorage clan, and I'd sworn to help him long before I ever knew Veronica existed.

At the moment, it looked for all the world like Orion was about to die—if he hadn't already. I grimaced and set the angle of my wings into a sharp dive. The grotesque, bleeding, hulking creature pivoted sluggishly in my direction. It ducked as I skimmed low over its head, barely avoiding the jagged points of its antlers.

Maybe that had been a little too close. One wrong pass could ground me for good. Nonetheless, I banked around in a tight curve and dove again. Up close, my target appeared to be in varying states of decay. White bone showed through strings of sinew and the patchy remains of a pelt. When it dodged, the creature wobbled dangerously.

I didn't want it to fall; I wanted it to leave. The last thing I needed was to deal with two potential corpses instead of one. "Come on," I whispered under my breath. "Get out of here."

On the third pass, it tried to swat me out of the air. Rolling nimbly out of the way, I watched the creature teeter nimbly on the very margins of its balance. The ground below was soaked in blood. I sensed the creature weakening little by little. But finally, the self-preservation instinct kicked in. With one last glare from its empty eye sockets, it limped off in the opposite direction of Veronica and the stranger.

I landed next to Orion's body. He was splayed out on his side; as I turned him over, I saw that he had turned an alarming shade of gray. This, I knew, was bad even for him. A vampire couldn't survive dying twice, no matter who he was.

And it certainly looked like Orion was headed that way. His eyes had rolled back in his head, irises barely visible. I propped him up on my lap, supporting his head as it lolled to the side. He would've been furious to know anyone saw him in such condition.

"Hey." I passed my hand in front of his face and shook him gently. "Anyone in there?" No response. "C'mon, Orion. Time to switch the lights on." With the flat of my hand, I slapped him lightly. Just enough to give him a jumpstart.

Probably the only time I'll ever get away with that, I thought, smirking wryly to myself. But he still lay absolutely motionless in my lap. His shirt and jeans were torn, perhaps by antlers, but I found no obvious wounds—and of course, there was no blood. Had he died of internal trauma already? Was that even possible?

"I thought you guys were supposed to be invincible," I muttered. "Or at least immortal."

He didn't answer. I laid my palm on his chest, took a deep breath, and closed my eyes. If there was nothing to be seen but a void, then we were in real trouble. But somewhere, far down in the depths of swirling shadows that threatened to eclipse him entirely, I saw a little spark of something.

I had been almost too late—but not quite. A river of energy flooded the darkness in which Orion's spirit floundered, bolstering its light and bringing it back from the edge of extinguishing. In a moment, that spark had blossomed into a flame, small but steady.

I opened my eyes, and so did he. He stared at me, briefly unseeing.

"Hello," I said. "You're welcome."

The vampire sat bolt upright. His gaze, suddenly frantic, swept around the ruined grove. The corpses of his clan didn't seem to register in his mind. I knew what he was going to say before the words left his mouth.

"Veronica," he growled. "Where is she?"

I braced for all hell to break loose. "Not here. She was taken."

Orion's eyes blazed with a fury that might have scared me if I believed he could stand under his own power. "The beast!" he bellowed. "That fucking devil. I'll tear it apart with my bare hands." He made an attempt to leap to his feet, which nearly ended with him flat in the dirt again.

"I don't think that's a good idea right now," I said calmly, holding him up.

He glowered. "Don't forget your place, angel."

"I haven't. That's why I saved your life." Slowly, I helped Orion stand. "And it wasn't the beast who took her. It was someone else. A man."

The vampire's face tightened into a rigid mask of rage. He ground his teeth, and I wondered if he was going to attack me just to have some way to vent the emotion swirling within. I didn't fear him in his current state; far from it. He was weak for the first time since I'd met him.

But he didn't know that, or else he wouldn't hear it.

"Let me go, Logan." The demand left his lips in a snarl. "I will not be disrespected in this way." He turned on me. "Did you recognize his face? Tell me the truth!" The unasked question hung between us, silent and yet perfectly understood: *Was it Seth?*

"I didn't know him." The only concession I made was to let go of the arm Orion kept trying to wrench from my grasp. "He was human, I think." The man's face floated vaguely in my mind's eye. I'd been too focused on other things to commit his features to solid memory. What I recalled the most was dark blond hair and broad shoulders. And strength, if the ease with which he lifted Veronica was any indication.

In other words, he was likely to be yet another rival in Orion's eyes. It was exhausting just to consider the possibility, and a glance at the vampire's expression all but confirmed it. If rage could have powered him on its own, he'd have taken off into the forest long ago.

"Where did she go?" he barked. "They can't have gone far." He lurched toward the trees. I let him go until one of his knees threatened to buckle under his weight, and then I followed reluctantly.

"I don't know," I said, keeping my voice calm and level. The urge to knock him out again rose with every outburst, but I held it in. Whatever was left of the clan would be lost completely if their leader fell. Did I care about that myself? I wasn't sure.

But deep down, I knew that Veronica might. And I still fully intended to track her down and get her back. For Orion, maybe, but at the very least, for myself.

"You don't know anything." Orion staggered. He fell forward, hard, into the churned-up earth. His fingers clenched around the soil. "Don't touch me. I'm fine."

He was obviously not fine. We both saw it. I knelt down at his side and gradually pulled him upright, slinging his arm around my shoulders.

"Let's go back to the house for now." Without giving him time to answer, I began walking toward the pathway out of the grove. It was clear that the eerie, necromantic magic that usually preserved him wasn't working at the moment. The best solution I could think of was to put him back in his tomb.

"I should be healing," he muttered. "Why isn't it working?" A note of panic stood out beneath the smoldering anger in his voice. That, I could understand; it'd probably been a few centuries since he'd felt what it was like to crawl closer and closer to death.

"You got your ass kicked," I told him. "That's why. Give it time."

Orion bristled. "We don't have time! Veronica—"

I cut him off. "If you don't shut the fuck up and let me get you back to the house, you are as good as dead. Won't be able to find her then, will you?"

He seethed into the silence but didn't say anything more.

15

VERONICA

$\mathcal{I}$ woke up to a foggy head, a body full of aches and pains, and a strangely familiar ceiling. The room spun when I tried to sit up, so that didn't last long. Reclining back against the pillows, I stifled a groan and tried my best not to puke.

"Are you positive?" Lian's voice, tense and questioning, filtered through the wall. I furrowed my brow and homed in on her words, wondering who she was talking to. Didn't take long for the answer to come.

"Yes, babe. I know what a wendigo looks like. I've seen them before." There was a pause. "Never here, though."

My eyes shot open immediately. A knot of anxiety twisted itself into my stomach. Even just the sound of Trent made me inexplicably nervous. Maybe it was because I couldn't even think of him without going back to the dark, rain-slick night on the streets of Seattle where it all began.

"What is he doing here?" I whispered. Then I remembered how Lian had never stopped being in love with him, and how she'd told me she was going to call him if I didn't get my shit together. And here I was, still a passenger on the hot mess express. I really had no right to be surprised.

Not about him, at least. The wendigo, though—that was a different story. After a few solid years in the field as a professional slayer, it was one of the few supernaturals I had never seen in person. Pictures, yes. Grisly, gruesome pictures. In hindsight, I kicked myself for not thinking of it sooner. But Trent was right; I'd never heard of a wendigo showing up in Alaska.

Why now?

"Look," Trent said, "believe it or not, the wendigo isn't the important thing right now. I'll take care of it. We need to know why she was there in the first place."

"You said the vamps were dead, right? Maybe she killed them." Lian was not convinced, but she was trying her best to give me the benefit of the doubt, yet again. I chewed my lip and wondered if there was any way on earth I could have been a worse friend to her.

"No. You saw how she was dressed." Trent scoffed. "Not exactly a work uniform."

"Unless she was trying to blend in," Lian retorted. The tension between them was palpable, even from the other side of the wall.

"I doubt it," he muttered.

Uncomfortable for a whole host of reasons, I shifted in the bed. The box spring let out a piercing squeak. I froze.

Apparently Trent and Lian did the same, because then he said, "Well, why don't you go ask her?"

I let out my breath. "Shit." Trent was pissed, and they probably both had a lot of questions I didn't really want to answer. The web of deception had been spun so intricately at this point that I wasn't even sure if I had a reasonable way out right now. Maybe I just had to live with it until I found what I was looking for.

Which is what, V? The holy trinity of supernatural dick? A forbidden orgy?

The door opened. Lian crept in. She saw me lying there with my eyes open and came quickly to the bedside. "Hey, V." Gently, she brushed a piece of hair out of my face. "How are you feeling? Welcome back to the land of the living."

I gave her a little smile and slowly sat myself up. "What are you talking about? I was totally fine." This time at least, the room didn't spin like a theme park ride.

She frowned. "You absolutely were not. Trent brought you in, and I thought you'd gotten yourself killed."

"Not quite." I chuckled wryly. "I don't think so, anyway." The memories were still a blur. I realized I had no idea how long I'd been out. "I'm surprised Trent didn't follow you in here. Figured he'd want to tear me a new one."

Lian sighed. "He does." She reached over and picked up my hand. "Veronica, I *need* you to level with me now, okay? I feel like you don't fully understand how deep in the shit you are. Trent told me about what he saw in the forest. About the vampires."

I gasped. The color drained out of my face as my memory finally kicked into high gear. It took all my willpower not to panic-shout Orion's name. The last time I saw him, he had just been tossed like a fucking rag doll. "The...the vampires?" I repeated, stunned into near-speechlessness.

Lian nodded solemnly. She squeezed my hand. "What the hell happened, V? Do you remember?"

"I..." I stared down at my lap. Inside, my mind was racing. *Is he dead now? Did Trent kill him?* My most pressing question I couldn't ask. "I guess you called him after all."

"Because you gave me no choice. I can't have you keeping secrets, V. Not when I'm the one who brought you up here. I thought we'd be doing this together, and lately I feel like you're trying to pull away." She shrugged. "It could be a slayer thing I don't understand. Trent does it too. So really, I need both of you to cut it out, please."

The guilt came back with a vengeance. "Sorry." I glanced away. "It's just...when I'm up to my neck in this bullshit, it's easy to convince myself we're all better off with me going it alone."

"Except you're not," she replied. "That's the whole point." She wrapped her other hand around mine. "And if it makes you feel better, that's not the *only* reason I asked Trent to come back."

"It's not?" Surprised, I looked up.

"My dad lost a lot of crewmen when the shifter tribe decided to bail. Business is way down." She shrugged slightly. "Trent pays me on the side to do desk work for his jobs. Research, navigation, whatever. I'm using the extra money to help with the boats."

"Fuck." I rubbed my eyes. "I forgot about that. I'm sorry, Li. This is all so fucked up."

"Yeah." She was quiet for a minute. "Which is why you have to tell me what was going on in the forest. Literally the last thing I expected was for Trent to come back with you slung over his shoulder like that. Scared me half to death."

I should have come clean right then, as she sat on the side of the bed in the guest room with me. That was my chance to lay everything on the table and own up to all the trouble I'd gotten in. Trent wasn't even there, though I had no doubt he could hear me if he wanted to, just like I was able to hear him. It was just me and her, like old times.

But for some reason, I couldn't force myself to open up. Not even after she asked me to as directly as she knew how. It made me feel like shit, and yet, I couldn't change the words that came out of my mouth.

"I don't recall anything beyond the wendigo crashing the party." That much was the truth. It also didn't answer her question.

"But what *happened*, Veronica? What were you doing there?" Her face had grown deadly serious. "You can't tell me there wasn't a real good reason and expect me to believe it."

"I was gathering intel." I spoke as casually as possible, as if I hadn't been hauled to safety by my best friend's boyfriend like a magical sack of potatoes. "Things got out of hand."

"Okay, but how did you get in? Who invited you?" The pressure was on. I felt her maneuvering me into a corner so that she could press me for as much information as I would give up. I looked at her hands, still holding on to mine, and wondered if Trent had coached her before she walked in.

"Listen, I get that you don't want me leaving you out of the loop, and I'm sorry it's kind of been that way lately. But I can't just tell you everything I know. Some of this stuff could put a target on your back, Li. Ask Trent if you need to hear it from him. He understands even better than I do."

She examined me searchingly. "I don't blame you, V. And I think some of what you're saying is the truth. But I also kind of think you're full of shit right now, and I don't get why." She paused. "This is why Trent came to Anchorage."

"I'm glad he did," I answered. "Honestly. I have zero practical experience with wendigos."

She was trying so hard not to roll her eyes into next week. "All right, all right, fine. Do you want to talk to him about it?"

"Only if you make him promise not to bite my head off." I wanted the knowledge Trent had, but not the lectures or suspicion that were sure to come with it. He wasn't wrong, per se, but he didn't need to know that.

"He won't," she said. "I made him swear he wouldn't play hardball—at least not right away."

I smirked. "I appreciate the effort."

Lian got up and went to the door, opened it, and stuck her head out. She said his name, and a moment later, Trent stepped into the bedroom. He and I stared at each other for a couple minutes that might as well have been days.

"Hey, Veronica." When he finally spoke, his tone was more subdued than I expected. "How are you feeling?"

"Uh…I'm okay." I shot Lian a glance that was half confused, half impressed. Trent had always been a little wild, a little unpredictable. Maybe she'd managed to tame him somehow. Or maybe life had done the heavy lifting for her in that regard. "Thanks for getting me out of there."

"Don't mention it." He sat down in a chair across from the foot of the bed. His eyes were exactly the shade of clear sea-green I remembered, but they were haunted now by ghosts of the past. The same ghosts who haunted me.

The quiet returned and soon became crushing. I was the one who broke first. "So…" A lame start, but one of us had to say something, or else the air would just keep slowly draining from the room.

Trent half smiled. "Been a long time, hasn't it?" he said.

16

ORION

I had no thoughts in my head that didn't concern Veronica. Where perhaps there ought to have been gratitude toward Logan for pulling me back from the edge of oblivion, I was filled with hatred for the one who had swooped in and stolen her away.

He was an outsider. He had to be. Not a soul in Anchorage, living or dead, would have shown me such blatant disrespect. And when I found this mysterious man, I'd make sure that taking Veronica was the last mistake he'd ever make.

"You didn't see his face?" I demanded yet again. Even I had long ago lost track of how many times that question had leapt off my tongue, but I couldn't let it go. My very sanity depended on unlocking the secret of the man's identity so that I could recover Veronica—and exact vengeance. "Think!"

Logan shook his head. "I saw very little," he said flatly. "As I've told you, my concerns were focused elsewhere at the time." At any other time, it would have been abundantly clear that his patience was being stretched thin. But I didn't care. I wasn't able to. Until Veronica was found, nothing else in the entire universe mattered as much as her whereabouts.

"How could he touch her?" Unable to stay still, I stormed around the first floor of the house, where Logan had forced me to stay. Anything that wasn't nailed down had been thrown or upended—broken objects littered the floor. The chairs in the dining room lay in a heap, and I snatched one of the legs as I went by, striking it against my palm. "Does he have any idea what he's done?"

"I doubt it very much." Logan's tone remained icy, detached. He stared at me with a bored expression, though his eyes tracked my movement closely. "But we both know Anchorage is full of people who can handle themselves in…unique situations."

I whipped around to glower at him. "What are you saying? That this was planned? That I've been tricked?" The very notion of a plot coming to fruition without my knowledge stoked the fire of my anger to a fever pitch. The humiliation of being outfoxed—by a human, no less—was a handful of salt in a fresh, raw wound.

The fallen angel sighed. He displayed no fear, only mild annoyance. "He could have had help." He paused. "Maybe from her."

The blow of his words left me stunned for a moment. I understood as well as anyone that Veronica and I had no formal contract, no relationship beyond the mutual attraction that kept drawing us together. Indeed, she'd made her stance clear just recently, hadn't she? We were free agents, as far as she was concerned, two bodies often passing in rapid orbit.

But my desire for her led me to make certain assumptions. Most prominently that she was mine, and it was simply a matter of time before I could make our bond official. Now, those plans had been tossed into jeopardy by this infernal interloper.

"I have to turn her," I muttered. The thought was so automatic and unconscious that I didn't realize it had escaped my lips until I noticed Logan looking at me. Immediately, I was on the defensive. "Not a fucking word. I can't risk losing her."

He was silent, for a while. Just long enough to make me think perhaps he hadn't heard me, or hadn't heard correctly.

Then he said, "You won't be able to do that. Not in the way you think."

It was the kind of insubordination I might have expected from Seth, but never Logan. The conviction in his voice, so cold and calm, was deeply unnerving. He made no move to explain further, and I found myself not wanting to ask. Maybe this was just another personal oddity, of which he had many.

That resolve lasted less than a minute. "What do you mean?" I snapped. I was in no mood for his typically enigmatic phrases. My body had barely begun to heal from the injuries I'd sustained in the encounter at the grove; I was impatient and on edge. Logan had picked the worst time to voice dissent I didn't want to hear anyway.

Still, something told me to bite my tongue, which I did with great effort. He took his sweet time formulating an answer.

At long last, he said, "It won't work."

And that terse, three-word response was the breaking point for me. My temper, already fraught with cracks like a flawed pane of glass, shattered into a thousand vicious shards. I wheeled and leapt at him, fangs suddenly bared.

"I have had *enough* of this bullshit!" I expected to land on top of him, seize him by the shirt. Instead, he outmaneuvered my dull reflexes, and I struck the chair where he'd been sitting as it toppled over. The edge of the seat slammed into my stomach.

From somewhere above me, Logan said, "With all due respect, you're not in any position to say so." He stepped up alongside me and hauled me to my feet. "Look, Orion. If you really want to fight about this, let's fight. But I'm just trying to warn you that what you want for Veronica isn't possible."

I didn't give him a proper answer; I just punched him in the face. It was not a strong punch, and Logan seemed to shrug it off immediately. The burst of exertion caused my surroundings to sway and shimmer. I felt my eyes threatening to roll back in my head. Why wasn't my fucking body cooperating? I hadn't lived for centuries to lose a skirmish against one of my own henchmen.

"Fuck off," I told him unconvincingly. "It was a mistake to think I needed either of you. Wherever Seth is, I hope you end up there too."

I might as well have been insulting a brick wall. Logan pulled back and returned the hit I doled out—except his was undiluted by weakness. My head rocked backward. I heard something crack. A tooth, perhaps, or maybe my neck. The as-yet-unheeded whisper of common sense in the back of my mind told me I was being uncharacteristically foolish, that he could kill me while the scales were so unbalanced.

Part of me wished he would. For the first time in ages, I was useless, incapacitated by unforeseen limits. And my rage was beginning to give way to a frightening level of despair. How had I come to rely on Veronica so heavily? Long ago, I swore it would never happen again, and yet here I was, locked in a grapple with a fallen angel, half on the floor of the house we shared.

Seen from the outside, the image must have been surreal. Logan had his hand on my throat, his grip solid as steel. His wings had come out when I sprang, and now they cast me in menacing shadow. His eyes, inches from my face, were placid, glacial.

"Take a moment to look around and see where you are," he said quietly. "And act accordingly." His thumb and index finger braced against the corners of my jaw. The heel of his hand pressed gently but firmly into my Adam's apple. It was no more than a warning. But I understood.

"I ought to kill you when this is over," I muttered. "I'd be doing both of us a favor."

"Yes," Logan agreed. "You probably would." He planted his knee down on my chest and let go of my face. "You're being naïve about Veronica, despite the years you've spent among mortals. She's more complex than you give her credit for."

"And you know this, how?" The storm of fury died down as quickly as it arrived. More disgruntled by the ease of my defeat than anything, I pulled the chair out from underneath my back and lay flat on the floor. Logan did not move. I supposed I couldn't blame him. Were I at full strength, he'd be a pile of sinew and bloody feathers.

"Her spirit is unique." He stared off into space as he talked about her. "Don't you feel it?"

"Of course I do." I tried not to sulk. It stung to know I wasn't the only one who thought Veronica special.

Logan nodded. "That's why you're obsessed."

I didn't bother denying it. "Whatever game we're playing, I'm going to win it. Veronica will join the clan." Formerly, my word was law, among clan members and other associates alike.

This time, Logan looked at me. "What clan?" he asked wryly.

I glared. "You've already won. For now."

He was quiet. After a few moments, he got up and backed away, keeping his gaze pinned on me. "Don't do anything stupid, Orion. We've just proven you're in no shape to pursue her, and contrary to popular belief, my goodwill isn't infinite."

"Yeah, yeah." I lay on my back and let my eyes drift closed. Rest was the last thing I wanted, but my battered body begged to differ. Pain had become almost a foreign sensation, but I savored it the same as pleasure. If only its presence didn't indicate that the magic I relied on for so long had nearly failed.

"Logan."

"Yes." His tone implied heavily that he wished I hadn't spoken. The single syllable was frosted with irritation.

"Thank you for bringing me back. You didn't have to."

He hesitated. "Yes, I did. You're lucky for it. And you are welcome."

With that, the choppy waters between us seemed to settle. Eventually, I sensed his eye drawn away, lured by boredom or perhaps by some ethereal thing I couldn't see. He hadn't left his post, but the bulk of his attention had wandered. I took a deep breath, opened my mind's eye, and began the search for Veronica.

Logan may have won the physical fight, but there was nothing across any plane that could keep her away from me. Veronica was mine, and she'd been stolen without honor.

I refused to let her go.

17

LOGAN

*T*hings had very nearly gotten out of hand. I went back over every detail of our little skirmish in my mind as Orion lay where he'd fallen on the hardwood, doing a remarkable imitation of a corpse. He could not, however, mask his now stable aura, the shroud of spirit and energy that flowed around him. Although he was weak, he had clawed his way back from danger. Even if he didn't feel it yet.

But it was still a fine balance to maintain. The fight, small as it was, had nearly wiped his reserves clean out. I would've been lying if I said I didn't think about ending things for good in the seconds he spent under my thumb. So simple to crush his windpipe, or cave in his chest with the point of my knee. What would he have done?

Nothing. He was helpless. I wondered how that felt to such an aged and powerful being, to be reduced to an animated shell of skin and bones. Did it scare him to be reminded of what it was like to be human; to be mortal?

I glanced at the chair he'd pushed away. Any of its four legs could easily be fashioned into an impromptu stake. He must have known how vulnerable he was, lying supine with his eyes closed, outwardly at rest. I imagined piercing his cold, dead heart, impaling him through into the floor.

A smooth, swift motion. Simple. Effortless, even.

Why not?

I looked around, startled. The thought had not come from inside my own head, but from somewhere beyond. The words had not been spoken as much as felt, projected into my consciousness. I called up my spirit sense, probing the glimmering veil between this realm and the next for their source.

Look at the bastard. He's probably half dead as is. You'd be doing him a favor.

"Ah," I murmured under my breath. Now I recognized him. "Where are you?" As I spoke, I kept one eye on Orion, just in case he decided to try and make a move.

I don't know. In a room with a bunch of mirrors. Think I finally figured out how to use 'em. There was a pause. *Well, sort of.*

"Is it cold there?" I asked. Talking out loud was unnecessary, but it helped to anchor me, so that I didn't just drift off in automatic pursuit of Seth's essence. Personally, I yearned to be somewhere, anywhere other than in the house with Orion in his current state. My dutiful obligation to him had faded.

Yeah, it's fuckin' cold here. You goddamned angels and your frigid hellscapes. I don't know how you live with this shit.

"I take it you're not enjoying yourself, then." I smirked. Couldn't help it. I had no visual on him, but even his voice sounded haggard, rougher than usual. A humbling experience for a prince of Hell—if he could be humbled in the first place.

I've been better, he grumbled. Then he said, *There's gotta be a way to cross back over from here. I need you to help me do it.*

"Oh, do you?" Just what I needed: another pushy, arrogant prick with a bad temper. But there was no denying that Orion had gotten himself into dire straits. I could admit that help of some kind would be useful. "What's in it for me?"

I'll help you find the slayer.

I'd expected him to bargain, or to have some kind of snarky retort at the ready. "You know she's gone?"

Saw it happen. The mirrors show me everything. I got a pretty good look at the guy who snatched her up.

I chuckled grimly. "Don't tell that to the leader." Neither of us needed to be told that Orion would lose his shit if he thought he had a chance to identify the man he considered a thief of his prize possession.

I don't plan on it. If he wants her, he'll have to find her himself. He paused. *Tell me how to get the fuck out of here, angel boy. Before I fucking freeze to death.*

"Give me a second to think about it." I leaned back in my seat, mulling over what I'd just learned. The long and short of it seemed to be that Seth was trapped in some layer of the Underworld—farther down, judging by the temperature. How he got there, I didn't know.

But I had spent considerable time in those frigid circles long ago, just after the fall that made me an angel, and I knew there had to be some way out, even for a person like Seth. No doubt he would immediately become a pain in the ass again once he'd returned to the mortal realm. Still, I wanted Veronica back. Preferably with as little involvement from Orion as possible.

"He might kill you if he thinks you're becoming competition," I warned.

The impression of a laugh echoed through the veil. *Who, the vamp? Let him try.*

That was when the connection between us began to waver. As he started to fade back into the ether, I reached out on instinct to try and grab him. At the same time, my anchor in the mortal realm slipped a little. For a moment or two, my concentration slipped, and I straddled the border between realms. The frigid rock walls of the Underworld loomed suddenly in front of me, and then they were gone.

"Shit," I whispered.

What was that? Don't tell me you fell through.

"No." Without opening my eyes, I ran a hand through my hair. "No, I'm fine. This might be a good sign for you, actually."

Yeah? It'd be the first in a while. Lay it on me.

I frowned. A thought had just occurred to me. If the paths were open enough to allow Seth to slip through, he likely wasn't the only one who would be trying. Maybe the monster running rampant in the forest wouldn't be the only one for very long.

"Are you alone?" I asked.

Was starting to think you forgot about me. Yeah, I'm alone...mostly.

I furrowed my brow. "What does that mean? Who else is there?"

No one special. Just some gremlins and angry spirits who want me off their turf. The usual.

"You'll have to take care of them," I told him. "We can't risk you being watched or followed."

At first, I thought he might object. Then I remembered who I was talking to. *No problem. Give me a minute. Two minutes, if they're lucky.* The aura of his presence melted away, and I opened my eyes. The passage of time had been blurred by intense concentration; stepping back into the physical realm came with an adjustment.

Suddenly, everything stopped completely, as if the great internal clock of the universe had just ceased its ticking. The spot where Orion had lain was empty. And there was no sign of him to be found.

I stood up so fast that the chair toppled over. "Damn it." Glancing toward the house's entryway, I saw that he had left the door hanging open, swinging slightly on its hinges. I had one foot on the porch by the time Seth came back to his side of the veil.

What the fuck are you doing now?

"Orion left." I grimaced. "While we were talking."

So what? Maybe he'll die out there. I saw what happened to him and his whole clan.

Of course he still didn't think of us as a team after he got shoved into that place, or probably much of anything outside himself. After taking in a sweeping panoramic view of my surroundings to no avail, I shook my head, gave up, and went back inside. Orion was hardly in the best shape he'd ever been, but if he felt well enough to bail out on his own, I reasoned that my priority had to be finding Veronica. Because I didn't really want him to get to her first.

"All right, listen. I'm assuming you can see things through those mirrors."

Yeah. You, him, the slayer girl, and the thing that kicked their asses.

"Her name is Veronica," I said. "And those are shitty choices, but they'll have to do." That particular arrangement of mirrors meant we only had one realistically viable option. Which, at the very least, streamlined the decision-making process.

I didn't know you cared. Seth sounded genuinely surprised, and perhaps even impressed. I could practically picture him standing on the frozen rock, eyebrow arched, arms crossed.

I shrugged. "Don't we all?"

Yeah. I guess we fuckin' do.

Unwilling to dwell on the subject, I pushed forward. "Anyway, pay attention. Each of the mirrors has a link to the person whose perspective they show, which means they're all linked to this realm. The realm you want to be in."

Uh huh. I think I get where this is going.

"Right now, those connections are stable and secure. But if you were to break one of those mirrors…" I trailed off, inviting him to fill in the blank.

You saying I might be able to bust my way through a broken link?

"Yes." I exhaled a sigh of relief. "The only thing is, breaking that connection won't be good for whoever you choose."

That right? He was quiet for a few seconds too long, clearly considering more options than I had. *Give me one good reason I shouldn't step on Orion's neck on my way in.*

I rolled my eyes. Was it always going to be such a dick-measuring contest with these guys? "Maybe you won't consider this a good reason, but I don't know what would happen to you if he died before you got all the way through. And honestly, I'm not sure he'd make it."

If you're trying to make me feel sorry for him, it's not gonna work.

"I could not care less how you feel about him," I admitted. "Or about him in general, frankly. But Veronica might."

Fuck. I got a very strong sense of Seth face-palming, holding his head in his hands. *Fine. I'll take the monster.*

Another wave of relief surged through me, for an entirely different reason. "Good. Warn me when—"

Predictably, there was no warning at all. The shockwave created by the shattering mirror reverberated across dimensions, briefly graying out the colors in my vision and making the world warp inward. The fabric of the veil, already stretched thin in many places, tore open, letting in a burst of spirit energy that threatened to destabilize the makeshift doorway I'd been straddling between the realms. A sharp pain rocketed through my temples. I gritted my teeth.

But the plan appeared to work. Once the sparks of light and pain stopped dancing behind my eyelids, I stretched out a curious feeler for Seth on the correct side of the veil. I found him exactly where I'd predicted he would land—deep in the forest that housed Orion's secret grove. His energy burned strong, like a flare on a moonless night. He was definitely in the right realm now.

The real question was, what had happened to the monster whose body he'd used as a vessel? Was it dead? And if not, was it angry?

As soon as I finished regathering my wits, I headed out the open door, closing it behind me. The bleak Alaskan landscape rolled out in all directions. I ran forward, unfurling my wings, catching the edge of the brisk, sharp wind. Beneath me, the land fell rapidly away, and I banked around toward the dark tide of woods blanketing the west.

Did I want to go anywhere near the vampire grove? Absolutely not. But I knew I had no choice. No point in helping Seth cross over if I was just going to leave him to die. Most likely, he thought he could handle himself without a problem. Every time I thought about turning back, though, the sight of Orion's crumpled body flashed through my mind, followed closely by the single glimpse I'd gotten of Veronica hanging limply over a stranger's shoulder.

We needed her back—if only because it was starting to seem like we might have finally stumbled in over our heads.

18

VERONICA

I had never felt so uncomfortable in the Zhou family home. It was so weird and wrong to be tense under their roof, considering how much time I'd spent basically living as a second daughter when I would visit as kids. But as I sat awkwardly in the bed, hands clasped in my lap, avoiding Trent's gaze, I just wanted to disappear. I should have known that Lian called her ex to get involved in my shit. Not that I can complain considering how badly crap went down at Orion's vampire meeting, but still. The moment I was dreading had finally arrived.

"Yeah." My voice came out raspy. I cleared my throat. If I could've, I would have paid Trent any amount of money to leave the room and never come back—at least not for the rest of the day. It was nothing against him as a person, really. He'd been my best friend's lover and obsession for years and years, and when they were on, he treated her like a queen. I should've loved him.

But he was too real, sitting less than ten feet away from me. I preferred him when he was traveling, because then it was easier to pretend all of the memories in which he featured prominently never happened, that they were masochistic fantasies in my head. Seeing Trent in any capacity meant confronting the past. Even if he didn't bring it up. He'd been close friends with my ex, Dylan, and had come up to Seattle many times to fight with us, to catch up.

Both of us were great at stewing in heavy silence. It drove Lian insane.

"Listen," he said softly. "I know this is weird. It's weird for me too, I promise." His eyes wandered around the room. I wondered what he was thinking. "I guess it doesn't help that we haven't spoken much since Dylan died."

I winced. As far as I was concerned, things would've been perfectly fine had he never once mentioned that particular elephant in the room. In fact, I'd gone so far as to assume the subject would remain unaddressed. I wasn't emotionally prepared to remember my ex-boyfriend's death, let alone examine it in granular detail.

"Trent…" I had no idea what the hell I was going to say—just that I had to say something, anything, to get him to veer off from where we were headed. "Hey, thanks for saving me back there. You didn't have to." The transition, if you could call it that, was about as smooth and graceful as a burning car rolling down an embankment. I might as well have worn a neon sign that read, DO NOT TALK TO ME ABOUT THIS.

He glanced at me, startled. "What?" Obviously, I had interrupted some invisible train of thought. A planned confrontation, maybe? The irrational paranoia invading my brain insisted that he was about to dredge up some serious mud, lay everything out on the line. We were suddenly a train speeding toward a moment of emotional catharsis. For him, of course. Not me.

I sucked in a breath, trying to disguise the evidence of my spiking anxiety. "You didn't have to save my life," I told him. "God knows you don't owe me anything." Despite my sincerest efforts, I thought of Dylan as I spoke, how he'd died in the rain-soaked street in Seattle so many years ago while I watched the life drain from his eyes, helpless. How Trent had arrived moments after to see me crying over Dylan's death as I lost sight of the vampires who dragged him away from me. Sharpness cut into my heart, slicing me over and over like Dylan's death just happened.

The air caught in my throat. I swallowed hard. Without even trying, I'd gone plummeting back to the place I'd been trying to escape since the night it happened.

Trent frowned. "What the hell are you talking about, Veronica?" The way he spoke was brusque, but with an undertone of empathy.

"You know." I cleared my throat again, struggled to push down the lump that kept trying to form. "You know exactly what I mean."

He didn't answer right away. I heard him sigh and run his fingers through his dark blond hair. From the outside, we must have looked like a scene from some daytime drama. Two old friends reuniting at last, a hatchet unburied between them. Except with us, the hatchet was a corpse belonging to someone we'd both loved in vastly different ways.

"It's not your fault," Trent said at last. "None of it. Okay? There was nothing you could've done to change anything that happened."

I laughed painfully, my lips twisting into a stark caricature of a smile. "I wish I could get myself to believe that." In my lap, my restless hands trembled. "I was right there, Trent. Right there. So close, and yet..." My voice trailed off. What else was there to say? Certainly nothing I hadn't said a million times before.

"I don't know how to help you," Trent admitted. "But all that stuff with Dylan—it's not on you, V. Who you are now isn't who you were back then. It's all in the past." He looked as if he was about to say something else, then changed his mind and stayed quiet.

"Yeah." I nodded robotically. "You're right. I just...have to keep telling myself."

"Every day," Trent agreed solemnly. "I get it." He stared out the window. "But that's not why we're here right now." The energy in the room shifted. A shiver ran down my spine. My hands squeezed each other tightly. I steeled myself.

"What do you want to know?" A loaded question. A dangerous question. If I had struggled omitting the truth from my conversation with Lian, Trent's slayer senses made lying all but impossible. Not only would he see right through me, he'd call me out on it too. Trying to talk my way to safety would be a futile exercise.

I was standing at the edge of a minefield, about to take the first step.

"The grove." He pulled exactly zero punches right out of the gate. "How did you get in?" Lian had asked the same thing, but Trent's tone carried much more weight. He had turned his full attention on me. I sensed the walls closing in.

"He invited me." Maintaining eye contact was excruciating, but necessary. I refused to seem vulnerable or afraid, even though there was a little bit of both simmering in my emotions. "And I'm trying my best to get inside his head, so of course I said yes."

"Who's 'he'?" Trent asked. "The clanmaster?"

I nodded casually. "Orion. No surname that I know of." *That's it, V. You're a colleague, not a criminal. Don't give him any reason to suspect you.*

"Yeah. They usually lose the family names after a couple generations, if they don't just ditch them entirely." He paused. "Did you find anything out?"

"Nah." I shook my head. "Unfortunately, the party was crashed before we got to the good stuff. And, well…" I shrugged. "Now most of them are gone, so whatever his plans were, they have a giant wrench thrown right in the middle."

"And he didn't tell you about those plans prior to the meeting?" Trent kept things cordial, but I could feel his interest ratcheting up. Here was where he expected to catch me in a lie, possibly the first of many. And to his credit, I was tempted.

"Well, I think there were more in the works," I said. "But he did say he wanted to go down to Seattle and issue a reverse challenge on their clan. Retaliation for them sticking their noses in Anchorage business, I guess. I assumed he'd be discussing the logistics of a clan-to-clan challenge at the meeting."

"But he never got that far," Trent finished.

"Right. Because a certain homicidal uninvited guest decided to show up last minute."

"Hm." Trent studied the floor, deep in thought. "You know, he's lucky he hasn't seen a wendigo up to this point. I'd think they'd be way into all the blood-drinking these guys are doing." He furrowed his brow. "Although is it technically cannibalism?"

I saw an opportunity to divert the uncomfortably hot spotlight and jumped at it. "Tell me about the wendigo. I really wish I'd gotten a better look." I had no idea we were dealing with a wendigo and now this started to explain the killings in town.

"No, you don't." Trent smirked grimly. "Those things are utter nightmares. I knew a guy who came face to face with one and was never the same. The fact that there's even one in the area is pretty bad news."

"You're telling me. It's been racking up a body count since before I got here."

"Not good," Trent murmured. "The more it kills, the stronger it'll be. No wonder it tore the vamps apart." He stood up abruptly. "Eventually it'll be unkillable. We've got to get to it first." He turned to me. "And by 'we,' I mean me. You shouldn't go anywhere for now."

"I'm fine," I protested, without really knowing if I was or not. "This is just as much my problem as it is yours, Trent. I'm not going to be shoved off the case."

"No one's shoving you off," he replied. "Just take it easy, for Lian's sake. She's—"

His sentence was cut short by the kind of scream that curdles human blood. We froze, and then both of us bolted from the bedroom. I was out of the bed so fast, I barely felt my feet touch the hardwood floor. The steps flew by at dangerous, breakneck speeds. There was only one other person in the house who could be screaming like that; the very person Trent and I wanted to protect the most.

Lian stood in the front entryway, barefoot, her hands clamped tightly over her mouth. The door to the house hung ajar, but I couldn't see what might be in the doorway. As we approached, Lian turned toward Trent and let him get in front of her. His eyes flicked forward, and then immediately to my face.

"What is it?" I asked. "Let me see."

Trent said nothing as I came within view of the porch. At first, my brain had a hard time making sense of what it was seeing. I thought I was looking at a large bundle of black rags, or an old blanket. A second later, however, the splayed limbs and glimpses of pale skin clicked into place.

And to my shock and horror, I recognized the face lying against the cold concrete.

"Stay back," Trent warned. "Looks like a vamp. He could be dead, but you know how hard it is to tell with these bastards." He stepped forward. "I'll take care of him in a second."

Instant panic flashed through my body. I had to force myself not to lunge at Trent to try and hold him back. Normally, Orion could've given even the most seasoned slayer a run for their money. But he looked like absolute shit out there. He didn't stand a chance.

"Trent, wait!" My exclamation was met by stunned silence. Trent and Lian both stared at me. An inscrutable expression crept into his gaze.

"For what?" He spoke slowly. "You want it to be a fair fight?"

"No." I put my hand on his arm. "Just wait, okay? Trust me."

It was a tall order, but he complied, albeit reluctantly. He moved back, and I bent down to get a closer look at Orion. The vamp was out cold, eyes half rolled back in his head, skin waxy and grayish. Had he come straight from the skirmish with the wendigo?

Not that it really mattered. I had way bigger problems than the wendigo now, including the fact that Orion had apparently turned up on Lian's porch to flirt with death. My mind raced as I attempted to figure out a solution. But the truth was, I had no idea what the hell to do. And my friends weren't going to wait forever.

19

SETH

The first thing I noticed upon my triumphant return to the mortal realm was the blessed rise in temperature. No longer did the bone-gnawing cold make every organ in my body ache, including my skin. I would've stood there for a while in the dank little cave where I'd landed, just enjoying the great thaw—except that something else snagged my attention as soon as I opened my eyes.

The beast whose eyes I had been borrowing lay at my feet, stunned, injured, or both. Its skeletal ribcage heaved, and I could see the glistening walls of its partially exposed heart contracting in a frenzied bid to keep it on this side of the veil. Despite its sorry state, or perhaps because of it, the thing was not happy to see me. It reared back its head and let out a plaintive, hollow cry.

"Really?" I stepped over one long, splayed out arm, dodging a weak attempt to snatch my leg. I had expected the possibility of a fight once I'd made it back to mortal soil, but this monstrosity was in such bad shape I couldn't bring myself to raise a hand against it. The light burning deep within its empty eye sockets flickered unsteadily.

Once more, it tried to grab me, and again I sidestepped. This time, I saw something caught on its long, vicious claws—a scrap of dark fabric. With one swoop of my hand, I grabbed the swatch and held it up. There was no mistaking Orion's distinctive, pompous aura. The cloth reeked of it.

"Should've fucking known," I muttered. To the wretched beast, I said, "I can't believe you let *him* do this to you, of all people."

It thrashed angrily by way of a response. Stepping away from the collapsed heap of bones and sinew, I began to search for further evidence of the vampire's trail. He wasn't the one I was interested in, of course. But I knew enough to surmise that if he was out in the forest tangling with eyeless skull-beasts after getting his ass kicked once already, it was probably because of the slayer.

Which meant finding him would invariably bring me that much closer to finding her.

Ten yards from the downed creature, I found another scrap of fabric among the debris littering the forest floor. Aside from some dirt, it was clean and bloodless, saturated with his energy. I turned it over in my hands, running my thumb across the material. Traces of the girl were in there too.

"You better hope I don't find you alive," I remarked to no one. "Or else you're never gonna live this down."

From behind, the injured beast called out again. I looked over my shoulder to see it struggling to stand, all fucked up and bent out of shape. One foot hung limply by the thinnest thread of tissue. Its baleful glare locked on to me, and I tensed without thinking. The charge that came next was slow and shambling, a mistake on the aggressor's part. Its warbling, unearthly cry seemed like a dying monster's last stand.

I felt kind of bad as I watched it come toward me. The spirit of its rage was still there, which I could appreciate, but the body was falling apart. Whatever challenge once existed had been beaten out by other opponents, leaving me with a broken-down shell of a creature hardly worth the effort of putting it down.

As its shadow loomed over me, I reached up and grabbed on to one of its curved ribs. The combination of my strength and its momentum tore the bone loose from its socket. The snapping of bone and tendon rang like a visceral gunshot through the trees.

The beast shrieked. There was something arrestingly human about the way it wailed, with notes of bereavement and rage in addition to injury. I jumped aside, still holding the broken rib. The creature had reared all the way back on its hind legs. Long fingers grasped urgently at the hole the rib had left.

"Sorry." I held up the bone. "You want it back? Come get it." Its surface was splashed with dried blood that flaked off onto my skin. I waved it a little, fully expecting its owner to make some attempt to reclaim it.

But the monster just looked between me and the jagged hole in the side of its chest. Then it turned and galloped unsteadily off into the dwindling space between the trees, in the opposite direction as his trail suggested Orion had gone. Normally, I might have pursued it until it either dropped or turned to finish the fight.

Now I had other things on my mind—one other thing, specifically. And I needed to find that bastard vamp before he got to her first.

Orion's lack of blood had never really bothered me until the moment I was trying to track him through dense forest. I tossed the rib away, keeping one ear open in case its owner decided to loop around for a second pass. No more scraps of his clothes turned up, but I could see patches of loose, recently disturbed debris on the forest floor. His energy stood out like a signal flare in these places.

In one spot, it appeared that he had lain or fallen prone for some time. I could see the outline of his body in the groundcover. That told me if I was lucky, I'd be happening upon a corpse not too far away.

I smiled a little. What poetic justice it would've been for that prick to die such an ignominious death. Alone in the woods, his clan in ruins, struck down by a creature he failed to control in the same way he manipulated so many others. I couldn't have written a more perfect ending myself.

But alas, it was not to be. I followed the spotty trail of Orion's energy through wilderness that did not thin until the moment I stepped out on the shoulder of a paved road. The transition between wild woods and evidence of civilization was jarring, but it took no time at all to regain my bearings. More concerning was the fact that the remains of Orion's energy trail were gradually growing fainter.

Could it be that he really was dying? I didn't let my hopes get *too* high. The trail, though diluted, stayed fairly consistent. Once out of the trees, he had made his way along the road. I saw where he'd stopped to rest, where he'd stubbornly lurched forward to carry on. Even after houses began to appear at the end of winding personal lanes, Orion kept going.

No doubt he was looking for the slayer. But what the hell was she doing here, of all places? I'd grown used to seeing and hearing of her in the shadows of Anchorage, the seedy places where her prey preferred to congregate. The homes at the ends of these lanes were symbols of wealth and prestige, arrogance and greed. The lethal spirit of Alaska's frontiers neutered by piles of money.

"I thought she was here to clean up the streets," I muttered. It appeared that the slayer might have a benefactor footing the bill for her noble quest.

It amused me to imagine what that person might think to see Orion on their doorstep, likely half-dead and demanding an audience with their hired help. Still moving cautiously, I picked up the pace. That was one show I didn't want to miss.

And as it turned out, I was just about on time. Approaching the mouth of the next private little drive, I heard a blistering scream. Instinct told me this was the place, and so I broke into a flat run, heading toward the as-yet invisible house. Gravel flew from under my feet, scattering off to either side. I started to notice similar impressions already pressed into the stones—Orion's footprints.

They were uneven, and I noted a few spots where it looked like he had fallen. When the house came into view, there was gravel tracked up the steps to the wraparound porch, leading straight to his body collapsed in front of the open door. There was a familiar man standing in the doorway, staring down at the unwelcome arrival.

"Trent, wait!" It was her voice that struck the chord with me, though. I stopped dead, half in the open, suddenly hungry for a glimpse of her. She didn't make me wait. But I bristled at the sight of her touching his arm, looking up into his eyes, speaking soft words to him.

Who the fuck is *this guy?* Moments after having the thought, it dawned on me how much I was acting like Orion. Couldn't exactly upbraid the guy for dragging his sorry ass to her door when I was standing thirty feet behind him for the same fucking reason.

The blond stranger who had come and collected V now stood near her and told V nothing in response. So she definitely knew him.

He ceded to her authority, and she knelt down beside Orion's body. Sensing an opportunity to get the hell out of there, I went to make my retreat, but I wasn't fast enough. My movement must have triggered her senses, because her head snapped up instantly, eyes homing in with laser precision on me.

"Fuck," I whispered. With nothing to lose, I bailed as fast as I could.

"Hey!" She had definitely seen me. I felt as much as I heard her tearing down off the porch after me, her heart racing in her chest. And whether it was subconscious or not, I slowed down just enough to let her catch up without too much of an effort. "Stop!" she shouted.

I turned around. The look on her face made me think she might keel over right there, out as cold as Orion.

"Hey," I said casually. "What do you want? I'd rather not stick around, if you don't mind."

She took a deep breath. "Seth?"

"Congratulations on remembering my name," I retorted. "Can I go before your friend comes and carves me up like a fucking roast?"

My words had little impact. "You're back," she said.

"Yeah, and I'm trying to leave again." To emphasize my point, I took an exaggerated step away from her. "Call me when you sort out whatever crazy shit is going on back there."

Panic struck her eyes for a split second, as if she'd just remembered the whole scene. "No, wait. Please wait." She let out her breath. "I need your help."

I laughed. "With him? Hell no. You think I don't know he hasn't spent a second looking for me? He's fine on his own, or at least he thinks he is."

"And he's clearly wrong about that." Her answer was quick and sharp. "Seth, please. I don't know what to do, and if I do nothing at all, he'll die. He looks like shit."

"Don't have to tell me twice." The last thing I wanted to do was expend a single drop of effort to aid Orion in any way. And yet, I could already feel my resolve weakening. She was right there, mere feet away from me, and I didn't have it in me to say no.

Which made no sense. There was nothing special about this fledgling slayer aside from her hair—except that there was, and I felt it whenever I had contact with her. As much as I worked to deny it, a connection was forming between us—which was why I was there in the first place.

"Just this once," she said quietly. "I'll make it up to you."

I wasn't typically one to do favors on credit alone. But it was becoming increasingly apparent that this girl was the exception to the rule. I glowered every step of the way up to the house, including while I slung Orion over my shoulder and started to haul him back the way I'd come. He was maddeningly heavy, the epitome of dead weight.

Veronica waited for me at the lower part of the gravel drive, just out of sight of the house. "Thank you," she said, and before I had the chance to respond, she leaned up and kissed me. "I won't forget this. Promise you'll make sure he's actually on the mend."

I glared at her, then softened. "Yeah, yeah. You better remember this for the rest of your life, girl."

"My name's Veronica," she answered. She was already retracing her path up the lane. "Maybe you should use it once in a while."

"God damn it," I muttered. Casting a sidelong glance at the vamp weighing me down, I frowned once more. "This is all your fucking fault, you dick."

I hadn't made the promise that I wouldn't let him die. Not outright. But I already knew I'd keep it, because she had asked me to.

20

LOGAN

Flying low to the treetops meant flirting with potential disaster, but the woods were so dense I couldn't see a thing from too far up. The undersides of my wings skimmed along tree branches, loose feathers cascading down in my wake. I peered down through the thick canopy, searching for signs of Orion or the monster coming to finish him off.

The flight gave me plenty of time to consider what I might do if I found one or the other. Would I step in and save Orion for the second time in the past day? Would I stand back and hope another beating could finally pound some sense into him? Would I let him be torn apart and then tell Veronica there was nothing to be done?

Just imagining the latter scenario made me cringe a little. I might have felt a staggering level of apathy toward Orion and his well-being, especially at the moment, but it was obvious that Veronica shared at least some of his fascination. She would not be happy to know that I had allowed some wild, murderous creature to beat him to a pulp.

By the time I drew near to the vampire's glen, I'd resigned myself to saving him all over again, if necessary. I wasn't looking forward to dragging him miles through the inhospitable wilderness, or to the verbal lashing that was sure to follow once he regained consciousness, but I owed it to Veronica to try and tend to the things she cared about, including him.

Orion was lucky she liked him so much. For more reasons than he realized.

But then, he wasn't anywhere to be found, and I wondered if his safety was already a moot point. Maybe I'd find him in pieces and have to bring him back to the house in a box. *Can vampires regrow if you plant them in their coffins one limb at a time?*

The only thing I could see from my vantage point was a trail of destruction carved through the trees, denoting a very specific pathway through the woods. Whole trunks had been split and scarred. I followed in the wake of obvious catastrophe, keeping an eye out for anything unusual, such as a bloodless, disembodied leg. If Orion managed to get himself wounded again, I doubted he could have made it very far.

Inexplicably, nothing stood out, even from the air. Half a mile past the far edge of the wrecked grove, I landed amid a broken tangle of trampled grass and splintered wood. The smell of churned earth lingered richly in the air. I could see remnants of supernatural energy splashed across the path in front of me. *Like blood,* I thought, *but probably worse.*

The path continued for another hundred yards or so, weaving and narrowing. I tracked the energy traces to the base of what looked to be the oldest tree in the forest. Thick, gnarled roots spidered out from a towering trunk. The branches threatened to blot out the last of the sun.

But the tree's sheer natural majesty wasn't what drew my attention the most. There was a space hollowed out where the roots began their spread. It didn't seem large enough to accommodate a creature of the size of the one fighting with Orion. And yet, into that dusky cavern was where the trail of energy led.

Not to be deterred, no matter how the situation appeared, I gritted my teeth and entered the low, earthy passage. Despite my misgivings, the passage proved to be easily as tall as a man, and it only widened the farther I traveled. By the time I noticed a sweetly rotten smell of decay seeping into the air, it was much too late to turn back. My footsteps uncovered glints of bone mixed in with the soil, fragments of skull, loose teeth.

None of these were great signs, as far as how much I could expect to enjoy whatever I'd find at the end of the hidden path. I knew before I got there that I was walking uninvited into some kind of lair. My only saving grace was the creature's grave condition, as indicated by the trail it left. I read the energy patterns like blood spatter at a crime scene.

Maybe this thing was breathing its last. Maybe it was already dead.

The path took a sharp turn, hooking around suddenly into the mouth of a cavernous, dark chamber. The stench of death invaded my senses. Piles of bones had been heaped all around, including a precarious monolith made entirely of skulls. Where there had been remarkably little blood up to this point, the floor of the large cavern was stained with it.

I peered forward into the depth of the cave's shadows. It was there, barely visible as a grotesque silhouette against some sourceless, ambient glow. The bestial head was bowed, antlers scraping the ground. For a moment I thought it might really have died after all, until I saw the thin glow still burning in its eye sockets.

The creature made no move to attack me, and as I approached, I understood why. Although it might technically have emerged victorious from its most recent spate of battles, it did not escape unscathed. Most notable was the gaping hole torn in its ribcage, through which blood and various innards continually threatened to spill.

"You're dying," I said quietly. The lair's still, stagnant air clung to each word. I was met with no denial, and no submission, either. The eyes watched me, full of suspicion and wounded rage. I stepped closer to the shattered husk lying in its final repose. Slowly, the energy that fed its vengeful spirit leaked out, drifted away. "Is this what you want?"

The question was mostly rhetorical. No creature of such pure hate and hunger ever *wanted* to die. It was driven by the power of its need. But that power could no longer sustain a failing body on its own.

I reached out my hand and placed it on the splintered ribcage so that I could feel its life force. In the same moment, I learned what to call this armature of bones and blood, this vessel of death.

"Wendigo." The uttering of its name seemed to buy me a certain level of grudging respect. I guessed it must have been a little-known fact, not high in the priorities of the monster's victims. "You don't have much time left," I told it now. "But you know that."

The wendigo grunted. Nestled among the broken ribs, its heart pulsated rapidly. Had I the inclination, I could have plunged my hand down and grabbed it, ripped it out of its web of veins and arteries. The thought was tempting in a cruelly merciful way. I had another idea forming at the back of my mind, though—one that could benefit us both.

What do you want, fallen one? The wendigo's voice resonated through my whole body, but its strength was waning. I could feel it slipping toward the edge of the veil between realms. *Have you come to mock me?*

"No." I met its hollow gaze. "I can help you. In exchange for a favor."

The wendigo stared into my face. *Is that a bargain you are permitted to make?* The question held a tinge of ironic amusement. I wondered if perhaps I was underestimating the creature's capabilities. A voice in the back of my mind warned to tread lightly.

"It's what I'm offering," I said. "There's trouble brewing on the horizon. A tide that may never ebb if we let it come in." I was referring mostly to the enduring threat of invaders from the south, but Orion's plans for Veronica tumbled around in my thoughts as well. Did I want to turn the full-fledged wrath of a restored wendigo upon him? Not particularly.

But there were things about Veronica I did not think he understood. Things that could spell disaster if he tried to claim her as one of his own. And it wouldn't hurt to have a hidden ace up my sleeve, just in case.

What will you give me in exchange for my aid? Even inches from permanent death, the wendigo eked out a deal. I didn't like the cunning resourcefulness lurking behind its words, nor the gleam in its dead eyes.

"Life." I shrugged. "That's all you need."

Hmm. The wendigo glanced away, pretending to think. As if it wasn't backed into the tightest possible corner, teetering on the razor's edge between existence and oblivion. I waited patiently, sure of the answer that was to come. A minute later, it turned back to me. *Fine. Consider these terms accepted.*

"Promise," I said. "You'll be there when we call."

I see little choice for me, the wendigo admitted. *For once, you are the one who wields the power.* It paused. *I will answer your beckoning, fallen one. But yours alone.*

I could work with that. "Then I'll uphold my end of the deal. This might hurt."

The wendigo scoffed. *Pain is fleeting.*

I knelt down, resting both palms on patches of exposed bone. The wendigo lay still, heartbeat and breathing irregular, shallow. Hauling it back from the brink would not be as simple as it had been with Orion—every second drew it closer and closer to the void.

There was no more time to waste. I closed my eyes, filled my lungs with the dank, rotten air of the cave, and settled in to the task at hand.

21

VERONICA

ian and Trent blocked me in the front hall. Just looking at them, I saw that my luck—and their patience—had run out.

Trent, in particular, had the kind of steely glint in his eye that I usually reserved for whomever I happened to be hunting. I did not enjoy being on the receiving end of that look, but I was also aware that it might be something I deserved.

"You better start talking, V," he warned. "And you better have a real good explanation for whatever the fuck we just saw out there, because I know what it seemed like to me, and it's not great."

I glanced at Lian. Under normal circumstances, she might have been quick to jump to my defense, but not this time. That was when I knew for sure that I'd really fucked up. She stared at me, her dark eyes somber.

"I asked you to tell me the truth, V. Correct me if I'm wrong, but that's not what happened, is it?"

The entire confrontation reeked of a rebellious teen getting caught in our current situation. *We're not mad. We're disappointed.* Except that no, Trent was definitely super mad. I was ninety percent sure he wouldn't fight me in front of his ex-girlfriend, but that rogue ten percent had me bracing for a surprise attack.

"Okay, look." I ran both hands through my hair and sighed deeply. "I'm sorry. I messed up. I thought…well, who the hell knows what I thought. But it was obviously not the right decision. If I come clean now, will you forgive me?"

Lian grimaced. She put her hand on Trent's arm. "Give her a chance. Only one, though." Reluctantly, Trent stepped back to let me cross through into the living room. It had been a long time since I'd seen him so willing to let Lian take the lead. For months after Dylan's death, he'd been way too overprotective of her, too scared to let her have agency in a world cruel enough to murder his best friend.

It was nice to see some of the balance being restored between them. Even if it meant they were teaming up against me.

I sat down on one side of the coffee table in front of the dormant fireplace. Lian sat opposite me, and Trent stayed standing. He said nothing more, but he didn't have to. The storm clouds gathering in his eyes told me everything about where I stood with him. Namely, on ice thinner than a sheet of paper. One false move, and I'd plunge straight through.

"Where do you want me to start?" I asked. It seemed prudent to let them steer the conversation as they saw fit; I was the one doing wrong, and so I deserved no power. My hope was that deferring to their moral authority might earn back some of the friendship, loyalty, and integrity I had so recently hemorrhaged.

"The beginning." Lian crossed her legs and leaned back on the sofa cushions. She arched her eyebrows. "Wherever that is." I had never blamed Trent for being so into her he couldn't extricate himself if he tried, and right then, it was apparent exactly why. My sweet, gentle, sometimes overly-accommodating friend had been replaced by some no-nonsense ice queen. All the time she'd set aside for my bullshit was up.

"Don't kill me," I began, "but he and I are...involved. With each other."

She furrowed her brow. Standing beside the couch, Trent let out an annoyed growl.

"Seriously, V?" he demanded. "You can't be for real with this."

I pressed my lips together into a thin, tight line. "Sorry. It just kind of happened."

"Wh—" Briefly, Trent looked like he was seconds from lunging across the table at me. His expression blazed with incredulous contempt. But Lian held up her hand, a gesture that demanded tempers be held. He receded into simmering anger, his gaze still locked on me.

"Stuff like that doesn't just *happen*," Lian said. "I know you're not naïve enough to assume we're going to accept that."

"I'm serious," I insisted. "We met in passing one night while I was downtown. I didn't have any intention of doing anything or going anywhere with him. Our paths kept crossing until..." I shrugged. "I gave in."

Lian frowned at me. "So you're saying this all happened because you were thirsty."

"Well, when you put it like that, it starts to sound pretty shitty." I'd meant it as a joke, but nobody laughed. Not even me.

Trent shook his head. I could tell he was struggling to wrap his mind around the kind of debauchery to which I'd just admitted. "You've been fraternizing with the goddamn enemy the entire time," he muttered. "Un-fucking-believable."

"Hey, credit where credit is due," I shot back. "It hasn't been the whole time. I didn't come here with an ulterior motive."

"You just came up with one all by yourself." He made no effort to hide the disgust in his voice. "What else are you hiding, Veronica? Don't bother denying it. Secrets are like roaches in this line of work; where there's one, there's bound to be a thousand more hiding in the dark." I didn't answer him right away, so he went on, unable to stop himself. "I can't believe you can even say Dylan's name while you're jumping in bed with a vamp!"

That one stung. I winced, and Lian saw.

"Trent." She looked at him. "That's enough. Cool it or leave."

He hesitated, annoyance momentarily large on his face. All three of us understood a line had been crossed, and I had no doubt he was sorry for it. But his anger wouldn't subside long enough for an apology to surface. He left the room without another word. I expected the door to slam shut behind him. It didn't.

"He shouldn't have said that." Lian rubbed a hand across her face. "But I can't blame him for being pissed, V. And I don't think you can, either."

"No," I admitted. "It's fucked up. But I couldn't help it." *I still can't*, I thought, wisely choosing not to say that last part out loud. "I'm so sorry, Li. All you have to do is say the word, and I'll be on the next plane back to Seattle. Paying my own way."

She stared past me, lost in her own thoughts. Finally, she said, "I want to trust you, V. I really do. You've been an amazing friend to me for so long, and I don't want to lose that. But I don't get this shit at all. Like seriously, explain to me what the hell you think you're doing, all wrapped up with a vamp. You know as well as Trent does what they're like."

I wished I had a better explanation than the number of orgasms Orion reliably gave me. Not to mention that I hadn't said a thing about Seth or Logan. "It's just...this weird allure. I can't resist it. Doesn't cancel out how unappealing and douchey he can definitely be, but it keeps me coming back regardless." I paused. "Also, Trent was right. There's more."

"Oh, God." Lian held her head in her hands. "Why would you *do* this to me, V? Why would you do it to yourself? There's no benefit other than making your life a hundred times more complicated."

"Trust me, I'm fully aware. The longer we spend having this conversation, the more I'm asking the same questions." Detailing my actions out loud really brought the insanity into full relief. Was I playing the long game somehow? Or was I just a fucking idiot? I knew what Trent would say. "He's got friends. And I've been with them, too."

Lian's eyes widened in morbidly fascinated horror. "Please do not tell me that's why you went to the clan meeting," she pleaded. "My heart couldn't take it."

"What?" I made a face. "No. Oh my God, no. Let's just say Orion is a very rare exception to the general rule. The other one isn't a vamp." I wasn't sure why I decided last minute to only mention one of the remaining two. Maybe it made me seem less like I was having some kind of psychotic break.

"That's...good?" Lian was not optimistic.

"He's a demon," I said. "Like, from Hell."

"Veronica!" Her jaw dropped. "I mean, actually, that's a little bit hilarious. But I'm still mad at you, and having sex with the spawn of Satan as well as a vampire is still the worst idea you've ever had."

"To be fair, I have no idea who his dad is." I smiled slightly. "But yeah, it hasn't worked out so great. They don't really get along."

She groaned. "Of course they don't. Do you realize how crazy this is, V? Look me in the eye and tell me you know what a shit show you're putting on here."

"It's a hot mess," I agreed. "I have no idea how I'm going to clean it up."

Lian let out her breath. She closed her eyes for a moment or two, probably thinking about what to tell Trent so that she wouldn't have to lie, but he wouldn't end up out for my blood. "Can I ask you something?"

"Shoot. I'm an open book." All except for Logan. He had become my last dirty little secret, and I couldn't even explain the compulsion to keep him to myself.

"Has this thing with the vampire changed your perspective at all?" She examined me keenly. "As in, do you feel like you understand him?"

I laughed. "Oh, hell no. I'm in it for the sex. Nothing else."

She hesitated. "Don't tell Trent I asked you this, but is it really that good?"

I made eye contact with her and nodded slowly. "I promise I wouldn't be within ten feet of him if it wasn't."

She snorted. "I'm gonna call the Grand and ask them to shut off all the hot water to your room. Cold showers only from now on, 'cause apparently you need them."

I'd graduated from telling full lies to half-truths. It was true that I craved sex with Orion on a shamefully frequent basis. But despite my insistence to the contrary, both to Lian and to myself, I kind of liked him too. He was charming, in an arrogant, exasperating way. And even though I hated his unyielding jealousy, I liked the feeling of being wanted so much.

Didn't tell her that, though. I just chuckled and said, "It's a little late for that."

Lian leaned forward and held out her hand. "Truce? I hate fighting with you, V. Honestly."

I smiled and took her hand in mine. "Truce. I know you do, and I'm sorry. This one's all on me."

She squeezed my hand. Then she got up, came around the table, and hugged me tightly. "I can't promise much as far as Trent's concerned, but I'll work on him, okay? I think he'll come around eventually."

"Thanks. Let him have all the time he needs. He's got every right to be furious."

"I'll tell him you said so." Lian gave my hand another squeeze. She smiled before she left. I felt like the biggest weight in the world had been lifted from my chest as I walked back to my room.

That relief lasted until the sound of knocking came at the window less than five minutes later. The curtain was drawn, but I could see the shadow of a figure waiting on the other side of the glass. When I pushed the curtain back, Seth's golden eyes burned into mine.

Against my better judgment, I opened the window. How was it that these damn supernatural men managed to subvert my convictions so easily? I knew it was a bad choice, and yet it was so easy to let him in.

"What are you doing here?" I asked.

He kissed me hotly. "You owe me. And I've got a pretty good idea about how I want to collect."

The rational voice in my head screamed at me to tell him no, to kick him right back out that window. It wasn't loud enough to override the intense heat washing through my body.

I stared at his chiseled, sharply handsome features and said, "Okay."

22

SETH

She was my first real taste of life back on this side of the veil, which was exactly how I wanted it. The soft, human warmth of her skin was almost like a drug to me. I drank her in, every part of her. The more I touched and tasted, the faster her heart beat, blood rushing through her veins.

Turning her on was a game. Not a difficult one, but I needed to win.

She let me take her shirt off before she realized that what we were about to do might not work out well for her. I knew there were other people in the house—I could feel their energy through the walls and the floor. I just didn't care.

"Wait." Veronica stopped me with her hands on my chest. She tossed her hair back, out of her eyes, and stared at me in what she must have thought was a serious, no-nonsense way. "We can't do this right now."

"Little late for that." I bent my head and kissed each of her rosy nipples. They stiffened against my mouth. Fuck I'd missed her so much. "Your body agrees."

She sucked in a sharp breath. "I mean it, Seth. Now is not the time or place."

I glanced up from between her breasts. "I hate to break it to you gorgeous, but it never will be. You're not exactly dealing with the kid next door here."

"Ugh." Veronica rolled her eyes. She pushed me backward toward the foot of the bed. "You have to go. This is my friend's house." Her gaze darted to the door. "She's home. And so is Trent." When she spoke the guy's name, her voice dropped to just above a whisper.

"So what? You got a thing for him?" Undeterred, I gave her another kiss.

"No!" She squirmed unconvincingly. "But if they catch us, we're probably both dead. Trent already saw Orion. He'd kill you without a second look."

"Huh." The threat of danger only added an edge to the fire already burning in me. I pushed her back on the pillows. "Then you'd better be quiet."

She was pissed at me for sure, but the slayer didn't put up much more of a fight. She writhed in ecstasy as I tasted her deeper, one hand clamped over her mouth, I made my way down her body, kissing her over clothes as my hand tugged up at her skirt. Every so often, a moan or a squeal would make it through her fingers. I gripped her quivering thighs, pushed aside her underwear, and plunged my tongue as far as I could. She smelled delicious and I lost myself to her, remembering why I couldn't get her out of my mind, why the fuck I needed her so insatiably.

Veronica grunted. She pressed her pelvis into my mouth. I sucked her; she yelped, and then she whispered, "Oh, fuck." And without giving her time to breathe, I changed positions. Up on my feet, I grabbed her gorgeous hips and spun her over onto her stomach, then dragged them back toward me. Kneeling forward, she stuck that gorgeous ass into the air, while I pushed her skirt out of the way, along with her thong.

If there was anything I had missed the most about the mortal realm, it was the tight, muscular softness that gripped me as I entered her slick warmth, and continued to grab at me with every following thrust. I rode her from behind, watching her slender back buck and flex. Her hands clenched into tight fists in the sheets. As she climbed toward orgasm, she seized a pillow and bit into it, hard.

"Come on, baby." I pounded into her. "Let it out. I know you want to."

Every muscle in Veronica's perfect body flexed. The force of her pleasure nearly knocked her out, drawing my own explosion. I hissed, pumping into her. Even her toes curled as she dove down into the mattress, I heard a long, muffled moan. Her hips gyrated hungrily on their own, drawing out every last sensation while I floated on ecstasy.

Something about the way she lay limply in the aftermath, half wrapped in the tangle we'd made of the covers, convinced me to stay by her side. Her eyes were closed, and she looked like a piece of art, even with her tousled hair and sweat gleaming on her skin.

"Goddammit," she muttered. Despite her efforts at low volume, her voice was still slightly hoarse. "I kind of hate you."

"Oh yeah?" I stretched out casually beside her. "Could have fooled me just now."

Veronica rolled over to face me. She ran her index finger up my arm, over my shoulder, and along the side of my neck. As if by some unseen magnetism, her body wrapped itself gently around mine, so that her cheek ended up nestled against my chest, our legs entwined.

"I know you're so warm because you're from Hell, and I really shouldn't be okay with that. And yet, here we are."

I smirked. "This from the woman who wanted me to leave half an hour ago."

"Consider me persuaded," she replied sleepily. Her fingers traced restless patterns on my skin. "Are you gonna tell me where you've been this whole time? Or are you just going to leave me hanging forever?"

"I'm surprised you're interested," I told her. "It's not really the concern of mortals where people like me end up after we get screwed."

"Why wouldn't I be?" She tilted her head to make eye contact. "First of all, I was having those crazy dreams, and I know it was you in them. Second..." She trailed off and shrugged her shoulders. "I guess I was worried about you."

When was the last time I'd ever heard anyone say that about me, let alone a girl like her? Mildly disturbed by the warm contentment suddenly kindling in my heart region, I squashed it down. "That was a waste of your time and energy, but I appreciate the sentiment."

She chuckled. "You're welcome."

We lay there in silence for a few minutes while I tried to figure out how to explain everything I'd been through over the past however long it had been. "There's..." I paused, shook my head, and tried again. "There are some places in this realm where the walls are thin. And sometimes you can make doorways in them and pass between places. I was, uh...on the other side of a door."

"But you could see me through it. And I could see you, sometimes."

"Only while you were asleep," I said. "Mortals usually can't see shit, even if they really try. Don't ask me why that is. You're just inferior that way."

She frowned a little. "I'm a slayer, though. That elevates me somewhat, doesn't it?"

I stroked her tender, fragile skin, feeling all the vitality just barely contained underneath. It would have been so easy to pierce that layer immediately and watch her life drain faster than she could slow it.

"Maybe… not sure," I said. I didn't add that it was one of the things I liked about her.

She kissed my neck. "It's still good to have you back. Does that mean you found a door that was open and were able to walk through?"

"Sort of." I remembered the mirrors, and the howl of agony that had sounded at the moment I broke through. "Let's just say I made my own."

She sighed. "For the sake of us both, I'm choosing to ignore that."

A new silence fell, one that lasted for a long time. She lay perfectly still, and I was beginning to think she'd fallen asleep. And then she shifted her weight and spoke up. "Okay, I need to ask you something."

"I don't need to answer, but you can try."

"Don't be mad," she said. It was such a strange, vulnerable response that I looked at her, trying to read her face. Veronica did not return my gaze. "Is Orion all right?"

Suddenly, I understood why she'd led with that particular stipulation. It was remarkable how quickly the mention of one individual could sour the mood. I took my arm from around her and sat up, putting some distance between us. She stayed where she was.

"As far as I know, he's going to be fine," was what I told her. The truth was, I had no idea what was happening to him as we spoke. My limited understanding told me that his stupid coffin ought to fix everything. But if there was a ritual involved, I sure hadn't done it.

"Okay." She took a breath in and let it out. "Thank you. For all your help."

"It wasn't much, to be honest with you." Against all reason, I felt my anger melting away. She had an effect I didn't understand. I could count on one hand the number of times I'd been soothed in my life. But I let her kiss me.

"It was enough," she said and smiled.

I stared at her. *When the fuck did I get to be such a goddamn sucker?*

She only gave me a little while longer to wonder. "Look, I'm sorry to kick you out so soon, but you really need to go now." She looked at the door. "They think I'm hurt, and they're going to check on me at some point. I know you think you're invincible, but I'm willing to bet Trent will want to prove you wrong."

"He'd fail, but I get what you're saying." Besides, she was right. I was already getting dangerously close to overstaying my welcome, if there was one to begin with. Trent, whoever he was, had been pissed from the moment I arrived, and his temper showed no signs of changing. I recognized that simmering cauldron of emotion; it was the same one I'd managed to put a lid on a few minutes earlier.

"That attitude is going to bite you in the ass someday," Veronica warned. She stole one more kiss as she pushed me toward the window.

I winked at her. "Maybe I'm into that."

If she replied, I didn't hear it. The outside air came with a refreshing sense of freedom so powerful that I wondered why the fuck I'd lingered so long in that damn house anyway. But then I looked over my shoulder at the room she was in—and I knew exactly why.

Because she was in there. And apparently, she was becoming a good reason for a lot of things.

23

———

LOGAN

*H*aving existed for so long in parallel with death itself, there was not much left in the mortal realm that could faze me —except the act of reviving another death spirit. As I worked to restore the wendigo, I could feel its energy trying to latch on to mine and drag me down into the strange purgatory where it lingered. Even in its dire state, it retained its eternal hunger.

There were a hundred moments during that struggle where I had the opportunity to pause and rethink the actions I had decided to take. If I had known, or tried harder to anticipate what could come of bringing a vengeful, devouring spirit back into the mortal realm, maybe I would've backed away before the process was complete.

But I was too focused on the way in which a perpetually starving wendigo could be geared toward becoming the solution to our looming problem. The Seattle clan wasn't going to wait forever to make their return, especially not once they found out the sheer numbers Orion had lost. We needed some kind of reinforcement as soon as we could get it.

And we were nothing if not beggars at this point, which meant being choosers was out of the question.

I came out of the revival with my head spinning, tendrils of nausea wrapped around my stomach. For a mercifully peaceful moment, I closed my eyes and breathed in—until the fetid odor in the air reminded me where I was.

"I need to get out of here," I muttered. Stumbling to my feet, I caught the briefest glimpse of the wendigo watching me. The glow in its deep black eye sockets was steady now, its bones no longer brittle and on the verge of breaking.

Now you flee, fallen one? Tempering your compassion with cowardice?

I shook my head. "No, I might—" Somehow, it felt wrong to inform a mystical being such as this, no matter how terrible, that I was about to throw up, so I just shut my mouth and went for the exit. Fortunately, the wendigo seemed to understand. Minutes after I had finally emerged into the gray dregs of daylight and the freshest air I'd ever smelled, it came out of its lair behind me.

I bent over with my hands on my knees. The scent of the forest washed through my nose and mouth, cleansing my body of the lair's foulness. I knelt, and then sat on the damp ground. Never had I been so thankful to simply exist in a different space.

"Don't forget the deal we made," I told the wendigo at length, once I was reasonably sure the sickness had ebbed. "I'll hold you to it."

The wendigo hunkered down onto its skeletal haunches. It looked much more bestial that way, less like a being capable of the kind of thought it displayed. I examined it carefully from where I sat. Despite my commitment to diplomacy for the sake of securing its aid in the future, I couldn't shake the feeling of sizing up a foe.

I will remember, it said.

Which left me to ponder the worth of a monster's promise as I stood up and got ready to leave. I'd half expected the wendigo to depart before me, but it obviously wasn't comfortable leaving me alone at the mouth of its den. I thought about trying to reassure it that I had no desire at all to revisit that location, then decided it didn't matter. My goals had been accomplished, and it was time to go.

For all I knew, Orion could be moldering in the earth somewhere, or wandering around an especially remote section of the forest, incapacitated by his injuries. Now that the wendigo was more or less taken care of, new and larger challenges rose up before me.

"Be safe," I told the wendigo. "I wasn't lying when I said we'll need you." Our alliance was new and tenuous, but it was there nonetheless.

The creature bowed its head, great, jagged antlers sweeping over the dirt. We locked gazes. I could sense its mind reaching out in the same way a mouth must be opened in order to speak.

Wait. The single word was followed by a long, pregnant pause. I wondered what the wendigo's depth of understanding really was. It knew enough to speak in grave platitudes and taunt me rather gracefully, but how much did it actually think?

As I found out, it had been thinking entirely too much.

"The deal has been struck," I said calmly. "If you want to change the terms, be ready to pay."

The wendigo continued as if I hadn't spoken at all. *I have a question.*

I raised an eyebrow. "Go on."

Slowly, the wendigo's whole body turned. Even healed, it wasn't much of a thing to behold, as far as beauty was concerned. The exposed teeth in its jaw grinned at me, starkly contrasting the rest of its expressionless features.

Who is she?

That was when I knew for sure that I'd probably made an incredible mistake. Temporarily frozen, I wracked my brain for an answer that might satisfy the creature without damning Veronica to a lifetime as the object of its twisted fascination. Orion's burning interest was passing in comparison. She would never be free of this thing, in life or in death.

"She is none of your concern." I kept my voice civil, though a few degrees cooler. "That is a fact. Not an opinion."

She is human. The wendigo tilted its head, bemused. *And she is not. Her spirit...* It trailed off, most likely imagining how it might feel to consume both flesh and soul of a slayer. I couldn't read its face, but whatever crumb of trust I harbored was long gone.

"Let me make something very clear." I stepped forward to emphasize my point. Directly into its line of sight. The baleful glowing eyes focused raptly on me. A stare full of ravenous hunger. "Do not touch her. If you harm her in any way, I will slaughter you, and we will find another way to deal with our problems." Orion's clan was in dire straits, but not so dire that I was willing to sacrifice Veronica.

It was a rare point on which I knew he and I agreed.

She is special. The wendigo nodded slightly. Some type of base recognition registered in that macabre face—how, I could not explain. *I see.*

"You could say that." I squared my stance. "There will be no escape from wrath should you pursue her." For the first time, the unspoken rivalry that had erupted between Orion, Seth, and me served a useful purpose. I was reasonably confident in our ability to unite, as long as Veronica might be at stake.

Still, it couldn't be anything but a worst-case scenario. Just imagining Orion's dramatics clashing with Seth's unbridled rage was enough to make my stomach turn again.

You would hunt me. The wendigo lifted its head, casting me in deep shadow.

"Not only that," I affirmed. "We would kill you. For good." Whether or not such a thing was truly possible, I wasn't sure. But I knew now that there was a place for things like wendigo spirits to go. And if it was anything like Seth's little Underworld vacation, it wouldn't be very pleasant.

The wendigo hesitated. It glanced off into the deep, dark forest, as if listening to sounds no one else could hear. The wind whistled softly through the gaps between its bones, playing a lonely, haunting song. How many souls had this beast trapped in its grasp? Were they not able to sate its appetite?

I knew the answer already, that a creature like the wendigo would never be full. And now I harbored an awful, nagging suspicion that all I'd really done was place Veronica squarely in its sights.

"Wendigo." I spoke its name sharply, with the sort of icy authority learned in the world of the fallen. It glanced back, startled. "Swear to me. The girl is not yours."

I understand your words, it answered. We stared at each other in defiant silence. The trickles of light filtering down through the trees had turned milky and silver, an indication that once I cleared the canopy, I'd be flying in the eye of the moon.

I thought perhaps the creature had more to say, but I was wrong. After a protracted stalemate, it finally turned and loped off. The way its whole grotesque form disappeared into the shadows was as impressive as it was unnerving. Where there should have been crashing through brush and tree branches, there was absolutely nothing.

I didn't like it.

Silver streaked the jet-black treetops of Chugach as I let the updraft carry me higher. Even though the moon was nearing fullness, there wasn't much to see. The only traceable aspect of the wendigo was its pervasive aura of death. I focused in on the echo of its raw, bottomless craving and began to follow it through the wilderness.

And almost immediately, I could tell by the sharply honed precision of its trajectory that the wendigo was on the hunt. It was more or less invisible to me, except for its energy signature, and yet the farther we traveled, the lower my stomach continued to sink. There were a lot of things I did not appreciate about what was beginning to unfold, not least of which was the beeline it was making for a side of the park that faced roads leading into residential areas.

But it kept going, and soon it was too late to stop it even if I had intended to try. I saw its otherworldly shape transition from the cover of the forest into the ambient darkness of the night, making little effort to avoid the growing signs of civilization.

I grimaced. Wherever this thing was going with such single-minded determination, there'd be hell to pay once it arrived. Cruising over the silent streets on the outskirts of Anchorage, I prepared to witness another murder.

24

ORION

The smell of earth drew me up from the bottom of a dreamless well, back toward the realm of the living and the mortal. I opened my eyes to the lid of my sarcophagus sitting askew, soil scattered all over the floor. When I made an attempt to stand, the whole apparatus teetered dangerously, spilling yet more soil across the floorboards.

It was all intensely sacrilegious. But right then, I lacked the capacity to care. My mind was disturbingly foggy, like the surface of an iced-over mirror. I knew, in theory, that things had happened—quite a lot of things, in fact. The details of those events eluded me by inches, skating just beyond my grasp.

But suddenly, the ice began to melt. Memories of the past few days came flooding back, and in an instant I understood everything—where I was, how I'd gotten there, and who was responsible for the dirt all over the floor. The answer wasn't as surprising as it was enraging. My first instinct was to find that fucking demon and send him straight back to the prison he'd escaped. It was the least he deserved, except I also understood he did it to save me. Even if it was in his own barbaric way.

And yet, the fact that Veronica had begged him to save me cooled my anger. Paradoxically, it bothered me that her persuasion worked so well; Seth obviously had a soft spot for her beyond his crass interest in

322

her body. But knowing he'd acted solely upon her request was just enough to put me in a more rational state of mind.

He hadn't *just* dumped me into my resting place like so many pounds of meat. He'd done it because Veronica pleaded for my life. And he didn't know yet, but that one fact made him the luckiest demon on Earth—and the accompanying knowledge that Veronica was somewhere relatively safe.

Besides, I had much bigger things to worry about. Any leftover beef with Seth paled in comparison to the problems the Anchorage clan was facing. Our numbers had just suffered massive depletion due to an outside force I failed to predict. Standing there in the dim bedroom, it dawned on me that I didn't even have a solid grasp on how many were left.

For all I knew, Anchorage could be facing clan extinction. Which meant that once the Seattle faction showed up again, as was inevitable, there would be no one to fight them back. I was proud, but not delusional about my chances against an army of my enemies. As it stood, Anchorage was on the verge of becoming my nemesis' latest acquisition.

"I'd rather Seth let me die," I muttered darkly. On my way downstairs, I put out a summons as far as it would go, calling my wayward cohorts back to my side. If I had harbored any fleeting notions that perhaps Seth's return could be attributed to a particularly vivid bad dream, they were soon dispelled by his prompt response.

Get back to the house, was the order. *This is a clan emergency.*

Oh, so you are still alive. Yeah, yeah. I'm on my way.

Logan didn't answer directly, but I could sense him moving in the right direction. His trajectory—heading from Chugach—confused me, but I didn't have time or space to worry about it at the moment. Waiting for them was agony on its own; by the time Seth showed up, I had migrated out to the front yard.

"Hey." He looked me up and down and did a decent job of hiding the smirk that threatened to jump across his lips. But his energy sliced through the air like a knife, carrying an unmistakable tinge of Veronica. I didn't have to speculate very hard to suspect the context of their meeting; not while he wore that smug grin on his face.

I glowered. "How was the Underworld? I have to say, I'm a little surprised you made it back so soon."

He chuckled. "Disappointed, you mean. You can say it." He paused.

"And jealous, I would assume." Every word he said was dripping with bait, the kind meant to goad me into starting a fight. There was little I would've liked more than to wipe the floor with him, but doing so would only consume precious time and resources. And was it him I was furious at, or that I'd lost my entire following?

I clenched my teeth. "The clan is fucked, Seth. We can't stand up to Seattle like this."

"So I've seen," he answered easily.

I took a deep breath, nearly choking on my pride. "Did you happen to see how many survived?"

"What? The attack by that thing?" He spoke as if there was anything else I could possibly be talking about. "Hard to say. There might have been a handful who came out of it all right."

It was almost impossible to tell if he was lying. He stared me in the eyes, his expression inscrutable. Not a flicker of emotion showed through. I could've punched him, but restraint barely won out.

"I need to find them," I said, keeping my tone even. "And then I need to make more."

The ambiguous implication of violence piqued Seth's curiosity. He raised his eyebrows. I felt his attention sharpen by a few degrees. "I'm listening," he said briefly. "Tell me more."

Neither of us noticed Logan approach until he had been there for an indeterminate amount of time, just watching us. "The clan must enter a phase of recruitment," I was telling Seth. "It hasn't been necessary in quite some time, but I'm afraid it's unavoidable now." My mind flashed back to the days of mass turnings, legions of thralls. The recollections were bittersweet, to say the least.

So many of those once-loyal servants were lost. It stung, but I refused to let it affect me.

"Why do you sound hesitant?" the demon asked. He was blunt, and I resented his perceptiveness. "I thought you guys were all about expanding your empires or whatever." He gestured in Logan's direction. "I mean, we're here because you don't want some other asshole taking over your turf."

"The process is complicated." I ran my fingers through my hair. "It causes unrest. Sometimes it can take months for those waves to settle again. Sometimes it takes years."

"It can take centuries," Logan interjected. His voice was flat, but the look in his eyes was intensely focused. For some reason, his normally ghostly skin looked even paler under the moonlight, which threw his features into sharp relief.

Seth turned to observe him. "What happened? You sick?"

Logan shot the demon a withering glance. "No." To me, he said, "Please continue."

I cleared my throat. "Well, that is true. In rare cases, the ramifications of a blood moon can span generations." Whole vampire dynasties had risen and fallen around blood moons of the past. The entire face of a clan could be shaped, or changed, by the ways in which its population waxed and waned.

"A *blood moon*?" Seth grinned. "Holy shit. That's the most interesting thing you've ever said to me." A keen glow sparked in his eyes. "I'm pretty sure I can help make this happen. No matter what it is."

I grimaced. The blood moon was at once incredibly profane and sacred in a strange kind of way. In my younger years, I had treated the birth of each new vampire into my clan as a blessed occasion, a celebration. This time, there was no such luxury. It pained me to have to involve two outsiders in what was perhaps the most intimate aspect of the clan's culture. Indeed, I'd intended to save the experience to be shared between Veronica and me.

But the gravity of the situation simply couldn't be ignored. To Logan, I said, "Seth claims there were survivors of the wendigo attack. Go and find them, and help them hunt down mortals to turn. As many as you can."

"You sure you want to be letting just anyone with a pulse into your club?" Seth asked. "I know your standards aren't real high to begin with, but this seems like a risky proposition."

I glared in his direction. "Don't fucking argue. You're the security. If you meet resistance, crush it." I paused. "I'll convert half the damn city if I need to."

"That's it? They do what we say, or they die?" Seth was incredulous. I knew full well that I had just handed him a dangerous set of orders. Depending on how compliant the population of Anchorage decided to be tonight, I could expect to wake up to blood running in the streets—maybe literally. His lack of conscience was the precise reason he'd been hand-picked for the job he was about to do.

I hoped all the hassle would finally pay off.

Nodding, I said, "Desperate times call for desperate measures."

He laughed. His teeth gleamed. "Ain't that the truth. I'm just glad you're finally loosening the leash a little."

"Don't get used to it." I frowned. *Especially not where Veronica is concerned.* It wasn't my intention to bring her up at all, in an effort to keep things civil, but as he and Logan were turning to leave, the urge peaked, and I was unable to help myself. "Where is V, Seth? Is she still in that house?"

"I thought you'd never ask." He looked over his shoulder. "Yeah, she's there. Nice place. Two other people. One of them's a guy, and he's like her." He winked. "I did a little recon for you. You can thank me later."

I saw a flash of red. "Who the fuck is he?" Had she been with him, too? I decided that once we were finally reunited, Veronica and I were going to have a talk about boundaries. She was sorely mistaken if she thought I was willing to share her forever.

The moment she became my sweet little vampire thrall, she was mine only.

Seth shrugged. "No idea. But I don't think he's banging her. Or if he was, they're not doing it anymore. He was pissed off the whole time I was there."

Somehow, that offended me too. More and more questions kept cropping up in my brain, but the part of me that wasn't focused solely on Veronica made me let him go. Wordless, I waved the two of them off and stormed back into the house. For now, much as it pained me, I needed to leave Veronica and everything about her in the background.

She would be dealt with the moment the Anchorage clan was back on its feet. And to that end, I pledged to grow it as fast as possible, through any necessary means. Maybe it was time at last to let Seth live up to his full homicidal potential. For all of my hard feelings towards him, I had absolutely no doubt that he could prepare an army of thralls as easily as they could be turned.

If we did everything right, we could practically bounce back overnight. Not as strong and stable as we had been before the wendigo struck, but powerful enough at least to hold our own when the Seattle tide came crashing in again.

All we had to do was buy enough time. Even at rock bottom, I still held the city in the palm of my hand. It was simply a matter of bending it, slowly and surely, to my will. And when that was done, I'd retrace my steps to the house where my Veronica was being kept away.

Because I had every intention of taking back what was mine.

25

VERONICA

Long after Seth left, I could still feel him on me as I lay in the bed, mulling over the string of bad choices I continued to make. As much as I tried to live in blissful ignorance, it was becoming very clear that these men each affected me in the weirdest ways. All my rationality and good slayer sense, the very things in which I had once taken so much pride, went out the window as soon as they got close.

And it was becoming a problem. I hadn't meant to sleep with Seth, or catch feelings for Orion, or get wrapped up with Logan too, and yet I'd done all of those things with a goddamn smile on my face. Groaning, I rolled over away from the window, locking both arms around my pillow.

"Girl, you are the hottest mess," I muttered, my voice muffled and practically unintelligible. "Like, seriously. We need to get our shit together." I cringed into myself, thinking about what Lian might say if she knew I was banging a demon literal minutes after our heart-to-heart. Trent would probably just toss me out on my ear. He'd never had much tolerance for bullshit, and I knew I was testing his capacity.

The only thing saving me was the fact that we were in Lian's family home, and he was nothing if not respectful to her agency. They fought about things like the amount of time they spent together and her allegiances to dumbasses like me. Not about her strong will or her need for independence.

All of the things I understood Orion trying to snuff out in me, Trent encouraged in Lian. And once upon a time, his best friend Dylan had been like that too. I squeezed the pillow tighter and let out a heavy, wistful sigh. In an alternate universe, the four of us were still a team. Us against the world, like we always thought it would be forever.

But Dylan was gone, and I was up to my face in a situation so complicated it defied mortal imagining. It was so stupid I almost had to laugh about it. Unfortunately, its stupidity didn't erase any of the very real feelings I had. To my disappointment, neither did my dirty little secret being out. I knew that my friends were pissed at me. It hurt.

Nonetheless, I allowed Seth to climb through that window. In my extremely weak defense, he hadn't given me a vast array of options, and I was not in a place to fight with him. My senses were still shot to hell; unsurprisingly, banging the shit out of a fire demon did not help. All I wanted to do now was curl up and sleep the rest of the night away. *Maybe things will be chill again when I wake up.*

But I couldn't get to sleep. I kept thinking about Logan and Orion, who had taken the place Seth previously occupied in my thoughts. It was kind of funny to imagine how mad Orion would be to know I'd seen him looking so bad, but I was also really worried. Even for a vampire clanmaster, he'd seemed to be inches from real, permanent death.

"I should have been more specific when I asked Seth to help him." For the first time, hours too late, I realized how crazy it was to beg Seth, of all people, to save Orion's life. Mortified, I covered my face. "They fucking hate each other!" How did I know Seth hadn't just dumped the body somewhere and come back to get laid?

I didn't. The trust I had in all of them was blind and foolish, but I couldn't help it. It was like they each filled a void in me that I wasn't aware of until they pointed it out with their presence. Logan especially carved out a tender place in my heart. He was too sad and gentle to carry the full hatred of which I knew Orion and Seth were capable.

Lying there in the calm dark of the bedroom, I closed my eyes and tried to stretch my senses, feeling for a response. Instead, I felt that the last twenty-four hours, or however many it had been, kicked my ass to Hell and back. Not even ten seconds into the attempt, a sharp, blinding pain sliced down behind my eye.

I sucked air in through clenched teeth. "Ah, fuck! Okay, okay, bad idea." As if scolding me, the stabbing in my eyeball remained as an echo after I eased off. Without my senses, there was no way to pinpoint exactly where the boys were. "I'm sure they're fine," I told myself, closing my eyes one more time. "They're strong. They're tough. They would want me to be resting right now."

Again, the thought, however true, failed to lull me down into the sleep I craved. The best I could manage was a light, fitful doze. Senseless half-dreams danced through my head. My spirit wanted to be with all three of them at once—I felt them pulling me in different directions. In those dreams, Orion was healthy, but pissed. He paced the yard of the house on the inlet, eyes dark, thoughts obviously racing.

I saw a glimpse of them together, Orion giving orders, Seth with that smug, cocky grin on his lips. The way he'd smiled at me as he came through the window. Floating in the purgatory of incorporeal space that's so frustratingly common in dreams, I strained to hear the words leaving their mouths.

"Is this real?" I wondered, half aloud and half in my mind. If it was, I received no answer. Neither vamp, nor demon, nor my strong and silent angel heard me.

Then, quite suddenly, my consciousness was jerked away to somewhere else. The field of view was under constant motion, and the images I was seeing looked strange. There were no bright colors, only varying tones of black and gray. The effect disoriented me completely at first; the struggle was so intense that it woke me up.

"What the..." I rubbed my eyes and sat up in the bed. "That was *so* weird." What I wanted was to wake up and get ready to jump back in the fray, because clearly the whole recuperation thing wasn't working out that well. I needed to be active, to be working in the field. All this time in bed was wreaking havoc on my brain.

It might be hard to get going at first, but I was down to risk it, confident my body would catch up soon. *Just don't take any insane risks for a while. It'll be fine.*

No matter how willing the spirit was, the flesh continued to refuse cooperation. The odd lure of that last dream pulled me back toward comfortable semi-consciousness. *You're not ready, V,* whispered a little voice in my ear. *You'll get your shit kicked in if you try getting out there right now. Just lean back, shut your eyes, and let the boys handle it.*

I wasn't convinced, but the energy would not be mustered. Before I knew what was happening, I had eased back down onto the pillows and was drifting off against my own will.

The moving grayscale images returned. They shifted left and right, as if looking around, and I was startled to find that I recognized the surroundings. My heart flipped sickeningly in my chest as I bounded across familiar wide, manicured lawns, passing through the shadows of huge, far-apart homes.

"What the hell," I whispered. "I think this is—"

Moments later, I broke through a line of trees, and all my suspicions were instantly proven. Lian's house stood less than a hundred feet away, and the distance kept closing. The second floor windows drew closer and closer, and I realized how unnaturally tall I was. Through the glass, I saw a bed, and a person lying on it.

My eyes snapped open. I bolted upright so fast the room spun. Still in bed, I spun to face the window, just in time to see the looming, grotesquely skeletal silhouette of the wendigo filling the frame. Its hand, long fingers outstretched, smashed through splintering glass and wood, reaching for me.

I stared. Time slowed to a crawl. I had enough time to see and understand exactly what was taking place, but not enough to escape. The wendigo wasn't hurt anymore; in my current state, I was no match for its speed and strength.

I remember a scream hit my ears as it dragged me over the jagged remnants of the window. It was only later that I realized that shrill, terror-driven sound had come from me. I thrashed in the wendigo's grasp, kicking and pounding with every last ounce of my energy.

The monster could not have cared less. It changed directions and swung me around, and right before it took off running, I got one final brief look into Lian's guest room just as the door came crashing in.

"Veronica!" Lian beat Trent to the window. She leaned out, and the last thing I saw was her face, frozen into a mask of horror and fear. *"Veronica!"*

BLOOD KISSED

CHOSEN VAMPIRE SLAYER

BOOK THREE

Torn by loyalty and the fiery desires of a conflicted heart, Veronica finds herself at a crossroads. What will she do if burning love turns into cold regret?

PROLOGUE

VERONICA

 had no idea how fast we were moving. All I knew was that if I looked down, the ground whipped by at a truly unsettling speed. And if I somehow managed to turn around, I was willing to bet Lian's house would be long gone, lost in the distance.

Okay, Veronica. Take a deep breath. You can figure this out.

I tried to follow my own advice and quickly discovered a deep breath was out of the question because of the way my ribs were being crushed in the vise grip of bony fingers. That left only step two to worry about: Figure this out before panic swallowed me.

Instead, I thrashed against the monster holding onto me, kicking and punching, which did nothing but make him move faster. His grip was iron, and I wasn't getting out of his hold easily.

"Oh yeah," I muttered under my breath. "No problem." Again, I glanced at the ground. We were far beyond the manicured lawns of Lian's neighborhood. Now there was black dirt and patches of snow. Rugged tree trunks flashed by, dangerously close to the top of my skull. I didn't want to lose my head.

The view in the other direction wasn't great either. I twisted my head around, shaking the loose hair out of my face. The dark silhouette of the wendigo loomed above me, glowing eyes fixed forward, exposed bones shining dully under a ragged pelt of skin and fur. Of all the shitty situations I'd gotten myself into over the years, this one definitely ranked among the ugliest.

Focus, V. The little voice in my head grew stern. *By the looks of this thing, once you get wherever the hell you're going, you won't have much time.* Staring up at the beast, I had to agree. But my current predicament was complicated. As far as I knew, there was nothing stopping the wendigo from crushing me to death at the slightest hint of insubordination. It sure didn't seem like I was destined to serve any higher purpose other than food.

Maybe I could get it to drop me...but did I really want that? The wind whipped my hair so hard I thought it might pull out at the roots. A fall from this height from the edge of the hill, at this speed, could easily kill me; if not now, a few agonizing minutes or hours later. Assuming I didn't die on impact, would I be able to get to safety?

So, yeah, it actually felt kind of strange to know I was on my own, at least for now. There was no doubt in my mind that the second Orion got wind of the current unfolding disaster, he'd be coming for me. And I'd be glad to see him.

But I had no way of predicting when that would be, or how long it would take him to track me down. For now, it was me, myself, and I against a feral undead monstrosity.

I tried to brace myself against the top of its hand without drawing any attention, but the moment I started wriggling to get out of its grip again, I felt those long fingers tighten. All the air rushed out of my lungs as if they were deflating balloons. My initial instincts were right on the money: It would just keep squeezing until I was dead.

"Shit," I gasped. My face was flushed with the effort each breath demanded. I could barely feel the blood rushing into my cheeks, they'd gone so numb from the cold. Wild as it was, I knew this part of Alaska like the back of my hand, and my gut told me we'd changed course. That probably wasn't good.

"God damn it, I need to get out of here." I sucked up as much oxygen as I could force into my lungs and pushed with all my might, until every muscle in my body screamed. My legs kicked out and connected with something hard. A searing pain shot through my foot. I squeezed my eyes shut. "Bad idea. Bad idea."

Suddenly, my perspective changed. The cold air sliced like a razor blade across my face, stinging my eyes with tears. I grimaced but kept up the struggle. The world spun wildly, end over end, and I realized that I was swinging as the wendigo made another turn. Another tree trunk whipped by, and almost as an afterthought, I reached out for whatever I might be able to grab.

Could I have broken my hands in a million places and screwed myself over completely? Yes. Fortunately, luck was at least a little on my side. I caught on to a branch, and the momentum of the wendigo's movement helped it tear free. Although it wasn't very clear how big my new weapon was in the shadowy darkness, it felt nice and heavy. And it was probably sharp on the end. Unbalanced, but as a present beggar, I couldn't afford to be a chooser.

I adjusted my grip on the broken branch. The right angle was hard to determine in the first place, let alone land. My hair flew all over the place, and I had this crazy, surreal thought that it was gonna take forever to get all the tangles out. As if I wasn't being slung around like a ragdoll by some otherworldly beast who'd just kidnapped me out of my bed.

"Hey!" The howling wind stole my voice right off my lips, and at first I thought the wendigo hadn't heard me at all. Then a shift in its rickety armature of bone and sinew sent shudders through the ghastly body, and I saw it turn its head to look at me. The eyes, glowing with a furious but empty fire, bored into me.

This was it; now or never. I clenched my teeth and took the only shot I knew I was ever going to have.

All I remember of the moments following the strike was the shrill, pain-driven screech tearing over the treetops. The wendigo recoiled from the branch now protruding from one of its eyes, and I had to squeeze mine shut in order to handle the g-forces put upon me by its frantic flailing. My ears rang. I fought to keep my head and neck steady. Yet with every swing of the creature's gangly arms, I felt everything grow dimmer and more distant.

It was like being drowned in violent, freezing water. My heart pounded in my chest. I struggled to breathe.

I hope it hurts, you bastard, I thought viciously through the pain. *I hope it hurts real fucking bad.*

But if I had hoped to get the wendigo to stop, or even slow it down, I was sorely disappointed. The ground continued to race by, although not as smoothly. The wendigo's movements had become erratic and unpredictable, perhaps owing to its new, half-blind condition. Occasionally it stumbled, and I'd be thrown haphazardly into the air as it attempted to regain balance. The lunging motion turned my stomach, but at least at the height of each dizzying swing, I could see far into the distance. This was the point at which I learned instead of heading back to the lair in Chugach State Park, we were traveling straight north.

"I knew it," I whispered. My lungs burned. The vague sense of triumph only lasted until my next glimpse ahead, which was when I realized exactly where we were going. In fact, its massive peak soared high above the horizon, gleaming white even in the dead of the Alaskan night. As correct as my instincts had been, the reality of our destination caught me off guard.

Why would a thing like this take me to Denali? The mountain embodied everything sacred about Alaska's wild frontier. It was steeped in ancient magic, mystical traditions older than memory, older than time. I was quite sure, even in my limited knowledge, that there was no place for a monster there.

I had to stop it.

"Hey!" I yelled again, squirming in the wendigo's grasp. "You want another branch to the face, buddy? 'Cause I can hook you up!" This time, instead of tightening, the wendigo's grip weakened for just a second. It was enough time for me to yank all but one leg free. I perched on the edge of its huge, bony hand, waiting for my next window of opportunity. "Trip again," I muttered under my breath. "I dare you. It'll be the last fucking time."

While I waited, my whole body tense as live wires, I scanned the surrounding environment for another improvised weapon. Ironically, the grievous wound I had inflicted on the wendigo worked against me, especially since I no longer had the anchor of its hand keeping me in place. One wrong move and I'd be splattered.

I frowned. Maybe that was better than the alternative. If I had to go out, I wanted to be able to choose my own terms. *Whoa there, V. Survival is still the best-case scenario. Don't go full fatalist just yet.* Although my eyes were trained on what I could see of the wendigo's ugly mug, my mind's eye wandered to the three faces I had come to admire so intensely.

Logan. Seth. And, of course, Orion. What would they do if I was killed tonight? How would they feel? Would they swear revenge, like I had after losing Dylan? Part of me kind of liked to think so. But an even bigger part didn't want to find out.

"Nope, no dying for Veronica today."

The wendigo pitched unsteadily forward. I braced myself.

"Sorry, man. I've got other things to do." Three other things, specifically. I decided right then and there that I couldn't die happy until I'd done each of them at least one more time. And that meant death was off the table.

The wendigo's loping stride faltered severely. I felt myself thrown forward into freefall as its hand opened, fingers fanning out. It looked like the chance I had waited for so patiently, and I got ready to seize it for all it was worth.

But then it all came crashing down. Instead of tucking and rolling onto the half-frozen, unyielding ground, I ended up dangling upside down, my calf pinched precariously between the tips of two claws. The luck that had come through so quick for me minutes earlier had just unceremoniously run out. Once my head stopped spinning, I rolled my eyes up and stared directly into the monster's baleful, one-eyed gaze. The tree branch still stuck brutally out from one socket.

"Let go," I growled, "or I'll do it again."

It lifted me slowly, inspecting me from all angles. I couldn't have looked like much of a prize, all disheveled, my hair in knots. For a moment, I thought it might toss its head back and drop me straight into its dark, skeletal maw. Then the claws opened, releasing my leg. I dropped roughly into the grasp of its other hand. My neck whipped painfully backward on impact.

"Fuck," I hissed. Stars exploded behind my eyes. "Not good." When I dared to look again, I saw the wendigo staring at me with its single good eye. And I felt its grip closing down on my torso, compressing my chest. The air came first in short bursts, then in ragged gasps, then not at all.

That blazing, hollow eye was the last thing in my view before it all went black.

1

———

SETH

*L*ogan was waiting for me outside of the Rabbit's Foot bar, half in shadow, quietly watching the world go by. I hadn't seen him in the flesh since the start of my little vacation in the Underworld. He looked at me as I approached, just a casual flick of the eyes.

"Hey," I said. "Been a minute." The way his cold blue eyes glowed in the darkness reminded me of some things I had seen on the other side of the veil. Kind of made me wonder how different angels and demons really were.

"Yeah." He straightened up. "Good to see you."

I smirked. "You're just saying that."

Logan chuckled. "You think I want to do all this shit by myself? Hell no." He stepped away from the bar and started down the street, his gaze picking over every face that passed us by. I followed suit, but in the washed-out light of the bars and streetlights, it was hard to tell a normal human from a vamp. They all looked sallow, sunken-eyed, and mostly miserable to me.

"I bet we won't find a single one of these idiots," I muttered. We were supposed to be searching for survivors of the clan massacre that I had witnessed through the mirror, which seemed ironic. Not because Orion had asked us to do it—wouldn't any shepherd want to track down his scattered flock? There was just something funny about a

341

legion of dead-ass vamps "surviving" anything. What did survival mean to someone who slept in a coffin every night?

"We'd better." Logan's face was impassive, but I could hear the edge of irritation in his voice. "I was tracking something when he called me back to the house."

I gave him a sidelong glance. "What do you mean by 'something'? You mean the thing that almost beat him and his whole cult to death?"

The angel nodded. "Yes. The thing you used as a gateway to get back here. It's a wendigo, by the way."

I almost stopped walking. "Man, fuck, Orion. If you had a bead on it, you should've just ignored him and kept on Wendigo's trail."

"That's not what I agreed to," he said calmly.

My temper flared, and I opened my mouth to continue berating him. I wanted to say he was weak, that he was a follower, that I hoped he enjoyed his life as a sycophant, because it was all he'd ever be. *Who fucking gives a shit about agreements anymore?* In my eyes, the loss of his clan had all but stripped Orion of the power he'd leveraged to rope us into his schemes.

Then again, there we were. Both of us—Logan and me. I told myself I wasn't doing anything for Orion anymore, only Veronica. But that still meant beating the pavement in the dead of night, hunting down what was left of his followers.

I closed my mouth and took a deep breath, willing the anger in my veins to cool. "Listen, I appreciate you helping me out like that. Thank you."

Logan glanced my way. "You could have stayed there," he said, smiling slightly. "Never would've seen Orion again."

"And he never would've missed me." I grinned. "Trust me, I thought about it. But somehow, slowly freezing to death in a barren wasteland seemed like the worse—"

That was when I felt it—a shockwave rippling through the realm. It hit me like an electric shock, mild but jarring enough to instantly grab my attention. I paused mid-stride and stared off into the distance. There was nothing to see except a cold, murky night, but I knew somewhere, something had gone wrong.

"You too?" Logan's voice sounded like it came from miles away. He stood beside me with the same expression of puzzled concern.

"Yeah." I ran my fingers through my hair. "I don't—"

Then suddenly, a bolt of understanding came down from out of the blue. In my mind, I could see the threads connecting us to Veronica straining under the pull of an unexpectedly violent force. The details were murky, but one thing was absolutely certain.

She was in trouble.

Just as I was thinking it, Logan spoke my thoughts aloud. "It's V," he said. "There's something wrong with her."

We had yet to locate a single wayward member of Orion's clan, but my priorities had abruptly shifted. I no longer gave a rat's ass about the clan—and this time I had a feeling the vamp might actually agree with me.

"I have to go," I told Logan. "Right now. Wherever she is, I need to find her." Without waiting for an answer, I spun around and headed in the direction my senses told me. I figured Logan would fire straight back to Orion and let him know I'd defected from our stupid assignment. But when I glanced to my left, he was rushing alongside me instead.

"You're not going alone," he stated flatly by way of an explanation. "I have a feeling you're going to need help."

"Thanks for the vote of confidence," I replied. Still, as much as it pained me to admit, I felt some measure of relief in the knowledge that I had backup. There was no telling what we were getting ourselves into.

"You're welcome," Logan said without a trace of irony. He paused briefly before continuing. "Actually, don't thank me yet. We have to tell Orion."

And there it was. The temper I'd wrangled into submission a few minutes ago threatened to rear its ugly head again. The absolute last thing I wanted to do was get the vamp involved. I could work with Logan. I could even peacefully coexist with him, despite the common assumptions about angels and demons. But all of my lenience toward Orion had been consumed by having to save his life.

"Do we?" I asked. My tone of voice made it clear as day that this was a plan I did not support. "All he's gonna do is take credit while we do most of the work."

Logan frowned. "Sounds like you think it'd be a good idea to hide information about Veronica from him until he inevitably finds out and shit hits the fan. Orion isn't as stupid or oblivious as you like to think, Seth. He's just as connected to her as we are."

"He was mortal, though," I pointed out. As far as I was concerned, Orion's human roots were a significant weakness. No amount of strength, speed, or immortality would ever fully erase the inferior being he had been in the past.

Logan, however, was unfazed. "And now he's not," he said simply. "Get over it." At the next intersection, he veered in the general direction of Orion's house. "I'm willing to work with you, Seth. The only thing I care about right now is Veronica's well-being, and if we're on the same page, great. But Orion needs to know what's happening as soon as possible. This is one of the few circumstances where I believe he might actually set aside differences and help."

I still didn't like it, and I grumbled under my breath even as I redirected my course to follow his. "Tell me it doesn't grind your goddamn gears to share her. I fucking dare you."

Logan shrugged. The moon broke through a cover of deep purple clouds, reflecting silver off his hair and skin. "As a demon, you ought to know it isn't that unusual."

I thought back to ages I had spent in fiery circles of Hell, surrounded by countless naked bodies in various states of ecstasy. The point he had made was one I had trouble disputing. "Fine," I said. "But with Orion specifically? I can barely handle sharing a house with him. Or space. Or, you know, air."

Logan didn't answer right away. "It's not my ideal," he admitted at last. "Mostly because I think Orion would claim her for himself if given half a chance." A flicker of some restrained emotion moved across his face. Was it annoyance? Disgust? Disdain?

I shook my head. "Someday, I'm gonna see you get pissed. And it is going to be fucking glorious." I had personally born witness to the devastation of which certain angels were capable. Deep down, I knew that quiet, unassuming, perpetually cool Logan had that kind of fury within him. I wanted to see him unleash it, preferably at Orion's expense.

He chuckled. "Not anytime soon. Let's go."

Before I could say anything back, he had lifted off, rocketing up into the sky. If I glanced overhead, I could trace the arc of his flight, his shape like a black meteor blocking out the faint sprinkling of stars. He pulled ahead, and I broke into a dead run on the ground. It wasn't a competition, but that didn't mean I'd let him win.

We reached the house in a matter of minutes, at about the same time. Part of me wondered why we had to come back to that place in person when Logan had the ability to break the news with his mind. But he didn't give me time to speculate; I watched him land, climb the steps, and throw open the front door.

"Orion!" The angel's voice resonated in a way I'd never heard. I stepped through the door and glanced at him sidelong. It was beginning to seem as though Logan had been holding out on me, or maybe on all of us. Clearly there was a lot I didn't understand.

"What?" Orion appeared at the top of the stairs, gazing down on us. He was, I thought, exactly where he liked to be, perched above the masses. His strange, metallic eyes glowed. "What are you doing here?"

Logan pulled no punches. "Veronica is in danger," he said bluntly. "She could be killed."

Orion's gaze immediately sharpened to a razor's edge. I swore the temperature in the whole building dropped by ten degrees. He swept down the stairs, stopping inches from Logan's face.

"Elaborate," he demanded. "Now. Where is she?"

"I believe the wendigo took her," Logan stated serenely. If he was intimidated by the vampire, he gave no indication. "That's all the information I have, and it's almost pure speculation."

"Fuck." Orion's fists and jaw clenched in unison. He turned to me, and for a moment, I prepared for him to lash out. Honestly, I was hoping for it, in a way. His irrational anger would allow me an outlet for the simmering rage I'd been harboring myself.

"She's moving," Logan added. "I don't believe it's voluntary."

Orion grimaced. The wheels turned in his head. I could see him weighing his options against the situation at hand. Finally, he said, "Forget about recovery. Forget about the clan. For now, Veronica is our sole priority."

"Agreed." Logan looked at me. "Seth has made a correct assessment. We need to find her."

"We should be finding her right now," I said. "Who the fuck knows how much time we have?"

Orion nodded. His eyes moved from Logan to me and back again. "What the hell are we standing around for? Let's go get her back."

There was no pushback from him regarding my involvement, no snarky commentary of passive-aggressive digs. The intensity of his focus kind of impressed me, as did his willingness to throw his clan by the wayside, at least temporarily. Did I trust Orion? Absolutely fucking not. But maybe he had a better handle on his priorities than I had first assumed.

For the first time, we were really, truly working together. And it was all for the sake of that damn slayer. The girl who should have tried to kill all of us on sight.

Veronica.

2

———————

ORION

$\mathcal{A}$ thousand thoughts ricocheted through my mind as the three of us stood outside the house on the inlet shore. The fact that Veronica could have been stolen out from under my nose, at a time when she should have been in my charge, filled me with all-consuming rage. With every last fiber of my being, I yearned to destroy until the moment Veronica was returned to my arms.

But as of right now, all threats of destruction lay idle. My attempts to home in on the connection we shared brought back muddled results. All I knew for sure was that she was traveling far and fast. Even the direction was a veiled mystery to me. I feared that soon, she'd be completely out of my reach.

"You said the wendigo took her?" I asked Logan. Though he claimed his insight was limited, he had spoken his theory with apparent conviction. Suspicion prickled in the back of my mind, but there wasn't time to pull on that loose thread. We couldn't afford to be sidetracked by infighting or divided by long-held grudges. Veronica superseded everything else.

"That's what I think." Logan's perpetual calm threatened to needle its way under my skin, but I forced myself to match it instead of blowing up. He added, "Not much else could carry her so quickly over such a long distance."

Visions of the creature's long, skeletal limbs flashed through my memory, its lanky height towering above my head. I knew he was right, a realization that only sharpened the edge of my anger. As mad as I was that she had been stolen, I also felt an undeniable burden of responsibility.

After all, Veronica was only away from my watch because I had personally failed her. My shortcomings in battle allowed her to be spirited away by another slayer, who was obviously not providing for her in the way I could have. How many precious hours did I lose to recovery following the massacre of my clan? And in what state had Veronica seen me? The idea that she'd witnessed my moments of weakness filled me with an emotion impossible to describe.

Was it shame? Indignance? Vulnerability? I didn't know, but I hated it.

"So what? Are we just gonna stand here like assholes while she's getting carted off to who-knows-where?" Seth demanded.

I jolted back to the present moment and glared at him. "Absolutely not." Then, remembering my pledge to put V above all rivalries, I softened my stance. "You're right. We've wasted enough time."

Logan frowned. "We don't have a plan. It's reasonable to assume that the wendigo has recovered at least some, if not all, of its power. It is not to be underestimated." He glanced at us. "I'm not sure we can find it alone."

I turned my glare on him. "Surely you're not suggesting we have time for a detour. There are three of us, Logan. I should hope we have a fighting chance against one wendigo."

"Yes. If we can *find* it," he repeated pointedly. "This land is vast and largely inhospitable. None of us have a reliable grasp on Veronica's exact location at the current distance. She might be long dead by the time we track the wendigo down."

The silence that fell was tense and heavy. I knew Logan at least had a point. As a slayer, Veronica rose high above the ranks of her mortal peers. But she still walked among them. Her body housed a beating heart that I feared was more fragile than it seemed. We all feared it, and so we all came to the same reluctant conclusion.

"Fine," Seth burst out suddenly. "So we need some fucking help. Where the hell are we supposed to find *that*?" He turned to me. "Look, man. I don't like being the one to tell you this, but there's no one out there. No one that we found, anyway." He paused. "The clan is gone. You're gonna have to build it from the ground up."

I stared at him. On the surface, those were the typical rash, uninformed words of an outsider, and it irked me to hear him offering any semblance of advice. But deep down, I feared the demon was right. Whatever remained of the clan had probably scattered to the winds in search of safety and a way to bide time until we could recover.

And that meant for now, I was more or less alone.

I grimaced. My wounded pride struggled to recover, though I would never have let him know it. "That isn't how this works," I told Seth curtly. "But if we need to rebuild, we will, no matter how extensive the damage may be."

"Whatever you say," he answered. "We're still exactly where we started. No V, and no help to get her back. And if we don't make a plan in the next thirty seconds, I'm going after her myself." His eyes blazed with defiance and conviction. A grudging sense of respect welled up in me.

"She'll die if you do that," Logan said simply. He looked at me. "You're not going to like this. But we really only have one choice."

"What's that?" The feeling of being backed into a corner was quickly becoming all too commonplace.

"The other slayer." Logan spoke gravely, as if he knew how severely his words would impact me.

I had braced myself in anticipation of his reply, and yet it still sent me reeling. "No," I growled once I'd recovered my senses. "Absolutely fucking not." There were certain compromises I had to be willing to make in dire times such as these, but working with a man who'd stolen Veronica from me was not one of them.

Logan's days of meek compliance, however, appeared to be over, or at least on hiatus. He didn't flinch as he shook his head. "He's all we have, Orion. More of us against the Wendigo, the better our chances."

Seth gave me no support. "Let's go," he said impatiently. "This is fucking stupid. I'm not fighting you over it. Which is the only time you'll ever hear me say that." He started to walk away, prompting Logan to follow. The threatened loss of my authority was galling, and my instinct was to stop such blatant insubordination at any cost. Then I closed my eyes for a moment and saw Veronica's face floating in the darkness.

Was she hurt? Was she frightened? Was she, as Logan predicted, already dying? I couldn't bear to consider any of those scenarios, and so I too turned and followed Seth away from the house, in the direction of the plush suburb where I had originally located Veronica—and from which she had been taken.

The journey was fast and somber. Logan flew while Seth and I retraced our steps from not too long ago before blazing across the all-too-familiar landscape. I was ever mindful of the dark horizon, knowing that it would eventually give rise to the sun and betray me, as always. Not that the dawn would stop me.

Nothing could have kept me from Veronica. I hoped she knew that. Once more, my mind reached out to hers, and I was dismayed to find that the distance between us had lengthened. A feeling of foreboding descended upon me. I picked up my pace.

Seth glanced over as I drew up alongside him. "Oh, now you're getting serious?" he asked. The remark was devoid of his usual flippancy. "Good."

"When I find that damned creature, I'm going to tear it to shreds," I muttered. There was so much helpless anger boiling in my head and heart. How could this have happened? Where was Veronica being taken? What would happen if we didn't get her back?

"That makes two of us," Seth said. Up above, Logan swooped forward, his great dark wings beating the air. Momentarily, he blocked out the pale eye of the moon, and we were cast in shadow. Seth tilted his head back. He grinned wryly. "Son of a bitch. Some people have all the luck."

The rain-scented wind blew in our faces as we came upon the wide lawn leading up to the house where Veronica had been held. Logan touched down just ahead. I watched his wings fold up and disappear. How strange he appeared in that brief instant, even to my eyes.

Then he approached me and said, "Stay back." As calmly as the command was delivered, I bristled. Who was he to give me orders as if the events of the past few days had changed the very core of who I was?

I drew up to my full height, meeting his cold eyes. "Why?"

Again, Logan didn't flinch. "Because the slayer will kill you on sight," he answered matter-of-factly. "And he can't be blamed for it. Such is his training, after all."

I could almost feel Seth smiling to my right. The spirit of passionate rage inside me yearned to lash out, but I stilled it for Veronica's sake. An invisible clock ticked down, minute by minute. There was no way to know how much time we had left.

"Be quick." I glowered, just to make my displeasure as evident as possible.

He nodded. To Seth, he said, "You stay too. If Orion can't show his face around here, you can't either."

The demon laughed. "That's fair." Logan set off toward the silhouette of the sprawling house in the middle of the lawn, and I saw Seth's face change. He was silent as we faded back into the night to await Logan's return.

The rain in the air began to fall in huge, cold drops. I barely felt it, barely felt anything other than the burning desire to find Veronica, sweep her into my arms, and never let her ago.

It was, I suspected, a sentiment the three of us had somehow come to share. The suspicion gnawed at my bones. I pushed it down. Veronica belonged to me—and yet I'd failed to save her on my own. Could I truly claim her in the face of the weakness I'd exhibited?

I clenched my teeth. This hunt for the wendigo would be one of vengeance and redemption, through which I would once again prove myself worthy. And as soon as I had her back by my side, the reconstruction of the Anchorage clan could begin in earnest.

3

VERONICA

It was the cold that woke me up, the kind of cold that slices straight to the bone and seems to freeze from the inside out. My skin felt like a layer of frost was forming on the surface, tiny crystals of ice crackling with every movement. I blinked against a current of fierce wind. Around my face, my hair flew in wild pink tangles.

Goddamn, I'm never going to be able to brush these out. That was my first groggy thought, as I tried to stretch my aching arms and legs. The back of my neck and shoulders hurt too, and I realized I'd been completely limp for who knew how long, suspended by my torso in the air. And then the memories came rushing back, and I knew where I was and what had happened.

"Oh, shit," I murmured. "How the hell am I gonna get out of this one?"

The wendigo had picked up speed while I was out. I looked down and saw the ground flying by beneath my dangling feet in a blur of white and gray and brown. We were no longer surrounded by the same dense cover of trees. The air smelled fresh, biting at the inside of my mouth and nose. Was it my imagination, or had the temperature plummeted since I passed out?

Squinting my eyes against the frigid air, I glared up at the wendigo. "I wish you had fur, you bastard. Then I might at least be warm." It paid me no mind at all as it galloped through a gently rolling, surprisingly open patch of land. Finally, the horizon caught my eye, and I let out a gasp that was snatched away on the wind.

The jagged blue peaks of the Alaska Range jutted from the earth, rising like great gems into the sky. They went as far as I could see, but the crown jewel stood directly in our path—Denali. Shocked and struck dumb by its sheer majesty, my jaw fell open. I had some vague recollection of knowing that this was where we were ultimately headed, but I had never seen the mountain in person.

Now I was barreling toward it at breakneck speed, in the grasp of an otherworldly death monster. Not exactly how I imagined my first visit to the sacred peak might go. Again, I wondered what the wendigo hoped to achieve by bringing me north to Denali. It had to have a plan because there was no slowing down. The world around me was a dizzying blur, except when I managed to catch a glimpse of the sky. Toward the east, the stars were beginning to fade into slowly lightening shades of blue and purple.

Soon it would be sunrise. I could hardly believe enough time had passed that another day was about to dawn. Wasn't I literally just tucked safely into the guest room at Lian's house, fresh off a clandestine rendezvous with Seth? Hadn't I just begged him to save Orion's life, much to his displeasure?

Funny how fast things were changing in my life. The wendigo lifted its arm, rocketing me high into the air. I held on to its bony fingers for dear life. Behind us, the great swath of land that we'd traveled spread out in the direction of Anchorage, two hundred miles or more. The distance was daunting, to say the least.

How long would it take for Orion, Seth, and Logan to find me, assuming they were all looking? And if I somehow managed to get out of this shitshow on my own, how long would it take me to find my way back?

An anxious foreboding hung palpably over my head like the clouds cloaking the top of the mountain.

It was getting harder to see where we were headed. My vantage point became a blur of cold fog, wet snow, and bursts of ice and rock that cascaded down every time the wendigo dug its claws into the mountain face. I shielded myself as best I could, but in no time, I was soaked. The howling wind whipped my hair and clothes stiff, scratching at my limbs and face.

Inside my body, my heart still beat strong. All things considered, I didn't feel too cold. If there was any time I had ever been particularly grateful for my slayer blood, it was right then. The wendigo bounded upward, scaling the cliffs as though they were paved pathways.

I squeezed my eyes shut tight. Ice melted off my eyelashes, running down my cheeks like pure, saltless tears. Nothing good would come of me accidentally drying my eyeballs out when the final destination was rapidly becoming clear. The wendigo, in all its fury, was headed straight for the peak of Mt. Denali. We were only going one direction now, and that was *up*.

The air grew thinner every minute. At first, as I became aware that it was getting harder to draw breath, I instinctually wanted to panic. The irrational desire was to claw more oxygen out of the air, or to open my lungs as wide as they would go. Certain kinds of mortal danger I knew how to face with a confident smile on my face. Fighting vamps? Sure. Wrangling werewolves? No problem. Suffocating on the side of a mountain, mid-ascent?

If I got the wendigo to drop me now, assuming I didn't immediately fall to my death off a sheer ledge, I'd be stranded in the middle of absolute nowhere, exposed to the elements, strong, but not invincible. Death would be agonizingly slow, my suffering great.

On the other hand, if I decided to let things play out according to the wendigo's half-baked plans, I might still end up dead or captive for an indeterminate amount of time.

I pressed my lips together. "They've gotta be searching for me by now, right?" I imagined Orion, wild-eyed and full of anger, Seth smoldering with ill-suppressed rage, and Logan, so cool and calm. The three of them had fought constantly in the days leading up to the present disaster. Could they really pull their shit together long enough to work as a team?

I hoped so. God, I hoped so. But I knew better than to count on it.

Suddenly, the wendigo coiled its haunches and leapt across one last crevasse. I made the mistake of glancing downward as we sailed from edge to edge, into a narrow, bottomless maw that went from white, to blue, to black. The knot already forming in my stomach tightened. I forced in another breath.

Then the gloom that had wrapped us so tightly in its arms receded all at once, like the tide moments before a tsunami. I looked up to see a brilliant plane of crystalline white snow, flooded by the light of a brand-new sunrise. For an instant, it was impossible to distinguish Denali from the edge of the sky. My heart stuttered in my chest.

The spell was broken when my field of view changed, and I realized the wendigo was putting me down. As my feet touched solid ground for the first time in hours, I almost fell to my knees. Arms out, flailing for balance, I staggered through unmarked drifts of snow. The pajamas I had borrowed from Lian stuck to my skin, drenched through with ice water.

One of the things I had always been taught as a slayer was never to turn my back on the enemy. That morning, on the peak of Denali, I made a rookie mistake. The wendigo couldn't have been out of my sight for more than twenty or thirty seconds, but that was more than long enough to grant it the upper hand. Later, I'd be ashamed to admit I never saw it coming. The last thing I remembered was the line between earth and sky coming back into focus.

Then my vision sank down into blackness. I had the surreal sensation of falling, although I never felt an impact.

Oh, fuck, I thought. *Not this again.*

4

LOGAN

The house glowed, casting shadows from the lights in the windows as I walked up the front path. It should have been warm and inviting, a symbol of luxury and prestige, nestled in the embrace of the most upscale neighborhood in the city. Instead, tension radiated from every beam. The windows watched me like baleful yellow eyes.

I could sense two people inside. Their energy was fraught with worry, one more than the other. There was anger, frustration, and betrayal mixed in with desperate concern. They too seemed to understand the gravity of Veronica's plight, for which I was thankful. We had no extra minutes to spend on explanations.

The door swung open almost before I finished knocking. The slayer stood in the entryway, blocking access to the house. He was tall, blond, and broad-shouldered; up close, I could see exactly why Orion detested him. The man was too confident, too powerful—and too suspicious of anyone like us.

He examined me carefully, poised for action. Behind him, I caught a glimpse of a young woman who was not Veronica but had been in her company before. Traces of Veronica's energy remained entangled with hers. I knew she was the one I needed to talk to if I wanted any hope of pleading my case, but that was not going to happen. The slayer kept her back.

"What do you want?" He squared his stance and folded his arms. I glanced at the girl. "Hey. I'm not going to ask twice."

Her gaze flicked uneasily toward him. "Trent."

The ice was obviously very thin and growing thinner by the second. I decided to be as direct as possible. "I need help."

Briefly, something other than guarded wariness flickered across his face. "That's interesting." He stepped across the threshold. "I'm listening. For now."

I gave no indication that Orion and Seth were there. My strongest chances of success hinged on two things: civility, and the appearance of neutrality. My companions weren't proficient in either of those.

"I need to find Veronica. She's in danger." At this, I noticed the girl perked up, suddenly invested.

She came forward. "What did you say?"

Gently, Trent placed his hand on her arm. "Give me one reason to trust you," he demanded. He stared through me as if he knew exactly who and what I was. "Do you know where Veronica is?"

"Not exactly." I took a deep breath. "That's why I'm here. She's moving fast, and I can't track her on my own."

He frowned. "I suppose you thought I wouldn't know you brought your friends along." He looked over my left shoulder, then my right. "They're not so great at staying hidden. Like you told them to."

The jig, or whatever we thought it had been, was up. I sighed and raised my hands, palms out, in a gesture of supplication. "We couldn't afford to make the wrong impression right off the bat," I said. "Are you saying you would *not* have gone straight for Orion's throat? Because I'm not sure I believe that."

"It's pretty ballsy of any of you to show your faces here again," Trent murmured. "Especially him." He moved another step closer to me. I held my ground. "You really want to help Veronica? Maybe she doesn't need weirdos like you screwing things up for her. Have you ever thought of that?"

Actually, I had. Many times, in fact. Pervasive self-doubt was one of the unfortunate hallmarks of the fallen, doomed as we were to question ourselves and our actions for all eternity. But I didn't say it out loud.

The girl interrupted. "Trent! We don't have time for this." She gripped his arm, her eyes boring into him. "Veronica's *gone*. If they have a lead, we have to take it." She paused. "Please." Her voice broke on the word.

I looked at her once more, and a wave of desperate sorrow broke almost violently over me. She was steeped in true fear for her friend, the kind that made her willing to take certain risks. Trent looked at her too, and a current of love swept across his aura. He softened a little, though not enough to back down.

"What have you got?" he asked brusquely. "And tell the others to show themselves. I'd rather we were all on semi-equal footing from the start, if we're really going to do this."

The girl kept her gaze trained on me as I signaled for the vampire and the demon to come up to the porch. I felt genuinely sorry for her, not just the condescending pity of a supernatural toward a fragile, mortal woman. She embodied the helplessness we were all fighting.

"I promise I am here to help," I told her.

She nodded. "I know." The slayer seemed not to like her stubborn confidence, but he chose, perhaps wisely, not to say anything. We were all silent while Orion and Seth flanked my position. Predictably, Orion was focused solely on the slayer, whom I was sure he viewed as his nemesis.

"The wendigo took her," I began once everyone had found their place. It was Trent's turn to nod. His distrust, particularly of Orion, showed plainly on his countenance, but he listened. "It appears to be running directly north, toward the mountains, at an alarming rate of speed."

"Toward the mountains?" Trent furrowed his brow. He and the girl exchanged a puzzled glance, and then his expression cleared. "The national park," he muttered. "That goddamned thing is taking her to Denali."

"What does that mean?" the girl interjected. "Is there something up there?"

"I don't know, but we're going to find out. Can you get us a car, babe?" Trent brushed past me while he spoke to her. He was suddenly all business, thinly veiled animosity aside. "Not all of us can fly like this one here."

I followed him down the porch stairs. Orion and Seth closed in on each side. Orion had yet to take his eyes off Trent for even a second. "I won't go ahead," I told them. "Nothing good can come of splitting us up right now." It would be a dream come true for the wendigo to pick us off one by one.

"Take the car in the garage," the girl called after us. "And drive like hell."

But we had barely made it ten feet from the house when I sensed the faint trill of Veronica's energy waver and go silent. Surveying the faces around me, I saw very quickly that I was not the only one. We froze in our tracks, none of us breathing. No eye contact was made.

"Oh, shit," Seth whispered. Without missing another beat, he broke into a dead run toward the garage. Orion and Trent did the same. I would have too, but the girl stopped me. She'd come down from the house upon seeing that something was wrong.

"What happened?" Her grip on my shoulder was surprisingly unrelenting, finely manicured nails digging into my flesh like claws. "Don't even think about lying to me." She had turned from scared to fierce in the blink of an eye.

Her strength compelled me to tell her the truth, as raw as it was. Far in the distance, I felt no trace of Veronica anymore—and since she was still a mortal, that could only mean one thing. I looked Veronica's friend in her sharp dark eyes.

"She's dead. Just now. I'm sorry."

All the color drained from the girl's face. She staggered backward, releasing my shoulder. Her hands flew to cover her mouth. "What?" she breathed. "No. Oh my God, no!" I saw her sway, and I thought she might faint, but by some Herculean feat of inner strength, she managed to remain upright. "That can't be. You have to have made a mistake."

I shook my head. "There's no mistake. She's become unmoored, drifting between realms. No longer present on the mortal plane." What I didn't voice was the depth of my own regret, nor my determination to somehow make things right. I wasn't sure she'd understand.

The girl stared at me, furious and heartbroken. "Fix this," she whispered. "I don't know how, and I don't care. Bring her back."

I said, "I will. I swear." A few tears leaked from the corners of her eyes, which she angrily wiped away.

"I'll hold you to it," she answered.

Orion's voice broke through the gravity of the pact we had just made. "Logan! Get moving!" Without another word, I left her standing on the front path in front of her house, gazing after me as I ran for the car.

5

SETH

We peeled out of there with the slayer behind the wheel. Logan got the front seat because his sense for V appeared to be the strongest at the moment, which left Orion and me to brood together in the back. Neither of us were particularly pleased with the arrangement, but we had little choice.

"Is there no way to travel faster?" the vamp demanded. "Veronica's life is hanging in the balance!"

"No, it isn't," Logan said. "Her spirit has passed fully through the veil. She's departed from the mortal realm. Her body is just a vessel now."

Orion fell silent. He had gone uncharacteristically pale, even for him. The tension in his neck and jaw was visible. "How long?" he finally growled. "How long to get to her?"

The slayer glanced in the rearview mirror. The car's engine revved as he caught our eyes and we shot forward down the road. "Not too long, I hope. But I'm gonna need you to strap in if you don't want to be left behind. We're not stopping if you fly out the rear windshield."

It was a joy I didn't know I needed to see Orion so angry and unable to do anything about it. He buckled his seatbelt with unnecessary force, and I had to suppress the urge to laugh. Honestly, at that point it was hard not to feel at least a little bad for the guy—who would have thought he'd go from king of the city to the back seat of a borrowed car in a matter of a few days? I was willing to bet not even Logan had fallen quite that hard.

"You're sure she was moving north?" Trent spoke over the roar of the engine as we sped along the quiet neighborhood road. Dawn had broken not long before, and the whole scene lay bathed in tranquil golden light. Hard to believe we were on our way to pry Veronica's wandering spirit back from the jaws of death.

"Yes." Logan paused. "A straight path. Purposeful. The wendigo knows where it's going."

"Hmm." Trent frowned. "That, or it's being drawn there for some reason. Either way, not good." The speedometer needle inched toward the far right side of the dial. The manicured neighborhood streets gave way to a highway that was just as empty. And we sat confined in the car like kids who'd gotten in trouble for fighting. As if we were being shipped off to prison, or military school.

"Hey, Logan," I said, mostly to break the silence. "How's this compare to flying?"

He chuckled. "It doesn't." Then to Trent, he said, "That's not a statement on your driving."

Trent's stony façade cracked a little. He smirked. "I appreciate the clarification." The temporary easing of tension was strange, but also welcome. I didn't like feeling as though we were piloting a hearse down the road at a hundred miles an hour, trying to head off a funeral. "You okay back there?" Trent asked. He was talking to Orion more than me.

Orion replied with little more than a sullen glare. He despised his lack of control nearly as much as the fact that Trent was the one who had taken over. "When Veronica is found," he said, "she is mine. No talks. No compromises. I'm taking her with me."

Trent's laughter carried an edge. "The hell you are, my friend." He turned back to the road. The engine surged. Outside the window, the world leapt by in a blur. "We'll be there in an hour," he said. "Maybe a little more."

I could tell Orion wanted to throw him out of the car. He gripped the seat so hard his knuckles stood out under his skin. Every so often, his eyes would dart around nervously, as if he expected something or someone to leap from the trunk or onto the windshield.

I bore it for as long as I could stand, and when I ran out of patience, I let him know. "Cut it out, man. You're making me fucking paranoid."

Orion stared at me. His voice was low and tight. "Need I remind you that we are inside of a car with the very same slayer who took it upon himself to remove Veronica from the sacred grove? It is still all too possible that we allowed ourselves to be played for fools, Seth. Even you." He stopped, presumably to let his words sink in. "Especially you."

I frowned. "What? Why especially me? What the hell is that supposed to mean?" I had to admit that I liked this new version of Orion even less than before.

"Because you're letting your guard down," Orion hissed. "You're trusting him. I can tell. And he might be leading all of us directly into a trap."

I rolled my eyes. "Blow it out your ass, Orion. You're here too, aren't you?" I gestured toward the driver's seat. "Listen, if this guy turns out to be a double-crossing prick, we'll kill him as soon as he betrays us. Just like that. No problem. Three of us, one of him." I raised my eyebrows. "Unless you're scared of him and that's what this is really about."

The vamp bristled. "Of course not." Out of the corner of my eye, I saw the edge of Trent's mouth twitch upward.

"Fine. Then it shouldn't be a big fucking deal." I leaned back against the upholstery and ran my fingers through my hair. "You're losing it without V around, man. A couple more hours of this and you'll be a stark, raving lunatic."

Orion grumbled, but he didn't deny it. He tried to maintain an expression of cold neutrality, but his face kept shifting, the veil peeling back on his emotions. I imagined that the man sitting beside me in that car was the real Orion—or maybe it was whoever he had been before making the transition to the night. Losing Veronica had clearly altered him in ways he barely understood.

"I need her back," he said softly. "No matter the cost."

"That makes four of us," I agreed. "Five, if you count the girl we left at the house."

"The way I feel for Veronica is beyond anything you could possibly understand," Orion declared. He sat up straighter, puffing out his chest. Finally, he'd found something to be smug and condescending about, which returned him closer to his natural, insufferable state. "She's destined to be mine."

Why was I relieved to hear him acting like a total dickhead again? *Don't tell me you were concerned about the guy,* I scolded myself with disgust. The idea of caring about him repulsed me. *Don't forget he would've left your corpse to freeze in the Underworld until the end of time.*

Still, every time I looked at or thought about Orion now, all I could see was the way Veronica had looked at me as she begged me to save his life. Of all the mortal opinions in the world, hers was the one I listened to most. And she obviously saw something in that pompous horror show, so I had somehow begun to entertain the idea that he might not be utterly useless.

Not that Orion would ever know I thought of him as anything other than an undead sack of air. And I had an important question for him. "What if other people were to challenge you for her?"

He narrowed his eyes. "They would fail," came the answer.

"Oh, it's that simple?" I kept an eye on the back of Logan's head in an attempt to gauge his reaction, but the son of a bitch never turned around.

"Yes." Orion lifted his head defiantly. "It is."

"Can I ask you something?" Trent drove with one hand now, although he hadn't slowed so much as a mile an hour. He guided the car down the highway with the deftness of a professional.

Grudgingly, Orion asked, "What is it?"

"Why do you talk about Veronica like she's a possession instead of a person? Something tells me she wouldn't be happy to hear you speaking like you own her."

The vampire's temper flared. "I can talk about her any way I please," he snarled. "These are rich words coming from a man who slung her over his shoulder and dashed off like a coward!"

"But I did that to save her life," Trent answered calmly. "She was unconscious, man. And so were you. Someone had to get her out of there."

Orion was angrily quiet for a few moments. "Veronica accepts me as I am," he countered. "If I have flaws, they don't affect my love for her."

"*If* you have flaws?" I burst out, unable to resist. "Come on, Orion. A perfect person wouldn't have gotten laid out by a wendigo."

"Nor would he have gotten captured and banished from the realm," Orion shot back. Then he turned to face the window. "Nonetheless, you are correct. I have failed in many ways in such a short time. It is a disgrace to my clan."

His candid admission caught me off guard. One thing I had never expected from Orion was humbleness, or any amount of vulnerability. Perhaps he was finally adjusting to his new position at the bottom of the totem pole, however temporary it turned out to be.

"Hey, no sweat," I said. "We're all a fucking disgrace in one way or another. That's how we ended up crammed in this damn car together." I jerked my thumb toward the driver. "Besides him, I guess."

Trent shook his head, smiling wryly. "No, no. Me too."

"See?" I reached over and patted Orion on the shoulder. "You're not special, boss."

He didn't answer.

6

VERONICA

The first thing I noticed was that the gnawing, ravenous cold was gone, and so was the wind. In its place lay the heaviest silence I had ever heard in my life. The still air was thick with it, a palpable hush. It reminded me, bizarrely, of attending a funeral where the deceased was too young and no one had anything to say.

Little did I know how much, or how soon, that wayward thought would come back to haunt me.

Slowly, I got to my feet. All my senses were on high alert, but there was nothing to sense. I'd never been in a place so completely devoid of life and sound. Despite everything I had learned over years of slayer training and field experience, I knew I wasn't prepared for whatever the hell this was.

"Where is this place?" Of course, there was no one to answer, but I felt better hearing a voice, any voice, even if it was just my own. I started to step carefully through the pitch blackness, and as my eyes adjusted, silhouettes began to emerge from the dark. I drew a sharp breath. Every muscle in my body tensed. They were humanoid shadows, and they were moving toward me.

Quickly, I felt for my staff. The cold hand of dread gripped my stomach; I didn't have anything other than the clothes on my back. Unarmed but undaunted, I clenched my hands into fists. *No weapon, no problem.*

But the shadows never seemed to take notice of me or get too close. They just shambled by at a distance, staring blankly ahead. And they didn't seem to be…real? No, that wasn't it. They were real like clouds were real, or steam on the surface of a mirror. I could almost see right through them.

"Okay, I don't know what the hell is going on," I muttered, "but I don't like it." Not that my personal preferences really mattered in this situation. Looking over my shoulder, I saw only the backs of the ghostly figures who had passed me, and nothing else except infinite blackness. There was nothing to do besides move forward.

So I kept on wading through the void, waiting for something to happen. The farther I went, the more people I saw, until there was almost a silent, shuffling crowd. Everything was shaded in grays and whites, and I wondered half-jokingly if I'd gotten trapped in some kind of old-time purgatory.

Then I saw it, cutting through the gloom like sunlight breaking through fog—a flash of normal color. Was I finally reaching the end of this bizarre dream world? Was it even a dream? Cautious excitement rushed through my body. The last thing I wanted was to be stuck in a nowhere dimension while there was a wendigo on the loose in Alaska.

As I picked up my pace, the slow-moving throng of spirits shifted, creating a rough path before me. I looked up. The air caught in my lungs. My heart skipped at least one beat, if not several. It took a minute or two to find my voice, and when I did, it came out as barely more than a whisper.

"Dylan?"

He glanced toward me at the sound of his name. For a moment, he appeared to be as surprised as I was, but the shock rapidly melted into the same smile I remembered: an almost shy grin that crossed his face halfway at a time. His eyes, green like emeralds, were bright in the dim ambience.

Weren't they blue before?

I dismissed the stray thought as nonsensical babbling from a blind-sided mind. Dylan had made regular appearances in my dreams for a while, but I never thought I'd actually get to see my ex-boyfriend again after he'd been killed by the vampires. Although I was thrilled beyond words, I found myself frozen in place, afraid he'd disappear if I moved. After his death, I wished for such a moment so much that it hurt. I cried, hated myself, blamed myself for not saving him… so to see him brought back all the broken emotions.

Then he said, "Hey, Veronica. You just gonna stand there?" And he sounded the same as he always had. Like no time had passed at all.

By the time I reached him, tears had spilled down my cheeks. I reached out and put my hands on his arms. Unlike the others, he was solid beneath my touch, so warm and real.

"I can't believe it's really you," I said.

His grin widened. "Me neither. C'mere." Dylan put his arms around me, and a part of my heart that had been frozen since his death immediately melted. I buried my face in his shoulder. He squeezed tight. We stayed that way for a long moment, as everything about touching him came back, how well I fit into his arms, how his breath always warmed my ear, and even his woodsy smell with a hint of vanilla lingered. My breath hitched all the way down to my lungs to be in his arms again.

I'd missed him so much.

Cried even more.

So I cherished that silent moment.

After a few moments, I pulled back and took a deep breath. "I thought you were dead. I mean, you are dead."

The grin faded a little. "Yeah, I am. And I hate to break it to you, but uh…you are too."

I blinked. "What?"

Dylan shrugged. "You must be if you're here." He gestured to the space around us. "Look at this place. It's not exactly for the living."

He was right, and I had known it on some level as soon as I opened my eyes, but the truth was hard to wrap my head around. "Huh." I frowned. "I guess that son of a bitch really killed me."

Dylan offered a wry smile. "Happens to the best of us. But there are upsides. One, I get to be with you again, and two, I think I know a way out."

The sweetness of his first sentence was overshadowed by the strangeness of his second. I stared at him. "How is that possible? You just said we're dead."

"Yeah, but that's the thing. It's not supposed to be like this. You know, this walking around, having conversations, existing together. I used to be alone, isolated from every other being I ever saw, no matter how many others there were. We couldn't speak to each other, couldn't hear anything, couldn't touch. But then I woke up."

I hesitated. An odd little seedling of doubt began to grow in the back of my mind. "What does that mean, you 'woke up'?"

Dylan looked at me, then looked away. "I can't really explain it," he said. "It's like everything came back into my world. All the color, all the feeling. The memories." His eyes returned to my face. "You."

Those tiny, whispering doubts didn't quite go away. But it was kind of easy to push them down while he was standing in front of me. How many times had I dreamt of this exact moment, asleep and awake? Whatever crazy opportunity had just fallen into my lap, I couldn't pass it up.

"Maybe we'll worry about the details later," I told him. "What's your plan?"

"This is going to sound insane, but hear me out." He nodded toward the nothingness stretching out forever in every direction. "I'm pretty sure we just keep walking and a door will appear somewhere."

I smirked. "That's your genius-level strategy?"

"Hey, I didn't say it was genius-level," he shot back, smiling. "That was all you." Dylan reached over and took my hand. "Come on. We might as well give it a shot, right? Not like either of us has anything better going on."

He had a solid point, and I loved the feel of his hand in mine, so I decided it couldn't hurt to go along for the ride. "All right. Lead the way."

We walked in silence for a few steps, each of us lost in our own thoughts. I kept wondering if this whole thing was some kind of cold-induced hallucination, brought on by the frigid peak of Denali. Or maybe the things I had always heard about the mountain's mystic sacredness were true, and I was on a spiritual quest—embodied by my dead ex-boyfriend.

I frowned slightly. Dylan raised an eyebrow.

"What's up?" he asked.

"Nothing." I shook my head.

"I guess this is weird, huh?" He chuckled. "It's weird for me too, but in a good way. A great way, actually. This is like, everything I ever imagined it would be." He squeezed my hand. "I can't stop thinking about how damn lucky I am to get a second chance at a future with you. You were always my dream girl, V."

I felt the blush creeping up into my cheeks before he finished talking. Even if they were nothing more than words, his sweet nothings filled a space I'd never really noticed. As much as I adored and craved my current cast of men, none of them spent an undue amount of time on compliments or optimism. I had really committed to the dramatic, mercurial, sometimes-strong-and-silent aesthetic.

Which meant being with Dylan was a breath of fresh air cleansing my spirit. Suddenly, it stopped mattering where we were. I could almost envision our old life, the way things had been back in Seattle. No bloody gang wars, no danger lurking around every corner, no sitting up at night waiting to see if he'd make it home. There was only the incomparable feeling of being young and in love.

But as quickly as the nostalgia appeared, it began to curdle and fade. I simply could not allow myself to toss aside the experience I'd had since Dylan's death in favor of rose-tinted glasses. A twinge of skepticism still needled at me, not least because the door he mentioned had yet to materialize. What if he was a figment of my imagination, a specter born of loneliness and grief?

Gently, I took my hand away. "That's sweet of you to say," I murmured.

Dylan slowed his pace. "Well, it's true." His expression turned apprehensive. "Listen, I know this is all strange, believe me. And I'm not asking you to take everything I say as pure gospel. But I promise it's me. I've never been able to lie to you about anything."

"Where's the door?" I stopped walking.

"I don't know." He looked genuinely perplexed. "I feel like it should be here any minute now." He took a few steps forward uncertainly.

"Is it possible we're both being lied to?" I asked.

He answered readily. "Sure it is."

His candor somehow managed to set me at ease and make me nervous at the same time. My heart wanted to accept him unquestioningly, but my head wasn't totally on board. I watched him while he wasn't gazing straight at me, and I noted his eyes again—green as summer grass. And yet, I could have sworn they were blue.

Weren't they?

"Look!" Dylan pointed to a spot in the formless dark. "There!" A spark had been kindled, and as we observed from a distance, it began to grow. Gradually, outlined in light, the shape of a portal began to emerge. I shielded my eyes.

"Is that—?"

Dylan broke out into a grin. "It's the door. It's gotta be! I can see something on the other side!" He ran for it. "Veronica, c'mon! I have no idea how long it will stay open!"

He was already halfway to the opening before I made my feet move. On the surface, the choice seemed more than obvious: Follow Dylan, reclaim the life I thought I lost years ago, ride off into the sunset, and live happily ever after.

But even then, I knew things were going to be far from easy. After all, there were at least three people waiting on the other side of that doorway who wouldn't be so happy to see a man I had once loved.

7

ORION

I had never been so happy to be out in the bitter, bone-aching cold. The ascent of Denali was a grueling, unforgiving trek, even for those of us who had come out on the other side of death. This was a cold that cut through all layers of mysticism, reducing us to equal vessels of misery.

Still, nobody complained. We were all grateful to be free of the confines of Trent's vehicle, which sat temporarily abandoned somewhere in the foothills. With our combined powers, it was faster to tackle the mountain on foot, although Logan didn't dare fly in the face of the slicing wind. I had intended to try and lose the slayer at the earliest convenience, but to my chagrin, he kept up remarkably well.

He also seemed to be fully aware of my schemes. "You disappointed, vamp?" he asked, cracking a grim smile. Despite the way in which he had softened a bit during the excruciating ride north, his eyes remained cold and calculating. I didn't trust him at all.

"That is not the way I would prefer you to address me," I informed him. There were a lot of things I did not prefer about him, to be frank. He was strong, fast, and surefooted as we raced over treacherous terrain, our footsteps sending sparkling showers of snow and ice down into bottomless ravines. I wanted to think it'd be easy to push him over the edge, but that was a fight I couldn't afford to pick at the moment.

Not because I feared that I would lose. Because of what it could cost Veronica.

The air grew thinner as we climbed, and every time I looked up, I saw the clear, hard blue of the sky stretching on forever. It was little wonder that the mountain was thought of as a holy place, rich in magic and secrets. I had to admit that if the veil was going to be thin anywhere, it might as well be here.

Logan was the first to reach the summit. He paused ahead of us and glanced back. "Brace yourselves," he warned in his quiet, solemn voice. "I'm not sure what we'll find."

"Keep going," I ordered. "I don't care."

Moments later, I ate my words. The four of us stood at what seemed like the top of the entire world, staring down at Veronica's body. The silence was deafening. Out of the corner of my eye, I saw the snow and ice melting at Seth's feet, streaming off the cliff face and down into oblivion. He steamed with rage.

I fought the urge to drop to my knees. The pain was a knife to the heart, a hammer to the ribs. How incredible that a physical sensation I hadn't fully felt in years still had the power to fell me. Though I didn't breathe, I found myself gasping.

"How could this happen? How?" The voice was barely recognizable as my own.

"Fuck." Anguished, Seth let out a roar to the uncaring sky. "Fuck! We're too fucking late!" His furious gaze swept around the semicircle, searching for someone or something to blame.

"Maybe not," Logan said. "She looks like she's sleeping. I can feel it. That could be a good sign."

I stared at him. "What can we do? Tell me."

"I don't fucking care what it is," Seth added. "You want me to obliterate this whole fucking mountain, I'll do it. I'm ready. Let's go."

The angel held out a hand. "No. Calm down." He closed his eyes for a moment that felt like an hour. "She's likely on the other side of the veil somewhere, wandering. Like I said, adrift. Unanchored."

"Not helpful, angel-boy," Seth growled. "How do we get her back?"

Logan didn't answer right away. It was the slayer who stepped in with an answer. "We may need to go in after her. I don't see signs of the wendigo anywhere, which means her body will likely stay safe while we're searching."

"Okay, so let's go." Seth stepped toward Logan, and I was quick to follow. "I don't know why the fuck we're standing around here with our thumbs up our asses. 'Cause I'm willing to bet her fragile mortal spirit isn't supposed to stay wherever she is for too long, right? Isn't that how this bullshit usually works?"

"Yes." Logan frowned. "I think it would be fairly easy to open a pathway from here. But it could be disastrous for some of us." He turned to me. "And by that I mean you, Orion. Since you're technically already dead, I have no idea what will happen once you step across the veil."

My response took no thinking whatsoever. "It doesn't matter. I will sacrifice every iota of my being for her. Open the path." Never had I spoken such undiluted, heartfelt truth. The occasion would have been auspicious under any other circumstances.

"You heard the man," Seth barked. "Get us through there. We'll deal with the consequences later." His eyes, blazing with anger and passion, met mine just long enough for him to give a nod of acknowledgement, perhaps also of thanks. Much as I tended to despise him, the joint loss of Veronica had kindled an unspoken bond between us. If nothing else, we were united in our efforts to save her.

"Agreed," said the slayer. "There's no time left."

Logan didn't hesitate any longer. He reached out his hand again, seeming to lay the palm flat against the air. His entire being glowed, channels of energy running like blood through veins throughout his body. The wind around us picked up to a cutting howl. As I watched the place where the fabric of the mortal realm began to rend apart, I held my breath.

But there was no explosion, no grand entrance or exit. The rift was there, but it was small, and it grew at a snail's pace. Each passing minute blew away in the miasma of snow whirling past. I waited until I couldn't physically bear it any longer.

"Logan!" I bellowed. "Let me through!" Engaged as he was in the opening of the path, Logan was powerless to stop me, although he saw me coming. "I'll rip the veil apart myself!"

"No!" The slayer lunged into my path, striking out at the center of my chest. The blow sent me staggering backward, but not for long. I put my head and shoulders down and charged him like a bull, completely intent on tossing him to his death if that was what it took. Not a single person in the universe could have kept me from Veronica.

"Get out of my way!" The words were stolen from my mouth by the howling wind. Trent grappled the brunt of my charge, locking his arm around the back of my neck and shoulder. I felt the power coursing through him, bestowed, as mine was, by some supernatural force. It was as if he had been placed there by divine intervention to stop me.

"Don't be an asshole," he shouted. "Logan is doing exactly what you told him to do. If you fuck this up now, our chances of finding Veronica shrink down to almost nothing. Hell, I don't even know if you'd survive long enough to see her again." He shoved me back. "Stand there, keep your goddamn mouth shut, and wait. There's nothing else we can do."

Seth caught me and set me on my feet. He glowered over my shoulder at the slayer, death in his demon eyes. "You motherfucker," he snarled. "You'd be fucking dead if I didn't know you were right."

I rounded on Seth. "This is bullshit. We don't have time for this!"

"You think the path between realms gives a shit about how much time we have?" Trent demanded. He gestured at the rift, which had widened slowly but surely. "This is the only way to keep it stable. Otherwise we have no way of knowing where we'll end up once we go through. Look, this is one thing you know absolutely nothing about, all right? Trust me. You need to swallow your vampire pride and let other people take point."

"He's right," Seth added. "As much as it fucking pains me to say."

I opened my mouth to argue, but before I could get any words out, a strange sensation washed over me. I threw back my head. Except for the squall Logan had kicked up, the sky remained empty, bright blue.

Then why could I sense a dark cloud passing through? In my mind's eye, it was a towering thunderhead, a herald of chaos and doom. And it was accompanied by foreboding so heavy it was nearly tangible. The very air at the peak of the mountain changed from barely there to thick and suffocating.

All of us felt it. The bickering ceased immediately. We exchanged glances. The slayer was the first to look toward the opening Logan continued to forge. That was when I began to suspect there was something wrong. The weight that I was feeling, that threatened to crush me into nothing, emanated from the path. I strained to see through to the other side.

"Logan—" I called. My yearning for Veronica had not subsided, but suddenly I was wary of the things that might be lurking beyond.

"Don't talk to him," Trent said. "It's too late. We have to let it happen." In the past few seconds, his confidence had turned into resignation. We all sensed a drastic shift, but none of us could name it.

"What the fuck just happened?" Seth grew wild-eyed. "What did you do, Logan?" It was his turn to be stopped by Trent, who wrangled the demon back into position.

"It wasn't Logan. Keep your cool." But Trent's gaze was glued to the ever-widening path now.

Then a flash of cruelly bright light erased my vision. I flinched away instinctively, protecting as much of my body as possible. The light carried with it a burst of energy, within which I picked out Veronica's very strongly. My soul leapt for joy—until I realized that she wasn't alone.

There was someone else with her. No, not just with her, *entwined* in her aura. Someone whose energy she gravitated toward in a way that did not please me. As the light subsided, my eyes refocused, and I saw two figures step forward from the place where the path had been. Belatedly, I noticed Veronica's body had disappeared from our feet.

She was beaming as she came toward us, harsh sunlight reflecting off her lustrous pink hair. In that moment, she was the most beautiful being in the universe, across all realms. I forgot everything in my burning desire to hold her in my arms.

Yet, indeed, she was not alone. My face darkened as I became aware of the companion she had acquired on the other side of the veil. He was a young man, perhaps her age in mortal years, or perhaps more, if he happened to be one of us.

I instantly disliked him, partially because the first thing he did was grab on to Veronica's hand. But there was also an imbalance in his manner and energy, subtle enough that I couldn't quite pinpoint the problem. All I knew for sure was that I wanted to send him straight back to wherever he had come from. And then I wanted to seal the path between the realms—for good.

8

SETH

"Who the hell is that?" I said to no one in particular. If there was one thing I hadn't expected out of this situation, it was for V to bring someone back from the dead with her. The kid stood close by her side, holding on to her hand as if he thought she was the one who needed to be afraid. His gaze landed briefly on every face.

At Trent, he stopped. The two of them stared at each other for a long time—too long, I thought. I could feel an odd tension simmering just beneath the surface. Obviously, Trent knew exactly who this guy was. How he felt about him was less clear, for some reason.

Finally, the new kid smiled. I narrowed my eyes, trying to determine what it was that freaked me out about his face, his stance, his whole demeanor. Something about him felt deeply wrong, but I couldn't articulate what, even in my own thoughts.

"It's been a long time, Trent." He had an understated way of speaking, a little too smooth. It didn't quite match his fresh, boyish features. "Good to see you."

"Yeah." Trent made no move to approach. "You too, Dylan." He took an extra few moments to size the kid up. I knew what he was thinking; the same as all of us. *What the fuck is going on here?* But then he seemed to relax enough to offer the kid his hand. They shook. Veronica's smile got bigger.

Logan, Orion, and I said nothing. To my left, I felt the vampire practically boiling in his skin. He hated nothing more than to be left out of the loop, especially when it came to V. And there wasn't much we could do at the moment except watch. Unless, of course, we wanted to attack. But I didn't need to be told how bad an idea that would be.

"Chill," I muttered out of the side of my mouth. "Look how damn happy she is. Let her be."

Orion grimaced. "That's what I don't like," he answered. "I don't trust him."

It was a sentiment widely shared among our motley crew, including Trent the slayer. I'd kind of gotten the impression that he knew Veronica's new friend at least as well as she did, if not better, and yet he didn't look too thrilled to see him walking the earth again. The next time Trent spoke only confirmed my suspicions.

"Don't take this the wrong way," Trent said, "but what are you doing here, dude?"

"I found him." V cut in before the kid called Dylan could reply for himself. "On the other side."

I studied her intently. She was still holding tight to Dylan's hand. Her aura shone huge and bright, but also a little shaky. Was she nervous? I frowned. *Why would she be nervous?* Did she know something we didn't yet?

"Where exactly were you?" Trent's tone was nonchalant, but the gears in his head were turning. He watched Dylan's every move with the intensity of a hawk.

Veronica faltered. "I'm not sure," she admitted. "It was dark and silent, and I saw a lot of people, but no one acknowledged anyone else. Dylan was the only one who could interact with me." She and Dylan looked at each other.

"We found your body here, Veronica," Trent said. Almost at the same time, all of us spectators leaned in to gauge her reaction. Orion was laser-focused on Veronica, like nothing else existed in the world. On the other side of me, Logan stood back impassively. He had gone quiet, but I knew he was absorbing every word.

V's eyes widened slightly. "That's..." She let out her breath. "That's really weird, Trent. I don't know what to say."

Trent continued. "You were dead."

"Yeah, I know." She lifted her chin a bit, the classic sign of defiance brewing in her spirit. "That's what Dylan told me."

"Okay, so you understood what was going on." Trent turned to Dylan. The paper-thin air was now composed entirely of awkwardness.

"I mean, not really." Dylan laughed wryly. "Is this an interrogation, or what? I saw her coming toward me, we talked, and then we found a way out. If that was a one-in-a-million stroke of luck, I won't argue with you. I'll just take it."

"Look, it was either this or we'd be stuck wandering that place for who knows how long? Maybe forever." Veronica squared up to Trent. She was ready to fight if necessary. The hard stubbornness in her expression stirred my blood. I'd always had a soft spot for women who stood their ground. "You don't have to be happy to see us," she said. "But that doesn't change the fact that we're here. And yes, it really is him."

Internally, I winced. I wanted to be in V's corner on this, a hundred percent. I wanted to step up between her and Trent and tell the slayer to fuck off and leave her alone. But the more I saw of this Dylan kid, the more alarms went off in my mind. I still didn't know how to describe the unrest he sparked in me, and that was saying a lot. There wasn't much capable of throwing me off.

But Dylan just set my teeth on edge. I would've liked nothing more than to see the last of him as he tumbled off one of the mountain faces surrounding the peak, and the fact that V was so dead set on defending him pissed me off. I wondered if he might have cast some magic on her, bewitched her somehow.

After a long pause, Trent relented. "All right." He backed up. "You're both fine?"

"Never been better," Dylan answered. Veronica grinned.

"Then let's get out of here." Trent turned.

I couldn't take it anymore. He only got a few feet before I blocked his path. "Absolutely not." I stared into his face. "That guy isn't coming with us."

Trent immediately folded his arms. "I beg your pardon?" he asked wryly.

"Seth..." Veronica's eyes found mine over Trent's shoulder. "Please don't." Her voice was full of pleading. "Please. I need you to trust me."

I ignored the disturbingly strong urge to back down rather than upset her. She had already been through a lot in the last few hours. But this was a level of apprehension I couldn't put aside. Pointing at Dylan,

I said, "He needs to go back to wherever the fuck he came from. Now, preferably."

Dylan's expression shifted from confusion to annoyance tinged with a hint of black anger. I could see something terrible in that subtle undercurrent of rage, something clawing to get out. Like hell I was going to stand by while these idiots brought it back to civilization.

"I'll take this opportunity to remind you, we're not a team," Trent said. "When we get back to Anchorage, you're free to do as you please. All of you. And what that means, is that you have zero say in the decisions I'm making for myself. Dylan's coming home."

I might've bought it if he hadn't hesitated right then. His eyes and his energy betrayed him—he doubted Dylan just as much as I did, if not more. Nonetheless, it was clear that for his own reasons, Trent's mind was made up.

"I trusted you, Seth. Why can't you have any faith in me?" V glared, her pleas replaced by hurt and indignance. "I'm safe. I'm comfortable and back from the dead. Thank you all for helping me, but now I just need some time to catch up with Dylan."

"Back off." Trent brushed past me. "Let's get out of here."

The two slayers and Veronica's mysterious friend went ahead. Orion, Logan, and I tailed them at a fair distance; not enough to lose them on the mountain, but enough to keep healthy space between us and Dylan.

"He's fucked up, right?" I asked the others. "It's not just me?"

Orion shook his head. "I want her away from him," he growled. "As soon as we're back in the city, I'll make sure they're separated. And if that slayer doesn't like it…" He trailed off. I tried not to imagine him and Trent waging war on the lush green lawns of that bourgeoise neighborhood. Normally, the thought would have filled me with chaotic glee. Now it made my stomach turn.

I'd already done a lot to fuck up my connection with V. She was mad, and why not? She thought the hollow-eyed monstrosity she had brought back from the veil was her newest Prince Charming. Until the delusion broke, if it ever did, everything I said made me look like the bad guy.

I hadn't been prepared for her withdrawal to hurt me in any way, much less so deeply. It took every ounce of my limited self-control to keep from snatching her up and trying to fight her head on straight.

Until Dylan showed up, I had convinced myself that V was worth all the trouble in the world.

But maybe I was wrong. Despite what I felt for her, which was real and true, the thought of getting wrapped up in this brand-new problem made my skin crawl. I had no desire to find out what was lurking under this new kid's human mask. *That wasn't in the goddamn contract!*

The game had changed, and suddenly, so had my perspective. Things were getting a little too hairy for my liking. I had an inkling that Dylan's presence would only lead to bigger messes. And we were already sort of up to our necks in shit.

I wanted V, badly. In a perfect, simple world, I could have had my cake and eaten it too. But I *didn't* want to mess with anything that wasn't strictly my business—or stay onboard a sinking ship. At the end of the day, I was always gonna look out for number one.

If that meant I had to leave beautiful, strong, fiery V behind—so be it.

At least, that was what I told myself.

9

ORION

Our excursion to Denali had gone from bad to worse in a remarkably short amount of time. We trudged back down the mountain in a formation that struck me as fundamentally incorrect and unfair. What were the supernaturals doing, following behind slayers like dogs? The further we traveled, the higher my irritation rose.

Never before had I allowed myself to be debased and humiliated in such a way. I could hardly believe it was happening now, except that Veronica's lithe form moved over the inhospitable terrain in front of me, a constant reminder of what I was working toward, of the reward awaiting me at the end of these long trials. I'd already lost close to everything, hadn't I? If swallowing my pride meant I could retain a shred of dignity on which to rebuild, I knew I had no choice.

But the consequences were nearly unbearable. More than anything, I hated to watch Veronica show attraction or affection toward a stranger. How could he have won her over so quickly? Were we really so late? A thousand questions consumed my thoughts, fueled by jealousy, anger, paranoia. A few days ago, I had been so sure that Veronica was mine and no one else's.

Now I battled my way through wind and snow, watching her go ahead arm in arm with another man. The urge to catch up and separate them coursed through my veins like blood, but I had seen how quickly her affection for Seth soured when he spoke his mind. Although the demon's effort was regrettably commendable, I had experienced enough of Veronica's temper to know he'd been foolish. The girl was strong-headed, stubborn as a mule.

And unless I wished to suffer the same kind of spurning, I had no choice but to keep my own mouth shut—at least until we were alone again. Alienating her was something I could not afford at this stage. No matter what else happened, I needed Veronica back. It seemed like that was going to be a challenge with the unwelcome arrival of this boy, but so be it.

Nobody spoke a word during the descent of Denali. We fanned out, each of us seeking our own space. I had no idea what the thoughts of my cohorts were as we came down from the sky, but on the way down toward the foothills where we had left the car, I noticed Logan and Seth both straying farther and farther from the path followed by Veronica and the others.

Where are you going? I asked, reaching out with my mind. *She can't be left alone with them.*

Seth was the first and only one to reply. *You think I'm fucking happy about this? I want to punch that kid's teeth down his throat. But V's stance is pretty clear at the moment, and there's no fucking way I'm gonna get in that damn car with him. We can meet in the city if you want.*

Logan, for his part, said nothing. I glanced in his direction and saw him soaring upward again, wings outspread, quickly becoming little more than a dark silhouette in the distance. He might have looked toward me as he flew off, but it was very hard to tell. Annoyed, I grimaced and shook my head. How far we had fallen in a matter of days. And where the hell was that angel off to, anyway?

"You." Trent's voice caught me off guard. He had stopped just up ahead, waiting for me with Dylan and Veronica behind him. My eyes caught V's for a split second before she looked away, but I'd seen the confusion in her eyes.

I raised an eyebrow to Trent. "What do you want?"

He watched me approach. "You're coming with us. In the car."

I frowned. "Absolutely not. I do not want to do that." The whole scenario struck me as absurdly unfair. Why should the others get to go freely while I was stuck under constant supervision from a mortal man? I longed to assert my rightful dominance over this arrogant human, and yet, Veronica's eyes had returned to me. I could feel her scrutinizing my every action.

"Yeah, well, I'm not giving you a choice," Trent said. "Because you're the one I can't predict."

A dark scowl crossed my face. "I'll take that as a compliment," I muttered.

He smirked. "It wasn't."

Boiling with rage and embarrassment, I submitted to being shepherded the rest of the way off Denali, reminding myself over and over that any amount of humiliation was worth keeping Veronica in my sights at all times. Other than a few passing glances, she seemed determined not to acknowledge me in the presence of her new man, with whom she was clearly infatuated. Something was very wrong here like she'd been brainwashed by him. As soon as the terrain leveled out, their hands linked and were never broken.

By the time we reached the vehicle, only a thin veil of cloud cover shielded me from the sun's rays. Veronica chose to sit with Dylan in the back, thereby relegating me to the front seat. I didn't even complain, my emotions rendered down to a bed of glowing coals. In the rearview mirror, I could see her smiling, gazing with sentimental eyes at the boy she had brought from the other side of the veil.

"Buckle up," Trent said, as the car's engine kicked to life. "It's a little bit of a ride back to Anchorage."

I sank back morosely into my seat. This had already turned into the longest, most arduous journey of my life, and I didn't see that changing anytime soon.

"So you really followed Lian to Alaska, huh?" Dylan grinned. "Man, I always knew you had it bad for her."

"I never made it a secret," Trent replied. His eyes moved back and forth in the mirror, constantly keeping tabs on everyone.

Dylan laughed. "You played it down. I'm glad she finally got you. Never thought I'd see the day, honestly."

"Good thing we just found out you're the luckiest man in the universe."

In more ways than one, I thought savagely. I hated how badly it stung to know I was replaceable in Veronica's mind and heart. Perhaps the history she shared with this mystery boy gave him something of an unfair edge, but I had always assumed that the connection we had was superior to all others.

"Or," Veronica said, cutting into my thoughts, "we're the lucky ones to have Dylan back." She giggled. My heart hurt. If there was one thing I hadn't missed from my earlier, more romantic days, it was the ache of longing for another. Those feelings had been far in the past for so long. But here they were again, and I lacked the luxury of privacy in order to work through them.

"We'll see about that." Something about Trent's tone caused me to eject from furious introspection to cast a sidelong look at his face. His expression was more or less blank on the surface, but I caught a subtle undercurrent of doubt, of heavy distrust—and not just toward me.

"Oh, come on, Trent. You have to admit this is totally unbelievable." Veronica spoke as if the current turn of events was undeniably a good thing. She sounded as though all her dreams had just come true at once.

"It sure is." Again, Trent's words were laced with the finest strands of doubt and apprehension. His gaze kept flicking over the back seat. Not that Dylan or Veronica noticed; they were much too involved in each other. "It's good to have you back, Dylan."

"It's good to be back, I think." Dylan pressed his finger to the window button and put his hand through the open pane. "I forgot what this all felt like. Hell, I was starting to forget your faces. Everything kind of runs together after a while in that place, you know?" He paused. "But you never forget about the moment of death. That shit stays with you forever."

"I'm sorry," Veronica said softly. "I wish I had done more save you. I would've done everything in my power..." She trailed off. I hoped she wouldn't speak anymore.

"It's not your fault. None of this is your fault."

I closed my own eyes and focused all my energy on a plan to separate them. There was only so much of this shallow nonsense I could take. Couldn't she tell that something was seriously wrong with him? Maybe with her too.

Of course, she couldn't. I didn't want to admit the truth, but Veronica had clearly been in love with this boy at some previous moment in time. Her judgment, normally sharp for a mortal, was being clouded by the passion that I admired so much when it was directed at me. Even if she knew he wasn't right on the inside, I wondered if she would care.

"I'm just glad you're here," she said.

"We're going to see her, right?" V asked. Her voice brightened further at the mention of her friend. "Like, you're taking us back to her house?"

Trent was quiet for a minute. "I'm not sure that would be the best idea," he said at last. "Not right now. She's been through a lot already over the last few days. I don't know how to explain this to her yet."

"Oh." Disappointment colored Veronica's tone. She recovered fast. "In that case, I'd like to formally request that you drop us off at the Grand Hotel."

My hackles went up. I sat up in the seat, suddenly tense. My jaw clenched as I waited for Trent's response. If he gave the wrong one, I'd handle things myself, restraint be damned. I refused to allow her to spend any time on her own with Dylan. None at all.

"Who's *us*?" Trent shot me a warning glance; he had seen my visceral reaction. I drove a hand into my hair, holding it there. All of my self-control had become abruptly dedicated to not jumping straight for Dylan's throat. The mere implication of Veronica being with him was almost more than I could handle.

"Dylan and me," she said innocently. "I thought he could stay with me at the hotel. It'd give you and Lian a break from hosting."

Trent laughed. "No. That is not happening."

"Dude, you sound like my dad," Dylan remarked. "When I was like fifteen. What's the big deal?"

"Seriously?" Trent's smile faded. "Both of you have endured some serious supernatural shit very recently. We have no idea what kind of trauma could be associated with dying, hanging out in an unknown purgatory space, and then bringing two spirits back into the realm of the living. You need to be under some kind of supervision for a while until we know that everything is really okay." He looked at Dylan. "Come on. You know how this works."

"Yeah, yeah. I was just playing." Dylan turned his face to the window.

"Then what are we going to do? We're not going to see Lian, so..." Veronica was irritated that her plans had been foiled. She chewed her lower lip.

I saw my chance and took it. "Veronica can come with me. Only Veronica."

"Normally, I'd say no," Trent said. "But this time, I don't think I can. As long as Logan will be there too, you guys can keep an eye on her."

"Yes," I grumbled. The mortals always adored Logan, for reasons I didn't fully understand.

"Excuse me! I don't need to be babysat, Trent." Veronica leaned forward.

"It's not babysitting," he said. "We're taking care of you, all right? Lian would lose her mind if she found out I let you go off on your own after you literally died on a mountain. Once we know it's all fine, you can go back to doing whatever you want."

She sighed. "You're right. Sorry."

"Thank you. Dylan and I will find a place to crash for tonight. I'll tell Lian we'll see her later, and we will figure this out in the meantime."

"Okay." She lapsed into silence without saying anything to me. I was annoyed at her, but still grateful that she was not going to be away from me any longer.

"Where are we going?" Trent asked me. "I'll drop you and V off first." I gave him the address of the house by the inlet, and he nodded. Then he looked at me—face to face, not in the rearview mirror. "If I catch you doing anything shady, and I mean anything, I know where to find you now."

"Ugh, Trent…" Veronica buried her face in her hands. "Can you just drive there, please?"

"You have my word." I had to pull the sentence out of my mouth one word at a time as if they were teeth. But I said it, and he seemed to accept the promise.

"Fine," he said. "Let's go."

10

VERONICA

Dylan looked at me and gave me that half-smile again, the one that made my heart go a million miles an hour. A smile I swore I'd never see again, and right now it felt like I've been given a chance to make up for the not saving him. Nothing seemed to matter now that I knew my time in Anchorage was all leading up to being able to see him, hear him, touch him.

Though I wouldn't lie that my feelings for Orion, Seth, and Logan hadn't changed. They'd just become complicated now with Dylan back.

"How's it feel to be back among the living?" I said quietly.

"I should ask you the same thing," he replied. Then he thought about it for a moment. "Honestly? It's pretty weird. Turns out you can get used to just about anything—even death. But I'm not complaining." He squeezed my fingers in his.

A rush of warmth surged through my body. "Neither am I." Actually, that wasn't quite true. I resented Trent and Orion's decision to keep us apart. *Of course, this is the one thing they come to an agreement on.* At the same time, I knew better than to rock the boat too much right away. We all needed time to get acclimated.

Soon Trent would see that Dylan hadn't changed a bit. He was the same loving, funny guy we'd always known. Sure, he'd been through hell and back, maybe literally, but at that point, so had we all. The strength of Dylan's spirit was reflected in the fact that he had come out on the other side unscathed.

Has he?

The thought burst into my mind with the force of a grenade, and to my immense chagrin, I couldn't make it go away. It was so hard to admit that anything could be wrong while he was right there in front of me, his chest rising and falling with every corporeal breath. And yet, there was the faintest trill of foreboding in the back of my head. This all seemed way too good to be true. That I was forgetting something. And maybe it was too good to be true.

All of a sudden, I had all the luck in the world. But I'd never been an especially lucky person. Particularly as far as Dylan was concerned.

"Uh, V?" He waved his hand gently over my face. "You're staring."

"Oh, sorry." I laughed and tried to convince myself that it was just the old paranoia rearing its head, and that I was being ridiculous. "It's so crazy. One minute I thought you were gone forever, and the next, here you are."

"Yeah," he said. "Here I am."

Trent just drove until the car pulled up the long driveway leading to Orion's house. Then he killed the engine and caught my eye, a stare whose meaning I understood immediately. *Get the hell out.*

"All right, all right. Fine. Even though I don't have any stuff with me, and I haven't eaten in like, a day and a half."

"Don't worry about it, V," Dylan told me soothingly. "I'll see you soon." He lifted his hand and touched the tips of his fingers to my cheek.

"Bye."

"Let's go." Orion spoke sternly. He punctuated the command by slamming the car door. I rolled my eyes, but left without a choice, and followed him up to the old porch stairs. Behind me, I heard Trent start up the engine again and pull the car out. I glanced over my shoulder. All I saw was Trent in the driver's seat, plus an outline of Dylan sitting in the back.

"That's weird," I muttered under my breath.

"What?" Orion pushed the door open. He stalked across the threshold, turned around, and glared at me.

"Nothing." I held up my hands in mock surrender. "Dylan and Trent used to be best friends. I figured he would want to sit up front after we got out. That's all." Orion eyed me up and down, plainly disbelieving of every word I said. I took a deep breath and let it go. "Thank you for coming after me, and sorry I was so distracted by Dylan. It's just that I never expected to see him again after he died… after I didn't save him. Anyway, you didn't have to come for me, but thanks."

"Yes, we did." He moved toward me abruptly, as if he was going to grab me by the shoulders, but at the last moment, his demeanor changed. I found myself wrapped in a tight embrace, possessive, but not unkind. "Don't act tough, Veronica. You needed us." Orion paused. "Both of you."

There was something so damn intoxicating about being in his arms. I closed my eyes and gave up resistance, leaning deep into his chest. His fingers ran through my hair, and I felt a twinge of guilt. Dylan and I had only just reunited, yet I could not stay away from my tall, dark vampire. There was no denying what I felt for him, but my mind felt twisted and so distracted by Dylan's return. I never realized how much guilt I held onto until I saw him again. How I wanted madly to make him understand that I wanted to save him. I hadn't worked out how I would deal with the old emotions awakening inside me for Dylan. Especially when recently, I'd found myself falling for three others… a vampire, a demon, and a fallen angel.

Nonetheless, Dylan stayed impossible to forget. His face drifted in the darkness behind my eyelids. I loved knowing that he was in a car at this very moment, heading to a hotel to spend a night catching up with Trent. But it was haunting too, in a way I couldn't hope to articulate.

"How are you feeling?" Orion finally inquired, a little brusquely. He led me from the front hall into the living room, which was empty and still. I looked around, ears open for any other signs of life.

"I think I'm fine." We talked casually, like I hadn't died and been resurrected hours earlier. "Where are Logan and Seth?"

He scowled. "I don't know. I can only assume they'll show up eventually. You should eat." Before I could protest, or even say anything else, a loud growl from my stomach answered for me. Orion promptly left my side for the first time since we exited the car and disappeared into the kitchen.

A few moments later, I followed. The energy between us was undeniably different, and I felt surprisingly bad about that. Alone with Orion, it was quickly apparent that whatever my feelings for Dylan were, they did not erase those I already had. My empty stomach twisted into a knot. The silence turned deafening.

"So…what do you think?" I leaned in the doorway, pretending I wasn't scared shitless of his answer. I had no idea what to do if he forced me to choose—between him, Dylan, Logan, or Seth. The longer I dwelled on it, the more I realized I might be totally screwed.

Nice fucking job, V. Getting entangled with four guys who hate each other's guts. I rubbed a hand across my face. No way this was going to end well.

Orion stopped. He was standing at the counter, and I could see him processing the question. Then he turned and tossed me an apple. "You don't really want to know," was what he said. "Trust me."

I caught the fruit and checked it over. Past experiences had taught me that immortal beings weren't always great at knowing about human staples such as expiration dates or over-ripeness. "No, I do," I said.

"You don't," Orion repeated. He guided me back to the living room sofa. "It will upset you."

"And?" I bit into the apple and almost collapsed under the sudden weight of its deliciousness. The sweet juice flooded my starved taste-buds. I sort of moaned through a mouthful of fruit. "Don't you like to argue?"

Orion actually chuckled. "Not while you're enjoying yourself so much. We will have time to argue in the future."

I took another bite. "I hate the sound of that. Would it kill you to stop being so damn cryptic and just speak your mind? I'm literally asking for it." It wasn't like him not to be offensively forthcoming with his opinions. I wondered what had happened during my little spiritual excursion. "Seriously. I won't be mad."

Orion sat on the sofa with his arm around me, full of thoughts but voicing none of them. Once I devoured the apple, his unresponsiveness began to grate. The moment I opened my mouth to press him, however, he said, "Are you in love with him?"

I blinked. "Is that somehow a trick question?" I had the distinct suspicion that he was trying to lure me into dangerous territory.

"Yes," he admitted. "I already know the answer."

"I…" I hesitated, which made me feel awful. "I was. Back in Seattle."

Orion's eyes narrowed slightly. "Not now, on Denali? Or in the Underworld, as you wandered together?"

The familiar note of challenge in his voice made me bristle. "We were in there for like five minutes. At least, that's what it seemed like. And…I guess I don't know how to answer that. I see him, and I feel the way I felt that last time, so many years ago. Maybe that is love."

He grimaced. "Or a shadow of it. A shell."

I frowned. "Jealousy doesn't look good on you."

"I'm not jealous," he lied. "You need to be careful, Veronica. Death affects everyone in strange ways, mortals most of all. You think you know whom you brought back to this realm, but do you?"

His ongoing questions wouldn't have bothered me so much if I had been a hundred percent sure of my own convictions. I knew that, and it made me mad. It made me want to take his arm from around my shoulders and put some distance between us on the couch. In the background, the seedling of skepticism I kept trying to kill threatened to take root.

"I think I'd know better than you," I retorted, fully aware of how my promise to not get mad inched closer and closer to breaking. "Dylan and I were tight, whether you like it or not. I know his heart."

I expected Orion's temper to flare at any moment. We were like a gas can and a match when we argued; it was only a matter of time before it blew up in our faces. This time, however, he simply regarded me with a strange, inscrutable expression on his maddeningly handsome face. Despite my brewing anger, I realized how much I'd missed him, and how thankful I was that he and the boys had come for me.

He leaned over and pressed his lips to my forehead. They were cool, in a familiar, comforting sort of way. "I've been there before," he said quietly. "Where you are. For your sake, I want you to be right. But I know that you are wrong."

"Well, you're not helping." I folded my arms.

"There's no way for me to help, even though I want to," he answered. I detected a weird hint of melancholy in his voice, one I had never heard previously. Not to mention the fact that this was the first time he had ever expressed a desire to help with anything.

"Yeah, there is." I nudged his shoulder. "You could order me some more food." It was easier to focus on resolving the ongoing problem of my hunger, instead of the tiny cracks already appearing in my new, deceptively perfect reality.

11

SETH

*L*ogan and I separated pretty fast on our way back to the city. One minute he was there in the sky, and the next, he was gone. I didn't think too much of it; if he had taught me anything, it was that fallen angels were some of the ficklest beings in the known universe. It was impossible to understand where he was or what he was doing, so I just shrugged and let it roll off my back. He'd turn up eventually.

Without him, I rolled up to Orion's house alone, having beaten the car by what I assumed to be a pretty wide margin. The fact that Logan was nowhere to be seen didn't surprise me at all—he wouldn't have bailed if not for his own secret purpose. But the solitude was a good thing as far as I was concerned. The moment I stepped through the door, fatigue hit me like a brick wall. I almost stumbled on my way up the stairs.

"Goddamn," I muttered. "Where the hell is this coming from?" Exhaustion wasn't an experience I was used to, nor did I appreciate it. But all of a sudden, I felt like I'd been run over by a truck from Hell. "All right, fuck it." I made my way to my room, yawning so wide my jaw crackled. "I guess it's time for a nap."

When was the last time I had taken one of those? But as soon as my head hit the pillow, I was out—for a minute.

At first, when I opened my eyes again, a sickening sense of familiarity punched me in the gut. The cold got to me first, dancing across my skin like a hundred tiny needles. "Ah, shit." I sat up, rubbing my face. "You've gotta be fucking kidding me." I glanced around at shadow-cloaked walls and wondered if I'd actually been asleep the whole time and was just now waking up for real. "If this is a joke, it's not funny."

My call received no response. Then I blinked, and everything disappeared. The walls, the floor, even the cold, all gone. I found myself floating in the midst of the deepest black void I'd ever seen. Everywhere I turned was dark emptiness.

"Okay." I took a deep breath. "Maybe it's not a joke."

It was hard to move through the nothingness, as if the air below my knees was made of something thick and viscous. I picked a random direction and started trudging. "If I ever find out who's behind this bullshit, I'm gonna fucking kill them." I stopped for a moment, glanced over my shoulder, then realized there was no way to measure how far I had gone. "Good. Great."

Then I faced forward and saw someone in the distance, just standing there. I should have been thrilled to find company for my misery, but the sight of that figure sent a prickle of foreboding up the back of my neck. Still, I kept moving closer; I'd already spent weeks working with a couple of assholes I didn't like. One more wasn't going to kill me.

At least, I hoped not.

"Hey," I shouted across the darkness. The figure remained motionless, staring blankly in my direction. "Can you—"

I stopped. The realization had just dawned on me that I recognized that face, and that there was something wrong with it. Veronica's creepy little boyfriend didn't look any better with blacked-out eyes. He opened his mouth to speak, and a trail of dark smoke leaked out.

"Oh, no." I shook my head. "No. Nope. Fuck this." As if on cue, the invisible floor fell out from under my feet, and I plummeted down into the belly of the void.

Next thing I knew, I was sitting bolt upright in my bed at Orion's house, catching my breath. I swore the temperature in the room had dropped by at least ten degrees. My suspicions had been pretty strong to begin with, but now I was dead certain. There was something horribly wrong with that kid.

"Fuck." I got out of the bed. "He's gonna fucking kill her."

The stairs creaked like mad on my way up to the vampire's room. If he was in there, he heard me coming a mile away, and I didn't even care.

On this particular playing field, Orion and I were equals, or as close as we could possibly get. For once, I was reasonably sure he'd understand exactly where I was coming from.

His door was cracked a little bit, but I still knocked. The look on his face when he saw it was me standing in the hall would have been a hundred times more satisfying if I hadn't resolved to be his civil ally for the time being.

"Seth." He frowned. "What is it? You look like shit."

"Yeah? I suppose you're speaking from experience," I retorted. A brief, wry grin flashed across his face. "Sorry." I sighed. "Look, can I talk to you about that guy V dragged in from the Underworld, or wherever the fuck she was?"

Orion's gaze and posture sharpened instantly. He stepped back from the door, motioning me inside. The door closed behind me. "What do you know?" he asked.

"Nothing!" I threw my hands up. "Not a goddamned thing, but I can take some guesses. And you know what? They're all bad!" I told him about the dream from which I had just woken. "That son of a bitch isn't human. I don't know *what* he is. But I think he's a danger to her, and I think he's got an agenda." Driven by anger, my voice began to rise.

Orion gestured for me to be quiet. "Be calm. She's here."

"What?" I shot a reflexive glance toward the closed door. "V? Where?"

"Down in the den." Orion grimaced. "She's angry. She wants to be alone."

"He isn't here too, is he?" I half-whispered.

"Of course not. That's why she's upset." He paused. "The other slayer would not allow them to remain together either. A rare show of mutual agreement." It seemed painful for him to admit he shared anything in common with a slayer, especially viewpoints.

"Okay. So we agree, he's fucked," I said. "I just don't know how, or why. And I don't believe for a fucking second that she just happened to find him out there on the other side of the veil. Someone made sure he was in the right place at the right time." I looked Orion in the eyes. "He's a puppet. He has to be."

I expected him to tell me flat-out that I was wrong, an idiot, and I hadn't thought things through. But this time, Orion simply nodded.

"I agree," he admitted. "Unfortunately, I don't have any more answers than you." He glanced away. "I'm at a disadvantage when it comes to matters beyond the mortal realm. However, we both know someone who isn't."

I had never heard Orion acknowledge any kind of deficiency whatsoever, and if we hadn't been in the midst of such a heavy discussion, I might have asked him to repeat himself. As it was, I had to take his unexpected candor at face value and nod back.

"Logan," I said. "Let's go get him."

That turned out to be easier said than done. Logan's door stood uncharacteristically open, his room empty. The window on the far wall was also ajar, curtains billowing in a light breeze. I could see the sun just beginning its descent toward midafternoon.

Orion folded his arms. "He always does this."

I ran a hand through my hair. "We should have known."

12

LOGAN

I hovered in the sky above the inlet, wings beating the air just enough to keep me high aloft. Shiny beads of sunlight reflected off the water. I closed my eyes, focused my mind, and conjured up the grotesque face of the wendigo. Ever since the arrival of Veronica's companion, I hadn't been able to keep the wendigo out of my thoughts. I couldn't explain exactly why, but questions about the creature consumed me.

Where had it gone? Why didn't it return? I knew better than anyone that the monster's condition was far too healthy for it to have died or disappeared completely. If it was banished somehow, I would've felt it. We should have seen some evidence of its ghastly existence near Veronica's body on the mountaintop. But the site had been clean; no blood, no footprints, no unduly disturbed snow. I had pressing questions, and in search of answers, I'd decided to go straight to the source.

The summons rang out loud and clear, resonating along the threads of energy that bound the mortal plane. There was no way the creature couldn't hear it if it was able. Now all I had to do was wait for a response. And initially, I received none. Turning in a slow circle, I scanned the horizon all around, searching for signs of a wendigo speeding toward my location.

Nothing. The half-wild Alaskan landscape rolled away in all directions, unchanged.

But then I caught the faintest glimmer of an echo coming from a place much nearer than I had expected. I kept turning, waiting for that tiny signal to sound off right in front of me. When it finally did, I looked down and furrowed my brow.

I was facing the house, so close I could see the window I'd left open in my room. The echo came from beyond, but not far. In the distance, I saw the outline of downtown, and I knew.

The wendigo's energy was there.

I returned to my room to find Seth and Orion standing in the doorway. They both looked at me expectantly. I folded my wings and shut the window.

Then I said, "The wendigo came back to the city. I don't know what's going on."

"Neither do we," Orion answered. "But we don't like it."

Seth stared at me. "You're sure that thing is here somewhere?"

"Yeah. It can't be far. If I call out, I can feel it." As a matter of fact, I still could, an almost magnetic pull drawing me toward the city. "I think it has something to do with the boy."

The expressions on their faces told me I didn't need to elaborate any further. The demon turned toward the hallway. "Can you take us there?"

I started to say yes, but Orion stopped me. "No." He gave Seth a meaningful glance. "Veronica can't be left alone. For now, we stay here. She's our priority."

Seth didn't like it, but he conceded. "Fine. For now." He shifted his weight impatiently. "Maybe if we all go, she'll talk to us."

Orion chuckled grimly. "I doubt it." He was quiet for a moment. "But it's worth a shot. Come on."

Together, we went down the stairs to the first-floor den. Veronica was curled up on the sofa, gripping a mug with both hands and staring out at a bright view that contrasted her gloomy expression. Her frown only deepened once she realized we were all there, watching her.

"Look who's here," she muttered unhappily. "What do you guys want?"

13

VERONICA

*E*ven though I was pissed at being stonewalled from spending time alone with Dylan, it was still exciting to see the trio come into the den and gather around me on the couch. I kept any visible emotion to a bare minimum, unwilling to give them the satisfaction. I wanted to keep believing they were the bad guys in this scenario; it made me feel better about the creeping doubts that still hadn't gone away.

"Just checking on you," Orion said mildly, as if he had no clue why I might be angry. "Seeing how you are."

"I'm fine. Feel free to leave me alone." Instead of bristling at the rejection, Orion leaned back against the couch cushions.

"No, I don't think we will," he said matter-of-factly. "Actually, I think we'll all sleep down here tonight. Just in case."

"Ugh." I picked up a nearby pillow and threw it at him. "What is wrong with you? Dylan isn't dangerous. He'd never hurt me. I'm sorry you're jealous, but I don't know what else to tell you." I hated the way those words sounded to my own ears as they rolled off my tongue. Like I was lying or covering for someone who was. Why was it so hard to get rid of the whispers of paranoia in the back of my head?

But I knew that if all three of the trio were concerned, there must be a problem. Orion had been overprotective literally from the moment I met him. And Seth could be too reactive, a hothead who acted before he thought. Logan, though? He was an oasis of serenity in the middle of a passionate maelstrom. I'd never seen him do, say, or think anything he didn't wholeheartedly mean.

And there he was, just as concerned as the others. In a way, it was sweet—not to mention surreal to see them pulling together for my sake. I inched further into the corner of the sofa to give them a little more room.

"Seriously, I'm good," I said, fully aware that any of my excuses were falling on deaf ears. "I just need some time to decompress and process everything that's been happening. 'Cause, you know…it's kind of a lot."

"Go ahead." Orion wasn't bothered in the slightest. "We promise not to disturb you."

"That's right," Seth added quickly. "Some of us are very good at brooding in silence." His gaze ricocheted between Orion and Logan.

I laughed before I could help myself. "Oh my God, stop it. Get the hell out of here." I pushed lamely on Orion's shoulder. He didn't budge. "You guys don't need to babysit me. I'm a big girl. I can take care of myself."

"That might not be the best thing to say when you're fresh off a kidnapping that resulted in your death." Seth was not impressed by my reasoning.

I rolled my eyes. "Okay, but I did come back."

"Logan brought you back," Orion pointed out.

I looked to Logan for some kind of help. He shrugged. Then he reached over Orion and brushed a loose strand of hair out of my face. Despite my annoyance, I melted a little. The fact that they still had such an effect on me—all of them—was frustrating and exciting at the same time.

"Thanks for that," I said glumly. "I guess I should be nicer to you, considering the circumstances. I just—" I heaved a huge sigh and let my hands fall to my sides. "Do you understand what it feels like to see a person you thought was gone forever, right in front of you like that?" Vulnerability was not part of my plan, but once I started talking about it, the words poured out. "I can't help but be drawn to him. It's like unfinished business, like there's so much I want him to understand. To see if he really forgives me."

Seth was biting his tongue, hard. I could tell by the way he watched me in silence, his lips carefully locked shut. He held out longer than I thought he would, but eventually, his patience and willpower expired. "You don't feel it?" he asked, exasperated.

"What?" I arched my eyebrows, challenging him. If he had shit to talk about Dylan, I wanted to hear it out loud.

"He's not right, Veronica." Seth's tone softened. "I'm not being a dick this time."

My conscience begged me to back down and agree with him, to embrace my own persistent misgivings. But the part of me that still loved Dylan and had grieved him every single day in the years since his death refused to let him be dragged through the mud.

"You don't know him like I do," I said defensively. "Just because he was a slayer doesn't mean you get to automatically assume the worst. I think I deserve the opportunity to catch up with him again."

"He was a slayer?" For a moment, I thought I saw worry flash across Logan's icy blue eyes. It passed as quickly as it might have arrived, and I tried to brush it off.

"Yeah, in Seattle. Years ago." I flicked my hair. I glanced out the window. "After Dylan died, Lian tried to help me heal. I'm not sure how well it worked."

"What exactly was it that you lost?" Orion kept his tone neutral. He talked slowly, choosing each word with care. I knew that he was trying very hard not to come off too harsh, though it must have pained him to hear me speak of another man the way I spoke about Dylan.

I decided not to pull any punches. "Everything." Reaching over, I took his hand. "You don't want to hear this, and I apologize for that. But I thought he was my soul mate. My other half. I expected us to grow old and die together."

"That didn't happen," Logan murmured.

"No." A lump threatened to form in my throat. "It didn't. Dylan died in a horrible, brutal way, and I never got any kind of closure. I just had to go on with life as if nothing happened." I swallowed hard, willing the tears not to come. "You know how fast people forget you when you die? Really fast." I let out my breath. "Really fucking fast."

They didn't say anything. I looked at their faces, and only Logan gazed directly back.

"It's true," he said quietly. "Mortal memory is cruel and limited."

"I had to honor him," I continued. "Somehow, in some way. I wanted him to know, wherever he was, that he hadn't been completely erased. So I became a slayer like he was, except I wanted to forge my own path.

I figured staying independent would keep me from meeting the same fate as he did." I laughed without humor. "It's worked pretty well so far."

"Let me ask you something." Seth blew a ring of smoke that drifted lazily up toward the ceiling. The sun reflected off his golden eyes, making them ethereal and vibrant. "What would you do if it turned out this man wasn't the person you thought he was?"

"What do you mean?" I attempted to keep the dread out of my voice.

"What if he didn't have the same soul?" Seth was calm as the surface of a still lake. "Or any soul at all. What if you found out he was hollow inside?"

"I don't know," I answered honestly. My voice wavered on the last word.

"That's enough." Orion sat up. He slipped his arm around my shoulders and drew me close. "All we want is to keep you safe, my love. There are many dangers lurking in the dark, and until we know for sure that you won't be harmed, we're going to keep you in our sight." He kissed my forehead.

Emotionally spent, I gave up and leaned into him. But his love and strength did not reassure me this time. I had an awful, creeping suspicion that we were all hurtling as one toward a point of no return.

14

ORION

I wasn't used to seeing Veronica in distress. Although I deeply resented Dylan's sudden, unwelcome presence in her life, it pained me to know that I had caused her grief. My reluctance to share her didn't mean a blatant disregard for her happiness. By the time night was beginning to fall, she'd settled down somewhat, but tension still lingered.

Late in the evening, Seth tapped me on the shoulder. "You get first watch," he said, arching an eyebrow.

"Can you all just relax?" Veronica cut in before I had a chance to reply. "Nothing is going to happen." She gave me a look that was equal parts fatigue and exasperation. "Wherever Dylan is right now, Trent's there too. He won't be letting Dylan out of his sight." She sighed. "Trust me."

"Consider it a precaution," I told her. "If he doesn't show up tonight, that's great. If he does, we'll be ready." She rolled her eyes but didn't protest any further. Seth, Logan, and I glanced at each other. "I've got this. See you in the morning." They nodded. I knew they would have preferred to stay with her, especially Seth, and I wondered briefly about the motive behind this uncharacteristic show of deference, courtesy, or whatever he might have called it.

"Night, V," he said as he left. "Sleep tight." Logan smiled at her and followed in his wake.

She waved as they left the room, and then she turned to me. "What, you didn't want all four of us sharing a room? I'm shocked."

"This wasn't my idea," I said. Which was true, but I couldn't deny that these new, intimate circumstances pleased me. It seemed like eternity since I'd been alone with her. I almost felt like an entirely different person.

Veronica narrowed her eyes. "Not sure I believe that. Everything is your idea around here."

I chuckled flatly. "Well, it used to be." We were silent for a moment, during which she studied my face with her raptly attentive eyes. I sensed her scrutinizing my face; what was she looking for? An ulterior motive? Traces of a lie? Little did she know that despite however she chose to interpret my intentions, I had practically nothing to deceive her over anymore. Yes, I still desired to turn her, but the new developments of the past few days, plus the rapid shift in dynamic between myself, the angel, and the demon had thrown a large wrench into my plans.

For now, everything I had so carefully designed was pushed aside—not forgotten, but unavoidably delayed. I needed my place of power back, and I needed to know that I had the support of a strong and willing clan.

"Is this about what happened in the grove?" Veronica said abruptly. A hint of compassion softened the bluntness of her tone. "Things are bad now, aren't they?"

I half-grinned at her. "That's awfully presumptuous of you, my darling. You could hurt my feelings if you aren't careful."

"I'm serious." She picked my hand up off her shoulder. "Don't take this the wrong way, Orion, but you don't feel the same. And..." She hesitated. "I could kind of tell that things have changed with the others too."

"Hmm." I glanced away. "I didn't know you were so perceptive."

Veronica shrugged. "Me neither." She ran the slender fingers of her other hand through her thick hair. I caught a mild draft of her scent, just enough to excite my spirit. How I still longed to possess her as my own! She was made to be my thrall. "But I can tell. And I don't necessarily think it's bad, to be honest."

"Why would you?" I frowned. "You're not the one who narrowly avoided losing everything in that forest." The gravity of the clan's situation hadn't struck me hard until that instant, as I sat on the old sofa in the den with Veronica nestled up against my side. My hand, holding hers, reflexively attempted to curl into a fist. She squeezed back.

"No, not this time. But I've been there." She gazed up at me. "And I *did* die today, so…"

"Okay. I'll give you that one." Her face, gentled by empathy, seemed to glow so close to mine, perfect features mapping out the shape of true beauty. I forgot everything, just looking at her. The next thing I knew, our lips had met.

She let me kiss her for a long time, until my starved appetite had been whetted by her touch, her taste. "You know," she whispered, after we finally eased apart, "this is really pushing your luck."

I kissed her again, drawing a delicate moan from the tip of her tongue. "If you don't want to be with me, say so now."

A beat passed. I felt her thinking. Then her hands crept underneath my shirt. She flattened her palms on my skin.

"I'm not going to do that." One swift, fluid movement pushed the shirt over my head, and her mouth found my neck and chest. The warmth of her skin burned mine as we shed our layers one by one. I could barely recall the last time I'd regarded anybody with such reverence, let alone a mortal one.

"How can you be so beautiful?" I murmured into the curve of her hip. My fingers had made their way between her thighs, to the soft valley where her pleasure was made.

Veronica shuddered. "Does it make you mad?" She watched me, chewing her lip, one hand tangled carelessly in her wild mane of hair. She wriggled out of her jeans and pants swiftly, pushing the clothes to the floor with her leg.

I stroked her clit. Her eyes closed. She made a low, guttural sound that rose from a deep, primal place in her chest. "Don't you understand that you are fragile? Temporary?" I traced the same path with my tongue. She was so wet and tasted delicious. "It is a truth that ought to haunt you."

Veronica arched her back. "Oh my God, shut up." She placed her hand on the back of my head, urging me to taste her deeper. "I thought you were going someplace sexy with that. We can talk about your existential philosophy later."

I obliged her request passionately. It was frighteningly easy to lose myself in her and go to a place where nothing except the frenzied entwining of our bodies existed. She grabbed at me, braced herself on the sofa, and let her head fall back. I saw her lips move occasionally when I came up for air, but her sounds were beyond words.

Every muscle in Veronica's lean, taut body tensed at the moment of climax. She cried out, perhaps louder than she meant to. Her fingers dug into my skin, and into the worn leather of the couch. A fine sheen of sweat made her glisten in the dim light as her body shuddered and her thighs clasped tightly around my head.

"Holy fuck, you are amazing." She relaxed, catching her breath. Her heart thrummed in her chest, the blood racing through her veins.

I could turn her now, I thought. *While she's vulnerable and her guard is down.* A month ago, I might have pounced on her without hesitation. Instead, I wrapped her in my arms. The drive to make her mine remained, but it no longer carried a hard, brutal edge. I didn't want to hurt Veronica. Maybe I didn't even want to own her. I wanted to love her.

"I missed you." She pushed her hair away from her face and sat up enough to kiss me fiercely. "Don't tell Dylan."

I caught her chin in my hand. "Tell me honestly. Can he give you this?"

"I don't know." She climbed on top and took me in her hands.

I would've replied, but a blinding flash of pleasure stopped me. I stared up at her, robbed of speech. "You and I are here, and that's all I care about."

Using her mouth and tongue, she sucked down on my cock. She brought me to the very edge of ecstasy, dancing along that fine line. She teased me until it ached sweetly, and then she lay back on the couch, spreading those gorgeous legs for me. Her inner thighs and pussy glistened from her arousal, and that only had my erection hardening. I took over from there; my appetite would no longer be denied. A few ravenous minutes later, and I leaned over her, pushing inside of her. She was tight, and her back arched, her body so responsive to me. I adored everything about her. One hand on the cushion, and the other on the back of the couch, I pumped into her, while she curled her legs around my hips, riding me. Her moans were addictive, and a vampire could easily fall deeper for a slayer as beautiful as V. It wasn't long before she screamed her second climax into a pillow, and we collapsed together.

"We both needed that," she said after a while. "Badly."

"Yes," I agreed. "And I could go again and again."

She rolled over and kissed me, laughing. A mischievous spark lit up her tender gaze. "Do you think they heard us?"

I stole another kiss. "It doesn't matter. They definitely know."

Veronica giggled. "Are you going to fight about it later?" She was tugging a little bit on my emotions, trying to get a rise out of me. I had no doubt about it, and for once I didn't care. The fact that we had all managed to unite for a single cause had changed my perspective by the tiniest bit, washed away some of the bitter jealousy.

"Do you want that?" I asked, amused. "I'm sure it wouldn't be hard to get Seth to throw a punch."

"No." She rested her head on my chest. "But it's nice to be desired."

Before long, her breathing had slowed into the pattern of sleep. A sharp, irrational thought intruded upon my consciousness: that I'd better keep an eye on her to ensure she didn't slip right back into the no-man's-land behind the veil. I kept one hand in the middle of her naked back, counting each rise and fall. Through the night that was how I kept time, too paranoid to sleep.

Veronica was alive, and she was precious. Holding her was like holding a cosmic treasure against my body, feeling its rhythm and trying to fall in sync. If I closed my eyes too, I could almost see my purpose realigning. I wanted her to be the only thing that mattered.

And yet, there were shadows accruing on the horizon. The state of his clan, the missing wendigo, the distant knowledge that far away in Seattle, plans for war were likely brewing. I could not afford to lose my focus.

But for the shortest of moments, I indulged in Veronica's love. She slept in my arms.

I waited for sunrise.

15

LOGAN

We walked half a mile into Bootlegger's Cove, to a café for breakfast with Veronica. The counter in the front was busy, the air thick with the scent of coffee. Veronica spent a while studying the menu board while we sort of hung around behind her and tried to look inconspicuous.

"Hey, are you guys being served?" The friendly young man behind the counter grinned at us. "The counter's pretty full, but feel free to take a booth if you'd like. Someone should be over soon to get your order."

"Anywhere?" Seth asked. He was making a real effort to act human and pretend he cared about things like manners, with varying degrees of success. His discomfort was palpable, but I had to give credit where credit was due; so far, he'd managed not to twist any heads off or scorch an innocent business establishment down to the foundation.

The guy nodded, making a welcoming gesture with his arm. "Anywhere you want. We'll be right with you."

Seth glanced at us. Veronica laughed. "What are you waiting for?" she teased. "You heard him. Pick a booth." As he awkwardly carved a path through the bustling diner floor, Veronica took Orion and me by one hand each and pulled us along in his wake. "This feels like a fucked-up sitcom," she remarked, her voice cheerful. "I don't think I hate it."

To no one's surprise, Seth beelined for a booth in the farthest possible corner of the restaurant. But then, Orion surprised everyone by backing off and letting me slide in next to Veronica. He wasn't thrilled about it, but there was a grudging acknowledgement of obligation in the way he said, "It's your turn." She looked between us, holding her breath, waiting for the tension to break.

I said, "Thanks" and reached for a menu.

"Wow," Veronica whispered under her breath. She turned for a moment to Seth, who shrugged. "Okay. I'm not going to pretend I understand why you're all suddenly playing nice, but you won't hear me complaining either." She leaned over, resting her cheek on my shoulder so that she could peer at the same menu. "Do you guys have pancakes in Hell or wherever? If not, you should definitely try some." She kissed my shoulder. "With syrup."

"Yeah?" I didn't know how to explain to her that my senses hadn't been the same for ages. I could eat, but food tasted like dust in my mouth, and the smells were more like memories of scent. Part of the atonement for my sins was a life dimmed of the joy that had been thrown away in my first life.

"I just realized I've literally never seen any of you eat anything. Except for Seth, but that's mostly alcohol."

The demon grinned. "So what? It's the only thing you got here that's worth ingesting. And by the way, it's not just 'Hell or wherever.' You've been there now; you ought to start learning what to call it."

Veronica sat up, suddenly intrigued. She disentangled her arm from mine and rested it on the table, propping up her chin in her hand. "Oh, this should be interesting." The way she eyed Seth was sort of challenging, as if she didn't quite believe he was about to tell her the honest truth. "Let's hear it."

"Listen carefully," he said. "I don't want to say this twice." After a quick survey of the room to gauge the potential for eavesdropping, he continued, "Underworld is the umbrella term. That encompasses everything, more or less. Which means the Underworld contains stuff like Hell and the weird purgatory you were in."

"So...that *wasn't* Hell," she mused.

"Didn't sound like it." Seth frowned. "There's plenty of shit living in Hell that would've been more than happy to talk to you for the rest of eternity. You know, bargain for your soul and things like that." He nodded toward me. "Logan's the one you want to talk to about cold, dark, and creepy."

I didn't deny it.

Veronica smirked. "What about Orion? He sleeps in dirt."

Seth barely managed to stifle a burst of laughter. His gaze moved straight to the vampire, who'd been uncharacteristically quiet up to now.

Orion rolled his eyes. "It's good for my skin." Then he added, "Contrary to popular belief, my darling, being a creature of night does not necessarily equal having an infernal nature. You're assuming Seth and I are of the same ilk, which is likely offensive to us both."

"Sorry. Slayer culture doesn't place a very heavy influence on differentiating between supernatural origin unless it has to do with specific weaknesses." She arched an eyebrow. "Just in case you forgot I'm supposed to be trained in how to kill all of you."

"I have to say, you're not doing a very good job." Whenever he spoke to V, Orion's voice lost some of its hard, habitually arrogant edge. He softened, and the thought occurred to me that perhaps this was what he was like before centuries of ruthless immortality took over.

"Let's just say my priorities shifted." Veronica winked. "As long as you're nice to me, that is."

We were interrupted by a waitress who promised to bring coffee and a mountain of pancakes. The conversation didn't immediately pick up again following her departure. I sensed a change in the atmosphere. Veronica's expression turned somber.

She said, "I wish you would be more accepting of Dylan. All of you." This time, her words weren't driven by an undercurrent of anger or spite. There was something else hiding below the surface, a deep, swirling pool of doubt. It dawned on me that she wanted us to approve of him so her own instincts could be quieted.

Seth shook his head firmly. "Sorry, honey. That's never happening." He had managed to develop a way of being blunt without being cruel, at least where Veronica was concerned. Aware of her feelings, and still completely immovable in his convictions.

"Why not?" She tried very hard to sound curious rather than petulant. Her heart rate had increased a little, her body noticeably tense. I gathered that this was a discussion she regretted as soon as it had begun.

"I can't tell you this without pissing you off." Seth leaned forward. "And I hate to be the bearer of bad news, but there's something messed up about him, V. Don't know what it is, but as long as I'm being honest, I don't want him anywhere near me or you."

She sucked in a deep breath. Her face was flushed. I could feel the heat radiating off her body. "That's not something you can just say about a person," she answered softly. "None of you understand what he's been through."

"Can I ask you something?" Seth spoke nonchalantly, as if we were talking about the weather.

"Sure." She lifted her chin slightly. We all knew what that tiny motion meant; she was getting ready to dig in her heels.

"How long ago did he die?"

The question made me wince internally. All of a sudden, I could see exactly where Seth's line of thought was headed, and I wasn't sure I wanted to go down that road. A few minutes ago, we'd been ordering pancakes in peace. Was it too much to ask for that tranquility to persist for one morning? But the way things were, I knew it was. Better to get the difficult confrontations out of the way sooner rather than later. Or so I hoped, anyway.

Veronica shifted in the booth. "Years ago," she admitted, hesitating.

Seth looked at me. "That's what I thought. There's no way, babe. No way he came back completely intact. Several years is too much time."

Veronica was staring at me too, her pretty face reflecting fear and desperation. As I gazed down at her, I sensed something strange and powerful underneath her energy. I had felt an echo of it long before, back when we had first met. Now this power was much stronger, dominating her aura.

"Say something, Logan," she whispered.

What I wanted to say was that her time across the veil, however brief, had clearly stirred some unknown magic to awakening in her spirit. I wanted to say that I was almost positive this beautiful woman with the candy-colored hair was far more than she had originally appeared to be. And for her sake, I wanted to wholeheartedly disagree with Seth's assessment of her situation.

Unfortunately, I couldn't.

"The integrity of a soul can't be preserved forever in those in-between spaces," I said. "There's nothing to anchor them into the life they lost. They forget who they are, slowly at first, and then fast."

Unshed tears brightened her eyes. She pressed her lips together. "I don't want to talk about this right now. Not in public."

"That's fine." Seth leaned back. "It won't change my stance on the matter."

Orion shot him a glare, and he fell silent. A moment later, Veronica's phone vibrated against the tabletop. She picked it up, examined the screen, and sighed.

"It's Trent," she said. "Because of course it is."

"What's he want?" Orion fought an endless battle to seem neutral. Inside, we knew he was seething.

Veronica scanned the text. She chewed her lip, twirling a lock of hair around her finger. When she finally spoke, it was to me more than anyone else. "He says Dylan wants to meet up later. He wants to see Lian too." Her worry proved impossible to mask. "What if she freaks out?"

"I wouldn't really blame her," I said.

"Neither would I, but…" Veronica let out her breath. "I guess I'm afraid she won't be happy."

Seth and Orion said nothing, but I could feel them listening.

"Why wouldn't she be, if you are?" I asked.

Veronica glanced away. "I don't know. And I hate that."

16

SETH

I kind of felt like shit for stepping on V's feelings while we were supposed to be taking her to breakfast. It was not my intention to bullshit her, ever, but I couldn't help thinking about whether there might have been a better way to voice my concerns. *I should have left it to Logan, goddammit.* He was a man of few words, but they always seemed to be better than mine.

Nonetheless, what was done was done. We ate a ton of pancakes, paid the bill, and got the hell out of there, all without purposely breaching any more touchy subjects. But the specter of Dylan and what would happen when he saw him again lingered over everything, especially since he kept trying to arrange a meeting.

"He says he wants it to be like old times," V told us. She furrowed her brow at the phone. "Him and Trent and Lian and me, just hanging out the way we used to every day."

"That makes it sound like we're not invited," I remarked.

"We must be," Orion interjected. For a moment, he was back to his old self, all stern and self-righteous. "I refuse to leave you alone with him." I hated that he was talking sense for once.

"We won't be alone," Veronica retorted. "Trent will be there, and so will Lian. You guys aren't the only ones who care about me, okay? I'm making my own choices whether you like it or not."

"You don't seem happy about it, though," Logan said.

She didn't answer him right away. I noticed her hand that was clutching the phone had gone white in the knuckles. "I'm just stressed." She ran her fingers through her hair. "At first, I was like, deliriously happy, but now…" Her voice trailed off. I watched her type something into her phone. The glow of the screen lit her features gently from below. Then she said, "He and Trent are going to see Lian by themselves. He wants me to meet up with them."

"That means you have two choices." I ticked them off on my fingers. "Either you can let us bug you so we can listen in, or we stake the place out in person."

"You have got to be kidding me," she muttered. She massaged her temples, as if attempting to ward off the mother of all headaches. "This is ridiculous."

"I don't think you mean that," Orion said.

"Oh yeah?" She scowled at him. "I'd love to know why."

He gazed at her evenly. "You haven't just left yet."

She covered her face with her hands. "Fucking hell. If I agree to this, you have to stay out of sight unless there's an emergency. A *real* emergency," she added pointedly. "Like, one of us has to be dying before you blow your cover. Understand?"

Orion grimaced, but he agreed. "As you wish."

"All right." She got up from the sofa and headed for the stairs. "Figure out your crazy plan. I need to get ready."

Once she was out of earshot, Orion and Logan turned to me. "This was your idea," the vamp declared. "You're taking point."

"Come on. Since when have I ever been the brains of an operation? You never had any problem taking over before." The truth was, I had no idea how to actually execute the terms of our agreement. Hell, she hadn't even told us where they were meeting.

"Times are changing fast," Orion replied. "Adapt or be left behind."

I grumbled. "Somehow you're still managing to be the fucking worst. Look, I was thinking we'd keep it as simple as we can. She goes to the meeting spot, we follow her to wherever that is, and then we keep real close tabs on his ass the whole time. I don't care if that fucker goes to take a dump. We need to be watching him."

Orion regarded me. "Do you know what he is, Seth? Your convictions against him are notable."

"It should be more than enough for you that he's back from the fucking dead, and he wants to be all over V. I do have a theory, though, now that you ask."

"Go on."

I detested the feeling of subordination Orion gave me, even when he wasn't meaning to. This time, however, I swallowed my objections and pressed on. In my head, I reminded myself over and over that Veronica meant more than nonsense bad blood between us. "I think he's a homunculus," I said. "Hollow. No soul. Like a puppet. Maybe he's fucking possessed, I don't know. But he's evil, and that's what matters here."

"Interesting." Orion steepled his fingers. "I believe he was resurrected by an as-yet-unidentified party. It would've had to have been a necromantic type of mage, and a powerful one at that. If he is a construct, he's well-made enough to fool Veronica. For now."

"What about you?" I said to Logan. "We shared our ideas. It's your turn."

He took his sweet time coming up with an answer, as usual. "I'm not quite sure," he said at last, "but the wendigo is key. I sensed its energy coming from the direction of downtown earlier. It isn't dead or gone." He paused. "And...Veronica changed while she was out of the mortal realm."

"Explain," Orion and I demanded simultaneously. I didn't like the sound of this at all.

"She has latent magical qualities that have remained dormant until now," Logan went on. "Beyond her capacity as a slayer and her associated training. What I felt was bound to her spirit. It's part of who she is." His calm, steady gaze moved to Orion. "You won't be able to turn her."

The vampire bristled. His veneer of tolerance cracked. "That's none of your concern," he said tightly. "I'll do with her what I please, provided she is in agreement."

I saw the opportunity to speak my mind on a sensitive subject, and I took it. "You will ruin Veronica if you make her into one of yours, man. She wasn't meant to be a vampire." More than imagining her locked in creepy vampiric matrimony with Orion for the rest of time, it got under my skin to think of her alive, yet essentially lifeless, her soft skin drained of color and warmth.

"That is true," Logan reiterated. "It can't be done without risking disastrous consequences."

"This is an irrelevant tangent," Orion protested. "A distraction from the most important task at hand. I suggest we focus on our common enemy for the time being, rather than dividing ourselves." It wasn't the worst point he had ever made, and while I was certain he just wanted to get out of the hot seat, I let him off the hook.

"Fine. That's fair." I cleared my throat. "We'll talk about that other stuff later." He had no way of turning her without detection at the moment anyway. We had reached a tacit agreement to function more or less as a unit while Veronica was under threat. "As far as this asshole Dylan goes, I think the plan remains the same. They meet, we follow, he never leaves our sight." Anything more than that would be stepping on V's toes, and I still wanted to respect her. "Like she said, no intervention unless absolutely necessary."

Why did I have a feeling that absolute necessity was on the horizon?

"We can do that," Logan stated. Orion didn't seem quite as confident, but he permitted no resistance. He just folded his arms and nodded, one eye on the stairs, watching for V's reentry.

"We don't really have a choice," I said. "Our only other option is to trust the other slayer to keep her safe, and I don't know how I feel about that."

"No," Orion said. "We're going."

I grinned wryly. "And there it is."

An hour later, we were fanned out behind Veronica as she made her way to the meeting spot her friends had chosen—another restaurant, not far from the one we'd just been at. Before she approached the doors, she checked to make sure we were all in a suitable position; in other words, that she couldn't see us.

Don't worry about us, I told her. *We're fine. Get going.*

She frowned in my general direction, but a moment later she disappeared into the entryway.

Get up high, Orion said immediately. *Somewhere that will let you see inside.*

I moved around the perimeter, peering with sharp eyes through the huge, modern windows. It didn't take long to spot her hair tumbling out of the cap she had worn as she settled down at a table with three other people. The scene looked like an alternate universe recap of the morning. Except they were all tense from the start. It was almost like V had walked in on three people attempting to defuse a bomb.

You guys feel that? I asked. *What the hell was going on before we showed up?*

Orion's voice murmured in my head. *I don't like it.*

They don't trust him either, Logan said. *Especially the other girl.*

I zeroed in on her expression. She had a stone-cold poker face on. Not the way she should have looked just after reuniting with a long-lost friend. Her dark eyes stayed trained on Dylan with the intensity of a laser. She was ready for him to do something reckless, stupid, dangerous, or all of the above.

Hold on tight, I said, half to myself. *We might be about to go for a wild ride.*

17

ORION

Veronica took a seat at that table, and the tension crackled through the air like electricity. We had split up to observe, but we all felt it as intensely as if we were sitting beside her. She must have sensed something too, because the first thing she did was look back and forth between the solemn faces of her friends.

The other girl, whom I assumed was the one known as Lian, acknowledged her with a quick, false smile. Her lips moved. I had to focus to hear her through the glass and the din of the other patrons.

"Hi, V. How are you feeling?" She spoke very deliberately, choosing each word with the utmost care. I got the strong impression that before Veronica arrived, Lian had been navigating a precarious social mine-field alone.

"Uh…fine." Again, Veronica looked around. "What's up with you guys? Are we going to a funeral after this?" She reached over and touched Dylan's arm. "How crazy is this, that we're all sitting at a table together somehow?"

He chuckled and shook his head. One of his hands found hers and squeezed it. "I gotta say, it's not something I ever imagined. I wished for it, when…" He trailed off, then cleared his throat. "Well, you know. And I can't believe my wish came true."

I turned my attention to Trent in an attempt to gauge his reaction. He sat back in his chair, saying nothing. His gaze traveled between every other person at the table. I could feel him thinking, mulling things over. The urge to jump in through the plate glass and ask him what he saw was nearly overwhelming.

As I watched the scene unfold, my hand curled into a loose fist. There was so much context I was plainly missing, cues I longed to understand. Was Dylan acting strangely? Had he said anything to arouse suspicion so far? What I really wanted to know was whether or not we'd be justified in leaping in and tearing him to shreds. Every inch of me itched to do just that.

If only such an intervention were possible! Nothing would have pleased me more, and it was a scenario at least Seth would also find agreeable. But Veronica had shown herself to be a naïve little fool in Dylan's presence; no doubt she'd be traumatized and start to despise me all over again. I couldn't bear the thought of losing her to the whim of mortal emotion, which meant I had no choice but to bite my tongue and bide my time.

"I'm sorry if I keep staring," Lian was saying. "I just can't wrap my head all the way around this yet. Where *were* you? How did you escape?" She paused. "How are you…alive?"

Even from a spectator's viewpoint, it was obvious that her questions made Veronica nervous. I watched my girl fidget subtly in her chair— touching her hair, turning the rings on her fingers, bouncing her knee gently underneath the tabletop. Was she anxious because she anticipated his answers and didn't want Lian to hear them?

Or maybe she feared what Dylan might say.

He better not slip up, Seth growled.

Personally, I wished he would. I wanted Veronica to see what she was choosing, to be forced to assess her own decisions without the rose-tint of nostalgia and lost love. Hints of who—or what—he truly was kept needling at me. She'd have to find out the truth sooner or later, and I had a feeling it wouldn't be pretty.

"It's hard to explain." Dylan talked calmly. He had an arm laid across the back of Veronica's chair, and every so often, his fingers grazed her shoulder. "I spent years just walking through an endless fog, with my memories drifting in and out. Sometimes I remembered myself, and I remembered you guys. But sometimes…nothing." He shrugged.

"That doesn't bother you?" Lian pressed. "Like, it's not hard to talk about now?" She looked over at Trent, possibly for backup, but he wouldn't take his eyes off Dylan. As if he expected his old friend to change into something unrecognizable at any moment.

Maybe he was smarter than I thought after all.

"I can't really explain that either." Dylan laughed, rubbing his forehead with the tips of his fingers. "It almost seems like a lifetime ago, even though I know it was literally yesterday. I guess my whole sense of time is messed up." He raised his eyes to stare at Lian. "How much does that matter? I'm here, aren't I?" The barest tinge of aggression colored his voice. He was apparently beginning to tire of the constant interrogation.

"Dylan, I'm not trying to be an asshole," Lian said immediately. "It's just...you came back from the dead. I think that matters a little bit."

"Yeah." Dylan took a deep breath and sat back. "You're right. Sorry. It's a shock for me too. I guess I have to adjust to the world of the living." He touched Veronica's shoulder and smiled when she looked his way. "I'd be lost if it wasn't for this girl right here."

Veronica smiled back. I felt her blush. "You're sweet," she said.

"Hey, I was thinking that maybe you and I could go out this afternoon," he added. "Just the two of us. Get some time alone." Somewhat sardonically, he addressed Trent, who still had not said a word. "Would that be okay with you, sir?"

Unamused, Trent frowned. "Not really."

"Come on." Dylan grinned, but there was a sharp edge forming on his demeanor. "Twenty-four hours of nonstop surveillance wasn't enough for you? I'm pretty sure if there was something wrong with me, it would've shown itself by now." He spread his hands on the table, palms up, to show they were empty. "Face it, bro. I'm back in business and there's nothing you can do about it."

The tone at the table had started to shift noticeably. The flavor of tension was turning slowly toward hostility. Trent's jaw was set hard as he regarded Dylan, his face expressionless.

"For what it's worth, I'd like that," Veronica said.

"See? Thank you, V." Dylan kissed her on the cheek. "It's what she wants, dude. We're all adults here. You can't just keep us locked away from each other until you're satisfied. We deserve a chance to reconnect."

There's no fucking way she's going anywhere alone with him, said Seth. *I'll climb a funeral pyre in the heights of Hell before I let that happen.*

Get ready to move, I replied. *In case they make a break for it.* I wanted to give Veronica the benefit of the doubt, that she wouldn't do something so reckless and stupid, but she could not be trusted to make wise decisions at the moment.

Oh, I'm ready. You there, angel-boy? Say something once a year so we know you're still with us.

They aren't leaving yet, Logan declared.

I refocused on the table, mostly to see if I could discern what the hell Logan was talking about. Lian sat with her chin propped on her hands, deeply pained. She couldn't stop scrutinizing Dylan. Suddenly, she sighed.

"You're not wrong," she admitted. "We wanted to make sure both of you were safe, that's all. People don't just casually move back and forth across the veil."

"I know that, Li," Dylan answered. His speech was terse now. "And I appreciate your concern. But I'm fine. We're fine."

"Watch it," Trent warned. "Look, I get it. I don't care what you do on your own time, which starts now. But I'm going to be checking in pretty regularly for a while. And if you don't answer the phone I gave you, I'll come looking."

"All right, all right." Dylan gave up an annoyed little smirk. "Jeez. I didn't know things had changed this much while I was gone. I guess I can't really blame you." Dylan pushed his chair back and stood up. He stretched, but when Veronica went to join him, he stopped her mid-rise. "We'll get out of here in a sec, babe. I need to make a pit stop first."

Her eyebrows arched slightly. "Okay."

His smile turned as reassuring as he could make it. "Having my body back means I need to empty the tank again. I'll be right back."

She snorted. "Gross."

I watched her watch him walk away. As soon as he was out of earshot, Lian leaned over toward Veronica. She kept her voice so low I had to concentrate to make out the words.

"Don't take this the wrong way, but are you absolutely sure that's Dylan?"

"What are you talking about?" Veronica snapped. Her quick leap to Dylan's defense told me conclusively that she still had lingering doubts. "Who else could it be?"

"I don't know." Lian backed off. "Never mind." She exchanged a glance with Trent. "You're okay with going out with him alone? It won't be weird?"

"No. It feels amazing to be with him again," Veronica insisted. She kept peering restlessly in the direction Dylan had gone.

Someone needs to follow that bastard, Seth cut in. *Orion, it should be you. Logan and I will keep an eye on V.*

I grumbled under my breath. He was right, but I hated to let her out of my sight. Reluctantly, I peeled away from the main setting in the dining room to track Dylan's path away. To my surprise, I found that he had gone out a back exit and was standing in the shadow of a dumpster behind the restaurant.

I can't tell what he's doing, I said. *Stand by.*

But then a voice came through, like a radio picking up a stray channel. It was unclear whether he knew he could be heard, and the things he said set my teeth on edge.

"Renfrew," Dylan intoned. "I've got her. Tell the others it's time."

The moment I heard that name, all my patience, restraint, and sense flew out the window. His mention of a man called Renfrew filled me with hatred and resentment. The Renfrew I knew had been my friend long ago, but he'd defected from Anchorage on the promise of prestige further south.

Now, he sat on the clan council in Seattle, at the right hand of a mortal enemy. And this tainted boy was summoning them all back here.

The last thing I saw before being consumed by rage was Dylan's face turning toward me, painted with a mix of shock and sudden fear.

"What the f—?"

18

VERONICA

He was taking way too long to get back. For the first time since laying eyes on him, I started to get a little mad at Dylan. Here I was, trying my hardest to stick up for him and be understanding of his whole situation, and he paid me back by acting even weirder. It was getting more and more difficult to explain his behavior away, and I didn't like it.

Finally, I looked at Lian and voiced a suspicion that was taking root in my head. "The bathroom isn't over there, is it?"

I hadn't been talking to him, but Trent immediately shook his head. "It's over there." He nodded in the opposite direction, and when I looked, I could see the sign, clearly marked and not at all the way Dylan had headed. "I think we need to see what's up," Trent added.

"I'll go. Stay with Lian." He looked like he wanted to object, but changed his mind at the last minute, which I thought was wise. At this point, there was not a lot that could have kept me from finding out what the hell was up with Dylan. I hadn't thought there were many secrets to be gained in a plane of lightless purgatory. Maybe I was wrong.

The apprehension grew steadily on my way toward the back of the diner, where I thought he had gone. The feebly optimistic, lovesick corner of my consciousness tried to pretend I might encounter a previously hidden second bathroom that would make this all okay. Of course, I didn't find one. All I found was an exit leading straight out into the back delivery lot. And as I approached that door, I caught sight of two familiar figures wrestling viciously on the ground.

The moment my brain registered what my eyes were seeing, I let out a bloodcurdling scream that echoed out across the empty lot. Orion had Dylan pinned to the pavement, his knee pushed down into the center of Dylan's chest. One thought flashed like an emergency sign in my mind: *He's going to fucking kill him!* My fight instincts activated even before I stopped screaming.

"No!" Without a second thought, I threw myself into the brawl, grabbed Orion by the shoulders, and tried to yank him back. His head whipped around, fangs bared in a primal snarl. In that instant, I glimpsed a snapshot of the monstrosity that was evident to everyone else. He hardly looked like the man I had come to love.

He looked like what he was: a vampire.

"Stay out of this, Veronica," he hissed. "This part is none of your concern."

"Like hell it isn't! Get the fuck away from him!" Keeping one hand latched on to him, I reached into my pocket for my staff with the other. Whatever feelings I harbored for Orion evaporated away in the face of furious betrayal. He *knew* how much Dylan meant to me, conflicted or not, and this was the choice he had made?

"Veronica!" Orion roared. He snatched the front of my shirt, tearing through the fabric, and shoved me backward. "Stop!" He glowered at me. "You know nothing, and you will only get hurt."

"Oh yeah?" I balanced on my back foot. The staff extended with a snap. I brandished it at him. "You know what? Fuck off. I thought you actually wanted what was best for me and didn't know how to express it. But now I see you're just fucking jealous because someone you've never met is suddenly more deserving of my attention."

On the ground, Dylan took the opportunity to shove Orion's knee off his chest. I reached out my hand; he grabbed it and got to his feet. Then he looked at me strangely, head cocked to the side.

"Jealous?" he said. "Why would he be jealous, V? He's a vamp."

I realized too late that I had let slip some pretty heavy inferences to the true nature of my relationship with Orion. And because Dylan was not a total idiot, he began to do the math pretty fast. Orion just eyed us both in silence. He, too, seemed aware that the game had changed, and he was just waiting to see what his next move had to be.

"You didn't notice he came to Denali to rescue me?" I asked Dylan, maintaining a tough exterior. *Don't back down, don't show weakness, don't look scared.* The three of us were a house of cards now, swaying in a dangerous wind. *This is not my fault.*

Obviously, that was a lie. This could not have been any more my fault than it already was.

Dylan's confusion morphed into shock and anger. I watched the emotions roll across his face like an unstoppable tide. "You were with him," he said softly. "He's jealous because you have fucking *been* with him and he thinks you're his!" The volume of his voice started to climb. "How could you?"

And just like that, the house of cards came down.

"Dylan, I—"

He didn't let me get more than those two words out. "No. Fuck no, V. I cannot fucking believe that you came to find me, and then you brought me back, into a world where you're riding a vampire's dick. Tell me it's not true, I'm literally begging you. Tell me this is all some crazy prank, and I'm gonna wake up at home in Seattle like nothing ever happened. Can you tell me that?"

I couldn't, and I couldn't bring myself to confirm what he now knew, so I kept my mouth shut.

He scowled. "I really wanted a future with you, Veronica. When I was walking alone in that place for God knows how long, the memories of you were the ones that returned the most. Of us together. They were my only escape from the void." He stared at me, his eyes abruptly hollow. "How could you do this to me?"

The lump in my throat was too big to speak around. Every muscle in my face had gone taut with the Herculean effort it took not to collapse in tears. "I'm sorry," I whispered. "This isn't what I meant to happen."

"Disgusting." He clenched his jaw. "Do you hear me? You're disgusting! I died, and after all this time, you didn't learn a fucking thing! I thought you were better than this, Veronica. I thought you were smarter."

The hot tears welling in my eyes finally spilled over. I held his searing gaze for as long as I could, but eventually the pain grew overwhelming, and I had to look away. As my head turned, I saw the back door of the restaurant opening to let Trent into the lot. He was quickly followed by two others—Seth and Logan. They stopped in their tracks for just long enough to assess the shitshow unfolding before their eyes. Then they broke into a run toward us.

"Really? You've got nothing to say?" Dylan's voice had taken on a taunting edge. "You're not even going to look at me anymore? That's pathetic." He chuckled grimly. "And to think, I almost defied all my orders for you."

The entire world stopped for me when he said that. I glanced up in slow motion, all sounds muted under a foggy hush in my ears. My lips and tongue moved, but it seemed like a long time before I heard the word that emerged from my mouth.

"What?" I blinked, again in slow motion. "What are you talking about?"

Someone yelled, "Get out of here, V!" But I wasn't able to listen, or even process what was being said. The jarring revelation Dylan had dropped on me was rooting my feet to the faded pavement. Our eyes were locked.

"That voice I told you about," Dylan said. "The one that told me the doorway out was going to appear after we found each other." A slight smile curved his lip. "He's the one who made it all possible."

"V!" I recognized the shouting as coming from Seth this time. He leapt in front of me, temporarily blocking my view of Dylan. "God damn, girl, you got a death wish or what?" he demanded. He grabbed me by the shoulders. "Get the fuck out of here before I throw your ass out. Go somewhere safe. We'll deal with this."

"No." I put my hands on his chest and pushed. "Let us finish talking. I need to find out what's going on here or it'll haunt me for the rest of my life."

Seth hesitated. He growled. "Fine. But he makes one false move, and we're killing him on the spot. I don't want to do that in front of you."

I sure as hell didn't want that either, but the notion of leaving without closure was unbearable. Seth stepped aside, and I looked at Dylan. "Can you just fucking cut it out with this cryptic bullshit and tell me the truth?"

"Why?" he asked. "I just found out you've been lying to me this whole time. Are you fucking all of them, V? Is that why they follow you around like some kind of messed-up entourage?" He sighed. "Honestly, maybe it's my fault for assuming you'd still be the girl I knew and loved. How easily we forget the ones we've lost, right?"

Every word was like a knife in my heart. "I never forgot you," I murmured.

"Lies!" Dylan exploded in a sudden bout of rage. "You're a fucking liar!" He lunged toward me, his face grotesquely contorted. The next thing I knew, the others had brought him down hard onto the ground at my feet. One of Seth's claws hovered at Dylan's throat.

"You fucked up big-time, kiddo," the demon said.

Dylan's face went blank, but only for a second. Then he started laughing, almost hysterically. The sound spiraled up from the parking lot into the sky, soaring out over the city. I knew I'd never be able to forget it.

"Me?" He was still laughing so hard that tears pooled at the corners of his eyes, and he had to catch his breath. "I'm not the one who fucked up." He nodded in my direction. "She is. She just doomed every single one of you." To Orion, he said, "Especially you, asshole."

My stomach dropped. I felt horribly sick. How *could* I have done this? And yet, I was unable to separate the seething, bitter person in front of me from the Dylan I'd known for so long. He still felt the same, in ways that really mattered.

But not even my lovesick heart could deny what was happening. Seth held Dylan's head up by his hair, one demon claw poised and ready. I kept waiting for him to pierce the skin, for the blood to start flowing and never stop.

Instead, they all waited.

Seth's eyes were riveted on me. "Say the word, or don't."

I knew that I should have instructed them to kill Dylan. Deep down, I understood that I had been fooled. No matter what I longed for, he was not the same. My Dylan would have died before he hurt me—in fact, he already had.

But I just couldn't bring myself to pull the metaphorical trigger.

"Spare him," was what came out. "Please. Until we can figure this out."

Seth wanted to protest. I could see how badly he wanted to defy me, and how wrong he thought I was. Truthfully, there was nothing stopping him except his own restraint, which he exercised. The claw was withdrawn from Dylan's neck. I breathed a sigh of sorrow, frustration, defeat, and relief.

Trent was the one who stepped forward to break the new silence. He gazed down at Dylan for a few long moments.

"Get up," he said. "Start talking. This is your only chance to tell us everything."

"And if I don't?" Dylan asked. His nerve pissed me off at the same time it appealed to my senses. I wished he hadn't just shattered my vision of him, for many reasons.

Trent shifted to reveal the long, cruel blade holstered at his waist. "Then I guess we might never know."

"Trent." I shot him a desperate, pleading look.

"Let him up," Trent said to Orion and his crew. Still restrained, Dylan staggered to his feet. A bruise was blooming on the side of his face that had been pressed to the ground. He and Trent glared at each other. "Speak," Trent ordered. "Now."

19

LOGAN

We made an impromptu circle around Dylan in the back lot behind the restaurant, a shield between him and the civilized mortal world. His eyes, flat and filled with mockery, stayed pinned on Trent, though I knew he could feel us all watching. He must have known, too, that we were primed to remove him from the mortal realm at a moment's notice—and we weren't inclined to be merciful. If not for Veronica, he probably would have been reduced to a corpse already.

Still, he smiled. A cruel smile, but one nonetheless. Part of me had to admire the absolute gall it had to take to grin in the face of four beings who didn't much care if he lived or died. But more than that, I was annoyed by him, by the things he'd done and the time he'd stolen.

We should have killed him on the mountain, I lamented.

Seth replied, *No shit.*

"Okay, look." Dylan tried to free his arms from Seth's grip and was met by a ruthless jerk of the shoulders that forced him to grimace in pain. "Here's the deal. Remember I mentioned that voice? He told me he was a shaman working for a guy in Seattle named Steele. I didn't get much more than that, but I mean, I've been around the block once or twice, right? I can recognize a vamp when I hear about one."

Orion let out a low, barely restrained growl. His eyes blazed. The thin veneer of humanity slipped away from his visage once more. "He sent you?"

"Maybe. I don't know who the fuck it really was, to be honest. And I don't care. The only thing I cared about was that I'd get to see Veronica." He paused. "Yeah, they told me to get rid of her, but up until now, I was undecided. Hell, I just told you I was about to throw it all away."

Veronica gasped. I glanced at her. She had a hand over her mouth, tears rolling silently down her cheeks.

"You changed your mind?" Trent asked. His stance and tone were both deceptively casual; his energy ran tense and hot like a live wire. He was prepared, like we all were, for anything.

"Well, yeah." Dylan turned his head to the side and spat on the pavement. "Obviously. Why should I give a fuck about what happens to a traitor?"

Veronica sank to her knees. On Dylan's right, Seth glowered, digging his claws into the flesh of the captive's arm and shoulder. A dark patch of blood began to bloom around new wounds, black instead of fresh red.

"Watch your mouth," Seth snarled.

Dylan laughed. "Oh, it's probably too late for that." Although he continued to jockey for advantageous positioning, he seemed completely unaffected by physical pain. The bruise around his eye was darkening rapidly, giving one side of his face a strange, almost skeletal appearance. "I've summoned the rest. They're coming. If you're lucky, it will be a matter of days—and this time there will be no one to stop them."

"You don't know that!" Orion barked.

Dylan looked at him with the same flat, baleful expression. "Tell me I'm fucking wrong," he retorted calmly. "Tell me it isn't just you and these two rejects sitting here in this shithole city, just waiting to be finished off for good. I saw what happened to your followers, man. All the bodies. The carnage." Another chuckle escaped his lips. "I bet you thought you were safe in the forest."

Orion was briefly stunned into silence. Seth and I exchanged a glance. A seed of realization had begun to grow in my mind. I wondered if anyone else could tell that I was starting to understand. The undercurrent of death and darkness surging through Dylan's energy. The trail of the wendigo leading downtown to exactly the area in which we now stood.

"How do you know about that?" Veronica's voice, subdued and shaken, struggled to be heard. She sat numbly on the ground, staring up at Dylan. A thousand raw emotions stormed across her face, sorrow shifting into disbelief, shifting into anger, and back again.

He scoffed. "And you call yourself a slayer? You were there! You were in it! I shouldn't have to explain this to you." He let out a pitying sigh. "But I will, for old times' sake. Not like I've got anything else to do. My job here is almost done."

"Hurry up," Trent ordered. His patience was running thin.

Dylan rolled his eyes. "Fine. So that thing, whatever it was, that tore your little clan apart? That was plan A, and it worked pretty well until little Miss V came along and tossed in a big old wrench. She would've been a problem if my shaman friend hadn't found a way to make her into a solution instead." His grin widened. "The shaman saw her for what she was: a massive weakness even after the rest of the clan had been obliterated. And so, plan B was born."

"Let me guess," Trent said. "That's you."

The gears that had been turning in my brain finally clicked into place. I could practically see it happening, the ritual binding Dylan's spirit together from scraps of dark and potent energy. Some from the shaman himself, some from Veronica's enduring memories, and some from the wendigo I had so helpfully restored to full health hours before chasing it to the peak of Denali.

That was why Veronica had to die—so that Dylan could live once more. She had been part of the fuel that stoked the fire of his spirit and propelled it back into the corporeal realm. The wendigo had disappeared after playing its part in the resurrection, its energy spent into nothingness.

But Veronica had endured. Not only that, she had somewhat thrived.

"Yours truly," Dylan announced with pride. "Poised to strike the killing blow, whatever it took. At first, I thought I'd just steal her away. Make her mine again and we'd live happily ever after." His face darkened. "But, no." He spoke directly to her. "You can fucking rot."

In the grand scheme of things, this last little jab wasn't much, a parting shot on the heels of a much greater betrayal. But for Orion, it was the last straw. He roared, lunging at Dylan in a dark flash of fangs and claws. Before Seth or I had time to react, slashes of scarlet ripped across the boy's face, narrowly missing his open eyes.

"Don't you dare speak to her!" Orion was nearly foaming at the mouth. "Not now. Not again. Not ever!" He went to seize Dylan by the throat, presumably to choke the life from him. But as it turned out, Dylan had other plans. Quick as lightning, he managed to tear himself free of Seth's grasp and shove Orion back. Caught off guard by the boy's apparent strength, Orion stumbled backward, catching himself on the asphalt.

"You want to dance, old man?" Dylan taunted. "C'mon. Let's dance." He swooped in low, driving his shoulder into Orion's midsection. Seth and I observed in silence for a few moments as the two of them peppered each other with a flurry of blows.

"We should help," I remarked casually.

"Not yet." Seth smirked. "For once, my money's on the vamp, but I want to see where this goes."

It didn't take very long to find out. Frustrated and nearing the point of blinding rage, Orion began to falter a little. He let himself get pinned in a corner of the lot, half on his back, braced against the full brunt of Dylan's onslaught. The remains of a broken bottle gleamed in Dylan's hand. He raised it high.

"Okay." Seth stepped forward. "Orion's about to get shredded. Now we intervene." The bottle embarked on a swift descent. At any moment, I expected to hear an incensed shriek of pain from our previously insurmountable leader. As before, I felt sorry for him. No one understood the pain of a fall from such high grace better than me.

But the shattering impact never came. Dylan's body jerked to a sudden stop, frozen in an unnatural position. Closing the distance behind Seth, I came up beside Orion and realized that he had plunged the claws on both hands deep into Dylan's chest. Adrenaline-fueled fury coursed through his body.

Dylan grinned, his teeth stained with blood. "Touché," he said. Less than a second later, Orion surged upward, hurling him through the air. His body made a hollow metallic sound as he struck the side of a dumpster.

Off to the side, Veronica shuddered. She hadn't said a word in five or ten minutes. Her cheeks were wet with tears. I moved toward her but was interrupted by Seth's voice.

"What the hell are you looking at?" he demanded brusquely. Too late, I spotted the small crowd that had gathered at the restaurant's back door.

"You got a lot of nerve, buddy," said a man at the front. "And you're gonna need it, 'cause the cops are on their way."

Seth spat; it sizzled on the pavement. "Goddammit," he muttered. "All right, all right. Let's go, you sons of bitches." He turned away from the back wall of the restaurant toward the dumpster where Dylan had fallen just in time to see the boy spring up and make a break for it. "Over my dead fucking body!" he barked.

We chased him together like a pack of wolves, some hungrier than others. Even Trent ran along, though I couldn't tell if he was in pursuit of Dylan, of us, or all of the above. Suddenly, the alliance we had forged on the peak of Denali seemed extra fragile, stretched thin by circumstance. What would happen between predators once we'd caught up with the prey?

Ultimately, Orion was the one who took him down—and fittingly so, since his temper flared the hottest. By the time Dylan came skidding to a halt, right on the edge of where the grass met the tree line, his shirt was a bloody tangle of cloth. He lay there, defiant even as he panted for breath, staring up at us with baleful eyes.

Seth planted a foot squarely in the middle of the would-be fugitive's back. "Nice try."

Dylan let out a slightly strained chuckle. "Worth a shot."

Orion withdrew his claws. "Take him back to the house. I'm going to get Veronica."

"I don't think so," Trent said.

Orion didn't hesitate. "I don't care," he answered. "He won't be allowed out of my sight until he is no longer a threat. Take that as you will—it's non-negotiable." He kept walking toward the parking lot, where I could still see Veronica sitting on the ground. "Your bond with him is obvious," Orion added. "Sooner or later, you'll give in to the past, as Veronica did."

Trent frowned. "No. Allegiance isn't the problem." He caught up with Orion and put his hand on his shoulder to stop him. "I don't want him returning to Seattle. We all know there's another fight brewing. You could lose track of him."

"You think me a fool, slayer?" Orion scoffed.

Trent smirked. "You know, it's actually hilarious that you think I, a *vampire slayer*, am somehow cool with Clanmaster Steele getting everything he wants." He ran a hand through his hair. "I'll admit, I'd rather not see Dylan murdered in front of my eyes again. But for once in both our lives, I'm not trying to double cross you here. I just won't give up custody of a dangerous fugitive to someone with whom there is no trust."

"He's coming to the house," Orion declared flatly. "And so is Veronica."

Trent sighed. "Listen, all I want is a promise that you're not gonna give me back a corpse. This is tough for a guy like you to understand, but Veronica and Lian and I are human, and so was Dylan at one point. We aren't like you in the way that you watch mortal lifetimes go by in the blink of an eye. We need closure. We need to know answers. We don't have all the time in the universe to get them. And we won't get shit if Dylan's dead."

Orion looked back at him, mulling over his words. I looked at Trent and wondered if he understood everything about Veronica after all. He spoke about her as though, at the end of the day, she was fragile and her time was limited. To be fair, I could see how he might make such assumptions. She'd been gravely injured in recent days. She had bled, and she'd need to recover.

But I no longer fully believed that Veronica was a mortal woman, or even just a slayer. Something previously unseen within the depths of her aura had started to bloom when she moved across the veil.

Maybe no one else knew it yet, but she had come back changed.

20

SETH

As good as it felt to finally release some of the urge for violence that had been pent up inside me for days, I knew implicitly that we'd fucked up. Our mistakes were written large in Veronica's thousand-yard stare, in the dull silence she maintained while we fled the scene of the brawl. The sirens approaching down the street couldn't follow us into the trees, and so they never quite caught up. I listened to them circle a few times, then fade.

We marched our captive through the woods, two in front and two behind—and V trailing after. She didn't want to come within ten feet of the weaselly bastard, but I saw her sneaking glances his way every now and then. The tears on her face had dried, and yet she looked as if she might erupt with new ones any second.

It was the first time I had ever seen her look anything close to fragile. I hated it, and I hated him for singlehandedly stealing her strength and confidence, however temporarily. Of course she'd get her damn groove back, but the fact she'd lost it at all was unforgivable.

Thirty feet from the house, Trent stopped the caravan. He stared Dylan in the eyes for a long moment, then turned to Orion. "Keep him for now," he said. "Not a scratch, and I'll bring you reinforcements to use against Seattle. Just like we agreed. Yeah?" In a show of good faith, he pushed Dylan toward the vamp and actually stepped back.

I had to give it to the guy; for a mortal, he sure was ballsy. Nothing was stopping Orion from grabbing the kid and ripping his throat out right where he stood. He wanted to—I knew that much beyond a shadow of a doubt.

Orion's face had been fixed in a permanent scowl ever since we escaped downtown. Now he aimed it at Trent. "Fine. Retrieve your woman and go. We will safeguard this…thing." He gestured to Dylan.

Trent started to nod and stopped partway through. "Don't talk about Lian like that," he said. "Take care of V. And keep them away from each other."

I laughed. "Oh, don't worry. He ain't going nowhere."

After that, Trent was gone, retracing his steps back to downtown. We had left the girl he clearly cared for more or less to fend for herself, and I felt kind of bad about that.

"Put him in the cellar," Orion said. He went to V, slipping an arm gently around her waist. She sort of sagged into him. Her skin was paler than usual; even her vibrant hair seemed to have lost some of its color. When his gaze fell on her, the darkness dominating his face gave way to worried tenderness so obvious that not even I could deny his feelings. "I need to take her inside," he said quietly.

"Yeah, yeah. Go on." I reached over and grabbed the prisoner by the collar. "I'll take first watch with this shitty piece of work." To Logan, I said, "You too. Don't worry about us. We'll be fine." I paused. "Or at least I will be."

"You heard the deal Orion made with the slayer," Logan replied serenely. "Not a scratch." He headed for the house, leaving me alone with my new best friend.

"Damn," Dylan muttered. "What's it take to get a rise out of that guy?"

I steered him toward the cellar doors. "More than you've got, asshole."

He didn't fight me on the way down the stairs. Maybe it was the way the place smelled—of damp and dirt, and a little bit like death. As a man who had come from beyond the veil, I hoped he could tell exactly what had happened here. *When you close your eyes, I hope you see us dumping that body into the inlet. Because with any luck, you'll be next.*

"Nice digs," Dylan remarked, glancing around. I suspected his nonchalant manner was little more than a bluff, though he voiced no outward complaints when I bound him and sat him against a pillar.

"Get used to 'em," I said. "Don't think you'll be seeing anything else of the city for a while."

"We'll see." He leaned his head back on the stone, staring up at the cobwebbed rafters. I went and closed the cellar doors, and the light shrank down to thin, pale slivers slicing across our faces. A hush descended. I could hear things skittering over the walls and the floor every now and then.

The sound made me wonder how long it'd take for the kid to crack. He talked a pretty mean game, and he knew it. But he had been human once. A human with mortal fears. I watched him out of the corner of my eye as seconds grew into minutes, inching slowly toward an hour. A quarter of the way there, he began to fidget. It was subtle; tapping of the fingers, the restless bouncing of the knee. I tried not to smile.

Finally, he spoke up into the quiet gloom. "What'd he have to promise to get you on his side?" Dylan didn't specify a name, but he didn't have to.

"None of your business," I answered easily. "But it *is* my business to ask you the same question. What are *you* getting out of this deal?"

Dylan smiled grimly. He dropped his head, grinning at the floor between his feet. The small space of the cellar seemed to amplify his unnatural energy.

"I thought I was getting Veronica," he admitted. "Or at least another chance to see her. And I guess if you want to be real technical about it, I did get that." He shook his head. "It wasn't supposed to be like this, though. I had a whole vision in my head of what was going to happen once I got back into a real body."

I folded my arms and leaned on the wall. "How's that working out for you?" The kid's eyes glinted.

"It's not," he muttered.

"Not to rub salt in the wound, but I could've told you it wouldn't. Any one of us could, including your friends. That's the crazy thing about the mortal realm. Nothing ever fucking shakes out like you think it will."

"That's easy for you to say." Dylan turned his head toward me. His gaze bored into mine, cold and steely. "You ever been anywhere worse than here?"

My mind flashed back to the Underworld, cold seeping through my bones as I walked blindly through the dark. "Yeah, actually I have. Thanks for asking. It doesn't make the things I just said any less true."

Dylan stared at me. The more I looked at him, the more convinced I became that he was hollow, missing something crucial. Whoever this mystery vamp shaman was, he hadn't gotten the resurrection ritual quite right.

A sudden thought made my skin prickle. *Unless this is what he wanted.*

"Then you should know what it's like to be in a place like that." All the casual levity had gone out of Dylan's manner in the blink of an eye. I had never seen a man in his predicament look so serious. "I forgot everything about who I was or who I had been. I felt it all slipping away, and there was nothing I could do." He paused. "Eventually, V was all I had left. My scattered memories of her, old feelings, her face..." His voice trailed off, then picked back up. "She was the only thing anchoring me to a shred of sanity."

"She thought you were dead," I reminded him.

"She wasn't wrong." He kept staring at me, practically unblinking. "But I wasn't gone either. I was just there enough to know she was on the other side of this wall keeping us apart. And to tell you the truth, I would've agreed to anything if she was the reward. In life, and in death."

"Huh." I arched my eyebrows. "She's certainly unique, and I don't know that I can entirely fault your logic, but...you've been taken for a ride." He was silent, so I continued. "There's no way in hell this shaman ever intended to make good on whatever he said to you. He works for a guy who'd like nothing more than to see Orion moldering in the ground. You gave them a way to try and make that happen." I stopped talking to let my words sink in. "Because you're an idiot."

The kid scowled. "I had a plan to double-cross them before they got a chance to fuck me over. As long as I had Veronica with me, it didn't matter if we were on the run for the rest of our lives. The important thing was that we'd have the rest of our lives in the first place."

A chuckle escaped my lips. "Pretty big dream for a guy who shouldn't exist at all. The way I see it, you ought to be killed. And if that doesn't work, you ought to be killed again." I glanced over. He wasn't looking at me. "How much of your old self do you think you really are?"

He shrugged awkwardly, the movement stunted by the bindings around his hands. "Honestly, I thought I was perfect when we first came through the doorway on Denali. The vibe was a little off, but that made sense. It's not like I was gone for a day or two and came back as if nothing happened." His expression darkened. "But then she let slip that she's been fucking around with you guys, and—" He sighed. "The rage wasn't normal, man."

"Let me guess." I smirked wryly. "You were never a violent person before."

"Well, it sounds stupid as hell when you say it like that, but I really wasn't. And yet at the same time, I mean, she betrayed me and everything I stood for while I was alive. I was martyred by a vampire, and here she is screwing one?" His face contorted into a mask of frustration. "I don't fucking understand it. Don't I have a right to be pissed off?"

"No," I told him without hesitation.

"Oh, please." He smiled. "I'd love to hear you explain this to me."

"Okay, fine." I straightened up. "This idea that she betrayed you is utter bullshit. Yeah, it blows that you were trapped in a horrible, timeless pocket of the ether, but guess what, buddy? Veronica wasn't! She was left to pick up the pieces and move on without you, because she had no choice. She didn't want to. She wasn't over it. She was just forced to keep going."

"The V I knew would never have jumped in bed with a goddamn vamp," Dylan insisted. "Especially not if she was going around calling herself a slayer."

"Then I guess you don't know her anymore," I said. "It's been a long time, kid. You can't expect her to stay exactly the same."

He was quiet for a few moments. Then he laughed. "What am I doing? You're a fucking monster, dude. You don't know anything about love."

"Maybe I don't. But I will not allow you to destroy Veronica's life all over again." My eyes locked with his. His restless leg stopped moving.

"That's noble of you," Dylan replied dismissively. "Too bad it's already too late."

21

ORION

What I wanted was to get Veronica inside the house without letting her see her little boyfriend get carted off to the cellar by Seth. But she was uneasy, and she wouldn't stop looking around, as much as I tried to keep her on a straightforward path. She glimpsed them veering off toward the cellar doors, Dylan's arms twisted behind his back in chains.

She looked at me then. "What are you going to do with him?"

"That depends on how he behaves," I said. In truth, I didn't really know yet. I did know, however, that if I showed a hint of weakness, she would feel it. Her unusually sharp perception was always there, despite how badly her world had just been shaken. I felt sympathy for her, and perhaps even empathy. I had suffered similarly, a long time ago. It was a kind of pain I no longer experienced, but the memory remained.

Veronica sighed. "Here's the part where I want to ask you not to kill him. A few hours ago, I might have begged, if that's what you really wanted." She dropped her gaze as I stopped to unlock the front door. "Now…I don't think I understand anything anymore."

I hesitated. The lost, raw vulnerability in her voice forced the realization to dawn upon me that we were crossing into uncharted territory. The familiar dynamic to which I'd become accustomed had changed. To my chagrin, there was no plan for that either.

Instead of swallowing my pride and admitting I was at a loss, I placed my hands on her shoulders, turned her gently to face me, and said, "Tell me what you need, Veronica. I'm here for you, and I will do my best."

She smiled a little. A spark of humor lit her pale eyes briefly. "Wow. That sounds a lot like compassion coming from you." Veronica reached up and wrapped her arms around my neck. She pressed her lips to my cheek. "Thank you."

I held her tightly. The urge to never let go was almost overwhelming. "I'm sorry that my actions in the parking lot upset you." I knew, implicitly, that I needed to apologize for something but couldn't bring myself to repent for the attack. As far as I was concerned, Dylan needed to be expunged from the realm sooner rather than later.

She smiled again, slightly wider. "Well, I'm proud of you for saying that." Then her gaze focused on a point over my shoulder. I should have known what was coming. "But you know what I need right now?" Her hand came to rest on my chest. "I need to be alone with Logan for a while."

Like I said, I should have known. She needed tender calm, two things I had rarely been over the course of our relationship. My love for her was wildly passionate, a storm of naked desire. Still, the request took me by surprise. I wasn't able to fully conceal the sting.

"That is not what I thought you would say," I told her. "Speaking in the interest of total honesty."

"I know." She inched me away, loosening my grasp on her waist. "But you asked, so I answered. I promise it's nothing personal."

"All right." The warmth I'd gotten from holding her quickly turned into a jealous ache. I turned away before she went to Logan so that I wouldn't have to see him take my place. He didn't say a word, and strangely, I envied that too. The stillness in his manner—that was why she wanted him now instead of me.

Why can't I be everything to her?

The thought came out of nowhere, and it left me physically unsettled, as if I had just been shocked. I pushed it down until the door of my chambers was closed and locked at my back. She was leading me down a dangerous road that skirted the edge of mortal emotion too closely for my liking. The mistake of loving a human too deeply was one I'd already made. And so was the catastrophic error of making my lover into my thrall.

And yet, the hunger to possess her gnawed at my eternal bones. I feared that it would never leave me, no matter where Veronica was or what she was doing. I could not fathom an immortal life of such intense yearning.

"I want to turn her," I muttered out loud. Hearing the words strengthened my resolve. "No, I have to turn her." A soft, doubting internal voice reminded me how Logan and Seth said it wasn't possible, that I'd ruin her. I would have been lying to say their reservations didn't concern me, at least more than they had in the past. But they failed to quell my desire.

There were greater things standing in the way of my ambition, namely the inevitable return of the Seattle clan. If I turned inward for long enough, I could sense the storm brewing on the horizon. They were far away at the moment, but that wouldn't buy us much time. Once the march began, it would be fast and relentless.

I knew it was only a matter of time. Under these circumstances, Veronica should have been little more than a second thought, a distraction to be saved for later. In theory, I had more important things to worry about. In practice, the only way I could tear her out of my thoughts was acknowledging that the Anchorage clan teetered on the edge of extinction. Everything I had worked for generations to build would be washed away like sandcastles in the tide.

Focus, fool! I closed my eyes, inhaled deeply, and cleared my mind as much as I was able to. The clarity I received was a dismal reality; my sole remaining option seemed to be a path I never would have chosen to take of my own free will. Step one—the uneasy truce with the human slayer Trent was already in place, however tenuously. I hoped that our alliance would be enough to sustain the lifeblood of the clan.

Step two was a little more complicated. Dylan's capture gave me a secret trump card for as long as it could be kept undiscovered by Seattle's prying eyes. I paced the length of my room, wishing I'd thought to interrogate him about the nature of his connection to Steele and his council of elders. If they could see him at will, I might already have been screwed; no doubt they'd want their mole back.

But if they remained ignorant for a while longer, I fully intended to use the boy as a bargaining chip to gain leverage in what I had to admit was a fairly one-sided debate. Someone higher in their ranks saw Dylan as a key to success, perhaps a tool that would allow them to kill Veronica and me with the same stone. And in that respect, he was undeniably a liability, which made him valuable to everyone involved.

Much as I detested the very ground he walked upon, Dylan was our sole advantage in the impending fight. It pained me deeply to leave so much of the clan's future in the reactionary hands of the enemy, but I was backed up to the edge of a cliff, one foot planted on thin air. The days of playing life like a chess game, always one move ahead, were behind me now.

The vampires of Anchorage had been culled, and then we became the hunted. There was nothing left to do except ensure that we did not lay down and die at the feet of our adversaries. And for the first time in a very long time, I had something other than power hunger and blood-lust fueling my determined rage.

Veronica had given me a cause. I would fight for my clan, of course, for our lands, and for my status as its rightful master. But I would also fight for her. Because she deserved everything that Steele and his army sought to take away.

22

VERONICA

"Wow," I said under my breath as Orion's footsteps faded up the stairs. "He actually left." I crossed into the den and sat down on the overstuffed arm of the couch, half-expecting to hear him turn around and come running back in a fit of jealous fury.

"There's been some self-improvement happening." Logan sat on the sofa beside me, his shoulder brushing my back. The ethereal shadow of his right wing touched between my shoulder blades, and my body released an involuntary shudder of something very close to pleasure. How was it that any one of these men had the power to awaken lust in me, no matter what else was happening? Orion could have done it too, but Logan was the one I needed. He was gentler than the other two, steady and calm. The rock in a vicious storm.

"Huh." I turned halfway and slung my arm across the angel's shoulders. "I didn't think he had it in him, honestly."

"We'll see." Logan smiled slightly. "It's incremental, so far." He caught my hand in his, kissed the back of it, and pulled me down into his lap. I landed sideways, my head nestled against the left side of his collarbone. He brushed some of my hair out of his face. "How are you feeling?"

"Ugh." I curled up in his arms. "I don't even know. It's like, on one hand I could write a fucking book about my emotions right now. But on the other…it wouldn't make any sense, because they're all messed up." I sighed. "Being human is stupid."

"Yeah." He stroked my hair idly. "What about being half human?"

I laughed. "I wouldn't know. I don't think being a slayer counts as a racial identity."

"That's not what I'm talking about." Logan lifted his left arm a little to prop me up higher. "Remember when we met in the woods and I did this?" He leaned in and kissed me on the lips. From the way he'd led into it, I thought it would be more or less chaste, but there was an undercurrent of sensuousness that would've made my knees weak if I wasn't already in his lap.

When he pulled away, I sat stunned for a second or two before realizing that my vision had changed. Energy swirled in the air, encompassing both of us in glowing auras. Over Logan's shoulder, I spotted an indistinct figure strolling past the doorway. The air in that direction turned cold.

A spirit, whispered a new, small voice in my ear.

"Oh yeah. Does Orion know his house is haunted?"

Logan shrugged. "I doubt it. He probably would have made me chase them all out." He looked at me. "See how that works, though?" I nodded, and he added, "It's not supposed to."

"What do you mean?" I asked. "You don't do this with every girl you meet at a crime scene in the forest?"

"Not every human girl," he replied. "Mortals weren't made to house power like that in their bodies. That's why they're mortals." With the patience of a saint, he watched my face, waiting for me to get it.

I frowned. "Okay. But I mean, I have slayer's blood now, so I'm not technically human. It still makes sense."

"The slayer's blood isn't the same. You've been augmented to be stronger, faster, more perceptive. To be sensitive to things a normal human would never see. But you shouldn't be able to do things like peel back the veil and see beyond, even if these abilities are given as a gift."

I stared at him. The implication in his words was obvious at this point, and yet I couldn't wrap my head around what he was saying.

"I'm not human?" I said finally. The question hung in the air, surreal.

"You can't be," Logan answered. "It's impossible." He paused thoughtfully, then amended his statement. "That is, you can't be *fully* human. Maybe you're half, or a quarter. But you aren't mostly human, either."

I was stone silent for at least a minute, dumbfounded, my mind racing, thinking of the vampire bite I survived when I was younger. How that was impossible, and yet here I was, still alive. I couldn't explain that or my strength for so long, so was this the reason? Then I let out a bewildered laugh. "What the fuck. How are you so sure about that?"

Just as patiently as before, Logan said, "I told you. The fact that you can accept any aspect of my power, let alone all of it, is irrefutable proof. A true mortal would either see nothing, or they would become overwhelmed and expire."

"Did you learn that from experience?" I had meant it as a light-hearted joke, but his answer didn't match my tone.

"Yes." He glanced away.

Instant guilt flooded in. "I'm sorry. You're right. You have to be right, I guess." The next question popped immediately into my head, and although I felt like a dumbass sending it out into the world, it had to be asked. "But if I'm not human, what the hell am I?"

"That I don't know yet."

I smiled internally. Of course that would be the one answer he didn't have. My head was still spinning, but I decided to have some fun with it. "What would you say if someone asked you? You've gotta have some idea."

He was quiet for a while, mulling it over. The hand working its way over and over through my hair paused in its tracks, so I held it. His fingers were long and slender, skin flawless and pale. Blue veins laced the underside of his wrist. *Like a living sculpture,* I mused. Just watching him exist was witnessing art in motion.

"A celestial being," he said at long last, nodding slightly. "Perhaps an angel."

I gazed up at his perfect features, long eyelashes shading those ice-blue eyes. "Like you."

Logan smiled. "No. Not like me at all."

I couldn't have related the events that followed in any kind of detail. I leaned up and kissed him again, and everything after that was a whirl-wind of clothes coming off, skin on skin, waves of intense, long-antici-pated pleasure. The next thing I knew, I was on my back, head flung backward, gripping the back of Logan's neck as he licked me until I wanted to scream. But not even the throes of impending orgasm could make me forget whose house we were in, nor who was upstairs at that very instant.

"Oh, fuck," I moaned. He leaned into me. My toes curled against the cushion. "Holy shit."

Logan tugged gently, easing away. "I'm sure you don't feel lucky at present, but you are." He ran his fingers down the soft skin on the inside of my thigh, leaving me trembling. "We don't have the same experiences that mortals do."

I opened my eyes. "Why not? You're missing out." I was at once intrigued and frustrated by his little aside. Leave it to Logan to drop knowledge as he edged me closer to the most intense climax of my life. The gradual buildup made it almost impossible to concentrate, despite my efforts. I really did want to know what he was going to say.

He licked his fingers, and when he put them inside me, my eyes rolled back into my head, and my brain filled with erotic sensation. Before I could stop it, a guttural groan escaped from deep down in my chest. He pushed in and out of me as he rubbed my clit with his thumb.

I moaned louder, my hips bucking as he never paused. To say I lost my mind was a rather accurate picture as I writhed against his touch, desire roaring within me. My heart thumped louder, and there was no way I was turning back now.

"I suppose it's a necessary benefit for them." His hand started to make slow, deft strokes. I squeezed it impatiently, needing him to go back to what he was doing before. "They're going to die, so it's only fair that they can find solace in pleasure."

My whole body trembled. "I appreciate what you're saying, but I cannot have this conversation with you right now," I told him with urgency. "I need you to make me fucking come."

Logan grinned and fingered me faster once more until I couldn't stand the agony of being right on the edge anymore. In response to my desperate, mostly wordless pleas, he pulled me on top of him with ease. The moment I felt him push into me, I almost shrieked with pleasure. He was huge and hard, and all mine. He covered my mouth with his, stealing my cries of pleasure.

"Fuck me like this all the time," I whispered into his lips. "Oh, fuck, I need it so bad."

His thrusts were smooth and powerful, practically lifting me off the couch with every motion. I arched my back and wrapped my shaking legs around his waist. Every pleasure center in my brain exploded with him inside me. He seemed to know exactly how I needed him to touch me.

Sweat glistened across his brow, a deep rumbling roared in his chest as his fingers dug into my hips as he thrust into me each time I rocked down on him. Lust dilated his pupils, and I loved seeing the hunger behind them. Logan was always the calm one who rarely showed emotions, so to have him succumb from being with me did things to me. It made me adore him more. I have no idea how things had escalated so far with these three men. Monsters I would have called them once upon a time, but that was before they'd crawled under my breastbone and found a place in my heart. I didn't want to think about such emotions. I couldn't when my life was just too complicated.

Logan groaned, driving deep inside me, each thrust edging me closer and closer to my climax.

Then it hit hard and fast.

The orgasm crashed over me like a tsunami when it finally arrived. I gasped incoherently, trying to keep from raising my voice. All thoughts exited, replaced by physical sensation. I kept coming for what felt like an eternity—a journey of sheer ecstasy. Logan growled, reaching his own high, both of us tangled together and breathless.

Afterward, I ached with satisfaction and collapsed against him He kissed me softly, wrapping me in his arms. In the fog of the afterglow, I also wondered how long he'd been holding out on me. *None* of them had ever fucked me like that before. I made a sleepy mental note to notify Orion and Seth that the bar had officially been raised.

"Thank you," I murmured, snuggling in close. "I needed that more than you'll ever know."

Logan kissed the top of my head. I felt him smile once more. "I know."

23

———

LOGAN

J hadn't meant to fall asleep on the sofa in the den, but when I opened my eyes, the light had changed. Veronica lay on her side, facing away from me. She only shifted a little as I carefully slipped out from underneath her body and pulled a blanket up around her shoulders. Her long eyelashes fluttered, but she didn't wake.

I leaned down and kissed her forehead. Any other night, I would have been happy to stay until she woke up on her own, but no matter where I was in the house, or what I was doing, I could feel Dylan's presence as tangibly as if he was following me around. He had been under Seth's supervision for a number of hours at that point; it was time for a shift change. And considering the reprieve I'd just been granted, I was willing to take on the next watch.

The cellar doors opened onto total darkness. Descending the stairs, I could see only the glowing yellow of Seth's eyes at first, and then the seated outline of our captive. He was hunched forward, his neck bent so that I couldn't see his face. I glanced at Seth.

"Don't look at me," the demon said. "There's nothing wrong with him. Nothing new, anyway."

At that, Dylan started to laugh. We stood there and watched his shoulders shake. Finally, he pulled himself upright and stared at us. His eyes were bloodshot, ringed with dark circles. "You guys are fucking idiots," he declared, still chuckling. "There's something wrong with me? You think it's that simple?"

"I mean, yeah." Seth rolled his eyes. "Fuck this. I've dealt with his bullshit long enough. I'm out." He patted me on the shoulder as he brushed past. "Good luck, angel-boy. I'll cover for you if you kill him."

He went up the stairs and was gone into the encroaching night. The doors creaked shut. I took up the post Seth had just vacated, and Dylan watched me with a keen gaze. "You never answered my question," he pressed. "Do you think it's as simple as me being fucked up?" He maintained a cool, irreverent tone, but I sensed some genuine curiosity underneath. As if he feared we might be right about him after all.

I let him stew in his own thoughts for a while. No part of me really wanted to engage with him on any level. I had a pretty good idea of where he had come from and what state he was currently in, and I wasn't particularly eager to have any theories confirmed. Then again, it wasn't like either of us had anywhere else to be.

I sighed. "No, I don't think that." After a moment's pause, I continued. "The vamp shaman didn't make a mistake. He used an unpredictable element."

"Interesting," Dylan muttered. Again, he made it seem like he was brushing me off. But a new wariness had entered his gaze. I wondered how much he really knew about his own resurrection.

"He didn't tell you how you came back, did he?" I asked. "In fact, I bet he just told you he was the one who did it, and that you should be grateful, because he granted you a second chance out of the goodness of his heart." Dylan issued no reply, which I took as confirmation. Except, I suspected I understood better how his return happened and where the wendigo vanished to. That the energy bringing Dylan back to life was a combination of the very creature that took Veronica's life and what remained of Dylan in the afterlife. I made a deal with the wendigo to aid us against the Seattle enemy that would return, which I believe had come in the form of a slayer. Leaning back on the cold cellar wall, I turned my eyes to the ceiling and smiled a little. "You were a slayer once. Do you remember what a wendigo is?"

24

SETH

She was sleeping where I assumed Logan had left her, wrapped up in a blanket, his energy coming off her in waves. Orion was nowhere in sight. I slipped down onto the couch beside her, and she opened those pretty eyes and smiled. Then she blinked.

"You're not the one I was expecting," she murmured. "Not complaining, though."

I kissed her on the mouth, long and deep. She purred against my lips. "Angel-boy came down to the cellar," I said. "He's on duty. I'm off. No idea where the other one is."

Suddenly Veronica frowned. She pulled back a bit, her hand braced on my chest. "Where's Dylan?"

I frowned back at her. "He's downstairs where we chained him up, V. And he's not going anywhere, so don't even think about it."

"Right." She relaxed, although the dismay was evident on her face. "God, it's so stupid to still be worried about him after all this." She laughed in a way that sounded like it was mostly to keep from crying.

I touched her face. "Yeah, it is. Don't feel bad. It's a human thing." She laughed again, more genuinely, and I hesitated. It seemed almost cruel to talk to her about Dylan in any capacity; no matter what I said, her image of him would end up shattered. But it bothered me more to lie to her, even by omission. "You know, we actually had a conversation down there."

"Oh yeah?" V tried not to sound interested and failed. She avoided making eye contact, resting her cheek against my chest. "That's surprising. I wouldn't have thought you two had much in common."

"We don't. I just wanted to know what the hell he thought he was doing, coming back from the dead only to get wrapped up in this mess." I wanted to wait for V to say something so I could gauge her emotions—to the best of my limited ability. Pain was a new thing for me, and yet I was determined to learn something about compassion for her sake.

She took a long time to answer, and when she did, I nearly didn't hear it. "It was me," she whispered. "He did it for me." She glanced up at me, eyes bright with unshed tears. "That's why it was so damn easy for the shaman. All he had to do was promise Dylan a way back to me."

I couldn't say she was wrong, and once she realized she'd pretty much nailed it, Veronica buried her head in my chest and sobbed. The sorrow overtook her like a storm. She clung to me, trembling. I didn't have anything else to do but hold her tight.

"It's not your fault," I murmured as reassuringly as possible. "We all have exploitable flaws." *All right, maybe that wasn't quite necessary.* "I mean, you couldn't have stopped them."

V brushed the hair from her face. She sniffled, wiping the tear streaks away with the backs of her hands. "I know what you meant." She leaned up and nuzzled the side of my neck and jaw. "And I know you're right. It's just horrible to deal with that kind of guilt. To think he hasn't been resting this entire time because of me."

I took her face in my hands, wiping the last stray tear with my thumb. "Listen, that's his problem, not yours. Sometimes the dead stay around even though the people they loved are trying to let them go. Half the time, that's how they end up in Hell. They won't cross over on their own 'cause they can't wrap things up, they get trapped in their own shitty negativity, and then boom. In Hell forever."

She regarded me closely. "Is that what happened to you?"

I laughed. "Me? Of course not. I never leave anything unfinished."

Veronica shifted into my lap. She straddled my hips, ran her fingers into my hair. "Prove it," she demanded.

Her appetite impressed me after such a heavy bout of raw emotion. Maybe physical pleasure was cleansing for her, a way to release all the bad stuff. It was definitely a coping mechanism I could get behind.

She kissed my neck. I felt the edge of her tongue, and the barest hint of her teeth on my skin. Instantly, a fire ignited in my loins. The woman was nothing if not persuasive. And I didn't need to be told twice.

25

ORION

The fact that Seth managed to get out of the cellar and see Veronica before I got back did not escape my notice. He wasn't there when I returned to the den, but her flushed skin and sensual aura told me everything I needed to know. Before, my instinctual reaction would have been an explosion of jealous rage, and I could not deny the urge to indulge in such anger. This time, however, something cautioned me to react in moderation. She had been satisfied, and she was happier than she had been. Wasn't that the least of what Veronica deserved?

"Hi." She reached a hand out toward me. The moment I touched her, I knew I'd gravely misunderstood her true emotional state. Perhaps the others had helped her release some tension, but she was not healed. Her eyes held worlds of sadness and confusion. I wondered if she had allowed them to see so deeply into her pain.

"Come on," I said gently. "Let's take a walk." She needed to get up and away from the place in which her past continued to fester underground. If I had my way, I wouldn't have let her return until the boy was removed from the premises. But of course, stubborn Veronica had her own ideas.

"Now?" She looked toward the window. "It's dark, Orion." She paused. "And...I know Dylan is still in the basement. I don't want to leave him." As if she was anticipating an unfavorable response, she added quickly, "Don't judge me. This has been hard enough already."

"I wasn't going to say anything," I half lied. "We won't go far. I think you could use the air." What I didn't say was that she seemed as though she'd been made from paper and eggshells—fragile, cracked, in imminent danger of collapse. I feared that the natural consequences of a slayer's decision to consort with her would-be prey were starting to catch up with her.

Veronica inhaled deeply and blew out her breath. "Maybe you're right," she finally conceded. She let me take her hand and pull her off the couch. Her fingers were cool to the touch. "I guess I'm just..." She trailed off. I waited, as I was gradually learning how to do. "I'm uncomfortable. Nothing's felt good for days."

Unable to help myself, I raised an eyebrow. "Nothing?"

Veronica cracked a smile. "That's none of your business," she said. "I've been taken care of, thank you very much."

"Not by me." I led her out onto the porch and down the steps, being careful to guide her as far from the cellar entry as possible. Her gaze still flicked uneasily to the doors, which were barely visible along the side of the house.

"This is a stupid question," Veronica said slowly, "but do you think he'll be okay?"

I tightened my grip on her hand. "He's not going anywhere."

She shook her head. "I mean after this is over." When I didn't respond, she gave me a look. "Come on, Orion. I'm not stupid. I know you weren't planning to keep him in your basement forever. And I *know* you'd never let his ass into the clan."

"At least you give me that much credit," I muttered. "But really, I don't know what will happen to him." I hesitated. Part of me wanted nothing more than to force some sense into her, even if the task required some harsh language. She was too exceptional a woman to be so prone to damaging emotional attachments. It was obvious to everyone else that the boy she'd brought back from the other side of the veil was an abomination. The fact that she refused his true nature frustrated me to no end.

And yet, I didn't want to inform her of my plans to utilize him for the clan's benefit in the impending clash with Seattle. We'd already gone through one potentially relationship-altering fight; I knew better than to purposely start another. As I rose slowly from the ashes of my clan, Veronica stood as a beacon in sudden darkness, the only light I welcomed. Now she needed me as much as I needed her, if not more. My duty and my desire was to be there.

She frowned, furrowing her brow. "It feels horrible to think this after what we've all been through...but I keep thinking I made a mistake when I let Dylan follow me back into this realm." Veronica tucked a strand of hair behind her ear. "At first I was so excited—and I'm sorry if that hurt you, by the way. It was like I forgot all about everything I already had."

I chose not to reinforce how badly her choices had affected me. "I won't pretend I fully understand," I said. "But I forgive you."

She continued quietly. "Maybe it was the grief that got to me. Maybe I never really got over it, despite how hard I tried. His death was so sudden. So tragic. So violent." A shudder ran through Veronica's body. "I still have nightmares about it sometimes. I thought that having him back was everything I ever wanted." A mirthless laugh escaped her lips. "I should've known better."

Yes, you should have. I bit my tongue hard. Rarely did Veronica allow herself to display this kind of vulnerability; in fact, her toughness was one of the things I adored the most. It was strange and uncomfortable to see her open up this deeply. I could wound her in this moment, if I so chose. We both seemed to acknowledge that. Instead, I squeezed her hand. She squeezed back, hard.

"So stupid," she whispered. "Like, of course he was going to be changed. He was marinating in fucking purgatory for so damn long." Abruptly, she stopped and turned to face me, taking my other hand in hers. The way she stared into my face was broken and desperate. "Did I keep him there? God, tell me I didn't."

Admittedly, I was the exact wrong person to ask, and I wondered briefly why she hadn't saved the question for Seth or Logan. Then it occurred to me that perhaps she had asked them as well and been unsatisfied, or unsettled, by their answers. At some point in the past few days, Veronica had morphed into a haunted soul, dogged mercilessly by demons she had set upon herself.

I took her beautiful face into my hands. She wrapped her arms around my neck, pulling close for comfort. "You didn't keep him," I said. "He stayed. That's his fault, not yours." I paused for emphasis. "Do you understand, Veronica? None of this is your fault." She closed her eyes, releasing a shaky breath. I pressed my lips to her forehead. "If you want someone to blame, I'll volunteer," I added.

Her eyes snapped open again. "What?" Our embrace loosened. A frigid wind cut between us.

"That night when I saw you for the first time on the street, I chose you," I told her. "I wanted you, and I knew that you would be mine. One way or another."

The apprehension eased out of her features. "Well, I knew that." This time, her laugh was much more natural. "You weren't very subtle about it." One slender finger traced across my lips. "But I'm not granting that particular wish in full."

I attempted not to grimace and failed. "That's…fine." Not long ago, those two words would have comprised a complete lie. As it was, they made up maybe half a truth. I'd already determined that nothing would stop me from keeping Veronica, including whatever unconventional arrangement she demanded. There would be time for negotiations later, once the clan no longer stood on the very cusp of oblivion.

"Is it?" Veronica's tired gaze sparkled with a hint of mischief. The phantom of a heart swelled in my chest. I ached for her to be free from the shadows plaguing her life, and I knew I would do anything to make it so.

"Yes." I nodded as convincingly as possible. "I can always kill Seth if need be."

"I don't know about that." She smiled and stepped back, prompting our walk to resume. "He's pretty strong. And so is Logan."

"Who's your favorite?" I pretended her answer didn't matter, that I was just asking because she'd brought us all up together. "You must have one."

"Come on." Her tone turned vaguely reproachful. "You're all wildly different, and exciting, and sexy. I honestly never imagined I'd be able to find anything like what I have with each of you." She grew silent for a minute. "There's something about…us…that Dylan never gave me. I think that's why I'm able to consider life without him."

"You've been living life without him," I reminded her. She winced a bit. I regretted the bluntness of my words.

"Yes." Veronica shook her head. "But I think this whole time I've been hoping deep down that he would miraculously show back up. And then he did, and it was too good to be true." Her voice broke. "The

Dylan in my head is perfect. He was the love of my life for so long. I don't know how to say goodbye to him for good."

The conversation had brought us down to the shore of the inlet, where we stood side by side on the bank and looked out across the dark water. Veronica sniffled, wiping tears off her cheeks. I slipped my arm around her. She leaned into me.

"He isn't giving you a choice anymore," I said. "Either you let him go, or you go with him." I could feel her watching me closely.

"I can't," Veronica murmured. "I can't go with him."

"I know," I said. "Because we would never let you. We would follow you to the ends of the earth, to the furthest corners of time and space. There is nothing that could spare him from our wrath."

Veronica snuggled into my chest. I sensed her smile, although her face was hidden. "I'm not afraid of you, Orion," she said softly.

I kissed the crown of her head. When she was in my arms like that, each beat of her pulse echoed through my body, the blood warm in her veins. The small, primal voice at the back of my mind commanded me to tilt her head to the side and claim her once and for all. The thought of my teeth sinking into her tender neck threatened to consume my consciousness.

But I forced the beast to stay dormant. The fangs in my mouth barely managed not to burst forth. I did not succumb to the raging tide of bloodlust.

"You don't need to fear me," I said to Veronica. "I don't want you to."

As we headed back up from the shore of the inlet, a shift in the air alerted all of my senses. A heavy, bitter current of energy had broken through from the south—the unmistakable warning of a storm on the horizon.

"Orion?" Veronica touched my face. "Are you okay?"

I glanced at her. "We're running out of time."

26

———

VERONICA

I was tired. No, not just tired—exhausted. The kind of fatigue that creeps down into the bones and grows roots, like a weed. Every part of me ached: my body, my soul, my mind. I had a million thoughts and no way to sort them out. The only real reprieve I could find was in mindless pleasure, and so even though I was worn the hell out, I clung to Orion fiercely as he claimed me, plunging into me. He was fast, passionate, and a little rough, and this time I was happy to let him have his way. I craved the pain, the pleasure, all of it to forget the rest of my deranged messed up life.

Orion's lips slid over my whole upper body, lingering on my neck and on the crown of each breast. He devoured me more gently than usual, but his vampiric hunger still permeated every touch, every stroke, every thrust. I choked on the moans that came out of my mouth.

"Oh, God." My hands clenched around the edge of his bed, which I pretended did not also double as a dirt-filled vessel during the day. *This is crazy, Veronica,* my conscience whispered in between jolts of pleasure. *Is this really the path you're going to choose?* Before I had the chance to dwell on any of my doubts, Orion found a spot, deep between my thighs that made me roll my eyes back and bite the inside of my cheek.

My emotions might have been all ruined, but on the physical front, he had Dylan beat. I felt my knees start to buckle as my third breathtakingly intense orgasm of the day built to its peak. Orion's grip tightened on my hips and stomach. Suddenly, his smooth gyrations became frenzied. I clapped my hand over my mouth to keep from crying out. Stars danced in front of my eyes. I thought I might faint.

"Holy shit!" I collapsed back onto the bed, inhaling its cool, earthy smell. Orion stayed deep inside me as I squeezed around him, my body convulsing with the aftershocks. But then, as abruptly as he'd driven us both to climax, he pulled away. I glanced over to him. "What's up?"

The look on his face was so jarring that it snapped me back from a state of hazy euphoria. I turned over on the bedspread, fighting an onslaught of dread.

"They're on their way," he declared solemnly. "Right now." Seemingly without missing a beat, he had started to put his clothes back on. "We have to get the others and go." And just like that, playtime was over. I nodded and pushed myself to my feet. Orion tossed me the same clothes I'd been wearing for the last three days.

I guess this is what I'm wearing to war, I thought offhandedly. Of course, I had known since they left that it was only a matter of time before the Seattle clan came back again. They were the vamps on my home turf—I liked to think I was at least as familiar with them as Orion, if not more. Stubborn sons of bitches, persistent as hell. And they absolutely hated to lose by any measure.

"Who do we have coming to back us up?" I asked as we moved out into the hallway.

"Trent." Orion looked uncomfortable calling Trent by name, but I was proud of him for doing it. "And whoever he has seen fit to bring." He gestured toward my pocket. "Call him. Let him know the timer has run down."

"I'm on it." I had the phone up to my ear on the way down from the third floor. My mind scrambled for the right combination of words to say. *Get over here, loser. We're going to fight the bad guys.*

Trent answered almost instantly. I could tell from his voice and the background noise that he was moving, and probably pretty fast. "We're almost there," he said. "Don't worry."

"Tell me you brought a goddamn army," I answered. "I have a feeling we're going to need one." In fact, the closer I got to the outside of the house, the stronger I sensed the disturbance that had caught Orion's attention. By the time we stood in the yard, it was practically suffocating. No wonder Trent hadn't needed me to call.

"I got everyone who would come on less than a day's notice," he told me now. It was not the kind of reply that sparked confidence.

"Where would you put our chances, if you had to guess? Assuming Orion and company are fighting on our side."

"Right." He paused for longer than I liked. "I think it will be enough."

The apprehension gnawing at my gut only intensified. "I hope so." It was my turn to hesitate. "Lian isn't with you, is she?"

"No, V. She's safe at home, although she's worried sick. You can come see her when this is all over."

I pressed my lips together. "If she can even bring herself to look at me." Never in my life had I felt like a worse friend, or a bigger piece of shit. How could I begin to make up for the staggering idiocy I had displayed over the past few weeks? Lian had called me for help, and what did I do? I came to Anchorage and fucked the local clanmaster. *Great job, V. I'm sure that's exactly what she had in mind.*

"Hey V, snap out of it." Trent's voice yanked me back into the present moment. "I need you to tell Orion that we're going to try to divert them away from the city—minimize collateral damage and all that. Meet us on the outskirts of Chugach, all right? The trees will give us some extra cover. Maybe we can use it to our advantage."

I already knew Orion wouldn't appreciate the change of venue. As far as I was aware, he hadn't stepped foot within park boundaries since the massacre in the grove. But Trent's thinking was logically sound. We needed all the advantages we could get, and if the city could also be spared the brunt of any potential damage, that was just bonus icing on the cake.

"I'll let him know," I said. "See you soon."

Orion stood frozen in the middle of the yard, eyes fixed on the slate-grey sky. His aura flared, absorbing energy from as far a distance as he could manage. The expression on his face had turned into a stony mask. When he heard me approach, his gaze flicked to the side, posture unchanged.

"What news?" he asked. *It better be good,* was the clear subtext of the question.

I arched my eyebrows. "Trent said they're drawing the Seattle contingent southeast, away from the city." He got my meaning before I mentioned the destination by name, but I did it anyway. "Toward Chugach. We need the cover of the woods."

Orion's sharp golden eyes narrowed dangerously. "The ground there is sacred to my clan," he growled. "Steele and his men wouldn't dare tread upon it."

I looked him directly in the face. "You and I both know damn well they would. And they will." I reached for his hand, turning east. "Let's go, Orion. Let Logan and Seth know that's where we'll be." The moment the words passed my lips, I froze for a split second, remembering that one or both of them had to be down in the cellar with Dylan at that very moment. A cold chill ran through me. I glanced at Orion again. Some of the bravado exited my voice. "What are we going to do about…him?" I nodded in the direction of the cellar doors.

Orion's face darkened. He glared sullenly at the cellar himself, and I knew he was consulting with the others, most likely excluding me on purpose. A little petty from my perspective, but at the same time, I couldn't really blame him anymore. My track record for acting rationally in Dylan's presence was pretty dismal, at best. A few tense moments passed. I wondered if Orion might risk leaving one of the boys behind—or, more importantly, if either Seth or Logan would allow it.

It turned out to be a moot point. "We have to bring him with us," Orion announced, in a way that made his displeasure very evident. He marched ahead. "They will escort him. You and I are proceeding on ahead."

The stupid, delusional, lovesick part of my brain, the part that still wanted to believe I could find a way to keep Dylan in my life without doing irreparable harm, urged me to stay behind and join the escort. I shoved it down and caught up to Orion in a burst of speed. For once, the correct choice was obvious. *You can do this, V,* I coached myself, as the house fell farther and farther away. *You can let go.*

But there was something else that slowed me down on the way out of Anchorage. Not Dylan, but a different voice slipping inconspicuously in between my thoughts. I recognized Logan's unfailingly serene energy right away.

Veronica. Wait for me in the forest. I need to speak with you. As usual, he gave no hints toward his intentions, good or bad.

"Oh, what the hell," I muttered under my breath. Apparently not even the threat of imminent battle was enough to keep a fallen angel from being weird and cryptic. Orion gave me a questioning look, but he was preoccupied, and when I said, "Nothing," he simply focused his eyes forward. I was grateful not to be pressed for details, and yet, Logan's comments needled at me the whole way out. Was he planning some-thing? Did he have doubts, or maybe suspicions? Had he discovered some earthshattering information he didn't want Orion to hear?

Every possibility I thought of made my stomach ball up into knots. I wanted to turn around and haul ass back to the house, just to demand an immediate explanation. But we were hurtling along toward the northern boundary of the park, and if I stopped for any reason at this point, Orion's burning fuse might just explode.

There was nothing to do but wait and wonder. And hope against hope that no more terrible secrets were about to emerge from the dark.

27

LOGAN

"They're here, aren't they?"

I could hear the sardonic smirk in Dylan's voice without looking at him. He walked behind me with his wrists tied in front. Seth was bringing him behind us.

"Don't try anything funny," the demon warned. "There's not much I'd like more right now than to beat the shit out of you." He spoke lightly, but each word carried an edge. His irritation was up, the hot blood in his veins creeping toward its boiling point. He, too, felt the electricity in the atmosphere.

"Maybe you should," Dylan chuckled coldly. "It might be good for both of us." Like Seth, he put up a nonchalant front that didn't quite mask the restless energy roiling beneath the surface. A multitude of mixed emotions colored his aura. I counted excitement, anger, resignation, and fear.

"Nah." Seth nudged the captive forward into the heavily overcast daylight. "I think you'd like it too much." He dropped the cellar doors shut with a resounding slam. "Just shut up and get moving."

Both Seth and I had received the message regarding the meeting point at Chugach. Dylan didn't comment as we steered him in that direction, though I wouldn't have been surprised if he knew exactly where we were headed. No telling how closely he was connected with the enemy.

During the journey to the park, I had the merciful luxury of flying high above and slightly ahead of Seth and Dylan. In theory, I was acting as a scout, in case the Seattle vamps had thought to try and catch us off guard. Mostly, however, I was just glad to get away from the dark cloud of tension enveloping all three of us. Seth had not exaggerated his level of animosity.

From my vantage point high in the murky gray sky, I could glance down and see the two of them making their way across the Alaskan terrain. Seth matched every move that Dylan made to a fearsomely precise degree. He was prepared to strike at any time, and I had little doubt he'd even think twice about dealing a killing blow. In many ways, it must have been easier to rationalize killing Dylan and answering to Orion for his recklessness than enduring another moment in the company of such an unpleasant individual.

I kept an eye on them at all times, half expecting to see Dylan's body collapse amid a scarlet arc of blood. Seth's temper was palpable, his volatile energy sizzling more ferociously the nearer we came to battle. I wondered how long he'd be able to keep himself in check, as well as how I might help him explain Dylan's smoking, eviscerated corpse.

But I knew the route to Chugach well now, and my mind was occupied by other, even more pressing matters. Veronica's identity—her true one, as defined by the kernel of magic nestled deep within her spirit, was a puzzle I'd been trying to solve for hours. I had been in casual denial for much too long—and for what reason? Perhaps the idea of adding yet more intrigue to an already complex situation was too exhausting to even consider.

Or maybe I had simply come to enjoy the way things were. As I knew her currently, Veronica was easy to admire and easy to understand. She was strong but mortal; her brief and tempestuous life little more than a ripple in the river of time. Their brevity was one of my favorite things about humans; it kept me from too much effort in the same way it kept me from pain.

If I was correct in my new assumptions about her, everything had changed. The scope of her future could be huge. Even a young celestial being had the right to laugh in the face of death. It occurred to me that she'd already done it at least once. Maybe more than that. I needed to talk to her.

Halfway to Chugach, heavy raindrops began to fall. They rolled off the tips of my feathers, plummeting like stones toward the landscape racing by below.

This is fucking bullshit, Seth growled somewhere underneath me.

Speed up, I told him. *Don't let them gain an advantage.* I leaned into my flight, beating my wings a little harder. The rain soaked my face and hair. It almost felt cleansing, in a strange way. A purification before the commencement of battle.

Oh, don't worry, Seth replied. *I did not come this far to lose to a pack of street rats.* The scowl was audible in his voice.

I shifted my attention forward, toward our destination. The rain had not deterred the oncoming forces—they pressed on in much the same manner as us, coming up from the south to clash at the border of the park. My window of opportunity to speak with Veronica was narrowing rapidly.

I'm going ahead, I told Seth. Without waiting for an answer, I bore down on my wings until the wind ripped by. My shoulders ached, but it didn't matter. The conversation I wanted to have could not wait until after the fight was over; in fact, the outcome might depend on it.

No problem, Seth barked back. *Don't bother warning me or anything. I'm sure we'll be fine.* He paused. *Actually, that gives me an excuse to whip this kid's ass into shape. Go as fast as you want.*

I had already left them in the distance. The voice of the wind had risen to a roar, drowning out all other sounds except my own thoughts. My worst fear was that the Seattle clan knew or had learned as much about Veronica as I thought I knew, and that they had beaten me to the punch in terms of creating a plan to deal with her.

There was a very good chance that she was in immediate danger. I wanted to tell Orion to protect her extra vigilantly, but his natural flair for the dramatic risked costing us time we didn't have. Instead of warning him, I resorted to pushing my body to its absolute limit in terms of strength and speed. The rain had turned to a thin coat of ice on my skin. Every color melted into a raging blur.

Then I spotted two figures half a mile from Chugach's edge. They were moving fast like me, flashes of deep black and the telltale pink of Veronica's hair. I angled down to swoop low over them, heading straight for the dense tree line. Veronica turned her face up as I passed, her eyes wide but knowing.

The landing I made carved a trough in the dirt ten feet long, and I ended with my body braced against the dark trunk of a tree that would have been happy to smash me to pieces. The world came back into focus.

"Logan!"

I turned around. A cloud of feathers, loosened by the wild flight, burst from my wings. Veronica ran toward me, concern etched on her face. She skidded to a halt beside my tracks.

I touched her face. "Hello. Walk with me for a minute."

She frowned. "What's wrong? You scared the shit out of me, coming in like a bat out of hell. Are you okay?" Her hands began to wander over me, searching for any signs of injury. Gently, I brushed her off.

"There's not a lot of time. They'll arrive very soon." I grabbed her by the hand, aware that Orion was coming up along Veronica's side. His eyes bored into me, burning with unasked questions. I paused just long enough to give him a meaningful stare. "Seth and the other one are on their way."

Orion didn't appear to fully understand what I was doing, and he didn't like it either. But he nodded, tight-lipped, and let me pull Veronica away without pursuing. I led her deeper among the trees.

"Logan…" she said again, her tone becoming vaguely wary. "What is this about?"

"Were you supposed to survive on the day that Dylan died?" The question was purposefully abrupt so that she was more likely to be honest in her surprise.

"I—" She stopped. "I don't know." The wariness in her gaze increased tenfold. "My memory of everything except his death is patchy."

"Did you get hurt?" My thoughts backpedaled to the most recent time I had seen her naked—was there any evidence of old wounds? Wounds that should have been fatal?

Veronica rubbed her jaw. Her eyes went hazy as she dove into the rawest, most painful part of her past. Suddenly, a spark of clarity kindled in her expression. She looked startled. "I think I might have. I remember Lian telling me she had to throw away the clothes I was wearing because of the blood. And I assumed she meant Dylan's blood, but she made a comment about how not all of it was his."

"You *were* injured." I ran a palm over the contours of her torso. "Where?"

"That's the weird thing," she said quietly. "I have no idea. If there was an injury, I don't recall it. Like, at all. I was devastated for weeks, but I wasn't hurt." Veronica took a step toward me. "Tell me what you're getting at. We're short on time, remember?"

"I don't think you're simply mortal." The words came out fast, because she was right, and anything other than pure directness would have been wasting seconds. "It's like I said before. You shouldn't be able to use my power. You shouldn't be able to bridge between realms. Those things aren't learned in the way a slayer's craft can be."

"You weren't joking, then." She gazed up at me. "Before we—"

I sighed. "Have I *ever* told you a joke? No, I wasn't joking. You are something more, and I believe we might need you to tap into that power very soon."

"What the hell!" Veronica threw up her hands. "I barely have any idea what you're talking about, Logan. How am I supposed to use this alleged power?"

"Let's see if this helps." I took her face in my hands and kissed her hard on her beautiful mouth. She grabbed my arms as a sudden wave of energy crashed through us both. The sensation was like that of a key unlocking, a practically tangible click.

We eased apart. "Listen," she said breathlessly. "I know we hooked up in the woods that first time, but I don't think—" Her eyes widened. Then they started to glow. "Wait. Whoa."

I smiled. "There it is."

Veronica drew in a deep, slow breath. "I can see...everything," she whispered. Her eyes roamed the surroundings. "Every shred of life. Every scrap of energy." She paused, facing south. "The Seattle clan is a mile away. There's a shitload of them."

"We're outnumbered?" I asked, though I knew the answer.

"Yeah." She chewed her lip. "Extremely."

I nodded. "That's why we needed to talk. You have to be operating at full capacity for us to have a fighting chance."

"Holy shit." She looked down at her hands and back at me. "Am I supposed to be giving off light?"

"Never seen a celestial who didn't," I answered.

The look she was giving me turned searching. "You must have been like this once too, weren't you?" she asked. "That's how you knew. And how you were able to awaken me just now, but Orion and Seth never did."

"A demon and a vampire aren't going to possess the keys to celestial power." I glanced away. "And...I suppose you're right. At some point, I may have been…" I gestured indistinctly at her. "But none of that matters after an angel falls."

Veronica touched my shoulder. "Will you tell me that story someday?"

"Not right now," I said. "We're wasting time."

She rolled her eyes. "That's why I said *someday*. Also, you get to explain this to Orion if he asks."

"He probably won't," I said. "Yet."

Orion didn't ask. But he was waiting impatiently on the edge of the thick woods where we reemerged. Instantly, he homed in on the difference in Veronica's aura, and I thought he might forgo the questions entirely in favor of fighting me on the spot. How he despised to be left out of anything, especially relating to her!

"Where's Seth?" Veronica asked, partially to defuse the influx of tension. She looked around again. "And…"

As if on cue, I heard the demon's voice.

If you want this son of a bitch alive, come take him off my hands. Fucker's trying to go rogue.

"Oh, shit," Veronica muttered. She bolted toward Seth's presence. Orion and I followed in her wake.

28

SETH

I could almost respect the time it had taken for the kid to do something incredibly stupid—that is, beyond the myriad ways in which he'd already fucked up. His stint in the cellar was remarkably peaceful; I had to admit that he had really tried to play nice. A few snide comments were nothing I couldn't handle.

But I had sensed him getting ready to rebel from the moment his Seattle buddies entered the scene. Their encroaching presence alone activated him like a guided beacon. *Stop being so fucking docile,* I imagined them saying. *Act like an asshole. That's your job.*

Still, well within my handling capabilities. The bastard had proven to be tougher than he looked, but I was fully confident in my ability to put him down like a goddamn dog, should the need arise. Not even Logan taking off to fly ahead fazed me, although I'd had better company in worse places. By that time, I'd begun to notice that the darkness in his aura was welling up and oozing out, sitting on the surface of his energy like oil on water.

Great. Exactly the kind of shithead I want to be babysitting. Logan was barely a speck in the clouds. I could talk to him if I wanted, but Dylan and I were more or less alone. That was when he started to watch me. The same way a caged animal watches its keeper, waiting for the perfect opportunity to make a break for it.

"I know what you're thinking," I told him calmly, "and you'd better stop, or else you'll be a dead man walking."

The kid laughed. "Don't we both know I already am?"

I scoffed, unimpressed. If he had any illusions about the type of man he was dealing with, I was prepared to dispel them real quick. As far as I was concerned, Orion might still be able to strike a bargain with the other vamps using Dylan's fresh corpse. And if that didn't work, we'd figure something out. Working under pressure was kind of my specialty, as a demon from Hell.

That was why I didn't panic when I felt his energy shift on approach to Chugach's boundary. No one needed to be there to tell me the little weasel was gonna try to cut and run. His intentions were clear as day—on his face, in his manner, in the way he subconsciously braced against the bindings on his wrists. He might as well have told me out loud that he was about to betray the unspoken agreement we had reached up to this point.

I was ready for it the instant he attempted to charge me and get away. He tucked in his arms and threw his shoulder forward. Maybe he thought the element of surprise was all he needed. It gave me immense satisfaction to know he was wrong.

The point of Dylan's shoulder struck my hands instead of my chest. I absorbed the impact and used his momentum against him, following his trajectory through in one swift push. His head snapped up in panicked realization a second too late; his balance had already passed the tipping point. I had the pleasure of standing back and watching him crash to the ground. Without his arms free to catch him, he hit hard.

"Dammit!" He slithered around to face me, pulling his legs up to shield his vulnerable stomach. I could've taken the opportunity to crush his balls or step on his throat, two options that both appealed to me. But then the amount of time I had spent suffering in his presence would amount to little more than an empty, annoying waste.

"That all you got?" I smirked. "Pretty weak. Get your ass up, and let's go. People are waiting on us." I chose not to give him a hand—it was much more satisfying to watch him struggle to his feet.

He spat at me. "Fuck off. It was worth a shot." I started to turn away, thinking we might actually make the remaining quarter mile without too much drama. Then I saw him out of the corner of my eye, flat-out making a run for it.

Maybe I should have held on to him after all. I frowned and took off in pursuit, bursting up to maximum speed. Smoke rose from the ground under my feet; each footstep left behind a charred print. I was gaining on him right away, but not as quickly as I expected, which was disturbing. What kind of deep sorcery had been pumped into him?

We tore a path parallel to the looming tree line. Every few seconds, the fugitive would toss a glance over his shoulder, as if he actually thought I'd let his sorry ass get away. He deserved a little bit of credit for forcing me to break a sweat, but his hobbled wrists messed with his equilibrium. One foot caught in a hole in the dirt, and he was sent stumbling. Even though he managed not to fall, the misstep slowed him down enough that I was able to land a flying tackle. I thought I felt something snap beneath my weight. The kid grunted.

"Next time, you're dead," I told him calmly. "I won't even chase."

He didn't waste a drop of energy on a reply. His whole body lurched as he tried to throw a punch in the general direction of my face. Once again, I was surprised by the measure of his strength. Unfortunately for him, it wasn't enough anymore.

"Are you kidding me?" I'd been doing my best not to inflict unnecessary violence or damage him any further, because I was certain it wasn't what Veronica would want. Now her little ex-boyfriend was wearing my limited patience thin. I took a deep breath and sent out a call to Logan and Orion. Not for help, per se—just to let them know the situation. He needed to become someone else's problem fast.

Dylan squirmed again, attempting to grab at me. One arm seemed dead, which pleased me and frustrated him to no end. He growled like a feral animal, his eyes full of black rage.

"I hope you fucking burn," he snarled. "You don't belong here, with her."

"That's funny," I said. "Neither do you."

29

ORION

The scene I saw playing out three hundred yards from where we'd been standing was Seth pinning Dylan down, pressing the side of his face into the earth. Seth looked bored, his expression a stark contrast to Dylan's obvious, burning fury. Veronica broke ahead of Logan and me. I could see a faint trail of her energy shimmering in the air behind her.

"It's not what it looks like," Seth told her flatly as she reached them. "Well, okay, it kind of is. Lover boy wanted to bail, but I said no."

"He's not my lover," she responded without a trace of breathlessness. She knelt down to look Dylan in the eyes. "I'm sorry that you had to spend so many years in a terrible place. And I wish things had turned out differently."

"That makes two of us," Dylan said bitterly. Seth took the pressure off his head, and he sat up, shoving space between himself and the demon. "Get off me, you hellrat."

"Hey." Veronica glared at him. "Watch your mouth."

"Really?" He laughed and shook his head. "I can't believe you're defending him now instead of me. I was an idiot to think we could just pick up where we left off, or that you'd be the same girl I remembered." He scrutinized her. "It's a real fucking shame, V. Some might call it a waste."

She winced. "We both know I'm not the only one who's changed."

Her voice was strong, but tight, the voice of a woman determined not to cry.

"You'd be nothing without your entourage."

I had heard enough. "Shut him up," I said to Seth. "Just grab his legs and drag him. They're close." For once, Seth was happy to oblige. He leaned over, seized Dylan by the ankles, and hauled him toward the trees. The captive put up some semblance of a fight, but his dragging right arm made all his efforts futile. I waited for Veronica as the others went ahead.

"I was going to ask what you're about to do with him," she said, rubbing her eye with the heel of her hand. "But then it would be even harder to convince myself I don't care anymore."

"Come on." I brushed her hair out of her face. "It's time to go."

At the edge of the woods, we stood watch, grouped around our prisoner like the actors in a sacrificial ritual. As shapes began appearing in the distance, moving toward us, I stepped away from the trees and into the open. Trent led the pack, and as he drew nearer, I realized he was running.

"Something's wrong." Veronica had come up behind me. She stared into the distance, brow furrowed, and then her expression suddenly changed. "Oh, fuck. They must have been ambushed." Over her shoulder, she called, "Let's go, you guys!" And with that, she was off, blazing a path straight toward our reinforcements.

Not wanting to be outdone, I stayed on her heels. She was wildly beautiful to me in those moments, permeating with a peculiar serenity, that we spent rushing to meet our reckoning. It met us in the form of a stampede of vampires, pale and ghastly in the overcast light, reeking of the grimy streets of Seattle.

The moment we were within striking distance, Trent swung around and bellowed to his fighters, "Turn!" Despite my skepticism that a human slayer was capable of holding a strong enough command, they turned as one, crashing back into the enemy like the angry tide.

The vampires shrieked, disappearing in a storm of teeth and claws. Almost immediately, I smelled blood misting in the air. Logan and Seth dove into the chaos. An enemy vampire, twisted with age and power, leapt toward my throat. I bared my teeth and ripped him out of the air.

His impact still knocked us both to the ground. I tore at him, feeling the snap of bone and the sickeningly satisfying tear of cloth and skin.

He was cold to the touch, his true strength belied by the gaunt appearance of a desiccated corpse.

"You!" the elder vampire snarled, baring ancient, blackening fangs. Yellow eyes, sunk deep into shriveled sockets, still gleamed with the fire of deep-seated hatred. "You will never be worthy of the master's title." One bony palm dug into my chest. His fingers curled over until the nails had pierced my shirt and raked against the skin beneath. "There is no place for you at the head of a clan, and for your indiscretions, you shall pay!"

For the second time that day, I had heard enough. Whatever drivel Steele was feeding his clan had poisoned their minds, made them casualties of his blind pursuit of power. I grabbed the elder by his scraggly throat and flipped him over. He wheezed in pain, but his glare remained unrepentant.

"Where is Steele?" I demanded. "This fight is ours, old man. Not yours."

He coughed in between spurts of uneven laughter. "I would die before leading you to him."

"Very well." I drove my hand straight into the left side of his chest, pushing aside flesh and bone. The cruel light drained from his eyes as quickly as the flipping of a switch. It was, at best, an undignified way to end a life so long. *Truly*, I thought, with some measure of irony, *we are masters of our fate.*

When I stood up, my mind singularly focused on the search for Steele, my gaze fell upon a panorama of chaos. The only thing I could tell with any certainty at a glance was that there were far more of them than there were of us. A bitter smile curled my lip. Perhaps some diplomacy would have been a wise investment.

But it was too late for regrets. I pushed my way through the battle, fending off a constant barrage of attacks, keeping my head as far down as I could manage. That first encounter had shown me that being recognized here would only end in disaster. Some might have called it foolish to seek out Steele alone, without protection. A reckless flirtation with death.

Nonetheless, I had no fear, only cold resolve. I had spoken the truth to the elder who now lay dead by my hand. This fight was between the two of us—no one else. And one way or another, it was going to end today.

30

VERONICA

I did not like to admit it publicly, but as a slayer, I was always kind of into a good fight. There was just some adrenaline-powered, sick thrill in beating the hell out of what usually amounted to the boogeymen from everyone's childhood nightmares. This attitude had changed since arriving in Anchorage, for obvious reasons, and yet I still felt an incredible sense of catharsis in the middle of the fray.

Maybe it had something to do with the fact that most of my opponents didn't really bleed. Even as I charged at a big, barrel-chested vamp, used my staff as a vault, and catapulted backwards off his pecs, striking the vamp rushing up behind me on the way down, the violence seemed almost like a cartoon. I speared the second guy through the chest and threw him at the big vamp, who stumbled back into another of his friends.

It was some grisly shit, but the pounding beat of my heart and the blood rushing through my veins washed it all away. I had long since learned not to think on the job. Once the training kicked in, it was like riding a bike. A screeching, violent bike that was constantly trying to kill me.

"What are you doing here, bitch?"

I whipped around at the sneering voice and came face to face with a woman who could have been any of the others. Her thin, sallow face contorted in disgust at the sight of me, and I got the impression that I was supposed to recognize her in turn.

Instead, I frowned and asked, "Do we know each other?"

She sniffed. "Oh, everyone knows you. Thinking you're such hot shit with your pink hair. Like you don't even need to worry about staying hidden, right? Because you're just *that good.*"

I stared at her in utter confusion. "What the fuck are you talking about?" My grip tightened instinctively on the handle of my staff. I wondered how fast I could stake her if she tried to make a move. In just the last few minutes, I'd been getting plenty of practice, so I thought the odds were in my favor.

She rolled her eyes. "You make me sick. Frankly, I'm impressed you showed up here. I didn't think you had it in you, since you're so good at running away." In a flash, her hand darted toward me. "And if you ever think about setting foot back in the city, you're a dead girl walking."

I knocked her hand out of the air. She hissed, drawing it back, and then she dropped all pretense and just lunged at me. Shifting my weight to my back foot, I jabbed the end of the staff sharply upward, exactly where I judged she would be.

She never completed that ill-advised leap. Her body crumbled off the edge of the weapon. I kept it at the ready, glancing around. "Anyone else?"

That was when I noticed something strange going on. The frenzy of fighting all around me had subsided, almost as if some of the vamps had been called off. A feeling of dread spawned in my stomach, and I looked around again, scouring the battlefield for anything out of place. My intuition screamed that we were about to be in big trouble.

Then I saw the man, a hundred feet away, walking calmly through a parting sea of vampires. I watched brutal skirmishes pause as he went by, often to the disadvantage of the vampire choosing to show reverence. His presence seemed to override the clamor of battle completely.

He was heading straight for me. It seemed like a terrible idea to move toward him, so I held my ground where I stood, staff at the ready. The closer he got, the more I sensed his aura permeating through the atmosphere. The magic brewing in his energy tugged at the corners of my mind.

Submit, it whispered. *It's not too late to join the winning side.*

I scowled. I caught his pale, powerful gaze. His expression betrayed no emotion whatsoever. Like Logan, but worse in a way I couldn't articulate.

"Fuck this," I said out loud. My voice carried unexpectedly; heads turned in my direction. The advancing figure gave no sign that he had heard me, although I was sure he did. He kept walking. It began to dawn on me that maybe I wasn't the one he cared about. As soon as he got in range, I stepped up to stop him myself. "I don't think I can let you go any farther."

He looked down at me. The top of his face was covered by a creepy mask of bone, pale white everywhere except for heavy black around the eyes. "I'm afraid you have no choice," he answered. Before I could react, he placed a hand over my face. I blinked, and when my eyes opened again, I was looking down at the top of my own head, a passive observer as my body crumpled to the ground. The man continued on his path as though nothing had happened.

"What the hell!" I shouted. My voice, which had carried so far only moments before, might as well have been muffled under ten pillows. Panic swelled in my chest. Was I dead? Was I unconscious? There was no way to know from there. Frantically, I kicked at the air—and to my surprise, I moved a little. Further experimentation showed that if I was careful, I could sort of swim back down toward my body. What happened after that, I didn't know, but it didn't matter.

I had seen where the figure was headed. He was going toward the thickest part of the trees, which was also the last place I'd seen Dylan.

Considering the circumstances, I couldn't call it a coincidence.

I clawed my way downward, full of determination and anger. *This is going to be the last walk you ever take, buddy. I fucking promise you.*

LOGAN

I had just finished off an enemy when I felt Veronica's spirit be pulled from her body. Instantly, all my senses were on high alert. I summoned my power in a desperate bid to call her back from wherever she was headed—but my calls were met with confusing silence. If she were truly dead, I should have seen her, should have been able to reach out and grab her. Instead, she was traveling away from me, on a trajectory at first parallel to the mortal realm, and then decidedly back toward it.

She didn't need me to rescue her from death again. She was doing it herself. An eerie calm began to spread over the scene of our endless fight. The signal of her spirit was slowly being diminished by a foreign energy, rare in its power. It made the hair stand up on the back of my neck; I knew that tranquility could be as bad an omen as any.

I pushed through the battlefield, tracking the path of Veronica's spirit. It wasn't long before I spotted her body. Even in all forms of death she was beautiful, as if she was merely resting. But the grim tableau didn't scare me as much as it might have if I couldn't also see her spirit struggling mightily to rejoin its vessel.

"Veronica!" I ran to where she lay and reached up to get her attention. Her spirit turned toward me, her expression a mix of surprise, relief, and delight.

"Oh, thank fuck you're here." She stretched an arm toward me. "I gotta go, or he's going to get away."

I grabbed her hand and pulled her earthward, using my body as an in-between to allow her to bridge the gap between the ether and the corporeal. She passed through me almost too quickly; the world spun for a moment or two. Then she sprang up off the ground.

"Who did this?" I asked. "I felt it happen."

"I don't know who he is," she said. "But I'm gonna fucking kill him." She turned to go, but quickly came back. "Hold on." Then she gave me a quick, passionate kiss. I sensed her drawing on my power just a little bit, enough to augment her own.

"Go get that son of a bitch," I said.

"I will." She winked.

That might have been the moment I truly fell in love.

31

VERONICA

I had never run faster or harder than I did that day, with Logan on my lips. He was my invigorator, my bulwark in a storm, and his power seemed to dovetail with mine in a way I hadn't noticed before. The energy in the air became a map showing me every step that bastard had taken. In places, I could literally see his footsteps pressed into the ground. My stomach sank when I noticed that each stride was lengthening.

He was picking up the pace, and so I did too. The trees formed a dark wall looming high over me, and the shadows they cast were long and dark. But he was in there—the footprints told me so. I leaned into my sprint, urging my body forward. Then the soft muttering of a disembodied voice touched my ears.

I didn't know how to decipher the words; they belonged to a language beyond my understanding. The tone, however, and the malice behind it, I could definitely register. The incantation floated from behind a cluster of trunks just ahead.

Was this where we left Dylan?

As soon as I asked myself, I began to pick out the subtlest threads of Dylan's energy, flowing alongside the route I was already tracing. My sneaking suspicions had just been confirmed. This asshole had been after Dylan the whole time.

And now he was trying to put something unknown into action. The chanting intensified, both arms lifting from his sides. His hands began to glow, dimly at first, and then the light crept along his arms, into his shoulders, centering in the middle of his chest. He lifted his eyes to the sky, shifted position, and I glimpsed Dylan's form sitting upright against a tree trunk.

"Shit," I whispered. At first, Dylan seemed limp and unresponsive, and I didn't know whether to feel dread or relief. Then, without any kind of warning, he picked up his head, and the dial turned all the way to dread. Still wasn't sure what was going on, but I knew I couldn't just stand by and watch. My window to act was small and constantly shrinking.

I took a deep breath, filling my lungs with cool forest air. Logan's taste still simmered on my lips, his power in my soul. I called mine forth the same way I had called his, dipping into the well of strength on the other side of the veil. Where there had once been little more than a slow but steady stream, I now found a river feeding into a deep, clear pool.

Sudden searing pain ripped through my shoulders. I bit my lip hard to keep from gasping—or swearing. My shoulder blades jerked backwards, and I found myself awash in gleaming feathers drifting down from overhead.

"No way," I whispered. It was impossible to contain the wonder filling my heart. The wings were heavy, and they kind of hurt. I flexed those muscles and winced. But they beat strongly, almost on their own. My feet lifted off the ground. I focused all my attention on my target, whose own ethereal trance had made him oblivious.

At his feet, Dylan had started to struggle against his bonds. It was now or never. As I drew my staff, the striking end exploded into a brilliant, flaming blade. At the same time that I shot forward on the force of my wings, I swung the blade up and then brought it down in a smooth, remorseless arc.

At the last second, all trances were broken. The man in the mask whipped his head around, but his reaction came a fraction of a second too late. I barely felt the blade cleave his body; all I saw was him falling to the ground. The blood pouring from the wound soaked the surrounding soil in tainted darkness. Faint trails of smoke ribboned up into the sky.

Soon, he'd be reduced to a pile of dust, and it would no longer matter who he was or what he did. At least, not to anyone who might come upon his remains before they were carried away on the wind. I was always glad to be rid of vamps so quickly, but it also annoyed me that winning a battle often meant losing all concrete evidence of their existence.

"You came back." Dylan grinned with one side of his mouth. He was dirty and disheveled now, and I could have sworn he looked paler. The dark circles under his eyes seemed to deepen every second.

"Was that him?" I asked. "Your benefactor?"

He nodded. "And you killed him without a second thought. Not sure how I feel about that—although I guess this new thing is pretty cool." Dylan gestured vaguely to the bright wings, the cascade of feathers. I couldn't tell if he was being sarcastic.

I rolled my eyes. "Stand up. I'm sorry we just left you here. Things got a little out of hand."

"You're right about that," Dylan said, "but you're not sorry."

"I am." I took him by the shoulder and helped pull him to his feet.

He turned to gaze at me, our faces inches apart. "How can you be sorry when you're about to walk me to the gallows?"

My heart clutched tight in my chest. Logically, I knew that I no longer had any obligation to care about what happened to Dylan at the hands of Orion, or any of the others. He had turned from the funny, confident, loving boy from my past to a bitter, hateful man so fast that I still had to process the emotional whiplash.

Nonetheless, I didn't quite have it in me to throw him to the wolves and look away. The idea that I would be the one to send him to his second death opened a yawning chasm of pain in my heart.

I let go of his arm and swallowed the lump in my throat. "Don't be so dramatic." I spoke with a false veneer of bravado. "I'm just not dumb enough to let you out of my sight again."

We stepped across the body of the slain shaman as the last of it moldered into the soil. Dylan glanced down at the ash seeping away into the dirt, but he said nothing. Part of me wanted desperately to know what he was thinking.

Part of me understood it didn't matter anymore.

32

SETH

*N*egotiations were the most boring part of any war, as far as I was concerned. If it were up to me, I would have skipped straight to the part where I got to enjoy the spoils of victory—that is to say, V naked underneath me in bed, bursting with pleasure. Maybe she'd be tied to the bedposts or handcuffed to the headboard. Or maybe I'd leave her loose and let her fingernails draw tracks all over my body. After this shitstorm had finally passed, we'd have all the time in the world to figure out exactly how good we could make each other feel.

But first I had to stand at the edge of a dust-bathed forest and listen to a bunch of vamps fight over Veronica's ex. The good news was that the Seattleite bastards had backed off considerably following the death of their great shaman. I had looked up from my latest victory to see V strolling out of the woods with Dylan in front of her and two huge wings flowing from her shoulders. A pang of wild jealousy shot through me; it was infuriating, but not altogether surprising that angel-boy was the one she ended up matching. They had a special connection that even I, a lowly prince of Hell, could not deny.

The bad news? The only deal the Seattle clan was willing to strike meant that Dylan would go back to Washington with them, and therefore, we would not get to kill him ourselves. Physical vengeance against him had been a burning desire of mine practically from the instant I made his acquaintance, and the base, violent section of my brain resented the loss of that opportunity. But I also understood that V hadn't quite put out her torch for the little rat, whether anyone else agreed with her or not.

She wouldn't want to see him die, and she especially wouldn't want to see us kill him. That fact alone was enough to grant him grudging clemency. I could tell from the way he looked at her that Logan felt the same. As for Orion, no words had to be said. It was not a secret that he'd been obsessed with her immediately.

Imagine how insane it was to realize I could actually comprehend the way he felt about anything, let alone a mutual love interest. As our connections to Veronica grew, my disdain for him had lessened alarmingly. Orion was an arrogant prick. He could be insufferable, and sometimes I had to leave the room to keep from punching him in the face. But he wasn't a villain, nor was he my rival.

He *was* currently excelling in his role as the least interesting vampire on the planet. Orion and the Seattle clan's third in command were at an excruciating impasse. They wanted Dylan back. He refused. They wouldn't budge.

"I have no assurance that he won't be used against me at a future date. Why shouldn't I simply eliminate him here and now?" he asked pointedly. It was a solid question from a negotiation standpoint. Getting rid of Dylan would also get rid of all the problems he had dragged into the mortal realm, whether or not he meant to.

And yet, we all knew without saying that the kid would be taken back to Washington unharmed, simply because none of us wanted to force Veronica to watch him die here. That girl had found a soft spot with all of us, and she wanted to stay there—with all of us. I had no idea how in the hell it would ever work, but it was probably going to be hilarious.

"Why not, indeed?" the Seattle vamp was saying smugly. His eyes flicked over Veronica. She stood with her head down, studiously avoiding the macabre scene in the midst of playing out. Her shining wings were gone. She looked full to the brim of tired sorrow.

Orion saw it too. He glanced at Logan, then at me.

I shrugged. *Kill him, and she'll never forgive you.*

He could be kept alive, Orion mused.

Where? Logan interjected. *In the cellar? We might as well kill him.*

Yeah, and she'll never fucking forgive us, I repeated impatiently. *Don't be an asshole, Orion. Let the kid be their shitty problem now.*

Logan said, *Agreed.*

Orion gave us both reproachful stares, but he ultimately turned around and told them they could take Dylan with them as long as they got the fuck out of Alaska, and fast. He was the one who facilitated the prisoner handoff; Veronica hadn't so much as looked Dylan in the eyes since she'd brought him out. As he was being led away, though, she lifted her head once, at the same time he looked over his shoulder. Their eyes locked for a good ten seconds.

Then he was gone, lost in the considerably diminished ranks of the Seattle clan. V seemed to deflate on the spot. She didn't cry, but she sat down right where she had been standing. The decision to let her be for a while was both instant and mutual.

Instead, the three of us held court with Trent and his people. The slayers had proven to be far more resilient than I'd given them credit for—they were worse for the wear, and down a few in numbers, but by no means had they been vanquished.

"Thank you for your aid," Orion stated gravely. He paused, then offered Trent his hand. "Your generosity will not be forgotten."

Trent shook the vampire's hand. "It's not over," he said.

Orion nodded once. "I know." He gazed thoughtfully at the rapidly receding line of the Seattle clan. "What will you do now?"

Trent didn't even have to think about it. "I'm going after them to Washington," he answered. "I don't know if this is fixable, but I have to try." He was quiet for a moment. "You?"

"We'll rebuild. And when we're done, Steele and I will have our reckoning. Whether he wants to or not." His attention turned to Veronica again, and the hard resolve in his face softened. "She will want to say goodbye to you," he remarked softly.

"She will." Trent ran a hand through his hair. "I won't be leaving right away. I figure I'll give them some time to settle in and try to make a plan. Maybe we'll get a fair fight next time."

Orion actually smiled slightly. He said, "I doubt that very much." There was no elaboration on what precisely he might have meant.

33

VERONICA

*L*ian looked at me from across her kitchen table. "So…how are you doing?" Her face and voice were full of genuine concern, and it made me think about how I would never be as good a friend as she deserved. After all the shit I had put us through, here we were in her kitchen, talking things over—or at least I was trying to. She'd even made me lemonade.

I sighed and shrugged my shoulders. "I'm okay, I guess. It's just…" I trailed off. In the two days that had passed since the Seattle clan had taken Dylan away, I'd spent hours struggling to figure out a way to decipher my emotions. There was a storm constantly brewing inside me, and sometimes I got overwhelmed, especially when I tried to talk about it. I shook my head.

"Yeah." Lian gave me a sympathetic, sad smile. "I think that's how I'd feel too."

I didn't know how to tell her I was haunted by the image of Dylan looking back at me as he was led away with his hands still tied. In theory, I understood he hadn't been betrayed, that in fact, he had agreed to betray me first. But it was still so hard to separate that version of him from the one I loved who had lived for so long in my memories.

"V?" Lian reached over the table and took my hand. "Are you okay?"

I realized I had started to cry. Not a lot, but enough. "I thought I would only have to lose him once," I said softly.

"Oh, honey." She got up, moved over to my chair, and put her arms around me. "I'm so sorry this is happening to you."

I hugged her back the best I could, with one arm. It felt like a metaphor for our friendship as of late. "I'm sorry, too," I said. "For a lot of things."

She laughed, squeezing me tighter. "Oh, please. Yes, I was mad about it at first, and let's be real, I still don't *get* it. But look, if you're happy and they're not hurting anyone, it's none of my business. I'm glad you found something that works for you."

"You have no idea how well it works for me," I replied.

Lian grinned. "That's gross." She stood up. "Want me to call you when Trent gets home? I think he'll be leaving in the next few days. He'll probably want to talk to you first."

"Yeah." To be honest, I couldn't imagine having a conversation about Dylan at the moment. That reopened wound was still too raw, as much as I tried to conceal it. I knew better than to love him now, but the loss was still mine to grieve. "I'll see you soon."

We lingered for a few minutes longer, and then she gave me a hug goodbye, and I went out into a surprisingly sunny day. The wind blowing across the lawn smelled fresh and clean, as if the world had been renewed overnight. I stood there for a second and let it wash away all the pent-up negativity that had been festering for days. It was time to go home, where I knew my three new loves were waiting.

I gasped, arching my back at the touch of Seth's tongue between my legs. He had tied my wrists loosely to the bedposts, and I strained against the bonds, wanting more. Orion sat behind me, his lips roaming my neck and shoulder. Logan caught my mouth in a deeply passionate kiss. Orion's hands cupped my breasts, teasing each nipple.

I moaned as Logan pulled away. My head fell back against Orion's shoulder. He lifted my chin to expose the delicate skin of my throat. I felt his teeth graze there gently.

"You better not bite me," I said. "Not like that, anyway."

Seth lifted his head, much to my annoyance that he wasn't still between my legs. "Don't even think about it. We talked about that."

Orion frowned. He shifted his hips, and I felt him pressing into the small of my back. The pressure of his cock made me ache to be pene-trated by any one of them.

"Is this the time?" he asked.

"No," I answered immediately. "Shut up and fuck me, please."

Seth leaned down and sucked me, hard. A jolt of wildly intense plea-sure made all my muscles seize. Both my hands clenched into fists of ecstasy. Orion smiled into my skin. Leaning into him, I worked one arm free so that I could reach for Logan and pull him closer. He kissed me again, his touch tender this time. The bed creaked dangerously under our combined weight, and then we heard a resounding crack from the frame.

Everybody paused. We looked at one another in silence until I burst out laughing.

"I told you guys we need a better bed!"

Logan ran his thumb down the edge of my jaw. "It's Seth's fault. He's very dense."

"Hey!" Seth smirked. "Let's talk when you've got your wings out. I bet they add at least forty pounds."

I looked up at Orion, whose face was a mix of annoyance and amusement. He kissed my forehead. "What do you think?" I said. "Is this reason enough to look for a new place?"

"In Anchorage," he said. "Where we can continue to rebuild the clan."

"Listen, as long as I get my own room, I'm not complaining." I stretched to touch his lips with mine. "We'll do whatever you want."

"That's it, I'm out." Seth started to stand up.

I giggled. "No, you're not."

He sighed. "You're right. I'm not. You guys are stuck with me—including you two assholes." When he sat back down, the bed began to list to one side, threatening to slide Logan onto the floor.

Logan nodded at the dipping edge of the mattress. "See? Dense."

Orion rolled his eyes and moved both of us over to make room for Logan. He had taken some time to warm up to this group arrangement on our first attempt last night. But I had insisted for the hundredth time that he needed to learn how to share. It made me happy to see him finally starting to take that to heart.

"We will find a new house," he agreed. "At my discretion. But...I'll make sure everyone's needs are met."

"Good," I said. "Now how about my needs, right now? Because I need at least one of you to make me come."

"Anything you want, princess." Seth's tongue went back to work, Orion and Logan put their hands and mouths on my body, and I let myself be immersed in waves of bliss.

Who would have thought that three men... these monsters... these creatures of the night would help me find love again. I sure as hell didn't but for the life of me I was so glad they never gave up on me.

LOST WOLF

Being rejected by my fated mate is the least of my problems...

I'm a half-breed, a Cursed. The wolf half gets me an alpha for a fated mate...the witch half gets me killed.

Or so they think.

Now four Viking Alphas are all that stand between me and certain death. They need my powers to take over the Savage Sector, and they'll hold my sisters' as leverage until they get what they want from me.

My wild magic, my heart.

My wolf calls to them, but I can't trust them to keep me alive once this is over.

I'm just an Omega to them, but that mistake may cost us all our lives

What the Viking Alphas want, the Viking Alphas get...

...and right now that's me and my wild magic.

ABOUT MILA YOUNG

Best-selling author, Mila Young tackles everything with the zeal and bravado of the fairytale heroes she grew up reading about. She slays monsters, real and imaginary, like there's no tomorrow. By day she rocks a keyboard as a marketing extraordinaire. At night she battles with her mighty pen-sword, creating fairytale retellings, and sexy ever after tales. In her spare time, she loves pretending she's a mighty warrior, walks on the beach with her dogs, cuddling up with her cats, and devouring every fantasy tale she can get her pinkies on.

Ready to read more and more from Mila Young? www.subscribepage.com/milayoung

For more information...
milayoungarc@gmail.com

www.ingramcontent.com/pod-product-compliance
Lightning Source LLC
Chambersburg PA
CBHW030836190726
48285CB00004B/1248